OXFORD WORLD'S CLASSICS

NANA

ÉMILE ZOLA was born in Paris in 1840, the son of a Venetian engineer and his French wife. He grew up in Aix-en-Provence where he made friends with Paul Cézanne. After an undistinguished school career and a brief period of dire poverty in Paris, Zola joined the newly founded publishing firm of Hachette which he left in 1866 to live by his pen. He had already published a novel and his first collection of short stories. Other novels and stories followed until in 1871 Zola published the first volume of his Rougon-Macquart series with the sub-title *Histoire naturelle et sociale d'une famille sous le Second Empire*, in which he sets out to illustrate the influence of heredity and environment on a wide range of characters and milieux. However, it was not until 1877 that his novel *L'Assommoir*, a study of alcoholism in the working classes, brought him wealth and fame. The last of the Rougon-Macquart series appeared in 1893 and his subsequent writing was far less successful, although he achieved fame of a different sort in his vigorous and influential intervention in the Dreyfus case. His marriage in 1870 had remained childless but his extremely happy liaison in later life with Jeanne Rozerot, initially one of his domestic servants, gave him a son and a daughter. He died in 1902.

DOUGLAS PARMÉE studied at Trinity College, Cambridge, the University of Bonn, and the Sorbonne. He later served in RAF Intelligence before returning to teach in Cambridge, where he was a Fellow and Director of Studies at Queens' College. He now lives in Adelaide, South Australia. He has written widely on French Studies and is a prize-winning translator from French, German, and Italian. He has edited Flaubert's *A Sentimental Education* (Oxford World's Classics).

OXFORD WORLD'S CLASSICS

For over 100 years Oxford World's Classics have brought readers closer to the world's great literature. Now with over 700 titles—from the 4,000-year-old myths of Mesopotamia to the twentieth century's greatest novels—the series makes available lesser-known as well as celebrated writing.

The pocket-sized hardbacks of the early years contained introductions by Virginia Woolf, T. S. Eliot, Graham Greene, and other literary figures which enriched the experience of reading. Today the series is recognized for its fine scholarship and reliability in texts that span world literature, drama and poetry, religion, philosophy and politics. Each edition includes perceptive commentary and essential background information to meet the changing needs of readers.

OXFORD WORLD'S CLASSICS

ÉMILE ZOLA

Nana

Translated with an Introduction and Notes by
DOUGLAS PARMÉE

OXFORD
UNIVERSITY PRESS

OXFORD
UNIVERSITY PRESS

Great Clarendon Street, Oxford OX2 6DP

Oxford University Press is a department of the University of Oxford.
It furthers the University's objective of excellence in research, scholarship,
and education by publishing worldwide in

Oxford New York

Auckland Bangkok Buenos Aires Cape Town Chennai
Dar es Salaam Delhi Hong Kong Istanbul Karachi Kolkata
Kuala Lumpur Madrid Melbourne Mexico City Mumbai Nairobi
São Paulo Shanghai Taipei Tokyo Toronto

Oxford is a registered trade mark of Oxford University Press
in the UK and in certain other countries

Published in the United States
by Oxford University Press Inc., New York

First published as a World's Classics paperback 1992
Reissued as an Oxford World's Classics paperback 1998

British Library Cataloguing in Publication Data

Data available

Library of Congress Cataloging in Publication Data

Zola, Émile, 1840–1902.
[Nana. English]
Nana/Émile Zola; translated with an introduction by
Douglas Parmée
p. cm.—(Oxford world's classics)
Translated from the French.
Includes bibliographical references.
I. Parmée, Douglas. II. Title. III. Series.
PQ2510.A36 1992 843'.8—dc20 91–22416

ISBN-13: 978–0–19–283670–0
ISBN-10: 0–19–283670–6

8

Printed in Great Britain by
Clays Ltd, St Ives plc

CONTENTS

Introduction vii
Select Bibliography xxvii
A Chronology of Émile Zola xxviii

NANA xxxi

Explanatory Notes 429

INTRODUCTION

NANA was the ninth in Zola's vast cyclical fresco of twenty novels, first planned in the sixties of the nineteenth century under the title of 'natural and social history of a family under the Second Empire'. Balzac's similarly vast project, the *Comédie humaine*, was always in his mind, and he was determined that his cycle dealing with several generations of the Rougon-Macquart family should be different. He had been impressed by the ideas of the positivist philosopher Taine, who stressed the importance of three so-called natural laws in determining personality: heredity, environment, and what he calls *le moment*, the dynamic momentum of a particular period. Zola's cycle was to be openly and consciously scientific, which he understood to mean giving the physical a predominant role in human affairs. For this method he coined the term 'naturalism'. He was even led to hope that he might turn the novel into a scientific experiment to prove certain hypotheses, though it would be indeed a strange science where the data, the development, and the conclusion depended on one man's imagination and choice. In *Nana*, though material and social pressures are given considerable emphasis, psychology is nowhere completely sacrificed to physiology; the main characters are far from single-dimensional, and minor ones, especially the women, are often markedly individual. The male protagonist, Count Muffat, is an excellent example: originally swept off his feet by Nana's physical beauty, his purely physical passion is gradually sublimated into tender devotion. What is more, by an ingenious twist, apart from being highly sexed, he is unsatisfied in his marriage and deeply, even mystically pious, almost a Baudelairean character for whom one of the pleasures of love seems to be the thrill of sinning and even the masochistic anticipation of chastisement. And this tormented man is not just anybody; he is the chamberlain to the Empress Eugénie, and as such can be made the scapegoat for Imperial society.

As part of his methodical approach to novel-writing Zola always prepared a preliminary sketch of his general intentions, of his characters, major and minor, and later even detailed chapter-schedules, though modifications would come while writing. The notes on *Nana* are very enlightening and very explicit: 'the philosophical subject is this: a whole society rushing to get sex. A pack after a bitch who's not on heat and despises the dogs following her . . . Nana dominates and crushes everything . . . the various episodes have only a secondary value.' To achieve this dominance of a sex-obsessed society she needs a beautiful body, and the reader is constantly present, almost as a voyeur, at her display, naked or nearly naked, on stage and off. She is, however, more than a body; the wily theatre-manager Bordenave who launches her in the first chapter, surely one of the most brilliant and intriguing chapters in any nineteenth-century novel, puts the reason for her success in a nutshell: she's got a voice like a corncrake, she can't act, but besides her obvious physical charms, she has 'something else', an indefinable, magical aura, and it is this that captures the public. It is a charm far from purely physical: in her last triumphal appearance on the Paris stage, in Chapter 13, although she is wearing only white tights and a gold belt, she is almost disembodied; she no longer tries to sing or act, not even to move: she stands in a grotto of sparkling mirrors gleaming with electric light, amidst cascades of diamonds and streams of glittering pearls, and strikes an 'artistic' pose. She has become a fairy princess. Someone who sees her describes her as 'like an image of the Good Lord'. Her vulgar, titillating display of sexual bravado is gone; she is, as Zola said in his notes, 'flesh, but flesh with all its grace . . . sex on an altar with everybody offering sacrifices to it.'

One thing is quite plain: she is no ordinary brothel inmate, though shown as no stranger to *maisons de rendezvous*, nor a street-walker, even if occasionally reduced to the streets when pressed for cash. There would in any case have been little point in writing a novel on such a well-worn theme. Zola had himself in his semi-autobiographical first novel, *La Confession de Claude*, dealt with this subject in 1865, where the torments of the idealistic Claude to reform a prostitute have similarities with Muffat's predicament in *Nana*. More recently, similar ground had been covered by two fellow-writers, Huysmans in his *Marthe, histoire d'une fille* of 1876, and Edmond de Goncourt in *La Fille Elisa* in the following year; the theme had obvious appeal to a society in which male sexuality was so deeply brothel-based. Nana is on quite a different scale: although an individual with strong personal characteristics, she is the epitome of a whole class of *courtisanes*, kept women, often associated with the stage, luxury articles which were so prominent a feature of smart society, the world of *galanterie*, of amorous intrigue, the *demi-monde*, where respectable women were never seen but only their wealthy husbands and bachelor men-about-town, a society which flourished during the Second Empire behind the official façade of hypocritical decency maintained by the censor and backed up by the law courts, an age which saw the prosecution of *Les Fleurs du mal* and *Madame Bovary*.

Zola detested the Second Empire, which he saw as an unholy alliance of an authoritarian police state and a triumphantly dogmatic, all-powerful Roman Catholic hierarchy, both of which he was able to encapsulate in Muffat. It was a society singularly propitious for the rise of the courtesans he had in mind, a world of festivity which was to reach its zenith in the World Fair of 1867, the year in which his novel starts, when royalty and notables flocked to Paris from all over Europe and beyond; ironically, the name of Bismarck turns up in many conversations—an irony underlined in the last chapter. But the surrender at Sedan was still three years away, and the Second Empire could still be seen as a brilliant regime that, having toppled a divided and discredited Second Republic in 1852, had launched into a career of galloping free enterprise and intensive industrialization, with its concomitant of rabid speculation and a booming—occasionally, of course, busting—Stock Exchange, a phenomenon which Zola was to examine more closely in his novel *L'Argent* in 1891. Paris itself was being revamped into its modern guise by the transforming genius of Baron Haussmann, whose splendid straight boulevards were not only grand but offered a clear line of fire in the case of any attempt by mob violence to overthrow an unpopular government. At the top of one of the grandest streets Garnier's almost outrageously grand opera-house was rising at the end of its Avenue—we see poor Muffat wandering around there in *Nana*. Paris was well on the way to becoming the capital of the world, gay Paree, *la Ville Lumière*, a centre of brilliance of all sorts, of which Zola was determined to expose the shady side. It was a cosmopolitan world; even the Empress Eugénie and court ladies derived much of their chic from Lincolnshire-born Mr Worth, the fashion designer. He also designed for the stage, a lucrative trade given the many 'little theatres' active in the environs of the *grands boulevards*, an essential ingredient of the hectic life of the capital and the principal backdrop of Nana's public career. Here were staged the sparkling *opéras bouffes* of Offenbach, also a foreigner, whose witty subversion of the regime Zola quite failed to grasp, viewing him instead, with great distaste, purely as the impudent representative of frothy frivolity—the show which launches Nana is obviously based on Offenbach's skits on classical antiquity. And to crown the Second Empire's brilliant image, it was also successful abroad: it had fought beside Great Britain in the Crimea against the Russians as well as in China, and had helped Italy in her war of independence against Austria. True, the attempt to establish a French protégé as emperor of Mexico was a disastrous failure; but French colonial ambitions flourished in North Africa and as far afield as Indo-China.

In sum, then, an age when the prosperous middle classes and a renewed and powerful aristocracy combined under a semi-dictatorial rule to form what Zola saw as a flashy, pleasure-loving plutocracy with money to burn; and what better and more pleasurable status symbol than a stunningly striking sexy young actress? For a basically materialistic society, she is a highly desirable sex-object to parade at a supper-party or at a race-meeting—Nana's appearance at the Longchamp racecourse in Chapter 11 represents almost the apogee of her career—or in expensive restaurants—though for professional or conjugal reasons, a discreet private room is sometimes better. You know that such appearances will be saucily reported in the gossip-columns of newspapers read by envious friends and competitors, all the smart people, *le Tout Paris, les clubmen*; it must not be forgotten that Nana's success is shown as stemming from male-group crass sensuality, though when she becomes fashionable even women are enticed into copying her.

Though Zola constantly asserts his intention of being the impartial recorder of the society of his time, engaged in a scientific endeavour, in fact there was inside him a social moralist constantly struggling to get out. One obvious moralizing intention in *Nana*—it had not yet turned into the preachifying of his disastrous later novels—can be detected in the choice of his heroine's status. This epitome of kept women has started life as a pretty working-class girl whose vitality—perhaps 'oomph' is the proper word—contrasts with the often enervated and effete males sniffing around her. Zola goes further; by breaking into this smart society, this poor working-class girl from a slum background becomes the symbolic instrument of its downfall, as is clearly—perhaps rather too clearly—spelt out in the Golden Fly article in Chapter 7. Through Nana, not only do male chauvinists receive their just deserts but the poor get their revenge on the inhuman bourgeoisie, men and women, held responsible for social injustice.

Such a clash between two social levels obviously fitted very neatly into Zola's belief in the importance of environmental factors. The second main factor of his naturalistic creed, heredity, which could easily have become a rigid formula, is not so much in evidence. It is true that when Zola first notes the existence of Anna, or familiarly Nana, Coupeau in a genealogical tree of the Rougon-Macquart family in 1868, before she had been thought of as the future 'heroine' of a novel, she had been described as having an inherited tendency towards drunkenness but there is little trace of such a weakness in the eventual Nana who, although she imbibes quite freely, is in no way an alcoholic. Environment thus remains the principal 'scientific' factor; Zola scatters important details of Nana's early life throughout the novel. He must also have been able to rely on the fact that many of his readers would be familiar with Nana's background from their knowledge of *L'Assommoir*[1], published three years earlier, where her past is abundantly detailed. It will, therefore, be helpful to make a brief reference to this work for a better understanding of Zola's intention.

In *L'Assommoir* Nana is born in a slum and brought up in appallingly traumatic conditions, which would have justified a plea for extenuating circumstances before any reasonable judge. However, she is a bonny baby, already heading for the plump juiciness which Zola is perhaps rather too much at pains to stress in *Nana*; a perennial problem: Zola was often accused of being a conniving voyeur. At the age of 3, by inadvertently causing her father, a tiler, to fall from a roof, Nana unwittingly sets him on the path of his alcoholism when he becomes idle and work-shy as a result of his injury. She turns into a noisy, mischievous child, good-natured though described as possessing a 'vicious curiosity', so that one night she sees her mother slip, half-naked, into the bedroom of her former lover while her husband, Nana's father, lies grunting in a drunken torpor in his own vomit. At 12, she is sticking pieces of paper into her bodice to enhance the shape of her breasts. Though expelled from catechism classes, she enjoys her first communion, chiefly because it involves receiving presents and wearing a lovely new white dress. At 15, doubtless influenced by her milieu, she is foul-mouthed and becoming keen on boys. She gets a job at a florist's, where she picks up all sorts of street wisdom from the chat of older girl assistants; she also develops a talent for making violet posies—hence, no doubt, the heady scent of violets which pervades her grand house in the Avenue de Villiers in *Nana*. She starts frequenting dance-halls—another taste she retains in later life—and hangs about in the streets. Finally, fed up with parental drunken brawling and parental disapproval, and especially with having her behind tanned by her alcoholic father, she runs away from home and takes up with a rich 50-year-old man who's been prowling around her for some

[1] The title *L'Assommoir* comes from a nineteenth-century colloquialism (from *assommer*, to stun, knock out) for a spit-and-sawdust pub where the working classes could drown their sorrows cheaply and drink themselves senseless.

time, but whom she then impulsively throws over in a sudden infatuation for a good-looking, penniless layabout; this sort of impetuous action against her own best financial interests is also repeated in the later novel; she is by no means an exclusively mercenary girl. Finally, she leaves home for good and disappears from *L'Assommoir*, though we have news that she's been seen driving round in a smart carriage and is later reported as having snaffled a viscount. From then on the ups and downs of her life depend on her relationships with men, usually for money. In any case, she's plainly now ready to embark on a wider world, where we meet her again in the first chapter of *Nana*, rather older than Zola's original birth-date warrants.

For a naturalistic novelist, perhaps even more than for a realist, authenticity and accuracy are prime considerations, both in general background and in the particular detail. Zola was fortunate in that, as a journalist of long standing, he had considerable familiarity with the theatrical world which provides the main background for *Nana*. He had done a good deal of dramatic criticism and in 1874 had himself been involved in putting on plays professionally, with an adaptation of *Thérèse Raquin*, one of his earliest novels. In 1878 a farce he had written had been put on in one of the 'little theatres'; it was, indeed, the utter failure of this play that sent him back to writing novels, and he started working on *Nana*. In a further search for authenticity we find him going behind the scenes of the Variétés theatre, where he shows Nana making her début in the first chapter. So his scenes in a green room, in various dressing-rooms, or at a rehearsal rest on solid factual knowledge.

His knowledge of the *demi-monde* was bound to be less direct; neither his temperament, his principles, nor, until the prodigious success of *L'Assommoir*, his finances could have made him familiar with the life of the high-class tart. However, his journalistic experience again stood him in good stead. As a writer of chatty articles for a number of Parisian and provincial papers he had picked up a good deal of gossip about these expensive ladies of pleasure. For example, in 1872 he tells the readers of a provincial paper about the suicide attempt of a man who had been squeezed dry and discarded by a certain Cora Pearl [*sic*], one of the most notorious kept women of the period, and of the actual suicide of a member of the smart Jockey Club, ruined by investing all his wealth in an unsuccessful racing-stables. Both these events have an echo in *Nana*; we must clearly beware of suspecting Zola of being over-dramatic in his incidents, even if the more lurid details are imaginary. And why not? Zola's naturalism never excluded poetic licence.

Zola also had far more reliable and direct sources of information than gossip. A friend of Flaubert, Edmond Laporte, and a fellow novelist, Henri Céard, were experts in this disreputable field and supplied great quantities of detail on it. Zola even commissioned Céard to write a series of reports on specific incidents that he'd witnessed, which Zola utilized extensively, sometimes using the very words and phrases of his friend. His preparations were so thorough that we can recognize, or make a good guess at, which real woman provided the model for Nana. From Zola's notes we learn that the splendidly named Blanche d'Antigny was also blonde, busty, impulsive, free-spending, superstitious, promiscuous (clearly a professional necessity), achieved success almost over-night, suffered a sudden infatuation for an actor, and made a trip to the East. Nana's Prince-of-Scotland encounter comes from Hortense Schneider's affair with the Prince of Wales, the future King Edward VII (still very much alive when *Nana* was published), when she was singing, rather badly but probably still better than Nana, in Offenbach's *La Grande Duchesse de Gérolstein* in the very same Variétés theatre where Nana is shown making her début.

Obviously such details of appearance, character, and career are merely bare bones to be fleshed out in accordance with his specific image of her. This image goes far beyond the social-moralizing conception of her as a deprived working-class girl. There is in Zola a strain of lyricism and a sense of the epic which is far from naturalistic. In this conception of Nana, she is not only the slum child, not even the representative of the grand Second Empire tart, but a combination of the Scarlet Woman, Sexuality personified, and an incarnation of the goddess of love, a living Venus. Her sexual frolics are shown in great detail, but our final impression of Nana is of something far grander and less fleshly. Chapter 11, which gives an account of a race-meeting at Longchamp, is a brilliant example of this sort of metamorphosis. It starts on a note of light-hearted frivolity, with amusing side-glances at Nana's tarts dressed up in various alluring *toilettes*, and glimpses of stuffy Imperial grandeur against a background of surging humanity; then come a few hints of menace laced with humour: the majestic bawd Tricon, whose sinister presence presides over many scenes of the novel; the flamboyant bookies; then the mad excitement of the Grand Prix, won by a mare named after Nana herself; this leads to an extraordinary final scene where Nana is acclaimed by the adoring, even worshipping multitude as she strikes the Venus pose which had made her famous on the stage. We have indeed moved very far away from the trivial concept of sex-kitten, though she is plainly no angel either; the mob isn't applauding a saint.

But even at her silliest and nastiest, the readers of *Nana*, and particularly those who know her life in *L'Assommoir*, are unlikely to forget how much she is a victim of society and that it is society, and above all the male elements of that society, which bears a great deal of responsibility for her deplorable behaviour. Nor does Zola neglect her endearing sides, her good humour, her frequent acts of kindness and disinterested charity. Zola did not want to risk alienating his readers by depicting too flawed a character.

He also succeeds in breathing life into minor characters. He was helped in this inasmuch as many had already existed in his consciousness before starting to plan *Nana*, and though they are collectively required to represent a particular type of smart society, he'd gathered sufficient personal details of character and situation to avoid making them too puppet-like, especially as he was always prepared to let his imagination rip on occasion; the novel was indeed, as he wrote in his notes, 'a *poem* about male desires'. The way he depicts these characters serves greatly to increase our sympathy for Nana: self-indulgent, deceitful, and selfish, they seem also uniformly, single-mindedly, and unrepentantly lustful, from the youngest, barely more than a schoolboy, to the oldest, the dreadful old state councillor and keen Sabbatarian the Marquis de

Chouard, passing through the vulgar comedian Fontan (modelled on the famous contemporary comic actor, the younger Coquelin), the vain *jeune premier* Prullière, the crafty, witty journalist and dramatic critic Fauchery, his cousin, the provincial coxcomb and would-be young blood la Faloise, the sex-crazy Jewish banker Steiner, and the civilized but effete Count de Vandeuvres—all recipients of Nana's favours (though the list is far from complete), and who all come, in one way or another, to a bad end. True, the women they patronize when Nana is not available, her colleagues and competitors, are no angels. Based, like the men, on a blend of real information and Zola's invention, they are bitchy, envious, and grasping; surrounded by male sharks, they surely have to be. They certainly seem rather kinder and, above all, less vindictive than their male partners. Vindictiveness seems, indeed, a hallmark of these smart young men: la Faloise, humiliated by Fauchery, enjoys getting his own back, or at least trying to; Fauchery, humiliated by Muffat, enjoys humiliating Muffat in turn; Labordette contemptuously depreciates Vandeuvres out of sheer bitchiness; and nobody has a good word for Steiner. On the other hand, the women—their 'ladyships' as Zola frequently refers to them—may squabble amongst themselves but they have far greater loyalty to each other: the men are prepared to let Vandeuvres sink without trace, but in Nana's last desperate hours her women friends rally round in support, at considerable danger to themselves, albeit perhaps with a certain morbid curiosity, while the men who've all enjoyed her favours wait in cowardly safety outside in the street below.

That sexuality involves struggle between the sexes is hardly an original concept, but there are other areas of sexuality explored by Zola which are far more novel, in particular lesbianism which, though it plays a very important part in Nana's life, has been little commented on by critics, perhaps because most of them are male. Lesbianism is by no means restricted to Nana herself; its prevalence in certain milieux is unfolded dramatically in a way that recalls Proust's similar exposure of male homosexuality in *Sodome et Gomorrhe* and *Le Temps retrouvé* a generation later. In *Nana* Zola dwells particularly on one centre of lesbianism, a restaurant in the

Rue des Martyrs—a street where Nana herself could have been seen lurking in *L'Assommoir* as an adolescent. This popular restaurant, based on a well-known existing establishment, is largely frequented by mature, burly, butch ladies who go there to wine and dine or perhaps pick up, at a price, more-or-less obliging young female partners; there are also a few young men and women of means and kinky curiosity who go slumming to observe the public behaviour of this peculiar, extremely animated fauna. A frequent visitor to this restaurant is Satin, a piquant young prostitute and former schoolmate of Nana; she copulates with men out of financial necessity, usually reluctantly, but with women by choice. It is through her that Nana gets to know this milieu, and after initial disgust she discovers the attractions of this form of love and forms a lesbian relationship with Satin, who is so taken by Nana that she becomes violently jealous of her friend's male companions, while Nana herself develops a love for Satin which is both passionately sexual and tender. They clearly experience a shared enjoyment and understanding which they do not find in their heterosexual encounters. Zola makes it plain that such relationships are to be considered vicious; he could hardly have done otherwise to avoid falling foul of the censor and public opinion; he was well aware that a banned and unread book serves no financial and little moral purpose. Similarly the clientele of Madame Piédefer's restaurant is depicted, not without flamboyant touches of humour, as shady and reprehensible. All the same, although neither Nana nor Satin gives up her wayward promiscuity, their relationship is something special and has a tenderness which Nana feels in only one of her heterosexual relationships which, interestingly enough, starts when the boy, Georges Hugon, is dressed in women's clothes—as Georges presses her, Nana is said to feel as if she were being pestered by a girl-friend.

But we must not enrol Zola too hastily in any feminist camp. The concept of *femme fatale*, implying a woman capable of causing havoc by sex-appeal alone, is a myth objectionable to feminists, female or male, even though it does represent a persistent belief; it seems indeed unlikely that Helen of Troy launched a thousand ships by her force of character, her spiritual qualities, or even her face alone and, rightly or wrongly, it does seem a myth central to Zola's moral and social intention in this novel. His treatment of sexuality elsewhere also bears a traditionally male stamp when he stresses the masochistic tendencies of two of his female protagonists. Nana and Satin have both had male partners who have shown them physical violence. At one point Zola has them settling down cosily to exchange reminiscences about their lovers' brutality, 'in a euphoric daze . . . wallowing in the tired warm feeling of being so outrageously knocked about'; and he adds that, although reluctant to admit it, they preferred those days 'when there were thrashings in the air, because it was more exciting'. Zola confessed to writing his novels in a state of repressed sexuality and he may here be indulging in private sexual fantasies, while his heated imagination is surely taking over in this description of the effect of repeated thrashings on Nana: she becomes 'as soft as fine linen, her skin delicate, her complexion peaches-and-cream, so tender to the touch and so radiant that she looked even lovelier.'(!) Despite such oddities, Zola maintains some claim to impartiality by not restricting masochism to the female sex alone. He gives a number of glimpses, one of them lifted straight from a play by the Restoration dramatist Otway, of various forms of this sexual pleasure enjoyed by male characters at Nana's hands. Muffat, the main recipient, accepts and seems even to need mental and physical chastisement, perhaps as a substitute for the divine punishment he feels he deserves, while la Faloise, for different, largely snobbish reasons, seems to enjoy having his face slapped by Nana as much as Nana enjoys doing it and as his cousin Fauchery enjoys watching it.

So perhaps the battle of the sexes is a drawn game, the blame distributed with a fairly even hand. On the whole, the women appear in a rather better light; their conduct is largely forced on them, and it is interesting to see that the woman with the least social or moral justification for her behaviour, Countess Sabine, is in many ways the least sympathetic of the female characters. Perhaps she gets a black mark from Zola for the whole-hearted pleasure she takes in her affairs, at least at the start; later, she too is shown as sinking into degradation. At this stage in his life, the puritanical Zola takes a very jaundiced view of sexual intercourse and depicts it largely as pure lust; he once stated that any love not aiming at producing children was basically debauchery. In *Nana* the sexual conduct—perhaps 'capers' is a better word—of his characters proceeds from boredom, envy, snobbery, ambition, a need for money, a desire for power, or to display wealth; it is, in the circumstances, not surprising that sexuality appears largely as joyless and that many of the characters are bedevilled by private torments.

None is more bedevilled, in the Christian religious sense, than Count Muffat. Although starting as an abstract idea—Zola needed a representative of authority, in league with the Church, and thus forced into hypocrisy when involved in an adulterous love-affair—the court chamberlain develops into a far more complex and dramatic figure than the other male characters also required for the logic of his plot. Muffat's strong sensuality which is the original cause of his falling for Nana's sex-appeal turns into an overwhelming passion, which is then considerably sublimated into a tender devotion akin to the religious fervour to which he has always been subject. There are further ingenious complications: Muffat's wife is as strongly sexed as her husband, but by an ironic mischance they have failed to hit it off in the nuptial bed; Muffat has been so strictly brought up by his mother that, still a virgin on his wedding-night, he seems to have muffed it. It is a complex, convincing situation, which greatly enhances the drama and deepens the pathos of Muffat's plight, and of course makes nonsense of the accusation occasionally levelled at Zola of being psychologically simplistic. We may, indeed, surmise that Zola could have fleshed out Muffat from self-knowledge, for at the time of writing *Nana* the novelist was himself a middle-aged man who hadn't sown any wild oats and was uncomfortable in his own marriage. Whether, in view of his negative attitude towards religion, he was in a good position to give a plausible account of religious agonies is another matter; not everyone will be satisfied with the portrayal of Muffat's pious ecstasies and contrition.

Never entirely puppets, the other males, apart from Labordette, appear more stereotyped than the women.

Labordette is a homosexual whose presence in the novel enables Zola to complete his full picture of types of sexuality and to show us what might be the position and status of such a man in the society of his time. Labordette is shown as a far-from admirable person: he is a parasite, with even a touch of pimp, always too ready to oblige everybody; but he is never shown as ridiculous; on the contrary, he enjoys general consideration, even respect, amongst his contemporaries; Muffat is prepared to accept his acquaintance, and he is certainly portrayed rather more sympathetically than most of the other men. Women are very fond of him: he is always courteously considerate towards them and can be relied on never to harass them sexually; if he helps them, as he frequently does, he won't expect, unlike their other men friends, to be paid in kind. He is also physically brave—he has fought a couple of duels—though in moral cowardice he seems to match the rest of the men. Altogether, he can in no way be considered a stereotype and Zola shows in him that he is ready to disregard a shibboleth.

In a fascinating coincidence, two considerable writers were called upon to express views on *Nana* simultaneously in February 1880, immediately after its first publication in book form; the not yet famous Henry James, in a review article, and the most famous living French novelist, Gustave Flaubert, in an enthusiastic letter to his friend Émile Zola; both views are extremely instructive. James cautiously pays careful lip-service to Zola's 'intrinsically respectable qualities', his 'incontestably remarkable talent', and even to 'the largeness of his attempt and the richness of his intentions'. He claims not to have been shocked by his choice of subject—perhaps a good example of *qui s'excuse s'accuse*. But when he comes down to specifics, the tone is very different; the novel is, he says, 'a combination of the cesspool and the house of prostitution'—no doubt metaphorically, for no brothel appears in *Nana*. He speaks of the 'singular foulness of [Zola's] imagination—never was such foulness so spontaneous and so complete!', a remark which completely disregards the Frenchman's painstaking technique of documentation. In a word, despite his denials, James's peculiarly delicate sensibility has been shocked by Zola's explicitness and this has thrown his judgement off balance; but one of his comments strikes so hard at our understanding of the novel that it is worth looking at more closely. Speaking in the name of the 'English reader'—presumably meaning 'English-speaking'—James was a New Yorker living in Paris—he writes: 'what will strike [him], if he has stoutness of stomach enough to advance in the book, is the extraordinary absence of humour, the dryness, the solemnity, the air of tension and effort . . . M. Zola would probably disapprove of humour, if he knew what it is'—a sentence which, whatever else it suggests, certainly proves that James had never read any of Zola's short stories.

No one will deny that there is in *Nana* an air of tension, effort, and even solemnity: Muffat's dilemma is surely no joke, nor is Nana's fate; a more positive way of expressing James's concern would be to say that the novel contains many dramatic situations, some pathetic, some tragic. Or does James harbour the conventional misconception that prostitutes are incapable of experiencing normal human emotions? But the truth is that in *Nana* there is humour in abundance: at the most elementary level, la Faloise, the provincial fop, is a figure of fun throughout as is the busty and obtuse Tatan Néné, most appropriately named—*néné* is a colloquialism for 'tit'. The impresario and theatre-manager Bordenave has a number of repulsive traits as a brutal macho, but his colourful bluntness, particularly when contrasted with his fawning obsequiousness before the Prince of Scotland, his behaviour at Nana's supper-party, and many other of his attitudes are rich in broad humour. The Mignons' unconventional mutual-benefit society, based on an actual married couple brought to Zola's notice by Ludovic Halévy, one of Offenbach's librettists, is obviously involved in funny scenes—Mignon's fight with Fauchery, his earnest educational concerns for his sons, his amazed appreciation of Nana's accumulated splendour—both of these last two scenes were picked out particularly by Flaubert in his extremely detailed letter to Zola. Even the tragic figure of Muffat is not entirely unrelieved by comedy: his preoccupied fumbling with a theatrical prop—a plaster egg-cup—as he awkwardly negotiates with his wife's lover on Nana's behalf, even some of his sexual antics, have a funny or grotesque side. The humour is frequently ironic: Nana's constant yearning for respectability, not only in society but on the stage, is a normal and touching desire, but ludicrous because of her manifest unsuitability in either case. Minor characters provide many more humorous incidents: Foucarmont's drunken boasting is only one of many retailed in the course of Nana's blundering attempt at giving a smart supper-party; Bosc's drunken gluttony matches Prullière's silly vanity; the portrayal of the massive Madame Piédefer (Ironfoot!) presiding over her fat, middle-aged lesbian flock; the furtive embarrassment of a large collection of males following Nana's miscarriage, each wondering uneasily if he is not the bereaved father—a scene which Flaubert singled out again unerringly but callously as adorable; and rather shamefully, as a hardened bachelor and something of a mysogynist, Flaubert, with all his aesthetic insight, made no mention of Nana's feelings, nor did he seem to appreciate the symbolism of the inability of Nana, the toy of a sterile male society and already the mother of a sickly child (whom she loved and who was to be the instrument of her downfall) to give birth to healthy offspring. In any case, while not all the ironical and humorous details are particularly subtle (Madame Maloir's hats here spring to mind), they are so numerous that we must convict James of reading with insufficient care or of himself lacking humour.

Flaubert's letter, written after a first and doubtless rushed reading, is in basic disagreement with James's article. Parallel quotations prove the point: James: 'this last and most violent expression of the realistic faith is extraordinarily wanting in reality'—we wonder what basis of knowledge James can muster to question, for example, the authenticity of the depiction of the theatrical milieu which Zola knew intimately. Here is Flaubert's statement: 'the characterization is remarkably truthful'—and no one can doubt Flaubert's familiarity, in 1880, with the Paris scene; he had kept a flat in Paris for the last twenty-five years. Above all, however, Flaubert has grasped Zola's grand design. For James, Nana was a 'brutal *fille* without a conscience or a soul' (had he read the beginning of Chapter 12, or in any way appreciated its irony?) 'with nothing but devouring appetites and ignorance' (had he read the country idyll between Georges Hugon and Nana? Had he considered her countless charitable actions?), '[which] has become the stalest of stock properties of French fiction . . . she is not made human'. This view might perhaps have had more substance had Zola stuck too rigidly to his preliminary notes, some of which we have already quoted, and it was partly echoed by some contemporary critics, one of whose major strictures was that Nana was too stupid and vulgar to represent the more polished image of the Second Empire courtesan, who was expected to charm by her social gifts and conversation rather than by her physique and erotic skills, a gift vaguely discernible indeed in one or two of the minor tarts, 'their ladyships'. James's view clearly fails to take into account all sides of Nana's character. Flaubert makes no such mistake: 'Nana', he writes in his letter, 'tends towards myth but never ceases to be real'. By real, he obviously means human: a woman of complex emotions and strivings; a mother, a woman who has to make her way in a frivolous, licentious society and who, in order to succeed, has to fight it with its own weapons, a woman still capable of disinterested affection which transcends purely physical attraction. Above all, Flaubert has realized the epic nature of her career; she has become, so to speak, the Helen of Troy of the Second Empire. Flaubert had already greeted Nana's apotheosis at Longchamp as 'épique, sublime!'; but it was the grandeur of the dramatic last chapter which most impressed him—so awe-inspiring and horrible that we are not surprised to learn that writing it reduced Zola to a state of nervous prostration—Flaubert was similarly affected after poisoning Madame Bovary. Nana's fate reduced Flaubert to almost inarticulate gasps of admiration: 'Chapter 14, unsurpassable! . . . Yes! . . . Christ Almighty! . . . Incomparable . . . Straight out of Babylon!' And he sums up: 'Worthy of Michelangelo!'

Flaubert's insight is once again unerring: this last chapter draws together all the threads of the novel. We see again Nana as mother caring for her sick child, the product of her early life in the slums, by whom she is fatally infected; we witness the loyalty of her women friends, even those who have been her rivals; we are reminded of the cowardice of the males while at the same time receiving further proof of her magical charm: all those who have known her, men and women, are drawn together as if by magnetic attraction; the mark she has left on them is indelible, particularly of course on Muffat who, as the one who has loved her most truly and tenderly, is shown as holding apart from the others whose love has been snobbish or purely physical. The wider implications of the novel are also set in perspective: Nana's radiant beauty of Chapter 1 has become a festering lump of flesh; she has reaped what she has sown, for it is through her flesh that she has corrupted and been corrupted by the society of her time, an inwardly rotten society whose decay becomes manifest in her; and that society, stupidly obsessed, which blindly acclaimed her at Longchamp, is now equally stupidly and blindly bellowing 'On to Berlin!' outside the windows of the hotel where she is lying, just six months before the Prussians will march victoriously down the Champs-Elysées; the Parisians have chosen another false god, the god of war, and in the same way that Nana's face is disfigured they too, in Mignon's picturesque phrase, will 'get their blocks knocked off'. The Empire will collapse as dramatically as Nana's beauty, and seeing their parallel fates we ask ourselves whether either was ever more than a glittering façade, an illusion of beauty in her, an illusion of grandeur in the Imperial society? As she lies on her bed, we ask ourselves what benefit did she either give or receive in her career; she certainly never achieved permanent happiness, any more than all the men lured by her charm. Was she more than a false Venus, created as much by the successful publicity of the entrepreneurial Bordenave as by any gifts of her own? Wasn't this 'something else' which the theatre-manager exploited, this indefinable charm, not the appeal of Venus but the false promises of the enchantress Circe[2] (though Nana's task was easier than Circe's, since her victims were already swine)? In any case, we know that the world of Nana and her society is coming to an end, though with no thought of any better one emerging; it has been a show and now it is closing down.

Fiction is, as we know, a craft and Zola's is considerable.

[2] *Circe*: a beautiful sorceress who transformed the companions of Ulysses into swine by a magic drink.

He started from an excellent base: the world of the theatre always fascinates, particularly when portrayed in authentic detail; it lends itself to humour, too, and actors and actresses are always good for a laugh; there is a sharp look at the feverish, fashionable Paris society at the height of its luxurious, legendary, Second Empire brilliance, and all-the-more interesting because of its hint of hollowness; that society's obsession with sexual activity, orthodox and less orthodox, is matched by an equal interest on the part of the author in the moral and social repercussions of such behaviour at various levels of that society. The care with which Zola drew up and worked out his plans, and his methodical gathering and ordering of the necessary material, is exemplary. He was particularly conscious of the need for variety of tone and scene, a factor which was rendered doubly important as the novel was written to appear as a serial: thus we find scenes devoted to particular forms of theatrical life, in the auditorium, before and during performances, at rehearsals, in the boxes and the foyer as well as backstage, in the wings, the green room and, most dramatically and pungently—*Nana* is full of odours of all sorts—in the dressing-rooms; life on the boulevards, in the charming, covered Paris arcades—a few still exist; scenes of street-walking; more domestic scenes in drawing-rooms, dining-rooms, a variety of flats and hotel rooms, and, naturally, bedrooms; a sober, aristocratic evening 'at home'; a noisy, drunken supper-party; a grand society private dance and a boisterous public dance-hall—Zola enjoys inviting comparisons; even a breath of fresh air away from the steamy atmosphere of the boudoir, though the air can be steamy here, too; and, of course, the splendid day at the races, whose background Zola researched very carefully. Zola's skill in bringing such scenes to life had been honed by long practice as a short-story writer[3] where he had, in particular, learned the art of building up suspense to a climax or anticlimax, essential to leave the reader of a serial with an exciting impression at the end of each episode, eager to learn 'what is going to happen next'.

[3] See, for example, Émile Zola, *The Attack on the Mill and other Stories* (Oxford, 1985).

In his preparatory notes Zola wrote: 'there's only sexuality and religion'; money, so central in *Nana*, is presumably considered as largely subsumed under sex. Religion is chiefly represented by the Muffat clan: the count himself; his father-in-law, a staunch upholder of religion for the lower classes; his surprising daughter Estelle, who proves conclusively and amusingly that a plain girl, as thin as a rake, can still make good when she determinedly brings the light-hearted Daguenet, one of her father's mistress's 'fancy men', firmly under her pious thumb after their marriage; the grey eminence of the family, the sinister but ultimately successful Venot, who brings the unhappy Muffat back into the fold; and there is also a most sympathetic portrait of Madame Hugon, who needs all her Christian fortitude to withstand the blows dealt to her family by fate, in the form of Nana. And it must be noted that, in spite of Zola's unbelief, Religion can in the end be seen to triumph over Sex. It is, however, safe to assume that this moral ending is not the main reason why, on its first publication in 1880, *Nana* went through more than fifty editions in a few weeks. A very vigorous publicity campaign by the publisher, perhaps taking a leaf out of Bordenave's book, certainly helped, but this would hardly explain the work's enduring success, the reason for which must surely be sought in the eponymous heroine. Not, of course, purely in sex-appeal, nor in the many scabrous situations in which her glamour, in every sense, placed her, but also in Zola's careful exploration of the career, at a psychological and social level, of a fascinatingly complex character, an unhappy corruptress corrupted by a closely observed luxurious and pleasure-loving society, brilliant, shallow, and doomed. Quirky, impulsive, and incalculable (whatever will she be up to next?—she doesn't even know herself . . .); ruthless and pitiful, generous and criminally wasteful, a Circe of epic proportions, Nana will surely continue to charm and outrage the prurient and the pious, the student of social and political relations or of the psychology of sex and crowds, the feminist (she is beginning to receive her due share of critical attention in this respect after years of male neglect), the male chauvinist, and of course the sturdy 'general reader', who will ensure that this will remain amongst the most widely read of Zola's novels.

SELECT BIBLIOGRAPHY

FRENCH editions of *Nana* are legion; a particularly good one is in the *Bibliothèque* de la Pléiade edition of Zola's novels, volume ii, with notes by the most distinguished Zola scholar Monsieur Henri Mitterand, to whom this translator is grateful to acknowledge his debt, and the Flammarion edition (1968) edited by Monsieur Roger Ripoll should also be noted.

In English there are a number of general critical works which include sections on Zola: Martin Turnell's *The Art of French Fiction* (Hamish Hamilton, 1959) and H. Levin's *The Gates of Horn* (Oxford University Press, 1963) are most likely to be available to the general reader. Judith Armstrong's *The Novel of Adultery* (Macmillan, 1976) contains references to *Nana*. Specific studies on Zola's life and work include: F. W. J. Hemmings' *Emile Zola* (Oxford Paperbacks, second ed., 1966), E. M. Grant's *Emile Zola*, in the Twayne's World Author Series of similar vintage, and P. Walker's *Zola* (Routledge and Kegan Paul, 1985).

For closer study there exists an excellent and exhaustive *Bibliographie de la Critique sur Emile Zola* produced by D. Baguley, published in two volumes by the University of Toronto Press, vol. i (1976): 1864–1970; vol. ii (1982): 1971–1980. David Baguley has also contributed an article on 'Zola the novelist' in the useful collection *Zola and the Craft of Fiction*, edited by R. Lethbridge and T. Keefe (Leicester University Press, 1990).

Other articles in English dealing specifically with *Nana* include: J. L. Beizer, 'Uncovering Nana: The Courtesan's New Clothes', *L'Esprit createur*, 25 (1985); P. V. Conroy, Jr., 'The Metaphorical Web in Zola's *Nana*', *University of Toronto Quarterly*, 47 (1978); J. C. Lapp, 'The Watcher Betrayed: Some Recurring Patterns in Zola', *Publications of the Modern Languages Association of America*, 74 (1959); G. Lukàcs, 'Narrate or Describe', in *Writer and Critic and other essays*, ed. A. D. Kahn (Merlin Press, 1970); H. Michot-Dietrich, 'Blindness to Goodness: The Critics' Chauvinism?', *Modern Fiction Studies*, 21 (1975).

Knowledge of the history of the Second Empire can increase understanding of *Nana*. Many such histories exist; here are three: J. P. T. Bury, *Napoleon III and the Second Empire* (Hodder and Stoughton, 1964); A. Cobban, *A History of Modern France, Volume 2: 1799–1871* (Penguin Books, 1961); W. E. Echard (ed.), *Historical Dictionary of the French Second Empire* (Greenwood Press, 1985).

A CHRONOLOGY OF ÉMILE ZOLA

1840 Émile Zola born in Paris of French mother and Italian engineer father, who died in 1847

1843 Family settles in Aix-en-Provence

1859 Émile twice fails the school-leaving *baccalauréat*

1862 Destitute in Paris, already writing poems and short stories, Émile obtains a job in recently-founded publisher's bookshop of Hachette. His poverty during this period makes him familiar with low life and slum conditions

1864 In charge of Hachette's publicity, Émile has *Contes à Ninon*, his first collection of short stories, published

1865 His first novel, *La Confession de Claude*, published: a semi-autobiographical account of a young idealist's attempt to reform a prostitute. Starts liaison with a florist, Gabrielle-Alexandrine Meley, whom he marries in 1870. Émile leaves Hachette to embark on a writing career, at first largely as a journalist (book-reviewer, drama-critic, short-story writer, feature articles, gossip columns), and continues to contribute to numerous Parisian and provincial papers and magazines for many years, particularly before 1880

1867 Frequenting artistic circles, which include his friend and fellow-Provençal Paul Cézanne and many Impressionists. Publishes the novel *Thérèse Raquin*, which he turns into a play in 1873

1870 Publication of *La Fortune des Rougon*, first of the twenty novels of the *Rougon-Macquart* series. Takes refuge from invading Prussian army in Marseilles; his journalism includes being parliamentary correspondent to French government which had retreated to Bordeaux

1877 Immense success of *L'Assommoir*, seventh in the cycle, brings fame and financial security, enabling him to buy a country property in Médan, a village on the outskirts of Paris

1878 Publication of *Une Page d'Amour*, which includes a genealogical table of the Rougon-Macquart family with the first mention of Anna Coupeau

1880 Publication of *Nana*

1885 Publication of *Germinal*

1887 Publication of *La Terre*. Émile starts lifelong liaison with Jeanne Rozerot, a servant of the Zolas, with whom he was to have two children; his marriage had been childless

1893 Publication of *Le Docteur Pascal*, last in the series

1894 Publication of the novel *Lourdes*, first of a trilogy, *Les Trois Villes* (the other cities were *Rome*, 1896, and *Paris*, 1898), concerned with social and religious questions; the first two went quickly on to the *Index*.

1898 Zola publishes his article *J'Accuse* asserting Dreyfus's innocence and is forced to go into exile in England to avoid imprisonment

1899 Publication of *Fécondité*, first in a proposed series of four didactic, social-humanitarian novels, of which only one more (*Travail*, 1901) was published in his lifetime; the third, *Vérité*, strongly anti-Christian, was serialized in 1902/3; the fourth, never completed, was to have been called *Justice*, and preached an end to war and the establishment of world peace

1902 On 29 September Zola is found dead, asphyxiated in his Paris flat overnight; there is evidence that his chimney had been deliberately blocked by a nationalistic Frenchman disapproving of Zola's political pro-Dreyfus stance

NANA

Chapter 1

AT nine o'clock the auditorium of the Variétés* was still deserted. The gas-jets of the chandelier were turned down and in the half-light a mere handful of people sat waiting in the rows of dusky red-plush seats of the stalls and dress-circle. The large red patch of curtain was in shadow, the stage completely silent, the footlights were unlit, the orchestra desks unoccupied. Only in the gods, at the very top, round the dome where naked women and children were depicted cavorting against a sky stained green by gas fumes, was there a steady buzz of voices punctuated by shouting and laughter, where rows of heads in caps and bonnets were stacked in tiers in the large, gilt-framed, round bays. An occasional usherette bustled in with tickets in her hand, propelling a man and woman in front of her, the gentleman in evening dress, the lady slim, with her back arched, slowly casting her eyes around before subsiding into her seat.

A couple of young men appeared and stood beside the orchestra pit, observing the scene.

'I told you so, Hector!' exclaimed the elder of the two, a tall young man with a small black moustache. 'We're too early. You could easily have let me finish my cigar.'

An usherette was going by.

'Oh, hullo Monsieur Fauchery', she said familiarly. 'The performance won't be starting for another half hour yet.'

'Then why did they put nine o'clock on the poster?' muttered Hector, screwing his long, thin face up irritably. 'Clarisse is in the show and assured me only this morning that it'd begin at nine sharp.'

They broke off for a moment to peer up into the dimly lit boxes, but their green wallpaper made them even darker. Below, under the dress-circle, the ground-floor boxes were shrouded in complete gloom. In the dress-circle boxes there was just one very large lady, relaxing over the plush-covered rail. The stage boxes on the left and right, with their long-fringed pelmets between tall columns, were unoccupied. The auditorium itself, white and gold picked out in a delicate green, was in shadow, as if filled with a fine haze by the dimmed lights of the cut-glass chandelier.

'Did you get Lucy her stage box?' asked Hector.

'Yes, but it wasn't easy', replied the other man. 'Oh, there's no danger of Lucy arriving early!'

He half-stifled a yawn, paused and then went on:

'You're lucky, you've never been to a first night before . . . [*The Blonde Venus* is going to be *the* event of the year. People have been talking about it for the last six months . . .] The music, old boy! Something really special . . . Bordenave, who knows what he's doing, has kept it for the World Fair.'*

Hector was listening closely; he asked:

'And what about that new star Nana, the one who's going to play Venus? Do you know her?'

'Oh God, here we go again!' cried Fauchery, flinging his arms in the air. 'People have been pestering me about Nana all day. I've met more than twenty people and it's been nothing but Nana, Nana all the time! What can I say? Can I be expected to know every little Paris tart going? Nana's been dreamt up by Bordenave. It's bound to be something pretty revolting.'

He calmed down; but the empty auditorium, the dim chandelier, the devout religious atmosphere full of whispers and slamming doors, was getting on his nerves.

'Oh no!' he exclaimed suddenly. 'This is adding years to my life. I'm going out . . . Perhaps we'll find Bordenave downstairs. He'll give us some details.'

Below in the large, marble-paved lobby, the public was beginning to collect beside the ticket-check. Through the three open entrance gates you could glimpse the bustling life on the boulevard, glittering and crowded with people on this lovely April evening. Carriages were rumbling up and halting, their doors were slammed, and little groups of people were making their way in, stopping to have their tickets checked and moving along up the double staircase at the back, where the ladies were lingering, swaying their hips. In the harsh glare of the gas-lamps outside, on the pale, bare façade, with its skimpy Empire decoration producing the effect of a cardboard temple peristyle, garish yellow posters were displaying the name 'Nana' in large black letters, read by men who looked as if their eyes had been suddenly caught as they were passing by; others were standing chatting, blocking the entrance, while beside the box-office, a burly man with a big, clean-shaven face was giving short shrift to the people who were pressing him for seats.

'That's Bordenave', said Fauchery as they were going down the stairs. The manager had spotted him.

'Well, what a nice chap you are!' he called out across the hall. 'So that's the publicity I get, is it? . . . I looked through the *Figaro** this morning. Not a single word!'

'Hang on', Fauchery replied. 'I'll have to get to know your Nana before writing about her. . . . Anyway, I didn't make any promises.'

To change the subject, he introduced his cousin: Monsieur Hector de la Faloise, a young man who'd come to complete his education in Paris. The manager threw him a sharp glance to size him up, but Hector was gazing at him, thrilled: so this was the Bordenave who put women on show and drove them like galley slaves, who always had some publicity stunt or other bubbling away in his head, shouting, spitting, slapping his thighs, a cynic with the mentality of a sergeant-major! Hector felt he ought to say something pleasant.

'Your theatre', he began in a piping voice.

Calmly, like a man who doesn't want any misunderstanding, Bordenave interrupted him:

'Call it my knocking-shop, will you?'

Fauchery gave an approving laugh but la Faloise was deeply shocked, with his compliment stuck in his throat, trying to look as if he appreciated the comment. The manager had dashed over to shake hands with an extremely influential drama-critic. When he came back, la Faloise was recovering; he was afraid of being thought provincial if he seemed too flustered.

He made another attempt, determined to say something:

'I've heard Nana has a delightful voice.'

'Her?' the manager exclaimed with a shrug. 'She's got a voice like a corncrake.'

'And a first-rate actress, I'm told', the young man added hurriedly.

'Nana? . . . She's a lump! She doesn't know what to do with her hands or her feet.'

La Faloise flushed pink. Completely at a loss, he stammered:

'I wouldn't have missed this first night for worlds. I know your theatre . . .'

Once again, with the quiet persistence of a man of strong convictions, Bordenave cut him short:

'Just call it my knocking-shop.'

Meanwhile Fauchery was calmly watching the women going in. Seeing his cousin standing open-mouthed, not knowing whether to laugh or be angry, he came to his rescue:

'Do oblige Bordenave and call his theatre what he wants, since he likes it that way. . . . And as for you, old boy, stop keeping us in suspense. If your Nana can't sing or act, you're heading for a flop, that's plain. Incidentally, that's what I'm afraid of.'

'Did you say a flop?' snorted Bordenave, going purple in the face. 'Does a woman need to be able to sing or act? Ah, my lad, you're too stupid. Nana's got something else, for Christ's sake. Something that makes everything else superfluous. I've got a nose for that sort of thing, and she's got oodles of it or I'm a Dutchman. You'll see, you'll see . . . All she's got to do is to come on stage and the whole audience will sit there with their tongues hanging out.'

In his enthusiasm he was waving his large hands about in the air; then, calming down, he grunted to himself, under his breath:

'Oh yes, she'll go far, yes, by God, very, very far . . . That skin of hers! . . . and all that flesh underneath it!'

Then, in answer to Fauchery's questions, he agreed to give some details, with a coarseness of language which embarrassed la Faloise. He'd had it off with Nana and now he was anxious to launch her on a career. At that particular moment he happened to be looking for a Venus. He never lumbered himself with any woman for long, he preferred to pass on the benefit to the public straight away. But he'd had a hell of a job in his outfit, where the arrival of this fleshy young piece had been causing quite an upset. Scenting a rival, his star turn Rose Mignon, herself a very gifted actress with a charming singing voice, had been threatening every day to leave him in the lurch. And what a fuss over the poster, heavens above! In the end it'd been decided to print the actresses' names in the same size letters. He didn't like being buggered about. When one of his 'little women', as he called them, didn't toe the line, he'd give her a kick up the arse. Otherwise life would be unbearable. After all, he knew what the sluts were worth, he sold them!

'Well, well', he said, suddenly breaking off. 'Mignon and Steiner . . . The heavenly twins . . . You know, Steiner's beginning to get fed up with Rose, so her husband won't let him out of his sight, in case he tries to do a bunk.'

The whole pavement in front of the theatre was flooded with light by a row of blazing gas-jets along the cornice; two small trees stood out in a lurid green, and on the brightly lit advertising-pillar in the distance the posters could be read as easily as in broad daylight; further on, where the shadows were already deeper, the confused, constantly moving mass of people on the boulevard was dotted with tiny specks of light. Many of the men didn't go in immediately but waited outside to finish their cigars; in the glare of the gas-jets their faces were ghastly pale, and on the asphalt their shadows were short and very dark. Mignon, an extremely tall, burly fellow, with the square head of a fairground strong man, was elbowing his way through the knots of people, dragging the banker Steiner along with him by the arm—a tiny little man, already pot-bellied, with a round face fringed by a greying beard.

'Well', said Bordenave to the banker, 'you met her yesterday in my office.'

'Oh, so that was her!' exclaimed Steiner. 'I thought it might have been, but as I was going out as she was coming in, I only caught a glimpse of her.'

Mignon was staring at the floor, nervously twisting a large diamond ring round his finger. He'd realized that they were referring to Nana. Then, as Bordenave started giving a description of his latest discovery which brought a glint into the banker's eye, he finally spoke out:

'Oh, come on, my dear chap, she's a slut! The public will

send her packing on the spot . . . Steiner, old man, you know my wife's waiting for you in her dressing-room.'

He tried to get him away. Steiner was reluctant to leave Bordenave. Behind them a queue of people were storming the box-office and the hubbub of voices was growing louder and louder, with the name 'Nana' providing a lively and melodious refrain. The men stationed in front of the billboard were spelling it out in full, while others mentioned it in passing, with a questioning note; the women, smiling uneasily, were whispering it quietly, with a look of surprise. Nobody knew Nana. Where on earth had she sprung from? People were telling each other stories. Jokes were being exchanged in whispers. The name sounded endearing, it had a nice familiar ring, everybody liked pronouncing it; merely saying it made the crowd cheerful and sympathetically inclined. Paris society was being gripped by a typically feverish curiosity, a sudden, stupid craze. People couldn't wait to see Nana. One lady had the flounce of her dress ripped off, a gentleman lost his hat.

'Oh, you're wanting to know far too much!' cried Bordenave, besieged by a score of men asking for information. 'You'll be seeing her . . . I've got to go, they need me somewhere else!'

He slipped away, delighted at having fired his public's interest; Mignon shrugged his shoulders and reminded Steiner that Rose was waiting to show him her first-act costume.

'Look, there's Lucy getting out of her carriage', said la Faloise to Fauchery.

It was indeed Lucy Stewart, a plain little woman, about 40 years old, with too long a neck, a thin, drawn face, and thick lips, but very charming, vivacious, and graceful. She had brought Caroline Héquet and her mother along with her; Caroline was beautiful; her mother looked like a highly respectable stuffed owl.

'Come and sit with us, I've booked an extra seat', she said to Fauchery.

'Oh no, thanks very much', he replied. 'I suppose you want me not to see what's happening! I've got a seat in the stalls, I prefer that.'

Lucy was annoyed. Was he afraid to show himself with her in public? Then she suddenly quietened down and changed her tack.

'Why didn't you tell me you knew Nana?'

'Nana? I've never even seen her!'

'Are you telling the truth? Someone swore you'd been to bed with her.'

But Mignon came up with his finger to his lips, warning them to keep quiet, and in reply to Lucy's query, pointed to a young man going by and whispered:

'Nana's fancy man.'

They all looked at him: a nice chap. Fauchery recognized him as Daguenet, who'd got through three hundred thousand francs on women and was now dabbling in the Stock Exchange so as to be able to offer them flowers and the odd meal. Lucy thought he had wonderful eyes.

'Ah, there's Blanche!' she cried. 'She's the one who told me you'd been to bed with Nana.'

Blanche de Sivry, a strapping blonde, with pretty features, showing signs of becoming rather blowzy, was coming in with a slightly built man, very elegant and distinguished-looking.

'Count Xavier de Vandeuvres', whispered Fauchery into la Faloise's ear.

The count shook the journalist's hand while Blanche and Lucy launched into a lively altercation, blocking the way with their heavily flounced dresses, one blue, the other pink. The name 'Nana' was coming up in such shrill tones that people started listening. Count de Vandeuvres took Blanche away; but now curiosity had become even keener, and Nana's name was being taken up more and more loudly all round the foyer. Weren't they ever going to begin? Men were pulling out their watches, late-comers were leaping out of their carriages even before they stopped, groups of people were coming in from outside where passers-by were craning their necks to look in as they dawdled along the now-deserted stretch of pavement under the glare of the gas-jets. A down-at-heel young tough came up whistling, stopped at the entrance in front of a poster, called out: 'Olé Nana!' in a husky, drunken voice, and went swaying off along the boulevard. People laughed and some very distinguished-looking gentlemen repeated: 'Olé

Nana!' There was a lot of jostling, a row broke out at the ticket-office, the buzz of voices was becoming an uproar as, in a heady wave of crude sensuality and stupidity typical of crowds, everybody began clamouring for Nana to appear.

Above the babel of voices the bell started ringing and the cry: 'It's the bell! It's the bell!' even spread to the boulevard outside. There was a general stampede, with everyone anxious to get in; more attendants were fetched to check the tickets. The worried Mignon at last managed to get hold of Steiner, who hadn't gone to look at Rose's costume. At the first sound of the bell, la Faloise had dashed off through the crowd, dragging Fauchery with him, determined not to miss the overture. Such eagerness on the part of the public annoyed Lucy Stewart: how rude people were, pushing ladies about! She waited till last, with Caroline Héquet and her mother. The foyer was empty; in the background, the rumble on the boulevard continued.

'As if their shows were always funny', Lucy kept saying as they went upstairs.

Inside the auditorium, Fauchery and la Faloise stood in front of their seats, once again looking round.

The theatre was ablaze with light. The gas-jets were now full on, and the huge, glittering, crystal chandelier was flooding the audience in a dazzling pink and yellow light from the proscenium arch down to the pit. The deep red of the seats had a silken shimmer, while the bright gleam of gilt was toned down by the soft green of the decoration running along under the garish ceiling paintings. The footlights were turned up and suddenly the heavy, dark red curtain glowed with the opulence of some fabulous palace, somewhat grander than the peeling gilt stucco surrounds, where patches of bare plaster could be seen. It was already hot. The musicians were tuning up at their desks; the light trills of the flutes, the muffled sighs of the horns, and the tuneful voice of the violins rose above the increasing buzz of conversation. The audience were all chatting, pushing, and settling down after the scramble for their seats; in the corridors, a jostling mass of people was jamming the doorways; the stream seemed endless. People were waving to each other, dresses were being crumpled, the parading skirts and hairstyles were interspersed with black frock-coats or tails. But the rows of seats were gradually filling up; the eye was caught by a pale dress, a face with a delicate profile bending forward, a flash of jewellery entwined in a chignon. In one box, a patch of bare shoulder gleamed white as silk. Other women were languidly fanning themselves, casting glances over the hustle and bustle; smart young men in low-cut waistcoats and with a gardenia in their buttonholes had stationed themselves beside the orchestra, peering through opera-glasses poised in their gloved fingertips. The two cousins were looking for familiar faces. Mignon and Steiner were together, side by side in a ground-floor box, resting their wrists on the velvet-covered rails. Blanche de Sivry seemed to have a stage box all to herself. But la Faloise was particularly interested in Daguenet, who was in an orchestra stall two rows in front of his own. Next to him sat a very young man, 17 at the most, a schoolboy playing truant; he had the look of a little cherub, with superb eyes which were popping out of his head.

'Who's that lady in the dress circle?' asked la Faloise suddenly. 'The one with the girl in blue beside her.'

He pointed to a large, tightly corseted woman, whose hair, once fair but now white, fell in a profusion of yellow-rinsed girlish curls over her round, puffy face plastered with rouge.

'That's Gaga', Fauchery replied simply and as his cousin appeared perplexed by the name, he added:

'Don't you know Gaga? . . . She was the darling of the early thirties.* Now she lugs her daughter around with her all the time.'

La Faloise didn't look at the girl; he was thrilled by the sight of Gaga and couldn't take his eyes off her; he thought she still looked wonderful, but was afraid to say so.

Meanwhile the leader of the orchestra was raising his bow and the musicians launched into the overture. People were still coming in, and the din and general commotion were increasing. In this first-night audience, always full of the same people, there were little private groups smilingly acknowledging each other, while the regular theatre-goers, still with their hats on, were exchanging waves and nods, relaxed and very much at home. This was Paris: the Paris of literature, finance, and pleasure; lots of journalists, a few authors, stockbrokers, and more tarts than respectable women; a strangely mixed bunch, comprising every kind of genius, tainted with every kind of vice, with the same look of feverish excitement and weariness painted on every face. In response to his cousin's questions, Fauchery pointed out the boxes occupied by newspapermen and members of clubs, then told him the names of the dramatic critics, one lean and shrivelled, with thin, malicious lips, and one especially, fat and good-natured in appearance, who was lolling against his neighbour's shoulder, an ingénue whom he was ogling with a loving, fatherly eye.

But seeing la Faloise bow to some people sitting in a box facing the stage, Fauchery stopped in surprise:

'Good Lord, do you know Count Muffat de Beuville?' he asked.

'Oh, I've known them for ages', la Faloise replied. 'The Muffats own a property close to ours. I often go and see them . . . The count's with his wife and father-in-law, the Marquis de Chouard.'

Flattered by his cousin's surprise, he smugly enlarged on the details: the marquis was a member of the Conseil d'État* and the count had just been made the Empress's chamberlain. Fauchery had picked up his opera-glasses and was looking at the countess, who was plump, with a fair skin, brown hair, and fine dark eyes.

'You must introduce me in the interval', he said finally. 'I've already met the count but I'd like to be invited to their Tuesday parties.'

The upper galleries yelled: 'Quiet down there!' The overture had begun, though people were still coming in. These late-comers were forcing whole rows of spectators to stand up, box-doors were being slammed, there were loud disputes in the corridors. The continued chatter was like the busy chirping of noisy sparrows at dusk. It was chaotic, a confused jumble of heads and waving arms, with some people sitting down and making themselves comfortable, others still stubbornly on their feet, determined to have one final look round. From the obscure depths of the pit there came a violent call to: 'Sit down! Sit down!' A thrill had run through the house: at last they were about to make the acquaintance of that famous Nana, whom the whole of Paris had been talking about for the last week!

Gradually, apart from the odd raucous outburst, the talking gently died down, and in the middle of this muffled murmur, as the noise subsided to a whisper, the orchestra burst into a lively sort of jig, a waltz with a rhythm as vulgar as a dirty laugh. The audience, titillated, started to smile, while the claque in the pit-stalls broke into wild applause. The curtain was going up.

La Faloise was still chatting away: 'I say, Lucy's got a man with her.'

He was looking at the dress-circle box on the right where Caroline and Lucy were sitting in front. At the back could be seen the dignified face of Caroline's mother and the profile of a tall, immaculately dressed young man with a superb mop of blond hair.

'Look', la Faloise insisted again. 'There's a gentleman there.'

Somewhat reluctantly Fauchery pointed his opera-glasses in the direction of the box and immediately turned away.

'Oh, it's Labordette', he said offhandedly, as if everyone would consider it natural and of no importance for that man to be there.

Behind them someone called out: 'Be quiet!' They stopped talking. From the stalls up to the top gallery the packed house now sat motionless and upright, intent on the stage. The first act of *The Blonde Venus* took place in Olympus, a pasteboard Olympus with clouds as side-wings and Jupiter's throne on the right. First of all, Iris and Ganymede, attended by a choir of celestial servants, had to sing a chorus whilst arranging the seats for a meeting of the gods. Once more, paid clappers broke into their planned round of applause; the general public, still somewhat at sea, suspended their judgement. However, la Faloise had clapped Clarisse Besnus, one of Bordenave's 'little women', who was taking the part of Iris, dressed in a delicate blue costume with a broad, rainbow-coloured scarf tied round her waist.

'You know, in order to get into that dress, she's had to leave off her slip', he said in a stage whisper. 'We tried it on this morning. . . . You could see her slip under her arms and down her back.'

There was a fresh stir in the audience: Rose Mignon had just come on stage. She was Diana, and being dark and thin had neither the face nor the figure for the part, but her adorably impish ugliness, so essentially Parisian, was charming, a sort of parody of the character. The words of her first song, in which she complained that Mars was on the point of deserting her for Venus, were unbelievably silly, but she sang them with such coyness and so many saucy innuendoes that the public warmed to her. Her husband and Steiner, sitting cheek by jowl, were tactfully laughing. And the whole house exploded when the highly popular actor Prullière came on stage: he was Mars, a Mars straight out of pantomime, dressed up as a general with a giant plume on his helmet and wielding a sword which reached shoulder-high. He'd had his bellyful of Diana; she fancied herself too much. At this, Diana swore she'd keep a sharp eye on him and take her revenge. Their duet ended with a comic yodelling song which Prullière brought off hilariously, in a voice like a squawling tom-cat, with the asinine self-satisfaction of a juvenile lead conducting a torrid love affair, rolling swashbuckling eyes in a way which brought high-pitched laughter from the boxes.

After this the audience became lukewarm again: they found the next scenes boring. Old Bosc, a moronic Jupiter with his head squeezed into an immense crown, barely managed to raise a smile in his domestic squabble with Juno over the cook's bill. The parade of gods and goddesses, Neptune, Pluto, Minerva, and all the rest, almost wrecked the show; the public was getting impatient; a sinister muttering was slowly spreading through the house as people started to lose interest and let their eyes wander round the theatre. Lucy was laughing with Labordette; Count de Vandeuvres was craning his neck behind Blanche's plump shoulders; meanwhile Fauchery was examining the Muffats out of the corner of his eye: the count was looking solemn as if he didn't know what was happening, the countess had a vague smile on her face and was gazing dreamily into space. But suddenly, at this awkward moment, the claque began loudly clapping, in time, like the rattle of gunfire. People looked towards the stage: was it Nana at last? She was certainly taking her time!

But it was a deputation of mortals introduced by Ganymede and Iris, respectable middle-class citizens, all deceived husbands coming to lay a complaint with the master of the gods against Venus, who was making their wives far too passionate. This chorus, sung in a mournful, simple tone, full of hidden admissions, aroused great amusement. Some wit made a comment which ran round the theatre—'the cuckolds' chorus', and the remark stuck. People started shouting 'Encore!' The chorus had funny faces and really looked the part, particularly one fat, moon-faced man. Meanwhile Vulcan came in, furiously demanding to see his wife who hadn't been home for the last three days. The chorus took up their refrain again, appealing to Vulcan, the King of the Cuckolds. This character was played by Fontan, a vulgar comedian, very clever and original, who lurched around crazily like a village blacksmith, in a flaming red wig and with bare arms tattooed with hearts pierced by arrows. In the audience a female voice blurted out, very loudly, 'What a hideous man!' and the women all started laughing and clapping.

There followed a scene which went on too long: Jupiter spent ages assembling a meeting of the gods to put the deceived husbands' petition before them. And still no sign of Nana! Were they keeping her just for the final curtain-call? This long-awaited event had finally made the audience irritable and the muttering started again.

'This looks ugly', Mignon said delightedly. 'There's going to be trouble, you'll see.'

At that moment, the clouds at the back of the scene parted and Venus appeared. Dressed as a goddess in a white tunic, with her long blonde hair hanging completely loose over her shoulders, Nana was very tall and sturdy for her eighteen years. With complete self-assurance, she advanced laughing towards the footlights and launched into her big aria: 'When Venus goes prowling at night . . .'.

She had barely reached the second line before the audience started exchanging glances. Was this a joke, one of Bordenave's calculated risks? They'd never heard a worse-trained voice, nor one singing more out of tune. Her manager had summed her up exactly: she sang like a corncrake. And she didn't even know how to hold herself on the stage—she was flinging her arms about in front of herself and swaying in a way that seemed both graceless and inappropriate. Oohs and ahs were coming from the pit and the cheaper seats, and people began quietly hissing; then a cracked voice, like a moulting cockerel's, in the orchestra stalls called out enthusiastically:

'Fantastic!'

The whole house gaped. It was the cherub, the schoolboy playing truant, with his eyes popping out of his head, his pale face pink with excitement at the sight of Nana. Seeing everybody looking at him, he went as red as a beetroot, realizing that he'd spoken out loud without meaning to. His neighbour Daguenet was examining him with a smile, and the audience, disarmed, started laughing, no longer having any thought of booing, while the smart young men in white gloves, also carried away by Nana's shapely curves, were clapping ecstatically.

'That's right! Wonderful! Bravo!'

Seeing the audience laughing, Nana had begun to laugh herself. The laughter became even louder. This splendid-looking girl really was funny. When she laughed, a delicious little dimple appeared under her chin. She stood waiting, relaxed and quite unembarrassed, establishing immediate contact with her audience; she seemed to be saying openly, with a wink, that she'd got no talent at all but it didn't matter, she'd got something else. And making a sign to the leader of the orchestra, as much as to say: 'Let's get going, old boy!' she began her second verse: 'At midnight Venus passes by . . .'.

It was the same vinegary little voice, but now it was rubbing the audience the right way and occasionally making them twitch. Nana was still laughing, her tiny red lips curling in amusement and with a twinkle in her large, bright blue eyes. In certain rather saucy passages her cheeks started to glow and she tipped up her dainty little pink nose; her nostrils were quivering. She continued to sway from side to side because that was the only thing she knew how to do; but now nobody found that at all ugly, far from it; the men were peering through their opera-glasses. As she was reaching the end of the song her voice gave out completely, and realizing she'd never be able to finish it, quite unperturbed, she gave a sideways flick of her hip, so that the curve of her buttock showed under the thin tunic and, leaning back, she held out both arms, thrusting her breasts out towards the audience. People started applauding, whereupon she quickly swung round and moved upstage; from the back, her red hair looked like the tawny mane of a wild animal. The applause became frantic.

The end of the act was less exciting. Vulcan wanted to slap Venus's face. The gods held a meeting and decided that, before satisfying the deceived husbands' demands, they'd go down and hold an enquiry on Earth. Overhearing Venus and Mars flirting together, Diana swore she'd never let them out of her sight throughout the whole trip. There was also a scene where Cupid, played by a little girl of 12, kept replying: 'Yes, Mummy . . . No, Mummy . . .' to every question, in a snivelling voice, at the same time sticking her finger up her nose. Then Jupiter, behaving like an irate schoolmaster, shut Cupid up in a dark cupboard, ordering him to conjugate the verb 'to love' twenty times. The finale was more enjoyable: accompanied by the orchestra with tremendous brio, the whole company sang a final chorus. However, at the end, the claque failed in its attempt to force a curtain-call; the audience were already on their feet making for the exit, and as they stumbled and jostled each other, jammed between the rows of seats, they exchanged their impressions. The general verdict was:

'It's idiotic!'

A critic was heard to say that they'd need to make a good few cuts. Anyway, the play itself didn't much matter: people were above all talking about Nana. Fauchery and la Faloise were among the first out, and in the stalls corridor they met Steiner and Mignon. It was stifling in the passage, which was lit by gas and as low and narrow as the gallery of a coal-mine. They stood for a minute at the foot of the right-hand staircase, protected by the curving handrail. The people from the cheaper seats were steadily thudding their way down the stairs in their heavy shoes; there was a constant stream of white ties; meanwhile an attendant was trying hard to prevent a chair which she'd piled up with clothes from being overturned.

'I know her!' exclaimed Steiner as soon as he saw Fauchery. 'I'm certain I've seen her somewhere . . . At the Casino de Paris,* I think it was, and she was picked up for being drunk.'

'Well, speaking for myself, I'm not sure', said the journalist. 'I'm like you, I've certainly met her somewhere or other.'

Lowering his voice he added with a laugh:

'At Tricon's place, perhaps?'

'Hell, yes, in some sleazy dive or other', Mignon exclaimed. He seemed exasperated. 'It's disgusting for the public to give that sort of reception to the first little slut that comes along. Soon there'll be no respectable actresses left . . . Yes, I'm going to end up having to forbid Rose from appearing on the stage . . .'

Fauchery couldn't suppress a smile. Meanwhile the heavy clatter of shoes coming down the stairs continued, and a little man in a cloth cap was saying with a drawl:

'My word, she's a plump bit! . . . And tasty, too!'

In the corridor, two young men with carefully frizzed hair, very spruce in their butterfly collars, were quarrelling with each other; one kept saying: 'Loathsome! Loathsome!' without explaining his reasons, the other kept replying; 'Absolutely divine! Divine!', similarly not bothering with any arguments.

La Faloise thought she was very good, merely venturing the opinion that she'd be better if she could do something about her singing. Then Steiner, who'd stopped listening, seemed suddenly to come to life. In any case, they'd have to wait; in the remaining acts everything might go wrong, and while the audience seemed quite well-disposed, they certainly weren't yet completely won over. Mignon was convinced the play wouldn't last out to the end, and as Fauchery and la Faloise were leaving them to go up to the foyer he took Steiner's arm and, leaning on his shoulder, whispered into his ear:

'My dear fellow, you'll be seeing my wife's costume in the second act, it's so sexy!'

Upstairs, the foyer was ablaze with the light of three chandeliers. For a second the two cousins hesitated; the glass doors were wide open and they could see the whole length of the gallery in which a heaving mass of faces was milling round in two streams. However, they decided to venture in. Five or six groups of men, talking very loudly and waving their arms about, were resisting all the pushing and shoving; the others were moving in lines, tapping their heels on the waxed parquet flooring as they did a right-about turn. Between the mottled marble columns on each side women were sitting on long red-velvet seats, wearily watching the crowd flow past, as if exhausted by the heat; their chignons were reflected in the tall mirrors behind them. At the far end, in front of the buffet, a man with a paunch was drinking a glass of cordial.

Meanwhile Fauchery had gone out on to the balcony in search of fresh air. He was followed by la Faloise who had been studying the framed photographs of actresses hanging between the mirrors. The lights running along the front of the theatre had just been put out; it was dark and very cool on the balcony, which seemed to be empty. However, the glow of a cigarette in the shadow of the right bay revealed a young man, all alone, leaning over the balustrade, smoking. Fauchery recognized Daguenet. They shook hands.

'What on earth are you doing out here, my dear chap?' the journalist asked. 'Here you are, hiding yourself away when you normally never leave the stalls on first nights.'

'I'm smoking, as you can see', replied Daguenet.

Trying to embarrass him, Fauchery said:

'Well, what do you think of our new star? . . . People don't seem all that enthusiastic, to judge by what I heard in the corridor.'

'Oh, that'll be men whom she's turned down', muttered Daguenet.

That was the only verdict he passed on Nana's acting ability. La Faloise was leaning over, looking down into the boulevard. Opposite, he could see the brightly lit windows of a hotel and a club; down below there was a dark mass of customers sitting at the tables on the terrace of the Café de Madrid; and in spite of the late hour the pavements were packed, people were picking their way along with tiny steps, and a constant stream was coming out of the Jouffroy Arcade; pedestrians were having to wait five minutes to cross the road because of the long queue of carriages.

'What a scramble! And what a din!' la Faloise was saying; Paris still amazed him.

A bell started to ring; the foyer emptied. People were hurrying down the corridors; many were still coming in after the curtain had gone up, to the annoyance of those already in their seats. There was an air of eager expectancy. The first thing la Faloise did was to look at Gaga, but to his surprise she had been joined by the tall fair-haired man who'd previously been in Lucy's box.

'What's that man's name again?' he asked.

Fauchery couldn't see him properly.

'Oh yes, that's Labordette', he said eventually, with the same unconcern as before.

The set for the second act was a surprise: it was Shrove Tuesday in The Black Ball, a low dance-hall in the seedy outskirts of Paris. Masked revellers were singing a sort of roundelay and tap-dancing to the refrain. The audience found this unexpected glimpse of low life amusing, and demanded an encore of the song. This was the place where the gods, misled by Iris, who'd boasted quite falsely that she knew the Earth, had come to conduct their investigation. To keep their incognito, they'd disguised themselves. Jupiter appeared as King Dagobert,* with his breeches on back-to-front and wearing a huge tin crown. Phoebus was the Postilion of Longjumeau,* and Minerva a wet-nurse from Normandy. Wearing an outlandish Swiss admiral's uniform, Mars was greeted by hoots of laughter which took on a very offensive tone when Neptune shuffled in, dressed in a workman's smock and matching tall puffed cap and slippers, with his temples plastered with kiss-curls, and smirking in an oily voice: 'What are you on about? When you're a good-looking man, it's wrong not to let 'em love you!' There were a few shocked exclamations and the ladies tried to hide their faces behind their fans. In her stage box Lucy was laughing so loudly that Caroline Héquet had to give her a tap with her fan to restrain her.

From this moment on, the play had no further fears; it was well on its way to becoming a great success. This carnival of the gods in which Olympus was dragged through the mud and the poetry and religion of an entire civilization was made fun of, was seen as a delicious treat. These intellectual first-nighters were beginning to revel in this avalanche of irreverence; legendary figures were being kicked around, images of antiquity were being smashed. Jupiter was a bit of a mug, Mars was weak in the head. Royalty was being turned into farce and the army was just one big joke. When Jupiter suddenly fell for a little laundress and started strumming a wild can-can, Simonne, who was taking the part, kicked her foot up under the nose of the master of the gods and addressed him in such a comical voice as 'my big Daddy!' that the audience went into fits of laughter. While they were dancing, Phoebus was buying Minerva one salad bowl after another of mulled wine, and Neptune was lording it over seven or eight women who were stuffing him with cakes. People were picking up all sorts of innuendoes, adding their own smutty comments, while perfectly innocent expressions were being deliberately misinterpreted by interjections from the stalls. The public hadn't been able to wallow in such stupid impudence for ages. They felt refreshed.

However, in the midst of all this crazy by-play the action was proceeding. Vulcan, dressed as a dashing young fellow in the height of fashion, all in yellow, with yellow gloves and complete with monocle, was continuing to pursue Venus, who finally came on stage as a fishwife with a handkerchief tied round her head, her breasts bursting out of her dress and covered in masses of gold jewellery. She had such a white skin, she was so plump, such an absolute natural for this broad-beamed loud-mouthed character, that she immediately won over the whole house. She outshone Rose Mignon, a delicious baby, with a wicker head-pad* and short muslin dress, who warbled Diana's grievances in her charming melodious voice. But the other woman, this strapping young wench who kept slapping her thighs and cackling like a hen, exuded an exuberant, overpowering sex-appeal that intoxicated the audience. By this second act she'd already got them eating out of her hand whatever she did, singing out of tune, holding herself awkwardly, forgetting her lines; all she needed to do was to turn round and laugh and people would cheer. Each time she gave her famous flick of the hips the stalls went into a frenzy, and the excitement was spreading upwards from one gallery to another, right up to the gods. When she took over the orchestra, she received a magnificent ovation. With her hand on her hip, she was really at home with her Venus—in the gutter and all set to walk the streets. And the music was just right for her vulgar voice, with its echoes of trashy fairground music, its snorting clarinets and squeaky piccolos.

Two more pieces were encored. The waltz from the overture, with the saucy rhythm, reappeared and captivated the gods. Dressed as a farmer's wife, Juno caught Jupiter red-handed with his little laundress and smacked his face. Diana overheard Venus making a date with Mars and quickly told Vulcan the time and place; he cried: 'I've got a plan!' The rest seemed rather obscure. The enquiry ended in a final *galop*, at the end of which, having lost his crown and his breath and dripping with sweat, Jupiter declared that the little women on earth were delightful and that the men were entirely to blame.

As the curtain fell, there were deafening calls for the whole cast, even louder than the cheers.

So the curtain was raised again and the actors and actresses came on holding hands, with Nana and Rose Mignon in the middle, bowing together. People were clapping, the claque were screaming: 'Bravo! Bravo!' Then one half of the audience slowly went out.

'I must go and pay my respects to Countess Muffat', said la Faloise.

'Right you are, and you can introduce me', said Fauchery. 'We can go downstairs in a minute.'

But it wasn't easy to get to the dress-circle boxes. The upstairs corridor was packed. To make any progress between the knots of people you had to slip sideways and elbow your way through. Leaning against the wall under a brass gas-lamp, the stout critic was passing judgement on the play to a circle of eager listeners. People were whispering his name to each other as they went by. In the corridor, it was being said that he'd been laughing throughout the whole act; however, he was now talking about good taste and morality, and adopting a very strait-laced attitude. Further on, the thin-lipped critic was being very benevolent, with a sting in the tail, like the aftertaste of sour milk.

Fauchery was peering into the boxes through the round hatch in their doors when the Count de Vandeuvres stopped him to ask whom he was looking for. They told him that they were going to call on the Muffats, and he pointed to Box Seven, which he'd just left. Then he whispered in the journalist's ear:

'I say, old man, that Nana must be the girl we saw one night on the corner of the Rue de Provence.'*

'Good Lord, you're right!' exclaimed Fauchery. 'I've been saying I knew her!'

La Faloise introduced his cousin to Count Muffat de Beuville, who greeted him very distantly. But, hearing Fauchery's name, the countess had looked up; she volunteered a discreet compliment on his articles in the *Figaro*. She was resting her elbows on the velvet-covered rail, and the movement of her shoulders as she half turned was charming. They chatted for a moment and the subject of the World Fair came up.

'It's going to be very fine', the count said; his square face with its regular features bore a fixed expression of official solemnity. 'I visited the Champs-de-Mars today and I came away very greatly impressed.'

'People are saying it certainly won't be ready on time', said la Faloise, tentatively. 'There's been some mix-up . . .'

The count's stern voice cut him short.

'It will be ready. The Emperor insists that it must be.'

Fauchery gave a lively account of nearly ending up in the aquarium, at that moment under construction, one day when he was visiting the site in search of a subject for an article. The countess was smiling. Now and again she would look down into the auditorium, lifting one of her arms in their white, elbow-length gloves and fanning herself more slowly. The almost empty house was half-asleep; in the stalls, a few gentlemen had opened newspapers; women were relaxing while their friends greeted them as if in their own homes. Under the chandelier, whose light had been dimmed by the fine dust-haze raised by the scramble during the interval, the only sound was the gentle murmur of well-bred voices. Men were crowding into the doorways to look at the women who'd remained in their seats, and as they stood there motionless, craning their necks, their shirt-fronts looked like large white hearts.

'We'll be expecting to see you next Tuesday', the countess said to la Faloise.

And she invited Fauchery, who accepted with a bow. No one said anything about the play; Nana's name was never mentioned. The count maintained the frigid, dignified attitude that you might see at a sitting of the Legislative Body. He explained their presence at the performance merely by saying that his father-in-law liked going to the theatre. The Marquis de Chouard had gone outside to make room for the callers; the door had been left open and he was standing there, a tall, erect old gentleman with a pale fleshy face under his broad-brimmed hat, following the passing women with his bleary gaze.

As soon as he'd received his invitation Fauchery took his leave, feeling that any mention of the play would be out of place. La Faloise followed; he'd just caught sight of the fair-haired Labordette in the Count de Vandeuvres' stage box, looking very much at home, in close conversation with Blanche de Sivry.

'Well, well!' he said when he'd caught up with his cousin. 'Does this man Labordette know all the women? He's with Blanche now.'

'But of course he knows them all', retorted Fauchery calmly. 'Where have you been all this time, old chap?'

The corridor was rather quieter. Fauchery was just about to go downstairs when Lucy called out to him; she was standing in her stage-box doorway, right at the end. It was boiling in there, she said; she was blocking the whole passage, together with Caroline Héquet and her mother, nibbling sugar almonds. An attendant was chatting with them in a motherly sort of way. Lucy had a bone to pick with the journalist: how charming of him to call on other women and not even bother to come and ask if they'd like a drink!

Then, changing the subject:

'You know, my dear, I think Nana's very good.'

She wanted him to stay in their box for the last act, but he managed to slip away, promising to pick them up in the lobby after the show. He went downstairs with la Faloise and they lit up their cigarettes in front of the theatre. A long stream of men had come down the front steps and gathered in a solid mass, blocking the pavement and breathing in the cool night air amid the hustle and bustle of the boulevard, which was now dying down.

Meanwhile Mignon had just dragged Steiner over to the Café des Variétés. Seeing Nana's success, he'd begun to talk about her with enthusiasm, carefully noting the banker's reactions out of the corner of his eye. He knew his man, having twice helped him to deceive Rose and then, when the whim had passed, brought him, faithful and repentant, back into the fold. There were too many people crammed round the cafe's marble-topped tables; some were gulping down their drinks on their feet; and this solid mass of faces was reflected to infinity in the large mirrors which made the narrow room look immense, with its three chandeliers, its imitation-leather seats, and its spiral staircase draped in red. Steiner went over to a table in the front room, open to the boulevard, whose doors had been removed rather too early for the time of year. As Fauchery and la Faloise were going by, the banker stopped them:

'Come and join us for a beer.'

But he had something on his mind: he wanted a bunch of flowers to be thrown to Nana. Eventually he called over one of the waiters, whom he addressed familiarly as Auguste. Mignon was listening and watching him like a hawk, so that he became embarrassed and stammered:

'Two bouquets, Auguste, and give them to an attendant, one for each of the leading ladies, at a suitable moment, tell her.'

At the other end of the room, a prostitute, 18 years old at the most, was sitting motionless in front of an empty glass, leaning her head back against the frame of a mirror, as if numbed by a long and fruitless wait. Her face, with its frank, velvety soft eyes, looked virginal under her mop of naturally curly, ash-blonde hair. She was wearing a faded green silk dress; her round hat had suffered from being knocked about;

in the chilly night air, she looked as pale as a ghost.

'Well, well, there's Satin', murmured Fauchery.

La Faloise asked about her. Oh, only a little boulevard whore, nothing more. But she was such an amusing little floozy that it was fun to get her talking. And raising his voice, the journalist called out:

'Hi, Satin, what are you doing there?'

'Getting pissed off', Satin replied calmly, without moving.

Charmed by this response, the four men burst out laughing.

Mignon kept reassuring them that there was no need to rush: the set of the third act would take twenty minutes to erect. However, having drunk their beers, the two cousins were keen to go back in; they were feeling the cold. Mignon remained alone with Steiner. He leaned forward with his elbows on the table and looked him in the face.

'OK? We'll go up and see her and I'll introduce her, fair enough? . . . This is between us two, of course. No need for my wife to know anything.'

When they got back to their seats Fauchery noticed a pretty, modestly dressed woman sitting in the second-tier boxes. She was with a serious-looking gentleman, a head of department in the Ministry of the Interior, whom la Faloise knew through meeting him at the Muffats. Fauchery thought she was called Madame Robert, a respectable lady who never had more than one lover at a time, and he was always respectable, too.

But they had to turn round; Daguenet was smiling at them. Now that Nana had scored a triumph, he was no longer lurking; in fact, he'd just been enjoying his own triumph in the corridor. Beside him the young truant, completely overcome with admiration for Nana, hadn't left his seat. Ah, that's what people mean when they talk of a real woman! He was going very red and he kept mechanically pulling on and taking off his gloves. Then, hearing his neighbour mention Nana, he ventured to ask:

'Excuse me sir, do you know that lady who's acting?'

'Yes, a little', Daguenet replied uncertainly, surprised by the question.

'So you've got her address?'

The bluntness of the question tempted Daguenet to slap his face.

'No, I haven't!' he replied sharply and turned his back.

Realizing he'd committed a breach of good manners, in his dismay the fair-haired boy went even redder.

The three knocks announced the beginning of the act. Laden with furs and overcoats, the attendants were insisting on returning them to the people coming back to their seats. The claque applauded the set, a grotto on Mount Etna, deep in a silver-mine, with walls gleaming like coins fresh from the mint; at the back, Vulcan's forge looked like a setting star. During the second scene Diana had come to an arrangement with the god, who was to pretend to be going away on a trip in order to leave the coast clear for Venus and Mars. No sooner had he left than Venus appeared. A thrill ran through the audience. Nana was naked, naked and unashamed, serenely confident in the irresistible power of her young flesh, her well-rounded shoulders, her firm breasts with their hard, erect, pink nipples which seemed to be stabbing at the audience, her broad hips rolling and swaying voluptuously, her plump golden thighs. Covered by a simple veil, her whole body could be seen, or imagined, by all through the diaphanous, white, frothy gauze. It was Venus being born out of the waves, hidden only by her hair. And when she lifted her arms, in the glare of the footlights you could glimpse the golden hair in her armpits. Now there was no clapping, and no one thought of laughing. The men had a strained, earnest look on their faces; their nostrils were taut, their mouths parched and burning. It was as if the softest of breezes had passed through, full of secret menace. This good-natured girl had suddenly become a disturbing woman offering frenzied sexuality and the arcane delights of lust. Nana was still smiling, but it was the mocking smile of a man-eater.

'Jesus!' said Fauchery simply, turning to la Faloise.

Meanwhile Mars, complete with plume, had rushed round to his rendezvous and found himself with two goddesses on his hands. Prullière played this scene very cleverly; while Diana made up to him in one final attempt before handing him over to Vulcan, Venus, stimulated by the presence of her rival, tried to get round him; he surrendered to all these advances with the smugness of a fighting cock. The scene ended in a grand trio, and it was at that moment that an attendant appeared in Lucy Stewart's box and flung two huge bouquets of white lilac on to the stage. The audience applauded, Nana and Rose took a bow while Prullière picked up the two bunches of flowers. Some people in the stalls turned with a smile to look at Mignon's and Steiner's box; the banker had gone purple, and his chin was jerking convulsively as if he had something stuck in his throat.

What now followed riveted the spellbound audience: Diana had flounced off in a fury and Venus immediately summoned Mars to join her where she was sitting on a mossy bank. Never before had such a daringly erotic seduction scene been put on the stage: putting her arms round Prullière's neck, Nana was pulling him closer when Fontan appeared at the back of the grotto comically mimicking the fury of a husband outraged at catching his wife *flagrante delicto*. He was holding his famous net of iron-mail, which he swung for a second round his head like a fisherman and skilfully trapped them, leaving them unable to move in their close embrace.

A murmur spread through the house like a rising wind. A few people clapped and every opera-glass was focused on Venus. Gradually Nana had asserted her domination over the audience and now she held every man at her mercy. She was like an animal on heat whose ruttishness had permeated the whole theatre. Her slightest movement aroused lust; a jerk of her little finger was sexy. Men were leaning forward with their backs twitching, as if their nerves were being vibrated by invisible violin bows, the warm breath of some mysterious woman was straying over the napes of their necks and setting the wisps of hair quivering. Fauchery could see the truant schoolboy half out of his seat with excitement. Out of curiosity he looked at the Count de Vandeuvres, white-faced and tight-lipped, and at the corpulent Steiner, whose apoplectic face seemed ready to burst; at Labordette, who was peering through his opera-glasses with the surprised look of a horse-dealer admiring a perfect mare; Daguenet whose ears were blood-red and trembling with delight. Then it occurred to him to take a glance over his shoulder, and he was amazed by what he saw in the Muffats' box: behind the pale, earnest face of the countess, Muffat was standing open-mouthed, his cheeks mottled with purple spots, while next to him in the shadow the bleary eyes of the Marquis de Chouard had turned into two phosphorescent cat's eyes speckled with gold. People were gasping, their hair was sticky with sweat. They'd been there for three hours, and the atmosphere was stuffy from their breath and the smell of their bodies. In the glare of the gas-jets you could see a thick haze of dust hovering under the chandelier. The whole house was in a trance, their heads were reeling from weariness and excitement, in the grip of that sleepy sort of lust that comes in inarticulate gasps from lovers' beds in the middle of the night. And facing this ecstatic audience of fifteen hundred people, all crammed together and overcome by the exhaustion and nervous prostration inevitable at the end of any show, Nana's body, as smooth and white as marble, was all-conquering, her sexuality powerful enough to destroy all these people and remain unscathed.

The operetta was drawing to an end. In response to Vulcan's triumphant call, the whole of Olympus paraded in front of the lovers, with many 'ohs' and 'ahs', full of amazement and suggestive undertones. Jupiter was heard to say: 'My son, I consider it frivolous of you to invite us to come and look at this!' Then there was a swing in favour of Venus. The chorus of cuckolds, once again introduced by Iris, beseeched the master of the gods not to accede to their request; now that their wives were at home all the time, life was becoming impossible for them; they preferred to be happy cuckolds; this was the moral of the comedy. So Venus was set free, Vulcan was granted a separation, and Mars went back to Diana. In order to have some peace at home, Jupiter sent his little laundress off into a constellation. And Cupid was finally let out of his dungeon, where instead of conjugating the verb to love he'd been making paper hats. The curtain fell on an apotheosis, with the chorus of cuckolds on their knees singing a hymn of praise to Venus, smiling and more splendid than ever in her captivating nakedness.

The public were already on their feet making for the doors. The authors were acknowledged and there were two curtain-calls, amid thunderous applause and frenzied cries for Nana from all round the theatre. Then, even before everyone had left, the house was plunged into darkness; the footlights went out, the chandelier was lowered, long, grey canvas covers slid out from the proscenium and hid the gilt of the galleries. The warm, noisy hall fell into a heavy sleep amid a rising, musty smell of dust. At the edge of her box, wrapped in her furs, Countess Muffat was standing, very upright, looking into the darkness and waiting for the crowd to disperse.

In the corridors, the frantic cloakroom attendants were being jostled amidst piles of clothes that had fallen on the floor. Fauchery and la Faloise had hurried away to watch the people coming out. Men were standing along the walls of the entrance-lobby, while two solid, endless streams of people were slowly and steadily making their way down the double staircase. Steiner had been carried off by Mignon, who was amongst the first to get away. Count de Vandeuvres went off, giving his arm to Blanche de Sivry. For a moment Gaga and her daughter seemed embarrassed, but Labordette quickly went to find them a carriage and politely closed the door after they'd got in. Daguenet was nowhere to be seen. As the schoolboy cherub, red in the face and determined to wait outside the stage-door, made a dash for the Passage des Panoramas, where he found the entrance locked, Satin, who was standing on the pavement, brushed against him with her skirt; he abruptly refused and disappeared despairingly into the crowd, his eyes full of tears of frustrated desire. Some of the audience were lighting up cigars and going off humming: 'When Venus goes prowling at night.' Satin had gone away to the Café des Variétés, where Auguste was letting her help herself to the lumps of sugar left by the customers. Finally, a large man who'd come out in a state of considerable elation went off with her along the dark boulevard, which had gradually gone to sleep.

There were, however, still people coming down. La Faloise was waiting for Clarisse. Fauchery had promised to pick up Lucy Stewart with Caroline Héquet and her mother. They appeared laughing loudly and occupying one whole corner of the entrance hall, just as the Muffats came past with an icy look. Bordenave had at that same moment come out of a little door and was making Fauchery promise to produce a notice of the play. He was sweating and beaming, as though intoxicated by his success.

'You're all set for two hundred performances', said la Faloise, trying to be friendly. 'The whole of Paris will be queuing up to come to your theatre.'

But jerking his chin angrily towards the public cramming into the entrance hall, a bustling mob of men with dry lips and bloodshot eyes, still helplessly enthralled by Nana, Bordenave shouted fiercely:

'I told you to call it my knocking shop, you obstinate bugger!'

Chapter 2

IT was ten o'clock the following morning and Nana was still asleep. She occupied the second floor of a large new house in Boulevard Haussmann which the owner was letting to single ladies until the plaster had dried out. She'd been set up there by a Moscow business man who'd come to spend the winter in Paris and had paid six months rent in advance. The flat was far too big for her and had never been completely furnished; the flashy, opulent, gilt chairs and console tables formed a violent contrast to the second-hand junk, mahogany pedestal tables and zinc candelabra pretending to be Florentine bronze. The whole thing had the feel of a little tart who'd been abruptly dropped by her first genuine protector then left to fall back on lovers of dubious character; a tricky start which had gone off the rails, made worse by shortage of cash and threats of expulsion.

Nana was lying on her stomach, her face pale with sleep buried in the pillow which she was clutching between her bare arms. The bedroom and dressing-room were the only two rooms decently decorated, by a local paper-hanger. There was a glimmer of light coming under the curtain, and you could pick out the Brazilian rosewood and the grey figured damask with the large blue floral design of the hangings and chairs. The atmosphere was stuffy and drowsy; Nana woke with a start, as if surprised to find an empty space beside her. She looked at the second pillow lying next to her own, still dented from someone's head in the middle of the lace edging. She fumbled for the electric bell at the bed-head.

'Has he gone?' she asked the chambermaid when she appeared.

'Yes, madam, Monsieur Paul left not ten minutes ago . . . As madam was tired he didn't want to wake her up. But he asked me to tell madam that he'd be coming tomorrow.'

While talking, Zoé was opening the shutters. Daylight

streamed in. Zoé was very dark, with her hair parted down the middle and small coils over her ears; she had a long face like a dog's, livid and bearing scarmarks, a flat nose, thick lips, and restless black eyes.

'Tomorrow? Tomorrow?' repeated Nana, not yet properly awake. 'Is that his day tomorrow?'

'Oh yes, ma'am, Monsieur Paul has always come on Wednesdays.'

'Oh no, I've just remembered!' cried the young woman, sitting up. 'It's all been changed, I wanted to tell him about it this morning . . . He'd meet up with my wog. We'd have a dreadful row!'

'Madam didn't tell me, so I couldn't know', murmured Zoé. 'When madam changes her days, it would be sensible to warn me, so that I know . . . So the old skinflint's not on Tuesdays anymore?'

'Skinflint' and 'wog' were the names they used between themselves, in all seriousness, for her two current providers, a shopkeeper from Faubourg Saint Denis, of a frugal turn of mind, and a man from Wallachia* who claimed to be a count and paid up only intermittently in money that didn't have a very nice smell. Daguenet had claimed the day straight after the old skinflint; as the latter had to be home by eight o'clock in the morning the young man would lurk in Zoé's kitchen, watching for him to leave, and then take over his place in bed, still nice and warm, until ten o'clock when he too had to go off to work. He and Nana found this arrangement very convenient.

'Can't be helped', she said. 'I'll write to him this afternoon. If he doesn't get my letter, you'll have to stop him from coming in.'

Meanwhile Zoé had been quietly moving round the bedroom, talking about yesterday's tremendous success. Madam had shown what a lot of talent she had and hadn't she sung well! Madam certainly needn't have any worries now!

Propped up with her elbow on the pillow, Nana was merely nodding in reply. Her night-gown had slipped and her loose, tangled hair was streaming over her shoulders.

'I suppose that's right', she said pensively.' But how can I manage to hold out? . . . I'm going to be in all sorts of trouble today . . . By the way, has the porter been up yet this morning?'

They both started to take stock, seriously; they were three months behind with the rent and the landlord was talking about evicting them. Then there was a whole avalanche of creditors, a man who hired out carriages, a linen-draper, a dressmaker, a coal merchant, and others as well who used to come and take up their stand on a bench in the entrance hall every day; the coal merchant was dreadful, the worst of the lot—he'd keep shouting on the staircase. But Nana's chief worry was her little boy Louis, whom she'd had when she was 16 and left with his wet-nurse in a village not far from Rambouillet.* This woman was claiming three hundred francs in order to return little Louis to his mother. In a fit of motherly love, dating from her last visit to the boy, Nana was in despair because she was unable to carry out a plan which had grown into an obsession: paying off the nurse and settling the little fellow with her aunt, Madame Lerat, in Batignolles,* where she could go and see him as often as she liked.

The chambermaid was hinting, however, that she should have told the old skinflint about her troubles.

'But I did tell him everything', exclaimed Nana, 'and he replied that he'd got too many bills coming up . . . He won't go beyond his thousand francs a month. The wog's skint at the moment, I think he's lost money gambling . . . And as for Mimi, the poor dear could really do with a loan himself at the moment, there's been a slump which has cleared him out; he can't even afford to bring me flowers any more.'

She was referring to Daguenet. Having just woken up, she was in the relaxed mood when she'd open her heart to Zoé, who was used to hearing all her secrets and was happy to listen with a politely sympathetic ear. Since madam was kind enough to talk to her about her business, she would take the liberty of saying what she thought. First of all, she was very fond of madam, she'd deliberately left Madame Blanche, and God knows the efforts Madame Blanche was making to try and get her back! There was no shortage of jobs, she was pretty well known, but she would have stayed on with madam even if she was in financial difficulties because she believed in madam's future. And she summed up her advice: when you were young you did stupid things, but this time she would have to keep a sharp look-out because men were only interested in having their bit of fun. Oh, one would turn up! Madam only needed to say a word to keep her creditors quiet and find the money she required.

'That's all very well but it doesn't give me three hundred francs!' Nana pointed out again, sticking her fingers into the untidy curls at the back of her head. 'I must have three hundred francs today, on the nail . . . It's crazy not to know anyone who'll let you have three hundred francs.'

She was racking her brains; she was anxious to send Madame Lerat down to Rambouillet, and in fact was expecting to see her that very morning. Her frustration at not being able to satisfy her whim was spoiling her sensational success of yesterday. To think that among all those men who'd given her such an ovation, there wasn't a single one who'd slip her fifteen twenty-franc pieces! And of course, you couldn't accept money just like that. Heavens, how miserable she felt! And all the time she kept coming back to her baby: he had angelic blue eyes and his funny way of lisping 'Mummy' could make you die with laughter!

At that moment they heard the brisk tinkle of the outside electric doorbell. Zoé came back and said in a confidential whisper:

'It's a woman.'

She had seen that woman twenty times before, but she pretended never to recognize her and to know nothing about her relationship with ladies who were hard up.

'She said she's Madame Tricon.'

'That woman!' exclaimed Nana. 'Oh yes, that's right, I'd forgotten. Show her in.'

Zoé showed in an elderly lady, tall, with ringlets and the look of a countess with a weakness for lawyers. She then slipped out unobtrusively, with the gliding, snake-like action which she employed when a gentleman came. In fact, she might just as well have stayed. Tricon didn't even sit down. Very few words were exchanged.

'I've got someone for you today . . . Do you want to?'

'Yes. How much?'

'Four hundred.'

'What time?'

'Three o'clock. Is it on?'

'OK.'

Tricon immediately moved on to the weather, which was dry and good for walking. She'd still got four or five people to see. And she went off, consulting a little notebook. Left on her own Nana looked relieved. Feeling a little shiver run over her shoulders, she gently snuggled down again into the warm bed, like a lazy cat which can't stand the cold. Slowly her eyes closed; she was smiling at the thought of buying Louiset some nice clothes tomorrow, and as she dozed off, in her confused dreams of the whole previous evening she kept hearing a never-ending thunder of applause, like a basso profondo which rocked her, tired as she was, to sleep.

When Zoé showed Madame Lerat into her bedroom at eleven o'clock Nana was still sleeping. The sound woke her up and straightaway:

'Oh, it's you. You must go to Rambouillet today.'

'That's why I'm here', her aunt replied. 'I've got time to catch the twelve-thirty train.'

'No, I shan't get the money until later', the girl said. She stretched and her breasts lifted under her night-gown. 'Have lunch with me and then we'll see.'

Zoé came in with her dressing-gown.

'Your hairdresser's here,' she said softly.

Nana didn't want to go into the dressing-room. She called out herself:

'Come in, Francis!'

Just as she was getting out of bed and showing her bare legs, the door was pushed open and a very dapper man came in who wished her good morning. Unhurriedly, she held out her hands for Zoé to slip them into the sleeves of her dressing-gown while Francis, quite unperturbed, stood waiting, with a dignified look, not turning his back. Then, when she'd sat down and he had started combing her hair, he said:

'Perhaps madam hasn't seen the papers . . . There's a very good article in the *Figaro*.'

He'd brought the paper with him. Madame Lerat put on her glasses and, going over to the window, read the article out loud. She was tall, held herself very erect, and looked something of a tartar; whenever she came to a saucy passage she wrinkled her nose. It was Fauchery's review written straight after the show, two spirited columns, mischievously witty on Nana as an artist and full of uninhibited admiration of her as a woman.

'Excellent!' Francis kept saying.

Nana couldn't have cared less about jokes concerning her voice. Fauchery was a nice chap; she'd reward him for his good turn. After reading the article, Madame Lerat suddenly declared that all men had devils in their legs and refused to elaborate further, pleased at her ribald, if cryptic, reference. Meanwhile, having finished putting up Nana's hair, Francis left, saying:

'I'll keep an eye open for the evening papers . . . Usual time? Five-thirty?'

'Bring me a jar of pomade and a pound of sugar almonds from Boissier's', Nana called out across the drawing-room as he was closing the door.

Left to themselves, the two women remembered they hadn't said good morning properly and deposited loud kisses on each other's cheeks. The article had stirred them up. Nana, who until now had still been half asleep, again became wildly excited over her sensational success. Well, Rose Mignon wouldn't be very happy this morning! As her aunt hadn't wanted to come along to the theatre because, as she put it, strong emotions gave her the willies, Nana began to tell her about the evening, embroidering the tale until you might have thought that the whole of Paris had been there applauding her. Then, suddenly breaking off, she asked with a laugh if anyone would have imagined that to be possible when they'd seen the bum of the skinny girl hanging round Rue de la Goutte d'Or.* Madame Lerat was shaking her head. No indeed, nobody would ever have foreseen that. Now she wanted to have her say, in an earnest voice, and calling her 'my daughter', because her real mother had passed on to join her daddy and granny, so wasn't she her second mother? Nana felt so sad that she almost started crying. But Madame Lerat said that bygones must be bygones, oh, they were such dreadful times, they certainly shouldn't be brought up every day. She'd not seen her niece over a long period of time because her family had accused her of ruining herself as well as the girl. As if something like that was remotely possible! And she wasn't asking her to reveal any secrets, she believed she'd always led a decent life. At present she was perfectly happy just to be seeing her niece once again in a good situation, and to know that she had the right feelings towards her little boy. In this world, the only thing, still, was to be decent and hard-working.

'Who's the father?' she asked suddenly, breaking off with a glint of curiosity in her eye.

Nana was taken by surprise. After a moment's hesitation, she replied:

'It was a gentleman.'

'Really?' her aunt said. 'People were saying it was a bricklayer who beat you up . . . Anyway, one day you'll tell me all about it . . . You know how discreet I am! . . . Never mind, I'll look after him as if he was the son of a prince!'

She had given up her job as a florist and was living on a pension of six hundred francs from savings which she'd put together cent by cent. Nana promised to rent a nice little flat for her and give her a hundred francs a month in addition. The mention of this sum made the good lady quite forget herself, and she exclaimed that now her niece had got them by the short hair she mustn't let go—she was referring to men. They both kissed each other again. In the middle of this happy scene, Nana brought the conversation back to little Louis; she suddenly seemed to remember something that depressed her.

'Isn't it a nuisance, I've got to go out at three o'clock', she muttered. 'What a pest!'

Just then Zoé came in to say lunch was ready. They went into the dining room where an elderly lady was already at table. She was wearing a dark dress of indeterminate colour, somewhere between brownish purple and yellowish green; she had kept her hat on. Nana showed no surprise at seeing her. She merely asked why she hadn't come into the bedroom.

'I heard people talking', the old woman said. 'I thought you had company.'

With her mannerly, respectable air, Madame Maloir's function was to be Nana's 'old friend', who would keep her company at home and outside. She seemed at first rather put out at the sight of Madame Lerat, but when she learned that she was an aunt she gave her an amiable look and a wan smile. Nana now proclaimed that she was famished and flung herself on to some radishes which she crunched away at, not bothering with bread. Madame Lerat, however, primly refused them: they gave you catarrh. Then, when Zoé brought in some cutlets, Nana toyed with the meat and sucked the bones, meanwhile casting surreptitious glances at her old friend's hat.

'Is that the new hat I gave you?' she enquired finally.

'Yes, I've altered it a bit', mumbled Madame Maloir with her mouth full.

The hat was preposterous, flared out over her forehead and decorated with a long plume on top. Madam Maloir had a mania for remodelling all her hats; she was the only one who knew what suited her, and with a flick of the wrist she could transform the most elegant head-dress into a shabby bonnet. Nana had bought this hat specifically to avoid having to feel ashamed of her and now almost lost her temper.

'Well, take it off, at least!' she shouted.

'No, thank you all the same', the old lady replied with a dignified air. 'It's not bothering me, I can eat very comfortably with it on.'

After the cutlets there was cauliflower with left-overs of cold chicken. But at each course Nana was making a face, humming and hahing; she'd sniff and leave everything untouched on her plate. She finished off her lunch with some jam.

They had a leisurely dessert. Zoé didn't clear the table before serving coffee; the ladies merely pushed their plates to one side. They were still talking about last night's wonderful success. Nana had rolled her own cigarettes and was lolling back in her chair and wriggling her bottom as she smoked. As Zoé was still hanging about, leaning against the sideboard with her hands dangling, they found themselves listening to the story of her life. She said that her mother was a midwife in Bercy* who'd run into trouble. Zoé herself had worked for a dentist, then an insurance-broker; but that sort of job didn't suit her, and with a touch of smugness she began to give a catalogue of the ladies where she'd been chambermaid. She talked about her mistresses as if she herself had controlled their lives. Certainly, there was more than one who'd have had big problems without her. For example, one day Madame Blanche was with Octave and who should turn up but the old man. What does Zoé do? She pretends to fall over while she's walking across the drawing room, the old man rushes to help her, fetches her a glass of water from the kitchen and Monsieur Octave makes his getaway.

'Oh, I say, isn't that smart!' exclaimed Nana who was listening with a sympathetic interest close to hero-worship.

'Well, I've been through all sorts of difficult times myself', Madame Lerat began.

And, drawing her chair closer to Madame Maloir, she started to confide in her. Both of them were dipping sugar-lumps in their brandy. But if Madame Maloir would listen to other people's secrets, she would never reveal any of her own. She was said to be living in a mysterious boarding-house, in a room where nobody was ever allowed in.

Nana suddenly flared up:

'Aunty, stop playing with the knives. You know that upsets me!'

Without thinking Madame Lerat had just placed two knives on the table in the form of a cross. However, the young woman claimed that she wasn't superstitious; spilling salt, for example, didn't mean a thing nor did Friday the thirteenth; but she just couldn't stand knives, they'd never proved wrong. Something unpleasant was certain to happen. She gave a yawn and with an utterly bored expression:

'It's two o'clock already . . . I've got to go out. What a pest!'

The two elderly women looked at each other. They all three shook their heads without speaking. No, it wasn't always fun, that was sure. Nana was sprawling back in her chair again, lighting another cigarette while the other two discreetly pursed their lips, very philosophically.

'We'll have a game of bezique while we're waiting for you. Do you play bezique, Madame Lerat?' asked Madame Maloir after a pause.

She certainly did and very expertly. There was no point in

disturbing Zoé, who'd disappeared; a corner of the table would do; they turned the table-cloth back, over the dirty plates. But just as Madame Maloir was going off to fetch the cards herself from a drawer in the sideboard, Nana said that before they started, it'd be very kind if she could write a letter for her. She found writing a bore and she wasn't sure of the spelling, whereas her old friend could turn out letters straight from the heart. She ran out to get some of her best writing-paper from her bedroom. An ink-well and a cheap bottle of ink were lying about on a chair, together with a pen thick with rust. The letter was to Daguenet. Without being told, Madame Maloir wrote 'My little darling' in her best cursive; she then told him not to come tomorrow because 'it wasn't possible', but that, wherever she might be, 'he was always in her thoughts'.

'And I'll end with "a thousand kisses"', she murmured.

Madame Lerat was nodding approval at every word. Her eyes were gleaming; she adored being involved in love affairs. And she even wanted to add a little touch of her own, whispering in a melting voice:

'A thousand kisses on your lovely eyes.'

'That's it, a thousand kisses on your lovely eyes', repeated Nana, as a blissful expression spread over the two old women's faces.

They rang for Zoé to take the letter downstairs to a messenger. She was, in fact, at that very minute chatting to the messenger boy from the theatre who had brought Nana the duty sheet which she'd forgotten to pick up that morning. Nana asked him up and gave him the letter for Daguenet. Then she asked him some questions. Oh yes, Monsieur Bordenave was very happy; they were already booked out for a whole week, madam couldn't imagine the number of people asking for her address since this morning. When the messenger boy had gone, Nana said she wouldn't be away for more than half-an-hour at the most. If anyone called, Zoé would tell them to wait. As she was speaking, the electric bell rang. It was a creditor, the man who hired out carriages; he'd stationed himself on the bench in the entrance hall. He could twiddle his thumbs until the evening; there wasn't any hurry.

'Ah well, I must buck up', said Nana sluggishly, with a lazy yawn, stretching again. 'I'm due there by now.'

However, she didn't stir. She was watching her aunt playing; she had just declared four aces. She was resting her chin on her hand and becoming immersed in the game; but when she heard the clock strike three she gave a jump.

'Oh, shit!' she exclaimed coarsely.

Madame Maloir, who was counting up the tens and aces, gently encouraged her:

'Well, my dear, wouldn't it be better to get it over with straightaway?'

'Don't be long', said Madame Lerat, shuffling the cards. 'If you can be back with the money before four, I can catch the four-thirty.'

'Oh, I'm not going to make a long job of it', Nana muttered.

It took ten minutes for Zoé to help her put on a dress and a hat. She couldn't care less how badly dressed she was. As she was about to go downstairs there was another ring. This time it was the coal merchant. Ah well, he could keep the carriage-hire man company; they could amuse each other. However, to avoid any fuss she went out through the kitchen and down the back-stairs. She often left that way, the only thing she needed to do was to hold her skirts well up.

'You can forgive a good mother anything', said Madame Maloir sententiously when the two ladies were left to themselves.

'Four kings!' announced Madame Lerat in reply; she was a passionate card-player.

They settled down to an interminable game.

The table hadn't been cleared; the room was full of a greasy haze of cigarette smoke and cooking smells. Our ladies had started dipping sugar-lumps in their brandy once more. They had been playing and sipping for twenty minutes when, after the doorbell had rung a third time, Zoé rushed in and started hustling them as if they were old friends of hers.

'Come along now, there's the bell again . . . You can't stay here. If a lot of people come, I'll need the whole flat . . . Off you go!'

Madame Maloir wanted to finish playing, but when Zoé looked as if she was about to swoop on the cards she decided to pick them up, without disturbing the game; meanwhile Madame Lerat removed the brandy bottle, the glasses, and the sugar. They both quickly made their way into the kitchen and settled down at the end of a table between the dish-cloths, still wet, and the bowl, still full of dish-water.

'That was three hundred and thirty points, wasn't it? You to play.'

'I'm leading hearts.'

When Zoé came back she found them once more absorbed in their game. After a pause, while Madame Lerat was shuffling, Madame Maloir asked:

'Who was that?'

'Oh nobody really', the maid replied. 'Just a boy . . . I wanted to send him away but he's so pretty, with blue eyes and a girl's face, not a trace of a beard, that in the end I told him he could wait . . . He's got a huge bunch of flowers that he refused to let go of . . . You feel like slapping his face, the young puppy. He ought to be still at school!'

Madame Lerat went to fetch a decanter of water to mix with the brandy; the sugar had made her thirsty. Zoé murmured that she wouldn't object to some either, as a matter of fact. She had a nasty bitter taste in her mouth, she said.

'So where did you put him?' Madame Maloir continued.

'Ah yes, in the tiny end room, the unfurnished one . . . It's only got one of madam's trunks and a table. That's where I dump the peasants.'

As she was heaping sugar into her brandy, the electric bell made her jump. Hell's bells, couldn't she even have a little drink in peace! That was a fine look-out if the ding-dong was getting going already. All the same, she dashed off to open the door. When she came back, seeing Madame Maloir looking at her questioningly:

'Nothing, just a bunch of flowers.'

And they all three took a gulp, giving each other a nod. The bell rang a couple of times more in quick succession while Zoé was at last clearing the table and taking the plates over to the sink, one by one. But it was nothing important: each time she kept the kitchen informed:

'Only a bunch of flowers.'

However, she made the ladies laugh in between two tricks as she described the looks on the creditors' faces when they saw all these flowers arriving. They'd be put on madam's dressing-table. What a pity they were so expensive and that you couldn't get a penny for them! Ah well, there was a lot of money wasted.

'Well', said Madame Maloir, 'I'd be glad to get per day the amount men spend on flowers in Paris.'

'I can see you're not difficult to please', murmured Madame Lerat. 'It'd only be pin-money . . . Four queens, my dear.'

It was ten to four. Zoé was showing surprise that the mistress should have been away so long. Normally when she found herself having to go out in the afternoon, she'd get through it in next to no time. But Madame Maloir pointed out that you couldn't always get things done the way you liked. Yes, life was certainly full of all sorts of little hitches, said Madame Lerat. The best thing was to wait; if her niece was late, it must be that she was detained on business, mustn't it? Anyway, they weren't doing anything very strenuous. It was very comfy in the kitchen. And as she had no more hearts, Madame Lerat played clubs.

The bell was ringing again. When Zoé came back she was all excited and even before she was through the door, lowering her voice:

'My dears, it's the great Steiner himself. I've put him in the little drawing-room.'

Madame Maloir explained about the banker to Madame Lerat, who wasn't familiar with all these gentlemen. Was he thinking of dropping Rose Mignon? Zoé was shaking her head, she knew all about these things. But then she had to go off to answer the door again.

'That's all we needed! What rotten luck! It's the wog. I tried to tell him she's out, but he's gone and installed himself in the bedroom. We weren't expecting him until tonight.'

By a quarter past four Nana still hadn't come back. What could she be doing? It didn't make sense. Two more bunches of flowers arrived. Zoé was fed up and looked to see if there was any coffee left. Yes, the ladies would be glad to finish off the coffee, it would wake them up. They were slumped in their chairs and dropping off to sleep as a result of interminably repeating the same action of taking cards from the stock. It struck half-past. Surely something must have happened to Nana? They were whispering together.

Suddenly, forgetting where she was, Madame Maloir screamed:

'I've got a five hundred! Quint to the ace in trumps!'

'Not so loud, for God's sake!' exclaimed Zoé angrily. 'What are all those gentlemen going to think?'

And in the ensuing silence and stifled whispering of the two squabbling old women, there was the sound of someone running up the back-stairs. It was Nana at last. She could be heard panting even before she opened the door. She bustled in agitatedly, red in the face. The loops of her skirt must have snapped and it was sweeping on the steps; its flounces had just got wet through from a puddle, some filthy mess that must have been sloshed down by that slut of a maid on the first floor.

'So there you are! About time too!' said Madame Lerat, pursing her lips, still put out by Madame Maloir's five hundred points. 'You're good at keeping people waiting, I must say!'

'Madam is really not being sensible', added Zoé.

Nana was already in a bad mood and these reproofs made her boil over. What a way to greet her after all the troubles she'd just had!

'Just leave me alone, will you?' she shouted.

'Sh! madam, there are people here', said the maid.

Speaking more quietly and almost at a loss for words, the young woman gasped:

'Do you think I got any fun out of it? It went on and on . . . I'd have liked to see you doing it . . . I could have smacked his face, I was so furious! And I couldn't find a cab . . . Fortunately it's just round the corner. All the same, I've been rushing like mad!'

'Have you got the money?' asked her aunt.

'What a question to ask!' replied Nana.

To rest her legs, she'd flopped down on a chair next to the stove and, still panting, pulled out of her bodice an envelope containing four hundred-franc notes, which could be seen through a large ragged slit she had torn with her finger to make sure they were all there. The three women round her were all staring at the envelope, a large, dirty bit of crumpled paper held in her dainty gloved hands. It was too late, Madame Lerat couldn't go to Rambouillet until tomorrow. Nana started going into lengthy explanations.

'There are people waiting to see you, madam', the maid reminded her once more.

Nana flared up again: those people could wait! In a minute, when she'd finished what she wanted to do. And as her aunt was holding her hand out for the money:

'Oh no, not the lot', she said. 'Three hundred for the nurse, fifty for the fare and expenses, that makes three-fifty . . . I'll keep fifty.'

The problem was finding some change. There wasn't ten francs in the whole house. Nobody bothered to ask Madame Maloir, who was listening dispassionately; she never had more than thirty centimes on her, for the bus-fare. In the end Zoé went off, saying she'd go and have a look in her trunk, and returned with a hundred francs in five-franc pieces. They counted them out on the end of the table. Madame Lerat left straight away, promising to bring little Louis back next day.

'You said there were people waiting?' Nana said, still relaxing in her chair.

'Yes, madam, three persons.'

And she mentioned the banker first. Nana made a face. If Steiner thought she'd let him bore her just because he'd thrown her a bouquet last night . . . !

'Anyway', she declared, 'I've had enough. I'm not going to see anyone . . . Go and tell them you're not expecting me any longer.'

'Madam shouldn't be too hasty, she must see Monsieur Steiner', murmured Zoé earnestly, not moving, annoyed at seeing her mistress acting foolishly again.

Next she mentioned the man from Wallachia, who must be starting to find time going rather slowly in the bedroom. Nana flew into a rage and became even more stubborn: no one at all, she didn't want to see anybody! Who on earth had saddled her with such a persistent bugger!

'Kick them out, the whole lot of them! I'd sooner have a game of bezique with Madame Maloir and that's what I'm going to do!'

While she was talking the doorbell rang. That was the last straw! Another pain in the neck! She forbade Zoé to go to the door, but the maid paid no attention and had already gone out of the kitchen. When she came back, she handed Nana two visiting-cards and said firmly:

'I've told these gentlemen that you're in and I've shown them into the drawing-room.'

Nana, who'd sprung to her feet in a fury, calmed down as soon as she saw the names: the Marquis de Chouard and Count Muffat de Beuville. She paused.

'What are they?' she asked finally. 'Do you know them?'

'I know the old man', Zoé replied, pursing her lips discreetly.

And as her mistress continued to look questioningly at her, she merely added:

'I've seen him somewhere.'

This remark seemed to decide the young woman. Reluctantly, she left the kitchen, that cosy haven where you could chat and let your hair down, with the smell of coffee heating up on the dying embers of the stove and where Madame Maloir had now settled down to a game of patience. The old woman still hadn't taken off her hat, but for greater convenience had loosened its ribbons and tossed them back over her shoulders.

In her dressing-room, while Zoé quickly helped her to slip on a dressing-gown, Nana relieved her feelings by muttering rude comments about men. The chambermaid was unhappy to hear her use bad language because she was sorry it was taking Nana so long to throw off her humble origins. She even ventured to suggest that she should calm down.

'Bugger that', Nana retorted coarsely. 'Men are bastards, they love that sort of thing.'

All the same, she put on what she called her 'Royal Highness manner'. As she was making her way towards the drawing-room, Zoé called her back and, without asking her permission, showed the Marquis de Chouard and Count Muffat into the dressing-room. That created a better impression.

'I'm so sorry to have kept you waiting, gentlemen', the young woman said, with elaborate politeness.

The two men greeted her and sat down. This was the most

elegant room in the flat; in the half-light filtering through the embroidered tulle blinds they could see the pale hangings, the marquetry cheval-glass, the Récamier sofa, the blue-satin armchairs, and the large marble dressing-table, which was piled up with a profusion of flowers: bouquets of roses, lilac, and hyacinths whose strong, all-pervasive scent competed in the heavy atmosphere with the sickly smell of wash-basins, and now and again with the more pungent perfume of bowls of crushed dry patchouli.

Sitting with her dressing-gown drawn tightly round her, Nana seemed to have been caught in the middle of her toilet, with her skin still damp, smiling and startled amidst her lace.

'We must ask you to forgive us for being so persistent, ma'am', said Count Muffat earnestly. 'We are collecting subscriptions. This gentleman and I are members of the neighbourhood charity committee.'

The Marquis de Chouard hastened to add, gallantly:

'When we heard that a great actress was living in this house, we determined to make a particular point of bringing our poor parishioners to her notice. Great talent and a good heart surely belong together.'

Nana looked coy, replying with little nods and thinking fast. It must have been the old boy who'd brought the other man along; his eyes had a very naughty look. All the same, she'd have to keep her eyes on the younger one as well; his temples were throbbing in a very peculiar way; he might well have come along of his own accord. Yes, that must be it: the porter had mentioned her name and the pair of them were manœuvring for advantage, each on his own account

'You were absolutely right to come up to see me, gentlemen', she said, very graciously.

But she could not prevent herself from giving a start when she heard the doorbell. Another caller, and Zoé was still going to the door, damn her! She went on:

'One is only too glad to be able to make some contribution.'

She felt secretly flattered.

'Ah, if only you knew what destitution there is, ma'am', the marquis continued. 'Although our district is one of the wealthiest in Paris, we have more than three thousand paupers. You cannot imagine the misery: children with not even a crust of bread to eat, women ill, completely helpless, dying from cold . . .'

'Oh, the poor people!' she exclaimed, deeply touched.

So great was her concern that tears came into her lovely eyes. Forgetting her pose, she leaned forward impulsively; her dressing-gown came open, exposing her neck, and as its flimsy material stretched tight over her knees, you could see the curve of her thigh. A patch of blood brought a flush to the marquis's ashen cheeks. Count Muffat, who'd been about to speak, dropped his eyes. It was too hot in this little room, a sultry heat like a tropical hothouse. The roses were wilting, the scent of the patchouli was overpowering.

It's in cases like this when one would like to be very rich', Nana went on. 'Ah well, we all do what we can . . . I assure you, gentlemen, that if I'd known . . .'

In her emotion she was about to blurt out something silly, so she left the sentence unfinished. For a moment she was embarrassed, as she'd forgotten where she'd put the fifty francs when she changed her dress. Then she remembered that they must be on the corner of her dressing-table under an upturned pomade jar. As she stood up, there was a long ring on the bell. Here we go again! There's no end to it. The marquis and the count had also got to their feet; the old man's ears had given a twitch as he listened in the direction of the door; no doubt he knew all about that sort of ring. Muffat glanced at him and they both looked away. In their embarrassment they both again adopted their stance of frigid formality, Muffat looking sturdy and strong, with his thick head of hair, while his father-in-law squared his skinny shoulders swept by a sparse fringe of white hair.

'My goodness, gentlemen', said Nana with a laugh as she produced the ten large coins, deciding to make a joke of it. 'I'm afraid I'm going to weigh you down. Please take these for the poor.'

The adorable little dimple in her chin became deeper. She looked good-humoured and unpretentious as she stood holding the pile of coins in her open palm and offering them to the two men as if to say: 'Well now, who'd like them?' The count had the quicker reaction; he took the money but one of the coins was left in her hand and in order to pick it up, he had to touch the young woman's skin; it was warm and resilient; a shiver ran down his spine. She was amused and still laughing.

'There you are, gentlemen', she said. 'Next time I hope I'll be able to let you have more.'

Having no further excuse for staying, they took their leave. Just as they were going towards the door there was another loud ring. The marquis could not repress a smile, while a shadow ran over the count's face making him look even more solemn. Nana delayed them for a few seconds to enable Zoé to find another spare corner. She didn't like people to run across each other in her house. All the same, it must be chock-full by now; she was pleased, therefore, to see the drawing-room empty. Had Zoé been stuffing them into the wardrobes?

'Goodbye, gentlemen', she said. She was standing in the doorway of her drawing-room, still laughing as she followed them with her bright blue eyes.

Count Muffat bowed, but with all his social graces he felt disturbed; with its stifling scent of flowers and woman, this dressing-room was making his head reel; he needed fresh air. Behind him the marquis, his face suddenly contorted, licked his lips, and realizing that he couldn't be observed he took a chance and gave her a wink.

When Nana went back to her dressing-room where Zoé was waiting to give her the visiting-cards and letters she was laughing even more.

'Well, there you are! They were so stony broke that they did me out of my fifty francs!', she exclaimed.

She wasn't annoyed, she just found it funny that men had managed to take money off her. All the same, they were swine; now she was cleaned out. The sight of the cards and the letters put her in a bad mood again. The letters weren't too bad, they came from men who had applauded her last night and were now making her offers. As for the callers, they could jump in the lake.

Zoé had put them everywhere; as she pointed out, the flat was most convenient, for all its rooms opened out on to the corridor. It wasn't like Madame Blanche's where you had to go through the drawing-room. And Madame Blanche had run into a lot of trouble as a result.

'You can send the whole lot of them home', said Nana,

pursuing her own train of thought. 'Start with the wog!'

'Oh, I sent him packing long ago, madam', said Zoé with a smile. 'He only wanted to tell madam that he couldn't come tonight.'

How wonderful! Nana clapped her hands; he wouldn't be coming, what a stroke of luck! She'd be free! She was heaving deep sighs of relief as if she'd just been granted a reprieve from the most dreadful torture. Her first thought was for Daguenet. Poor dear, she'd just written to tell him to wait until Thursday! Quick, Madame Maloir must write him another note! But Zoé told her that Madame Maloir had slipped away on the sly, as always. So, after talking of sending a messenger, Nana hesitated. She was very weary. A whole night's sleep would be so nice! The idea of such a treat finally decided her. She could afford this luxury, once in a while.

'I'll go to bed as soon as I get back from the theatre', she murmured greedily. 'And you're not to wake me before twelve o'clock!'

She raised her voice:

'So off you go and down the stairs with the lot of them!'

Zoé didn't move. While she would never have taken the liberty of advising her mistress, she did contrive to give her the benefit of her own experience whenever she was in one of her more headstrong moods.

'Including Monsieur Steiner?' she enquired tersely.

'Certainly', retorted Nana. 'Do him first.'

The maid still lingered, to give her mistress time to reflect. Wouldn't madam enjoy taking this very wealthy gentleman, so well known in Parisian theatrical circles, away from her rival, Rose Mignon?

'All right, but hurry up, my dear girl', Nana said, taking the point. 'And tell him he's a nuisance.'

Then, suddenly, she had another thought: she might well be wanting him, even tomorrow; she gave a laugh and, screwing up her eyes like a little street urchin, exclaimed:

'As a matter of fact, if I do want to have him, the quickest way is still to kick him out!'

Zoé looked extremely impressed. She gazed at her mistress with sudden admiration, and without further ado went off to 'kick Steiner out'.

Nana meanwhile delayed for a few minutes to give her time

to make a clean sweep, as she expressed it. What an extraordinary onslaught it had been! She poked her head into the drawing-room. Empty. Dining-room, empty too. But as she was pursuing her investigation, her mind now at rest and feeling sure there was no one left, all of a sudden, pushing open the door of a tiny study, she came upon a diminutive young man perched very quietly on top of a trunk, looking very well behaved and holding an enormous bunch of flowers on his knees.

'Good Lord!' she cried. 'There's still one left!'

As soon as he saw her the little fellow jumped down, as red as a beetroot. Not knowing what to do with his flowers, he was shifting them from one hand to the other, breathless with emotion. His youthfulness, his embarrassment, and his funny juggling with his flowers softened Nana's heart and she burst into a peal of laughter. So children were doing it now? Men were calling on her straight out of the cradle! She couldn't contain herself, she was slapping her thighs and feeling all motherly. To pull his leg, she asked him familiarly:

'Would you like me to blow your nose, ducky?'

'Yes, please', the boy answered eagerly, in a whisper.

This reply made her laugh even louder. He was 17, his name was Georges Hugon. He'd been at the Variétés last night. And he'd come to see her.

'And are those flowers for me?'

'Yes.'

'Well then, give them to me, stupid!'

But as she was taking them, with that wonderful impulsiveness of youth he pounced greedily on her hands. She had to give him a tap to make him leave go. Well, here was a young puppy who went straight to the point! But while telling him off she'd gone pink in the face, and she was smiling. She sent him away, giving him permission to come again. He was stumbling and had trouble finding the way out.

Nana went back to her dressing-room, and almost at once Francis came in to dress her hair for the night. She never got dressed until the evening. She was sitting in front of her mirror, quietly day-dreaming, when Zoé entered.

'There's a man who's refusing to go away.'

'OK, let him stay', she replied calmly.

'And there are more people still coming.'

'Who cares! Tell them to wait. They'll leave as soon as they get too hungry.'

Her mood had changed. She was delighted to be keeping these men waiting. She had one final idea to amuse herself: she slipped away from Francis and double-bolted the door of the dressing-room; now they could form a queue outside—they wouldn't break the wall down, she imagined. Zoé could come in through the little door leading into the kitchen. Meanwhile the electric bell was working overtime. Every five minutes you could hear its cheerful tinkle, as regular as clockwork. For fun, Nana started counting them. Then she suddenly remembered something.

'What about my sugar almonds?'

Francis was also forgetting the sugar almonds. He pulled a bag out of the pocket of his frock-coat with the perfect discretion of a man of the world offering a present to a lady friend; all the same, each time he sent in his account he added the price of the sweets to his bill. Nana put the bag between her knees and started munching, twisting her head in accordance with Francis' directions.

'Hell!' she muttered after a pause. 'Here comes a whole gang of them.'

There had been three rings in quick succession, and now they started to come thick and fast. Some of them were discreet, rather tremulous, like a first, modest declaration of love; others, produced by the pressure of some uncompromising finger, vibrated loudly; and others were hurried, quivering as they shot through the air. A real ding-dong, as Zoé called it, a ding-dong which could upset the whole neighbourhood, a bustling throng of men all lining up to press the ivory bell-button. That tease Bordenave had really given her address to far too many people, the whole of last night's audience must be joining in.

'Oh, by the way, Francis', said Nana, 'can you manage a hundred francs?'

He stood back, examined his handiwork and then, calmly:

'A hundred? That depends.'

'Oh, you know', she went on, 'if it's guarantees that worry you . . .'

And without completing her sentence, she gave a broad wave of her hand which included the adjacent rooms. Francis handed over five gold twenty-franc pieces. When she could find a spare moment, Zoé was getting her mistress's clothes ready; soon it was time for her to dress Nana while the hairdresser waited to give the finishing touches. But the maid was continually interrupted by the doorbell and had to leave her mistress half laced-up or with only one shoe on. In spite of her long experience, she was beginning to lose her head. After putting men more or less everywhere, using any spare nook or cranny, she had just been forced to park three or four in the same room, which was against all her principles. Anyway, it couldn't be helped, and if they gobbled each other up it'd leave more room for the rest! And safely bolted in, Nana kept poking fun at them, saying that she could hear their heavy breathing; they must look very odd, all with their tongues hanging out like so many lapdogs sitting on their backsides in a circle. This pack of men who'd tracked her down was the continuation of last night's triumph.

'As long as they don't start smashing things up', she muttered.

All this hot male breath filtering through the cracks was beginning to make her uneasy, and she gave a sudden cry of relief when Zoé showed in Labordette. He wanted to tell her about an account that he'd just settled for her in a magistrate's court. She didn't listen.

'I'm carrying you off with me', she said. 'We'll have dinner together and then we'll go on to the Variétés. I don't come on stage until nine-thirty.'

Good old Labordette, turning up just when he was needed. *He* never asked for anything. He was just the women's friend, and he'd always undertake to do small jobs for them. For example, as he came in, he'd got rid of the creditors waiting in the entrance hall. Anyway, they were nice blokes, they didn't want to be paid, far from it; if they'd insisted on coming along it was merely to congratulate the lady and personally offer their services for the future, after her great success last night.

'Let's be off', said Nana, who was now dressed.

And indeed, at that very moment, Zoé came in, exclaiming:

'I give up, madam, I'm not letting anyone else in... There's a whole queue on the staircase.'

A queue on the staircase! Even Francis, who always tried to keep a stiff upper lip, had to laugh as he was putting away his combs. Nana had caught hold of Labordette's arm and was pushing him into the kitchen. And so, finally rid of men, she made her escape, happy in the thought that you could have Labordette to yourself, by himself, anywhere, without any fear that he might do something silly.

'You must bring me home', she said as they went down the backstairs. 'I'd be safe that way... Just think, for one night, one whole night, I want to sleep all by myself... A crazy idea of mine, my dear chap!'

Chapter 3

COUNTESS Sabine, as people had taken to calling Madame Muffat de Beuville to distinguish her from her mother-in-law, who had died last year, was at home every Tuesday in her town residence in the Rue Miromesnil,* on the corner of the Rue de Penthièvre. This huge, square building had been occupied by the Muffat family for more than a century; the tall, sombre façade with its large slatted shutters, rarely opened, looked asleep, as melancholy as a convent; in the tiny, damp back garden the trees had grown so tall and puny in their search for sun that their branches were visible above the slate roof.

By ten o'clock on this Tuesday in late April there were barely a dozen people in the drawing-room. When only close friends were expected, the countess did not open up the small drawing-room or dining-room. It was cosier chatting round the fire, for the drawing-room was very large and high-ceilinged, with four windows looking out on to the garden, which on this rainswept evening was making its damp presence felt despite a big log-fire. The sun never managed to penetrate down to this room and the greenish light of day did little to relieve the gloom; but at night, with its solid mahogany Empire furniture, its hangings, and chairs in yellow-patterned velvet boldly embroidered in gold, in the light of the chandelier and the lamps, it merely looked solemn, with an atmosphere of dignified formality, of bygone customs, heavy with the piety of a vanished age.

However, facing the armchair in which the count's mother had died, a square, stiff, wooden chair covered in hard-wearing material, Countess Sabine was sitting in a deep, red-silk upholstered armchair as soft as an eiderdown. It was the only modern piece of furniture, a little note of personal, whimsical taste which clashed violently with everything else.

'So', the young woman was saying, 'we'll be having the Shah of Persia.'

They were talking about the foreign royalty who would be visiting Paris for the World Fair. There were a number of ladies gathered in a half-circle round the fire. Madame Du Joncquoy, whose brother had served as a diplomat in the Middle East, was giving details of the court of Nazar Eddin.*

'Is there something the matter, my dear?' enquired Madame Chantereau, the wife of an ironmaster, seeing the countess go pale and give a slight shudder.

'Oh no, nothing at all', she replied with a smile. 'I felt a sudden chill . . . This drawing-room takes so long to warm up.'

She ran her dark eyes over the walls and up to the high ceiling. Her daughter Estelle, a wispy, insignificant girl of 16, that awkward age, got up from her stool and quietly went over to pick up a log which had slipped. But Madame de Chezelles, a friend of Sabine's since their convent days, but five years younger, exclaimed:

'Well, I must say I'd love to have a drawing-room like yours! At least you can give parties . . . They're only building little boxes these days! I wish I were you!'

She was talking without thinking, waving her arms about, explaining how she'd change the curtains, the chairs, the whole lot; then she'd give dances that would attract the whole of Paris . . . Behind her, her husband, a judge, was listening with a solemn look on his face. It was said that she openly had love affairs, but people forgave her and continued to invite her because she was considered crazy.

Countess Sabine merely gave her wan smile and murmured, 'That Léonide!', completing her sentence with a listless gesture.

She'd certainly not be making any changes in her drawing-room after living there for seventeen years. It was going to remain exactly as her mother-in-law had wanted it to be during her lifetime. Returning to their conversation:

'I've been told that we're definitely going to have the King of Prussia and the Tsar as well.'

'Yes, they've promised to put on some splendid receptions', said Madame Du Joncquoy.

The banker Steiner, recently introduced into the Muffats' house by Léonide de Chezelles, who knew everybody worth knowing, was sitting chatting on a settee against the wall between two windows, cleverly trying to pump a member of the Legislative Body about a possible movement in the Stock Exchange which he felt might be in the air; Count Muffat was standing in front of them, listening in silence and looking even more forbidding than usual. Near the door, four or five young men were forming another group round Count Xavier de Vandeuvres, who was talking in a low voice, no doubt telling them a smutty story, because they were stifling their laughter. In the middle of the room a fat head of department from the Ministry of the Interior was sitting all by himself, slumped in an armchair and sleeping with his eyes open. Then one of the young men seemed to be doubting Vandeuvres's story and the count raised his voice:

'You're too much of a sceptic, Foucarmont. You'll ruin your pleasures.'

He laughed and came back to the ladies. He was the last of a fine old family, a witty and effeminate young man who was in the process of polishing off a fortune in a mad, insatiable pursuit of pleasure. His stud of horses, one of the best-known in Paris, was costing him unheard of sums; he was losing alarming amounts each month at the Imperial Club; his mistresses were swallowing up, year in, year out, a farm and a few acres of arable land or forest, a sizeable slice of his vast estates in Picardy.

'You're a fine one to call anybody a sceptic', said Léonide, making room for him to squeeze in beside her. 'You don't believe in anything yourself, it's you who's ruining his pleasures.'

'Exactly!' he retorted. 'I want to let others benefit from my experience.'

He was told to shush: he was shocking Monsieur Venot, and as the ladies drew aside they revealed a little 60-year-old man with bad teeth and a sly smile huddling in a sofa, looking very much at home, listening to everybody and never opening his mouth. He waved a hand to signify that he wasn't shocked. Vandeuvres again put on his grand manner and said, in a serious voice:

'Monsieur Venot is well aware that I believe in what must be believed.'

He had made a confession of faith. Léonide herself looked satisfied. The young men at the end of the room had stopped laughing. The tone at the Muffats' was very prim and they didn't find it much fun. A cold breeze had just swept through the drawing-room, and in the ensuing pause Steiner's nasal twang could be heard; the deputy's discretion was beginning to make him angry. Countess Sabine gazed into the fire for a second and then resumed the conversation:

'I saw the King of Prussia in Baden last year. He's still very vigorous for his age.'

'Prince von Bismarck will be coming with him', said Madame Du Joncquoy. 'Do you know him? I had lunch with him at my brother's, oh, ages ago, when he was the Prussian minister in Paris. I find his recent successes* rather difficult to understand.'

'Why do you?' asked Madame Chantereau.

'Well, my goodness, how can I put it? I just don't like the man. He looks brutal and ill-bred. And in my opinion he looks stupid.'

They all now started talking about Prince Bismarck. Opinions varied considerably. Vandeuvres knew him and guaranteed that he was a first-rate toper and gambler. The discussion was at its height when the door opened and Hector de la Faloise appeared, followed by Fauchery, who went up to the countess and bowed:

'I've availed myself of your very generous invitation, Countess.'

She gave him a smile and a friendly word. Fauchery went over and shook hands with his host and then stood for a moment uncertainly in the middle of the room, where the only person he recognized was Steiner. But Vandeuvres turned round and came up to him. The journalist was delighted to see him and, feeling a need to talk, drew him closer and said in an undertone:

'It's tomorrow, are you going to be there?'

'I wouldn't miss it for worlds!'

'Midnight, at her flat.'

'I know, I know . . . I'm bringing Blanche along.'

He was trying to get away and go back to the ladies to provide further arguments in favour of Bismarck, but

Fauchery hadn't yet finished:

'You'll never guess whom she told me to invite.'

And he gave a little nod in the direction of Muffat, who was at that moment engaged in discussing a budgetary matter with the deputy and Steiner.

'You're joking!' said Vandeuvres, amazed as well as highly amused.

'Honest! I had to promise to bring him along. That's one of the reasons I'm here.'

They exchanged a quiet laugh, and Vandeuvres hurried back to the ladies, exclaiming:

'No, on the contrary, I assure you that Prince von Bismarck is extremely witty . . . Listen, one evening I heard him make an absolutely delightful remark . . .'

Meanwhile la Faloise had overheard the whispered exchange and was looking at Fauchery, hoping for an explanation, which was not forthcoming. Whom were they referring to? What would they be doing at midnight tomorrow? He kept close to his cousin, who had taken a seat. Fauchery was particularly interested in Countess Sabine. He'd often heard her name mentioned and knew that she'd been married at 17 and must now be 34, and during that time had been living a cloistered life between her husband and her mother-in-law. Some people in her set thought she was rigidly pious and others felt sympathy for her, remembering her cheerfulness and laughter, the glow in her large, dark eyes, before she'd been shut up in the depths of this old mansion. Fauchery was eyeing her uncertainly. On one occasion a captain friend of his, just a day before sailing for Mexico* where he'd died quite recently, had blurted out, after a farewell meal, the sort of crude admission which even the most discreet of men sometimes let slip. But his recollection was a trifle blurred; it had been after a very good dinner; and looking at the countess in this venerable drawing-room, in her black dress and with her relaxed smile, he had his doubts. She was plump and dark, with delicate features which he could see in profile against the lamp behind her; only her mouth, with its rather thick lips, hinted at a compulsive sensuality.

'What are they going on about with their Bismarck!' muttered la Faloise, who claimed to find social gatherings tedious. 'This place is deadly dull. What a queer idea of yours to want to come here!'

Fauchery flung a sudden question at him:

'Tell me, doesn't the countess go to bed with anyone?'

'Good Lord no, no, certainly not', he stammered, obviously jolted out of his pose. 'Where do you think you are?'

Then, realizing that his indignant reaction was rather provincial, he added, sinking back into the settee:

'Well, I said no but I'm not really sure . . . There's a little man over there called Foucarmont who creeps around here all the time. Obviously, there've been queerer things than that . . . Personally, I couldn't care less . . . Anyway, one thing's certain, if she does enjoy a little bit on the side, she must be pretty smart because it doesn't get around, nobody talks about it.'

Then, without further prompting, he told Fauchery what he knew about the Muffats. With the ladies' conversation continuing in the background round the fire, they were both having to lower their voices, and in their white gloves and bow-ties they looked like two men engaged in an elegant discussion on some weighty topic. Well, old Ma Muffat, whom la Faloise had known well, was an impossible old trout, always stuck with priests; and incidentally, a very grand manner: one wave of her hand and you did as you were told. As for Muffat, he was the late-born son of a general whom Napoleon I had made a count and thus naturally *persona grata* after the coup of December the second.* He was a dull dog too; but he had the reputation of being a very honest and high-principled man. And his opinions were straight out of the Ark to match; he'd such an exalted idea of his duties at court, and of its dignity and virtues, that he carried his head as if it were a sacramental offering. It was old Ma Muffat who'd given him this marvellous upbringing: confession every day, no wild oats, no concessions to youth of any sort. He was a regular church-goer, and his crises of religious fervour were full-blooded, as painful as a raging fever. To complete the picture, la Faloise whispered a final detail into Fauchery's ear.

'It's not possible!' exclaimed the other man.

'No, honestly, they swore it was true! He was still one when he got married.'

Fauchery laughed as he glanced towards the count, whose face, framed in whiskers without a moustache, seemed squarer and harder than ever now that he was quoting statistics to Steiner, who was attempting to argue back.

'My word yes, he's got that sort of look', he muttered. 'What a wedding present for a wife! . . . Poor little girl, how boring she must have found it! I bet she doesn't know anything about anything!'

In fact, at that very moment Countess Sabine was addressing him; he was finding Muffat's case so amusing and extraordinary that he hadn't heard her. She repeated her question:

'Haven't you written a profile of Prince Bismarck, Monsieur Fauchery? Have you spoken to him?'

He scrambled to his feet, went over to the ladies, and quickly recovering his composure he replied smoothly:

'I'm afraid I have to confess, countess, that I did that profile using information from biographies of him published in German . . . I've never met the prince personally.'

He stayed with the countess, still pursuing his train of thought while continuing to chat with her. She seemed younger than her age; he wouldn't have taken her for more than 28; her eyes in particular had kept a youthful glow, shadowed by the blue of her long eyelids. Having grown up in a broken home, spending alternate months with the Marquis de Chouard and the marchioness, she had married very young, when her mother died, no doubt egged on by her father, who found her presence embarrassing; the marquis, although extremely pious, was a dreadful man, about whom strange stories were beginning to circulate. Fauchery asked if he would be having the honour of meeting him. Yes, her father would certainly be coming but not until much later. The journalist thought he had a good idea where the old man spent his evenings, but he kept a straight face. He was struck by the mole on the countess's left cheek, close to her mouth; Nana had an absolutely identical one. That was funny. Curly little hairs were sprouting out of the mole, but while Nana's were blonde hers were jet-black. Never mind, this woman wasn't going to bed with anyone . . .

'I've always wanted to meet Queen Augusta',* she was

saying. 'She's said to be so kind and devout . . . Do you imagine she'll be coming with the king?'

'She's not expected to, countess', he replied.

So, she was definitely not sleeping with anyone, that was plain. You only needed to look at her, sitting next to her daughter, that little nonentity perched so stiffly on her stool. This tomblike drawing-room, with its churchy smell, was sufficient evidence of the iron hand and rigid way of life which dominated her. She'd not brought anything of her own personality into this ancient, gloomy building. It was Muffat, with his pious upbringing, his penances, and his fasting who was the unchallenged master here. But, for Fauchery, his sudden discovery of the little old man with the bad teeth and sly smile sitting behind the ladies was even more conclusive. He knew this person: Théophile Venot, a former lawyer whose speciality had been ecclesiastical lawsuits; he'd retired very wealthy and led a rather mysterious life, accepted on all sides with the greatest respect and even a touch of fear, as if he represented some powerful occult force which you could sense behind him. However, he put himself forward as a very humble man; he was a churchwarden at the Madeleine,* and had refused to accept any grander post than that of deputy mayor of the ninth arrondissement, purely, he said, in order not to be idle. Hell! The countess was well protected on all sides; there was definitely nothing doing there!

'You're right, this place is deadly', observed Fauchery to his cousin once he had succeeded in slipping away from the group of ladies. 'Let's go.'

But Count Muffat and the deputy had just left Steiner and he was making his way towards them, sweating and angrily grumbling under his breath:

'Good God, if they don't want to let on, they needn't . . . I'll find people who will.'

Then, changing his tone, he pushed the journalist into a corner and said triumphantly:

'It is tomorrow, isn't it? I'll be there, young fellow!'

'Will you?' exclaimed Fauchery in surprise.

'So you didn't know? . . . Oh, it was a bit of a job to find her at home! And Mignon was hanging on to me like a leech!'

'But the Mignons are going to be there.'

'Yes, so she told me . . . Anyway, she let me in and she's invited me . . . Midnight sharp, after the show.'

The banker was radiant. He winked and added, emphasizing his words:

'And everything all right with you?'

'All right?' replied Fauchery, pretending not to understand. 'Oh, she did call on me to thank me for my article.'

'Aha . . . You're lucky, you lot. You get a fee . . . And talking of that, who's paying tomorrow?'

The journalist spread his arms to signify that no one had been able to find out. Vandeuvres was calling over to Steiner, who knew Bismarck. Madame Du Joncquoy was almost convinced, and finally said:

'Well, he created a bad impression on me, I think he's got an evil face . . . But I'm prepared to concede he may be witty. That would explain his success.'

'No doubt', said the banker with a wan smile; he was a Jew from Frankfurt.

Meanwhile la Faloise was pursuing his cousin, determined to get an answer out of him this time. He whispered over his shoulder:

'So there's going to be a supper party tomorrow night at some woman's place? Who is she? Come on, out with it!'

Fauchery made a sign that there were people within earshot and they mustn't forget their manners. The door had just opened again and an old lady was coming in, followed by a young man whom the journalist recognized as the truant schoolboy who, at the first night of *The Blonde Venus*, had uttered that famous shout of 'Fantastic!' which people were still talking about. The lady's arrival caused a stir. The countess had quickly gone over to greet her, grasping both her hands and calling her: 'dear Madame Hugon!' Seeing that his cousin's curiosity was aroused, la Faloise, hoping to make him more forthcoming, briefly put him into the picture: Madame Hugon was the widow of a solicitor and had retired to Les Fondettes, an old country estate, while keeping a pied-à-terre in Paris in a house she owned in Rue Richelieu; she was spending a few weeks there at the moment to set up her younger son during his first year as a law student; she had been a great friend of the old Marquise de Chouard, and after the birth of the countess used to have the girl to stay with her for months at a time until her marriage; and she'd remained on very close terms with her.

'I've brought Georges to see you', she was saying to Sabine. 'I hope he's grown up a bit!'

The young man had clear eyes and his blond curls made him look like a girl dressed up as a boy; he greeted the countess very naturally, and asked her if she remembered the game of shuttlecock they'd had at Les Fondettes a couple of years ago.

'Philip's not in Paris?' enquired the count.

'No', the old lady replied. 'He's still stationed in Bourges.'

She had sat down and began to talk proudly of her elder son, a strapping young man who, after impetuously deciding to join the army, had been very rapidly promoted and had just been made a lieutenant. The ladies were all listening with friendly respect. The conversation was now proceeding on a more amiable and sensitive note, and looking at Madame Hugon's motherly, honest face set between its large coils of white hair, Fauchery thought he'd been ridiculous to suspect Countess Sabine even for a second.

However, he'd just noticed the padded, red-silk chair in which the countess was sitting, and was struck by its capricious and disturbing effect and how greatly it clashed with the smoky black atmosphere of the drawing-room. It was certainly not the count who'd introduced this voluptuous and slothful piece of furniture. It was like someone flexing her muscles to embark on a life of pleasure and gratification. And he slipped into a day-dream, going back in spite of himself to that vague admission heard one night in a private room of a restaurant. It was sensual curiosity which had prompted him to wangle an invitation to the Muffats' and since that friend had failed to return from Mexico . . . ? Who knows . . . ? He'd have to find out . . . No doubt he was being stupid, but the idea still nagged away, his instincts were stirring, he was tempted. That large armchair had a saucy look, its back was tipped up in a way which, on reflection, was amusingly suggestive.

'Well, are we going?' asked la Faloise, inwardly promising himself that once outside he'd get to the bottom of this woman's supper party.

'In a minute', replied Fauchery.

He was now in no hurry to leave, giving himself the excuse of the invitation he'd been asked to pass on, which was not going to be easy. The ladies were discussing a girl who'd just become a nun; the ceremony had been very moving, and the case had provided an emotional topic of conversation in Paris society for the last three days. The girl who'd felt this irresistible vocation and joined the Carmelites was the eldest daughter of Baroness de Fougeray, and being a vague cousin of the family Madame Chantereau was describing how the mother had been so distraught that she'd had to keep to her bed the next day.

'I had a good seat', said Léonide. 'I found the whole thing odd.'

Madame Hugon expressed her sympathy for the poor baroness. How terribly sad for a mother to lose her daughter like that!

'People accuse me of being pious', she said in her quiet, frank way, 'but that doesn't prevent me from finding it very cruel of children to insist on committing that sort of suicide.'

'Yes, it's a dreadful thing', murmured the countess, with a chilly little shiver, huddling even deeper into her chair in front of the fire.

The ladies launched into a discussion, keeping their voices down, though the earnestness of their conversation was broken now and then by quiet laughter. Under their pink lace shades, the two lamps on the mantelshelf were casting a very subdued light, and since there were only three other lamps, placed some distance away, the huge drawing-room was shrouded in gentle shadow.

Steiner was feeling bored. He was telling Fauchery about an affair of that little Madame de Chezelles, whom he referred to simply as Léonide; a hard-boiled bitch, he said, lowering his voice, for they were standing behind the ladies' chairs. Fauchery looked towards her, oddly perched on a corner of her chair, in her long pale blue satin dress, as slim and bold as any boy and he found himself feeling surprised at seeing her there: guests were better behaved at Caroline Héquet's, where her mother had set her up impeccably. There was the subject for a whole article there. What a strange world this Parisian society was! The most strait-laced drawing-rooms were being invaded. The silent Théophile Venot, who did nothing but smile and show his bad teeth, must have been a relic from the old countess, like the elderly ladies Madame Chantereau and Madame Du Joncquoy, and four or five aged gentlemen sitting in frozen attitudes in odd corners. Count Muffat would bring along those senior officials who displayed the propriety deemed desirable by the Imperial court; these must include the clean-shaven and dead-eyed head of department, still sitting in splendid isolation in the middle of the room, so tightly buttoned into his tailcoat that he didn't dare move. Most of the young men, and a few upper-crust dignitaries, had been introduced by the Marquis de Chouard, who had maintained close contacts with the Legitimists* after he had made his peace with the Second Empire on joining the Conseil d'État. That left Léonide de Chezelles, Steiner, and a whole shady element in stark contrast to that serene and kindly old lady, Madame Hugon. Fauchery, who was already composing his article, decided to call it the 'Countess Sabine element'.

'On another occasion', Steiner was saying in a low voice, 'Léonide brought her tenor down to Montauban.* She was living in the château of Beaurecueil, five miles away, and she used to come round to see him every day in her two-horse buggy at the Golden Lion where he was staying. The carriage waited outside and she'd be there for hours, while the locals all gathered round looking at the horses.'

There was a sudden pause in the conversation, and for a few seconds time moved solemnly across the lofty ceiling. Two young men who'd been whispering became silent too, and the only sound was the muffled steps of Count Muffat crossing the room. The lamps seemed to have dimmed, the fire was dying down, the old family friends, ensconced in the armchairs which they'd occupied for the last forty years, were swallowed up in an austere shadow. It was as if, while they were talking, the guests had sensed the count's mother and her icy, haughty manner returning to haunt them. Countess Sabine broke the silence.

'Anyway, there was a sort of rumour to that effect. The young man was said to have died and that would explain the poor girl's going into a convent. And in any case people were saying that Monsieur de Fougeray would never have given his consent to the wedding.'

'People were saying lots of other things as well', said Léonide, scatterbrained as ever.

She gave a laugh but refused to expatiate. Her laughter was infectious: Sabine had to put her handkerchief to her lips. And in this vast, solemn room this laughter shocked Fauchery; it was as if someone had broken a piece of cut glass. Certainly something was beginning to crack here. Everybody started talking again. Madame Du Joncquoy was protesting, Madame Chantereau knew that a wedding had been arranged but nothing further had happened. Now even the men started to offer their views, and for a few minutes the drawing-room was filled with a confused babble of voices from the various factions as Bonapartists and Legitimists competed with the society sceptics. Estelle had rung for more firewood, the footman turned up the lamps; it was like a reawakening. Fauchery was smiling, as if reassured.

'Good God, they become brides of Christ when they can't be anybody else's!' Vandeuvres muttered between his teeth; he'd just rejoined Fauchery and was bored by the whole discussion. 'Have you ever seen a woman become a nun if she's loved by some man?'

He didn't wait for a reply, he'd had enough. He continued in an undertone:

'Tell me, how many of us will there be tomorrow? The Mignons, Steiner, you, Blanche and I . . . Who else?'

'Caroline, I think . . . Simonne . . . Probably Gaga . . . You can never really tell, can you? At this sort of party you expect twenty and thirty turn up . . .'

Vandeuvres was looking at the ladies; he abruptly changed the subject.

'That Madame Du Joncquoy must have been pretty good fifteen years ago . . . Poor Estelle has shot up a bit more . . . Flat as a board! Fancy finding that in your bed!'

He broke off and switched back to the party.

'The bore of all these jamborees is that it's always the same bloody women . . . We need some new blood . . . Do try and whip something up . . . Ah, I've just had an idea! I'm going to ask that fatso to bring along that woman he took to the Variétés the other night.'

The 'fatso' was the portly head of department, dozing away in the middle of the room, still looking very dignified. Vandeuvres sat down beside him and for a moment both seemed to be engaged in a serious discussion of the topic being debated, the real feelings and motives behind a girl's decision to shut herself up in a nunnery. Then Vandeuvres came back.

'Nothing doing . . . He swears she's a respectable woman and wouldn't play . . . Yet I'd make a bet I've seen her at Laure's.'

'Really? So you go to Laure's?' exclaimed Fauchery with a quiet laugh. 'You risk going to places like that? . . . I thought it was only poor devils like us . . .'

'Ah, my dear fellow, you have to learn how the other half lives!'

And with a glint in their eyes they grinned and proceeded to exchange impressions of the restaurant in Rue des Martyrs where the massive Laure de Piédefer offered a three-franc meal for hard-up little women. What a dive! The little women would all kiss Laure on the mouth. And as Countess Sabine looked over towards them, having picked up a word or two of their conversation in passing, they beat a retreat, squeezing against each other, highly amused and a trifle titillated. They hadn't noticed Georges Hugon listening close beside them and blushing bright pink from his ears down to his girlish neck, a fascinated and embarrassed baby boy. Ever since his mother had let him loose in the drawing-room he'd been prowling round Madame de Chezelles, the only woman who came up to his idea of chic. And yet Nana was miles better!

'Georges took me to the theatre yesterday evening', Madame Hugon was saying. 'Yes, to the Variétés, where I hadn't set foot for ten years. The dear boy adores music . . . It didn't amuse me very much myself but he was so pleased. They're putting on very odd plays these days. In any case I'm not particularly keen on music, I must confess.'

'What, not keen on music?' cried Madame Du Joncquoy, casting her eyes heaven-wards. 'Is it possible not to like music?'

The ladies all exclaimed. Nobody mentioned the show at the Variétés which Madame Hugon had failed to understand; they all knew everything about it but weren't going to let on. They immediately started displaying their good taste and sensitivity in their fanatical admiration for the great composers. Madame Du Joncquoy loved only Weber, Madame Chantereau was for the Italians. Round the fireside, their voices became muted and gently wistful; they sounded like people in church, singing a discreetly ecstatic song of praise in some little chapel.

'Now look', muttered Vandeuvres, leading Fauchery back into the centre of the room, 'we really must unearth a woman or two for tomorrow. What about asking Steiner?'

'Well', said the journalist, 'when Steiner's got hold of a woman it means that everybody else has finished with her.'

Vandeuvres was still casting his eyes around.

'Hang on', he said, 'the other day I met Foucarmont with a charming blonde. I'm going to tell him to bring her along.'

He called Foucarmont over and exchanged a few quick words. Some complication must have arisen for, picking their way carefully over the ladies' skirts, they went over to another young man and continued their conversation in a window-bay. Left by himself, Fauchery was just deciding to make his way towards the fireplace where Madame Du Joncquoy was revealing to all and sundry that she could never listen to Weber without immediately seeing lakes, forests, and the sun rising over landscapes soaked in dew, when a hand was laid on his shoulder and he heard someone say:

'That's not at all friendly of you.'

'What isn't?' he asked, turning round and recognizing la Faloise.

'That supper party tomorrow . . . You might have wangled an invitation for me.'

Fauchery was finally deciding to own up when Vandeuvres came back.

'Apparently she's not one of Foucarmont's women. She belongs to that man over there . . . She's unable to come . . . Our bad luck! All the same, I managed to rake in Foucarmont. He'll try and get Louise at the Palais Royal.'

'Monsieur de Vandeuvres', called Madame Chantereau in a loud voice. 'Didn't they boo Wagner* last Sunday?'

'Oh, abominably, Madame Chantereau', he said, going towards her with his usual exquisite politeness.

Then, as they didn't detain him, he went back to the journalist and continued whispering in his ear:

'I'm going to round up a few more . . . Those young men are bound to know some of the right sort of little girly.'

Smiling affably, he went across to the men, chatting with them all round the room, murmuring a quick word or two over their shoulders before turning away with a wink and conspiratorial nod. It was as if, in his smooth progression, he was transmitting a password. And the news was going round, arrangements were being made while all the time this hectic but discreet flesh-peddling exercise was being covered by the gushing outpourings of the ladies on the subject of music.

'No, don't talk to me about your Germans', Madame Chantereau was insisting. 'Singing means being lively and cheerful . . . Have you ever heard Patti* in the *Barber*?'

'Fantastic!' breathed Léonide, whose only musical interest was strumming operetta tunes on her piano.

Meanwhile, Countess Sabine had rung; when there were few callers on Tuesday tea would be served in the drawing-room itself. While she was telling the footman to clear a little table, the countess was following Vandeuvres with her eyes. She was still wearing that vague half-smile which gave a glimpse of her white teeth. As the count went by, she questioned him:

'What are you plotting, Monsieur de Vandeuvres?'

'Me?' he replied blandly. 'I'm not plotting anything.'

'Ah! . . . I saw you looking very busy . . . Anyway, you can make yourself useful.'

She handed him an album to put on the piano. However, under his breath he contrived to whisper to Fauchery that they'd be getting Tatan Néné—the finest tits going in Paris that winter—and Maria Blond, the one who'd just made her début at the Folies Dramatiques. However, la Faloise kept blocking his way each time he moved, hoping for an invitation. Finally the young man himself volunteered; Vandeuvres signed him on then and there but made him promise to bring Clarisse along, and when la Faloise pretended to have qualms, he reassured him:

'The invitation's coming from me, there's no need to worry!'

Nevertheless, la Faloise would still have liked to know who the woman actually was, but the countess had again called Vandeuvres away to tell her about the English method of tea-making. He made frequent visits to England, where he raced his horses. In his opinion the Russians were the only people who could make tea properly, and he explained their method. Then, as if he'd been following an inner train of thought while he was talking, he broke off and asked:

'And by the way, what of the marquis? Wasn't he supposed to be coming?'

'Yes indeed, my father promised solemnly he'd be here', the countess replied. 'I'm beginning to worry. He must have been held up by his work.'

Vandeuvres smiled discreetly. He too seemed to suspect the sort of work the Marquis de Chouard might be involved in. He recalled a handsome woman the marquis sometimes took off into the country. They might perhaps be able to enlist her.

Meanwhile Fauchery considered that the time was ripe to risk inviting Count Muffat. It was getting late.

'Are you serious?' enquired Vandeuvres, suspecting a joke.

'Absolutely. If I don't do what she's ordered, she'll have my guts for garters. It's just one of her crazy whims, you know.'

'In that case I'll help you, my dear fellow.'

It was striking eleven. The countess, helped by her daughter, was serving tea. As the guests were almost all close friends, the cups of tea and the plates of little cakes were being passed round quite informally. Even the ladies didn't bother to move, but sat sipping their tea and nibbling at their cakes daintily poised in their fingertips, in their armchairs round the fire. From music the talk had turned to catering: Boissier's was the only place for rum truffles and Catherine's for ices, though Madame Chantereau stood up for Latinville's. Conversation was starting to flag, the room was becoming somnolent and weary. Steiner had again cornered the deputy on a two-seated sofa, and was quietly having another go at him. Monsieur Venot's bad teeth must have been the result of eating too many sweet things: he was tucking into one cake after another, making little nibbling noises like a mouse, while the head of department was gulping down his tea with his nose stuck in his cup. The countess was moving unhurriedly from one guest to another, never insisting, saying nothing, merely stopping for a second or two to look questioningly at the men before moving on with a smile. The glow of the fire had made her pink in the face; she looked young enough to be the sister of her daughter, so bony and awkward in comparison. As she approached Fauchery, who was chatting with her husband and Vandeuvres, she noticed that they ceased talking; she went on without stopping and handed the cup of tea she was holding to Georges Hugon, standing a little further away.

'There's a lady who'd like you to come to her supper party', Fauchery was saying breezily to their host.

The count, who'd had a dismal expression all the evening, looked very surprised:

'What lady?'

'Nana, of course?' Vandeuvres interjected, trying to force his hand.

The count looked even more earnest. For a mere second his eyelids quivered while his forehead contracted uneasily, as if he'd felt a touch of migraine.

'But I don't know the lady', he objected.

'Oh, come now, you have been to her house', Vandeuvres reminded him.

'What? I've been to her house? Oh, of course, the other day, on behalf of the charity committee. I'd forgotten . . . All the same, I don't know her, I can't possibly accept.'

His voice had taken on an icy edge to make it plain that he considered this a joke in very poor taste. It was completely inappropriate for a man in his position to sit down at the table of such a woman. Vandeuvres demurred: this was a supper party for actors and actresses, and talent didn't need any justification. But when Fauchery started pointing out that at one dinner party the Prince of Scotland,* the son of a queen, had sat cheek by jowl with a former music-hall star, the count, forgetting his excellent manners, waved his arguments away with an angry gesture, refusing to listen.

Standing nearby drinking their tea together, Georges and la Faloise had overheard this exchange.

'Well, well, so it's Nana', muttered la Faloise. 'I should have guessed it.'

Georges said nothing, but he was all on fire and so worked up and overwrought by the vicious atmosphere surrounding him for the last few days that his blond curls were tousled and his eyes were sparkling like fireworks. So he was finally going to penetrate into the world of his dreams!

'The trouble is, I don't know her address', la Faloise went on.

'In Boulevard Haussman, between Rue de l'Arcade and Rue Pasquier, on the third floor', blurted Georges in one breath.

And seeing the other man's look of amazement, he added, very red-faced and bursting with mingled embarrassment and childish self-satisfaction:

'I'm going to be there too, she invited me this morning.'

There was a stir in the drawing-room, and Vandeuvres and Fauchery had to stop pursuing the count. The Marquis de Chouard had just come in and everybody was bustling around him. He shambled in uncertainly and stood, pale-faced and blinking in the middle of the room, dazzled by the lights, as if he'd just come out of a dark little side-street.

'I'd given up hope of seeing you, Father', the countess said. 'I would've been worried all night.'

He looked at her without answering, as if he failed to understand. His extremely large nose stood out on his clean-shaven face like a swelling full of pus. He had a pendulous lower lip. Seeing him looking so utterly worn-out, the charitable Madame Hugon said, sympathetically:

'You work too hard. You ought to take a rest. At our age, we must leave the work to the younger ones.'

'Work, ah yes, work', he faltered after a pause. 'Always lots of work . . .'

He was beginning to recover, straightening his bent back and running his hand in a familiar gesture over the white hair curling in wisps behind his ears.

'But what were you working at so late?' asked Madame

Chantereau. 'I thought you were at the Finance Minister's party.'

The countess came to his aid:

'My father had to examine a proposal for a new law.'

'Yes, that's right, a proposal for a new law', he said. 'That's exactly what it was, a new law proposal. I'd shut myself away in my room. It's about factory workers. I'd like to make sure that Sunday is a day of rest. It's absolutely scandalous that the government refuses to take active steps. Fewer and fewer people are going to church, we're heading for disaster . . .'

Vandeuvres had thrown Fauchery a glance. They were both standing behind the marquis and they could smell him. When Vandeuvres managed to take him to one side and asked him about that lovely lady whom he had the habit of taking off into the country, the old gentleman professed to be greatly surprised. He must have been seen with Baroness Decker, he sometimes spent a few days at her place in Viroflay.* Vandeuvres got his own back merely by saying suddenly:

'I say, what have you been doing? Your elbow's all covered in spiders' webs and plaster.'

'My elbow?' he mumbled, slightly confused. 'Oh yes, I see . . . A bit of dirt . . . I must have rubbed against something coming downstairs at my place . . .'

A number of guests were leaving. It was nearly midnight. Two footmen were silently collecting the empty cups and plates. In front of the fire, the ladies had formed a smaller circle. The evening was drawing to a close, the conversation was becoming freer, people felt more relaxed. Even the drawing-room was drowsy, the walls shrouded in gentle shadows. Fauchery talked of leaving, but when he looked at Countess Sabine he started day-dreaming again. She was relaxing from her duties as hostess, sitting silently in her usual place, staring at a glowing ember; her face was so white, so inscrutable, that once more he was seized by doubt. In the glow of the fire the black hairs sprouting from the mole in the corner of her mouth looked blonde. Exactly like Nana's, even to the colour! He couldn't resist making a whispered comment to Vandeuvres. Good Lord, that was right! Vandeuvres had never noticed it before. And the pair explored the comparison further: they thought there was a vague similarity between the chin and mouth, but the eyes were quite different; moreover, Nana looked cheerful and good-natured whereas you couldn't tell with the countess, she was rather like a cat with her claws retracted and her paws quivering slightly in a nervous twitch.

'All the same, she's eminently bedworthy', said Fauchery.

Vandeuvres was undressing her with his eyes.

'Yes, she's bedworthy all right', he said, 'but I'm a bit suspicious of her thighs. Will you take a bet, she's got lousy thighs?'

He stopped; Fauchery was vigorously tugging at his elbow and nodding in the direction of Estelle in front of them on her stool. Without noticing, they had been raising their voices and she must have heard them. However, she was continuing to sit stiff-backed, not moving an inch, and with not a single little hair out of place on her skinny neck, the neck of a girl who'd shot up too fast. They moved two or three steps further away. Vandeuvres was positive the countess was a woman of the highest principles.

At that moment the ladies round the fireside raised their voices. Madame Du Joncquoy was heard saying:

'I've conceded that Prince von Bismarck may be witty . . . But if you're claiming he's a genius . . .'

The ladies were back at their original topic.

'Good God! Still on Bismarck', muttered Fauchery. 'This time I really am going.'

'Wait a second', said Vandeuvres. 'We must get a definite yes or no from Muffat.'

The count was talking to his father-in-law and a few serious-looking men. Vandeuvres drew him on one side and repeated the invitation, adding that he would be going, too. A man could go anywhere, nobody would ever think of seeing anything wrong in it; at the most, it'd be put down to curiosity. The count listened to his arguments non-committally, looking down at the floor. Vandeuvres could sense a certain hesitation. The Marquis de Chouard came up with a questioning look. When he learned what it was about and Fauchery included him in the invitation, he glanced furtively at his son-in-law. There was an embarrassed silence, but they were prodding each other and would no doubt have ended by accepting had Count

Muffat not caught a glimpse of Monsieur Venot staring at him. The little old man had lost his smile, his face had an ashen look, and his eyes were as bright and sharp as steel.

'No', said the count at once, so curtly that any further persuasion was out of the question.

The marquis refused even more curtly. He talked of high principles: the upper classes had to set an example. Fauchery gave a smile and shook hands with Vandeuvres. He'd not wait for him, he had to be off straight away to go to his newspaper.

'Midnight at Nana's, OK?'

La Faloise was also departing. Steiner had just taken his leave of the countess. Others were following his example and the same words were going the rounds, everyone was saying 'Midnight at Nana's' as they went off to pick up their overcoats in the hall. Georges was going to have to wait till his mother left, but he had stationed himself in the doorway and was informing them of the exact address: 'third floor, door on the left.' However, before leaving, Fauchery had one last glance: Vandeuvres had again taken his seat amongst the ladies and was having a joke with Léonide de Chezelles. Count Muffat and the Marquis de Chouard were joining in the conversation, while kind old Madame Hugon was dropping off to sleep with her eyes open. Concealed behind all these skirts, Monsieur Venot had retreated into his shell; he was smiling again. Slowly, in the huge, solemn room, the clock struck twelve.

'What's that?' Madame Du Joncquoy was screeching. 'What are you saying? You think Bismarck is going to make war on us and win? Oh, that's really rich!'

And indeed, people round Madame Chantereau were laughing; she had just repeated a remark which she heard someone make in Alsace, where her husband had a factory.

'Fortunately, the Emperor is there to protect us!' said Count Muffat in his solemn official voice.

This was the last thing Fauchery was able to hear as he closed the door, after taking one last look at the Countess Sabine. She was calmly chatting to the departmental head, and seemed to be interested in the fat man's comments. No, he must definitely have been mistaken, there was no sign of a flaw. What a pity.

'Well, are you coming or not?' la Faloise called up from the hall.

And as they parted on the pavement, they said to each other: 'See you at Nana's tomorrow.'

Chapter 4

SINCE morning Zoé had handed over the flat to a man from the catering firm of Brébant,* with a staff of assistants and waiters. Brébant was to provide everything, the food, the crockery, the cut-glass, the table linen, the flowers, even the chairs for the supper party. Nana wouldn't have been able to dig even a dozen table napkins out of her cupboards, and not having yet found time to set herself up properly in her new career, she had rejected the idea of a restaurant and opted to bring the restaurant into her own home. It seemed the smarter thing to do. As the dining-room wasn't big enough, the caterer had laid up the table in the drawing-room for twenty-five people, leaving not much elbow-room.

'Is everything ready?' asked Nana when she came home at midnight.

'Oh, I don't know', reported Zoé brusquely; she seemed furious. 'Thank God I'm not responsible for anything. They're creating havoc in the kitchen and the whole flat, too! . . . And I've had a row to cope with . . . The two others came back again. I've just kicked them out, neck and crop.'

She was referring to her mistress's two earlier gentlemen, the shop-owner and the man from Wallachia, whom Nana had decided to send packing now she felt her future was assured; to use her own words, she was keen to turn over a new leaf.

'What a pain in the neck they are, the pair of them', she muttered. 'If they come back, threaten to go to the police!'

She called out to Daguenet and Georges who were hanging up their coats in the entrance hall. The two had met at the stage-door exit in the Passage des Panoramas, and she'd brought them back in her cab. As no one had yet arrived, she called to them to come into her dressing-room while Zoé was tidying her up. Without changing her dress, she hurriedly got Zoé to put her hair up and stuck white roses in her chignon and on her bodice. The dressing-room was crammed with furniture from the drawing-room which had been packed in there, a mass of small tables, settees, and armchairs with their legs in the air; and just as she was ready, her skirt caught on a caster and tore. She swore furiously: that was typical, things like that were always happening to her! Fuming with rage, she took the dress off; it was made of flimsy white foulard, very simple, which flowed round her like a long chemise. Then, as she couldn't find anything else suitable, she put it back on again, almost in tears, saying she looked a frump. Daguenet and Georges had to pin up the tear while Zoé re-did her hair. All three were bustling around her, especially the boy, who was kneeling on the floor with his hands in her skirts. Eventually she calmed down when Daguenet reassured her that it was certainly not later than a quarter past twelve, since she'd rushed through the last act of *The Blonde Venus* at such a tremendous rate, gabbling her lines and skipping whole verses.

Anyway, it was far too good for that bunch of idiots, she said. 'Did you see what a lot of ugly mugs there were in the audience tonight? . . . My God, just in time! There's someone at the door.'

She dashed out. Georges was still kneeling, his coat tails brushing the floor. He blushed when he saw Daguenet watching him. All the same, they'd taken a liking to each other. They rearranged their bow-ties in front of the cheval glass and brushed each other down; they were all white where they'd been rubbing against Nana.

'It looks like sugar', murmured Georges with his greedy, baby-like laugh.

A footman hired for the night was showing each arrival into the small drawing-room, a tiny room furnished with only four armchairs to enable all the guests to be packed in. From the large drawing-room next door there came a clatter of plates and silver cutlery; a bright streak of light shone under the door. When Nana went in she found Clarisse already ensconced in one of the armchairs; she was escorted by la Faloise.

'Good Lord, you're the first here', exclaimed Nana, who ever since her own success had taken to treating her as a close friend.

'That's because of that man', replied Clarisse. 'He's always scared of not getting somewhere . . . If I'd listened to him, I wouldn't have had time even to take my make-up and wig off.'

The young man was meeting Nana for the first time. He bowed, offered his congratulations, mentioned his cousin, and hid his excitement under an exaggerated display of politeness. Not bothering to listen or discover who he was, Nana shook hands with him and rushed away to greet Rose Mignon in an extremely genteel voice.

'Oh, dear Madame Mignon, how very kind of you . . . I was hoping so much that you'd be able to come . . .'

'Oh, the pleasure's entirely mine, I assure you!' Rose replied in an equally friendly voice.

'Do take a seat . . . May I offer you something?'

'No, thank you . . . Oh, I've forgotten my fan . . . Do go and look in my right pocket, will you Steiner?'

Steiner and Mignon had followed Rose in. The banker went off to fetch the fan, while Mignon gave Nana a brotherly kiss and insisted on Rose's kissing her too: weren't they all members of the same big happy family in the theatre? Then he gave a wink of encouragement to Steiner, but the latter, daunted by Rose's sharp eye, was happy merely to kiss her hand.

At that moment, the Count de Vandeuvres appeared with Blanche de Sivry. There followed much bowing and scraping, and with great ceremony Nana conducted Blanche to an armchair. Meanwhile Vandeuvres was laughingly explaining that Fauchery was having a row with the porter for not allowing Lucy Stewart's carriage into the courtyard. In the hall, Lucy could be heard calling the porter a lousy yob. But when the footman opened the door she came in with a smile, gracious as always, and announced herself, clasping both Nana's hands and telling her she'd liked her from the start and thought she was very, very gifted. Full of her new role as hostess, Nana thanked her: she was too kind. However, since Fauchery's arrival she seemed preoccupied. As soon as she could get close to him she asked in an undertone:

'Is he coming?'

'No, he didn't want to', the journalist replied abruptly, taken unawares, though he had concocted a story to explain Count Muffat's refusal.

When he saw Nana go pale he realized his stupidity, and tried to rephrase his answer:

'He couldn't come because he's taking his wife to the Interior Minister's ball.'

'All right', muttered Nana, suspecting him of not trying hard enough. 'You'll pay for that, young man.'

'Oh, come on', he protested, offended by her threat. 'I don't like that sort of errand. You should get Labordette to do jobs like that.'

They turned their backs on each other in annoyance. At that same moment Mignon was urging Steiner to approach Nana. When the actress was standing by herself, he whispered to her, with the cheerful cynicism of an accomplice anxious to oblige a friend:

'He's panting for it, you know . . . Only he's afraid of my wife. You'll protect him, won't you?'

Nana looked as if she didn't understand. She was smiling and looking at Rose, her husband, and the banker. Then she said:

'Monsieur Steiner, I want you to sit on my right.'

But gusts of laughter and whispering could be heard coming from the entrance hall, cheerful, chatty voices, as if a whole lot of convent girls had suddenly been let loose. And in came Labordette, trailing five women behind him, his boarding school, as Lucy Stewart maliciously described it. There was the majestic Gaga, squeezed into a blue velvet dress, Caroline Héquet, always in black ribbed silk trimmed with lace, Léa de Horn, dowdy as ever, then big, fat Tatan Néné, a cheerful blonde with udders like a cow whom everyone made fun of, and finally tiny Maria Blond, a little girl of 15, as skinny and vicious as a street urchin, who was just being launched on her career at the Folies Dramatiques. Labordette had brought the whole bunch of them along in one cab and they were still giggling at being packed so tightly, with Maria having to sit on the others' laps. But, pursing their lips, they now made their way round shaking hands and greeting the others very primly. Gaga was being childish and lisping, in an exaggerated effort to be well-behaved. Only Tatan Néné seemed uneasy: on the way here they'd been telling her that Nana had engaged six buck niggers to wait at table stark naked and Tatan was asking to see them. Labordette called her a silly clot and told her to shut up.

'And what about Bordenave?' inquired Fauchery.

'Oh, believe it or not, he can't come!' exclaimed Nana. 'I'm so sorry.'

'Yes', said Rose, 'he got his foot caught in a trapdoor and gave himself a nasty sprain . . . You should have heard him swearing, with his leg bandaged up and stretched out on a chair.'

Everyone said how much they'd miss him. He was the life and soul of any party. Anyway, they'd have to see what they could do without him. And they'd already changed the subject when they heard a loud voice outside:

'What's all this? What's all this? So that's how you tuck me underground, is it?'

There was a shout and they all turned round: it was Bordenave, huge and very red, standing in the doorway with a stiff leg, leaning on Simonne Cabiroche's shoulder; this was his current sleeping-partner. She was an educated girl who played the piano and spoke English, a charming, plump, dainty little blonde, so dainty that she was bending under Bordenave's massive weight, but still smiling and uncomplaining. He stood there posing in the doorway for a second or two, feeling that the pair of them made a nice tableau.

'Eh? I really have to be fond of you lot', he continued. 'The truth is I was afraid of getting bored so I said to myself: I'll go!'

He broke off and swore:

'Bloody hell!'

Simonne had stepped forward too fast and he'd been obliged to put some weight on to his foot. He jolted against her and she cringed like a dog expecting to be beaten, though still smiling and supporting him as well as she could. In any case everybody was eagerly rallying round, with loud exclamations. Nana and Rose brought up an armchair into which Bordenave collapsed, while other women slipped a second armchair under his leg. And of course all the actresses kissed him. He was grumbling and sighing:

'Bloody hell! Bloody hell! . . . Anyway, there's nothing

wrong with my stomach, you'll see!'

Other guests had arrived. In the room there was no space to move. In the drawing-room the rattle of crockery and cutlery had ceased, to be replaced by the sound of quarrelling; you could hear the angry voice of the man in charge. Nana was growing impatient; she was not expecting any more guests and she was surprised that they hadn't begun serving. She had just sent Georges along to see what was happening when she was amazed to see more people, men and women, come in. They were complete strangers to her and, somewhat embarrassed, she questioned Bordenave, Mignon, and Labordette, who didn't know them either. When she enquired of the Count de Vandeuvres, he suddenly remembered: they were the young men he'd recruited at Count Muffat's. Nana thanked him: good idea! But it was going to make it a jolly tight squeeze. She asked Labordette to go and get seven more places laid. Hardly had he gone than the footman announced three more people. Oh no, this was becoming ridiculous! They wouldn't all be able to get in, that was sure! But when she saw another two people arrive, she started to laugh; it was too funny for words! Never mind! They'd squeeze in somehow or other. Everybody was standing; only Gaga and Rose had seats, as Bordenave needed two armchairs all to himself. There was a buzz of voices; people were talking in undertones and stifling slight yawns.

'I say, my dear', called Bordenave, 'how about a spot of supper now? We're all here, aren't we?'

'Oh yes, you can say that again!' she laughed. 'We're certainly all here!'

She was running her eyes round the room. Suddenly she looked earnest, as though surprised not to see someone. No doubt there was a guest missing whom she was not going to mention. They'd have to wait. A few minutes later, the guests noticed in their midst a tall, very distinguished-looking man with a superb white beard. And the most astonishing thing was that nobody had seen him come in; he must have slipped into the small drawing-room through a bedroom door which had been left half-open. There was silence, people were whispering among themselves. Count de Vandeuvres certainly knew who the gentleman was, for they had discreetly shaken hands; but when questioned by some of the ladies, he merely smiled. In a stage whisper, Caroline bet that he was an English lord who was returning home the following day to get married in London; she knew him; she'd had him. The story circulated amongst the ladies, but Maria Blond claimed to recognize a German ambassador; she knew this because he often went to bed with one of her friends. The men were doing a rapid assessment: looked a man of substance; could be paying for the supper—this was probable; you had the feeling he might be . . . And what the hell! As long as it was a good supper! In the end people were still uncertain, but they were already forgetting the white-bearded old gentleman when the head waiter flung open the door of the large drawing-room:

'Supper is served, madam!'

Steiner offered Nana his arm, which she took, apparently not noticing the old gentleman's move; he followed behind her. People were, in any case, having trouble organizing the way they filed in, and in the end they all went in higgledy-piggledy, exchanging polite jokes at this lack of formality. A long table ran from one end of the huge room to the other, with no other furniture; and even this was too short, for the plates were touching. On the table were four candelabra, each with ten sconces, and in the middle a silver-plated epergne with sprays of flowers on each side. It was the sort of luxury you find in restaurants, gold-lined china with no monogram, silver worn and dull from much washing-up, glasses which didn't match, the sort sold in any cheap bazaar. It suggested a house-warming party inadequately organized, prematurely celebrated, and paid for with money acquired too fast. One chandelier was missing; the candelabra, with their very tall candles showing hardly any wick, were casting a pale yellow light on the fruit dishes, plate-stands, and bowls of *petits fours* and preserves placed alternately in a symmetrical pattern.

'Sit down wherever you like, you know', said Nana. 'It's more fun like that.'

She was standing at the middle of the table. The unknown old gentleman had placed himself on her right while she kept Steiner on her left. As the guests were starting to take their seats, there was a volley of oaths from the small drawing-room; Bordenave had been left behind and was finding great difficulty in getting up from his two armchairs; he was yelling for that little bitch Simonne who had dashed into the other room with all the others. Full of sympathy, the women rushed to help, and Bordenave appeared supported, almost carried, by Caroline, Clarisse, and Tatan Néné. There was a great fuss while they decided where to put him.

'In the middle, opposite Nana!' people were shouting. 'Bordenave must be at the head of the table, put him in the middle!'

So the ladies deposited him in the middle. He needed a second chair for his leg; two women lifted it and put it down, sticking out. Never mind, he'd have to eat sitting sideways.

'Bloody hell!' he grumbled. 'It's damned awkward. Daddy needs your help, my little darlings!'

He had Rose Mignon on his right and Lucy Stewart on his left. They promised to look after him. Everybody was now finding a seat. Count de Vandeuvres put himself between Lucy and Clarisse; Fauchery was between Rose Mignon and Caroline Héquet. On the other side, Hector de la Faloise had plopped down next to Gaga, ignoring Clarisse's appeals opposite; Mignon was sticking close to Steiner, with only Blanche in-between them, while Tatan Néné was on his left. Labordette was next. Finally, the young men and the women were at the two ends, all jumbled together; Daguenet and Georges Hugon were both there, and beginning to find they had more and more in common; both kept continually smiling towards Nana.

Meanwhile people were teasing two women who'd failed to find a seat; the men were offering to sit them on their laps. Clarisse, who had no elbow-room at all, was telling Vandeuvres that she was relying on him to feed her. And what a lot of room Bordenave was taking up with those two chairs! After one last effort everyone found a seat; but they were all packed like sardines, damn it, exclaimed Mignon.

'Cream of asparagus à la comtesse or consommé à la Deslignac.' The waiters were moving round behind the guests, quietly offering platefuls of soup.

Just as Bordenave was loudly recommending the consommé, there was a loud outcry; people were protesting angrily: three late-comers, a man and two women, had just come through the door. Oh no, they really couldn't pack any more people in! Nana didn't get up, but screwed up her eyes to see if she could recognize any of them. The woman was Louise Violaine. She'd never seen the men.

'Oh, Nana, my dear', said Vandeuvres, 'this gentleman is a friend of mine, Monsieur Foucarmont, a naval officer whom I've invited.'

Quite unembarrassed, Foucarmont bowed and said:

'And I've taken the liberty of bringing along one of my friends.'

'Oh, delighted, I'm sure', said Nana. 'Do sit down. Clarisse, surely you can move back a bit, you've got lots of room there . . . There you are, where there's a will . . .'

They squeezed a little more tightly together, and Foucarmont and Louise managed to find a small corner for themselves; the friend, however, had to sit such a long way from the table that he could eat only by stretching his arms out between his neighbours' shoulders. The waiters were removing the soup plates and serving truffled rabbit crépinettes and Parmesan gnocchi. Bordenave nearly caused a riot by saying that he'd half thought of bringing along Prullière, Fontan, and old Bosc. Nana snapped scornfully that they wouldn't have enjoyed their welcome, and if she'd wanted to have colleagues she'd have invited them herself. She could do without ham actors. Old Bosc was always tipsy, Prullière far too pleased with himself, and as for Fontan, his rowdiness and stupid behaviour made him quite unfit for decent company. And in any case, hack actors like that were like fish out of water in the company of gentlemen.

'Yes indeed, very true', agreed Mignon.

The gentlemen in question, sitting round the table, looked very proper in their white ties and tails, and the tired expression on their pale faces added to their air of distinction. With his leisurely movements and sly smile the elderly gentleman seemed to be chairing a diplomatic congress. Vandeuvres's exquisite politeness to the ladies next to him would not have been out of place at the Countess Sabine's. As Nana had remarked to her aunt that very morning, as far as men were concerned, you couldn't find anything better: all aristocrats or rich; in a word, the smart set. And the ladies themselves were behaving very well. A few—Blanche, Léa, Louise—had come in low-cut dresses; only Gaga was revealing rather too much, particularly as at her age she'd have done better not to reveal anything at all. Now that people had finally found seats, the laughter and joking had subsided. Georges was thinking to himself that he'd been present at livelier dinner parties in middle-class houses in Orléans. There was little conversation; the men who didn't know each other were eyeing each other, and the women were sitting quietly; this was what Georges found most surprising. They all seemed terribly humdrum; he'd imagined they'd all start kissing each other straight away. As the next course was being served—Rhine carp Chambord and saddle of venison à l'anglaise—Blanche said loudly:

'Lucy my dear, I met your Olivier last Sunday . . . Hasn't he shot up!'

'Well, after all he is 18', replied Lucy. 'And that hardly makes me any younger . . . He left to go back to college yesterday.'

Her son Olivier, of whom she was very proud, was a student at Naval College. They started talking about their children; the ladies became sentimental. Nana mentioned how delighted she was that her baby, little Louis, was now with his aunt, who brought him round every morning at about eleven; and she'd take him into her bed where he'd play with her terrier puppy Lulu. It was really comical to see them both snuggling right down under the blanket. You couldn't imagine what a sharp little kid Louis was already.

'What a day I had yesterday', said Rose Mignon, making her contribution. 'Can you believe it, when I went to pick up Charles and Henri at their boarding-school, they absolutely insisted on being taken to the theatre that evening . . . They were jumping around, clapping their little hands, shouting: "We'll see mummy acting! We'll see mummy acting!" Oh, it was such a hullaballoo!'

Mignon was smiling sympathetically, his eyes dewy with fatherly affection.

'And at the performance', he said, continuing the story, 'they were so funny, as serious as grown-ups, watching Rose with their eyes popping out of their heads and asking me why mummy had bare legs like that!'

The whole table exploded in laughter. Mignon was bursting with paternal pride. He loved the little chaps, his only concern being to ensure that they'd not be short of money later on, for which purpose he kept careful check, like a faithful steward, over any monies earned by Rose in her dramatic, and other, activities. When he'd married her, he was the leader of the orchestra in a café where she was a singer. They'd been passionately in love with each other. Now they were still good friends. They'd reached an agreement: she worked as hard as possible, exploiting her acting ability and her beauty to the full; he had abandoned his fiddle to keep an eye on her success as an actress and as a woman. You couldn't have found a more middle-class or more united couple.

'How old's your eldest?' enquired Vandeuvres.

'Henri's 9', replied Mignon. 'Oh, he's such a fine young lad!'

Then he began quietly teasing Steiner, who wasn't fond of children, even going so far as to tell him that if he'd been a father he wouldn't be throwing his money away so stupidly. While speaking, he watched Steiner closely over Blanche's shoulders to see if he was hitting it off with Nana. However, for the last few minutes he'd been irritated by the sight of Rose and Fauchery engaged in very private conversation. Surely Rose couldn't be so silly as to waste her time like that? If so, he'd certainly have to put a spoke in their wheel! And his fine strong hands, with a diamond ring adorning the little finger, dealt decisively with a slice of venison.

Meanwhile the topic of children was still being pursued. Greatly excited by sitting so close to Gaga, la Faloise was enquiring after her daughter, whom he'd had the pleasure of seeing at the Variétés with her. Lili was well but still such a little monkey! He was surprised to learn that Lili was rising 19. It made her mother seem even more remarkable in his eyes. He asked why she hadn't brought Lili along to the party.

'Oh dear me no, I never would', she replied stiffly. 'It's only three months since she insisted on being allowed to leave her convent school . . . I was planning and hoping for her to get married straight away. But she's so fond of her mother that I've had to take her back at home with me, quite against my will.'

Her eyes, with their blue shadows and burnt lashes, were sparkling as she talked about setting up her 'young lady'. If at her age she hadn't been able to save a penny, though still working and still having men, above all men so young they could have been her grandsons, it proved that there was nothing to beat a good marriage. And she leaned towards la Faloise, who blushed as he felt her massive naked shoulder, plastered with powder, crushing against him.

'If she takes to doing that sort of thing, it won't be my fault, you know', she murmured. 'But young people get such odd ideas into their heads.'

There was a great stir round the table; the waiters were bustling around to serve the next course: poularde à la maréchale, fillets of sole ravigote, and slices of foie gras. The butler, who up till now had been serving Meursault, switched to Chambertin and Léoville.* In the slight disturbance caused by the change of service, Georges, who'd been more and more surprised, asked Daguenet if all those ladies had children like that. Daguenet was amused at the question and gave him some details. Lucy Stewart was the daughter of an Englishman working as a greaser at the Gare du Nord; she was 39 years old, with a face like a horse but adorable, suffering from TB, but still going strong, the smartest of all those ladies, having notched up three princes and a duke. Caroline Héquet had been born in Bordeaux. Her father, a minor office clerk, had died of shame, but she'd had the luck to have a hard-headed mother who, after first of all disowning her, had had second thoughts and a year later had joined up with her again, anxious at least to make sure that her money would be safe; the daughter was 25, a cold fish, with the reputation of being one of the loveliest women you could get for a price that never varied. Her mother was highly efficient, kept a strict account of income and expenditure, and managed the household's affairs from a small apartment two floors up from her daughter's, where she'd also set up a dressmaker's workshop to supply her dresses and lingerie. As for Blanche de Sivry, she was from a village near Amiens; her real name was Jacqueline Baudu, she had a superb figure, was stupid and a liar, claiming to be the granddaughter of a general and refusing to admit she was 32 years old; very popular with Russians, because she was plump. Daguenet added a few details about some of the others: Clarisse Besnus, brought to Paris as her maid by a lady from Saint-Aubin-sur-Mer,* whose husband had launched her on her career; Simonne Cabiroche, daughter of a furniture-dealer in the Faubourg Saint Antoine* and educated in an excellent boarding-school to become an elementary-school mistress; as for Maria Blond, Louise Violaine, and Léa de Horn, their entire education had come from the streets of Paris, whereas up to the age of 20 Tatan Néné had looked after the cows in her native Champagne Pouilleuse.* As he was listening, Georges watched these women, shocked and excited by these devastatingly frank and crude disclosures which Daguenet was whispering in his ear. Meanwhile behind them there came the steady murmur of the waiters:

'Poularde à la maréchale . . . Fillet of sole sauce ravigote . . .'

'Steer clear of the fish, my dear chap!' said Daguenet, laying down the law with the weight of his experience. 'It's not the time of year to eat it. And stick to the Léoville, it's not so insidious . . .'

The room was growing warmer and warmer from the candelabra, the food in the dishes, and the whole tableful of thirty-eight people struggling to breathe. The waiters were becoming distraught as they rushed to and fro, covering the carpet with grease-spots. But the party was hanging fire. Their ladyships were picking at their food, leaving their meat half-eaten. Only Tatan Néné was stuffing everything down voraciously. At this late hour, people's appetites were uncertain, their stomachs unsettled; they were full of fads. The old gentleman beside Nana was refusing every dish; he'd taken just one spoonful of soup and was sitting in front of an empty plate, silently watching. There were stifled yawns; here and there eyelids could be seen drooping and faces becoming ghastly pale; in Vandeuvres's words, the whole thing was deadly dull, as always. In order to be fun, supper parties had to be dirty. Otherwise, if you put on a show of high principles and good form, you might just as well be in good society, where you wouldn't be any more bored. But for Bordenave's incessant bellowing, people would have dropped off to sleep. With his leg comfortably stretched out, the theatre manager, always uncouth, was letting his neighbours Lucy and Rose serve him and looking like a sultan. He was their sole concern; they were seeing to his needs, pampering him, making sure his plate and his glass were never empty, which didn't prevent him from grumbling:

'Who's going to cut up my meat? The table's miles away, you can't expect me to do it myself!'

Simonne was getting up all the time to cut up his meat or his bread. The women were all taking an interest in what he was eating. They kept calling the waiters back and stuffing him until he was bursting. When Simonne wiped his mouth and Rose and Lucy gave him a clean knife and fork, he said that was very kind of them and finally condescended to show his appreciation:

'That's fine! You're on the right track, my dear girl... That's just what women are made for!'

People woke up a bit, a general conversation got under way. They were just finishing the mandarine-flavoured water-ice. There was a choice of roast fillet of beef with truffles or cold galantine of guinea fowl. Nana was amazed at her guests' dullness, and started talking very loudly:

'The Prince of Scotland has already booked a stage box for *The Blonde Venus* when he comes over for the World Fair, you know.'

'I hope all the visiting princes come', commented Bordenave with his mouth full.

'The Shah of Persia is expected to arrive on Sunday', added Lucy Stewart.

This remark led Rose Mignon to start talking about the Shah's diamonds. He wore a tunic completely covered in precious stones, absolutely fabulous, a glittering star worth millions. Pale, their eyes sparkling with greed, the ladies all leaned forward and listed the names of the other kings and emperors who would be coming. They all had one dream: a sudden fancy, a night in a royal bed that would leave them rich for life.

'I say, my dear', asked Caroline Héquet, leaning forward and addressing the Count de Vandeuvres, 'how old is the Tsar?'

'Oh, he's ageless', the count replied with a laugh. 'Not a hope for you there, I warn you.'

Nana pretended to take offence. His remark seemed rather objectionable; there were muttered protests. But Blanche was starting to give details about the King of Italy, whom she'd once seen in Milan; he wasn't much to look at but that didn't prevent him from getting all the women he wanted, and she was peeved when Fauchery said that Victor Emmanuel would definitely not be coming. Louise Violaine and Léa had a weakness for the Emperor of Austria. Suddenly little Maria Blond piped up:

'What an old bore the King of Prussia is! I was in Baden last year. He was with Count Bismarck all the time.'

'Ah, Bismarck', Simonne broke in. 'I knew him . . . What a charmer!'

'Just what I was saying yesterday', exclaimed Vandeuvres. 'They wouldn't believe me.'

They spent a great deal of time discussing Bismarck, exactly as Countess Sabine's guests had. Vandeuvres produced the very same words. For a moment, it was like being at the Muffats'; only the ladies were different. And the company even went on to the subject of music. Then, as Foucarmont happened to let slip a remark about the controversial retreat into a convent of Mademoiselle de Fougeray, Nana became interested and insisted on hearing the details. Oh, the poor girl, to bury herself alive like that! But then, if she'd suddenly felt the call! The women round the table were very touched. Bored at having to listen to the same old things again, Georges was starting to question Daguenet about Nana's habits when the conversation again inevitably came back to Bismarck. Tatan Néné bent forward and whispered into Labordette's ear to inquire who this man Bismarck was; she didn't know him. Without batting an eyelid, Labordette started telling her horrendous stories: Bismarck lived on raw meat; whenever he found a woman close to his lair, he'd sling her over his back and carry her off; as a result, he'd already got thirty-two children by the age of 40 . . .

'Thirty-two children at only 40!' exclaimed Tatan Néné,

flabbergasted and believing every word. 'He must be pretty exhausted for his age!'

There was a burst of laughter. She realized that her leg was being pulled.

'How idiotic you are! How could I know you were joking!'

But Gaga was still on the subject of the World Fair. Like the rest of the ladies, she was looking forward to it and getting ready. It'd be a good season, with people pouring in from the provinces and abroad. After the World Fair she might perhaps at last be able to retire to Juvisy,* where she'd had her eye on a little property for a long time.

'What can one do?' she said to la Faloise. 'One's not getting anywhere . . . If only one had love!'

Gaga was becoming sentimental as she felt the young man's knee pressing against her own. His face was very red. She was lisping and sizing him up with her eyes. A little man, not very substantial; but she'd stopped being choosy. La Faloise obtained her address.

'Just look at that', whispered Vandeuvres to Clarisse. 'I think Gaga's grabbing your friend Hector.'

'I couldn't care less!' retorted the actress. 'That young man's a cretin . . . I've given him the boot three times already . . . It's disgusting to see little boys falling for old bags.'

She broke off to point to Blanche, who'd been leaning forward in a very uncomfortable posture since the start of supper, giving herself airs and anxious to show off her shoulders to the distinguished old gentleman sitting three places away.

'You're being discarded too, my dear man', she added.

Vandeuvres gave a gentle smile with an unconcerned wave of his hand. He certainly wouldn't stand in the way of poor Blanche enjoying a little success. He was more interested in the spectacle Steiner was making of himself in front of everybody. The banker was well known for his sudden infatuations; this formidable German-Jewish tycoon, who dealt in millions, turned into a complete idiot each time he fell for a woman. And he wanted them all; no woman could appear on the stage without being bought by him, whatever the price. People used to quote figures. His insatiable appetite for actresses had already twice ruined him. As Vandeuvres remarked, these tarts upheld morality by cleaning out the till. A big operation on the salt-pans in the Landes* had again made him a power in the Stock Exchange, and for the last six weeks the Mignons had been taking big bites out of the proceeds. But bets were beginning to be made that it wouldn't be the Mignons who'd finish off the job; Nana was sharpening her lovely white teeth. Steiner had once again been taken over, so effectively that he was sitting beside Nana like someone who'd been knocked on the head, barely eating, with a blotchy face and sagging jaw. She had only to name her figure. However, she was in no hurry, playing with him, puffing little laughs into his hairy ear, enjoying the quivers which kept running over his heavy features. There'd be plenty of time to wrap up this little job in two shakes of a lamb's tail if that dolt Muffat continued to be so stuffy and puritanical.

'Léoville or Chambertin?' the waiter murmured, sticking his head between Nana and Steiner just as the latter was whispering something to her.

'What?' he stammered, completely lost. 'Oh, I don't mind, anything you like.'

Vandeuvres was gently nudging Lucy Stewart with his elbow. She was extremely spiteful and savagely witty once she got going. Tonight Mignon was getting on her nerves.

'He'd be the pimp, you know', she whispered to the count. 'He hopes to bring off the same coup he managed with young Jonquier . . . You remember, Jonquier was with Rose and suddenly fell for that big girl Laure . . . Mignon got Laure for Jonquier and then brought him back to Rose, all good friends together, like a hubby who's been let off the hook for a quick bit of fun on the side . . . But it's not going to work like that this time. Nana's not the sort of girl to give back any man she's been lent.'

'Do you see the stern look Mignon's giving his wife?' said the count. 'What's the matter with him?'

He bent forward and saw Rose casting very affectionate glances at Fauchery. So that was why his neighbour was in such a rage . . . He said laughingly:

'What the devil? You can't be jealous surely?'

'Jealous?' replied Lucy furiously. 'Ah well, if Rose wants Léon she's welcome to him. What's he good for? . . . One bunch of flowers a week, if you're lucky! . . . You see, all these theatrical women are the same. Rose wept with anger when she read Léon's article on Nana, I know that for a fact. So you see, she wants her article too and she's prepared to earn it . . . As for me, I'm going to kick Léon out, you'll see!'

She stopped to speak to the waiter standing behind her holding two bottles:

'The Léoville.'

Then she lowered her voice and went on:

'I've no intention of making a fuss, that's not my way . . . But all the same, she is a real bitch. If I were her husband, I'd tan her arse for her . . . Oh, she'll not get any good from it. She doesn't know Fauchery, he's a dirty swine as well, who attaches himself to women to help him in his job . . . What a prize bunch they all are!'

Vandeuvres endeavoured to calm her down. Neglected by both Rose and Lucy, Bordenave was growing annoyed, and complaining that they were letting Daddy starve—and what about something to drink? This provided a lucky diversion. The party was flagging; everybody had stopped eating; whole platefuls of cèpes à l'italienne and banana pasties Pompadour had been left untouched. However, the champagne that the guests had been imbibing ever since the soup was going to their heads and making them increasingly edgy. People were starting to let themselves go. The women were resting their elbows on the table, which was beginning to look like a battlefield; men were pushing back their chairs in order to take a breather; their black tailcoats were wedged between the pale bodices and gleaming, silky, bare shoulders half twisted towards them. It was too hot, and the smoky light of the candles on the table was becoming more and more yellow. From time to time, the nape of a neck, golden under its wisp of tiny curls, would bend forward, revealing the sparkle of a diamond brooch glittering in the chignon caught up high on the head. There were sudden guffaws, laughing eyes, a glimpse of white teeth, the gleam of the candelabra reflected in a glass of champagne. People were making loud jokes, waving their arms about, asking questions without waiting for answers, shouting across the room. But it was the waiters who were making the most noise, thinking they were in the corridors of their restaurants, barging into each other and uttering loud, guttural grunts as they served the ices and dessert.

'Now, my little darlings', called Bordenave, 'remember we've got a show tomorrow! . . . Take care! Go easy on the bubbly!'

'Well, I've had every conceivable sort of drink in every part of the world', proclaimed Foucarmont. 'Absolutely extra-ordinary things, spirits that could kill a man on the spot . . . Well, it never had the slightest effect on me. I can't get tight, I've tried, I just can't manage it!'

He was very pale, quite unruffled, leaning back in his chair as he went on steadily drinking.

'All the same', murmured Louise Violaine, 'don't go on, you've had enough . . . It'd be silly if I had to look after you for the rest of the night.'

Drink had brought a hectic, consumptive flush to Lucy Stewart's cheeks, while Rose Mignon was becoming maudlin and tearful. In a stupor from having eaten so much, Tatan Néné was laughing vacantly at her own stupidity. The others, Blanche, Caroline, Simonne, Maria, were all talking together, telling each other about themselves, a quarrel with their coachman, a proposed excursion into the country, complicated stories of lovers stolen or recovered. But when a young man next to Georges tried to kiss Léa de Horn, he got a sharp rap and a thoroughly indignant: 'Careful, you! Who do you think you are?' And Georges, very tipsy and excited, was in two minds about whether to proceed with an idea which he'd been seriously considering, of crawling on all-fours under the table and nestling at Nana's feet, like a little dog. Then Léa asked Daguenet to tell the bold young man to behave, and Georges suddenly felt very miserable, as if he'd just been told off himself; how stupid and sad everything was, nothing was nice . . . However, Daguenet started teasing him, making him drink a tumbler of water, and asked him what he'd do if he was alone with a woman when three glasses of champagne were enough to knock him out.

'Now in Havana', Foucarmont went on, 'they make a kind

of spirits from a wild berry. It's real fire-water. Well, one night I drank more than a litre of the stuff and it didn't do a thing to me . . . And more than that, once on the Coromandel* coast the natives gave us a mysterious concoction of pepper and vitriol, and even that didn't have any effect. It's impossible for me to get drunk.'

In the last few minutes he'd taken a dislike to the face of la Faloise sitting opposite. He was sneering and making uncomplimentary remarks. La Faloise's head was spinning. He was snuggling up to Gaga, unable to keep still. His nervousness had just been increased because someone had taken his handkerchief, and with drunken stubbornness he was demanding its return, questioning his neighbours and bending down to search for it under the chairs and people's feet. When Gaga tried to reassure him, he mumbled:

'It's stupid, it's got my monogram and coronet in the corner . . . It could be used to compromise me.'

'I say, Monsieur Falamoise Lanafoise Malafoise!' bawled Foucarmon, feeling very witty at deforming the young man's name in as many ways as possible.

La Faloise took offence. In an unsteady voice, he spoke of his ancestry. He threatened to throw a decanter at Foucarmont's head. Count de Vandeuvres had to intervene and assure him that Foucarmont was just being funny. Indeed, everybody was laughing. Shaken, the bewildered young man agreed to sit down, and when his cousin loudly ordered him to get on with his meal he started eating like an obedient little boy. Gaga made him snuggle up close to her again, but he still kept anxiously casting furtive glances at the other guests to see if he could find his handkerchief.

Still intent on showing how witty he was, Foucarmont now started on Labordette, speaking across the whole room. Louise Violaine was attempting to keep him quiet, because she said that when he went for people in that way it was always she who suffered in the end. He'd got it into his head that it was funny to address Labordette as 'Madame'; he must have found it most amusing for he kept on repeating it, while Labordette gently shrugged his shoulders and replied each time:

'Do keep quiet, my dear fellow, you're being very silly.'

But when Foucarmont persisted and started being insulting, for no apparent reason, he stopped answering him and turned to Count de Vandeuvres:

'Please get your friend to stop . . . I don't want to lose my temper.'

He'd already fought a couple of duels. He was accepted everywhere and no one would ever have thought of snubbing him. Everybody was up in arms against Foucarmont; he might be witty and make people laugh, but that was no excuse for ruining the party. Vandeuvres's fine-drawn features were slightly flushed; he insisted on Foucarmont's withdrawing his aspersions on Labordette's sex. The others, Mignon, Steiner, and Bordenave, were also keen to have their say, and were drowning his voice with the sound of their own. Only the old gentleman sitting forgotten beside Nana retained his grand manner and tired smile, as he silently observed this disastrous climax to the dessert through his pale eyes.

'How about taking coffee here, my little chickabiddy?' asked Bordenave. 'We're very cosy.'

Nana didn't reply at once. Ever since they'd sat down she'd had the feeling of being a stranger in her own house. She'd been dazed and submerged by all these people, with their loud voices, their calls to the waiters, making themselves at home as if they were in a restaurant. She herself was even neglecting her duties as hostess, paying no attention to anyone but the fat banker beside her, who seemed liable to throw an apoplectic fit at any moment. She was listening to him, turning his proposals down with a shake of her head, a plump blonde with a provocative laugh. The champagne had made her pink, with moist lips and shining eyes; and each time the banker saw the flirtatious twist of her shoulders or the voluptuous little rolls of flesh on her neck as she turned her head, he increased his offer. Next to her ear there was a dainty little patch of skin as smooth as silk, which was driving him to distraction. From time to time Nana roused herself and remembered her guests, trying to be agreeable and show she was capable of being a good hostess. Towards the end of the meal she was extremely tipsy; what a pity champagne went straight to her head. She was suddenly struck by a maddening thought: these women were trying to do her down by behaving badly in her house. Oh, she could see it all quite plainly! Lucy had given Foucarmont the wink to set on Labordette, while Rose and the others were egging the gentlemen on. Now the hullaballoo was deafening, and everyone would be able to say that at Nana's parties you could do whatever you liked. Well, she'd show them! Tipsy she might be but she was still the smartest woman there, and the most ladylike.

'Nana, my little darling', Bordenave was saying, 'do tell them to serve coffee here. That'd suit me, because of my leg.'

But Nana had sprung to her feet, muttering to the amazed Steiner and the old gentleman:

'It's my fault, that'll teach me to invite slobs like that.'

She pointed towards the dining-room and added loudly:

'If you want coffee, you can get it in there.'

They all stood up and pushed their way towards the dining-room; no one noticed Nana's anger. Soon the only person left in the drawing-room was Bordenave, holding cautiously on to the wall and cursing these bloody women who didn't give a bugger for Daddy now that they were full. In obedience to the head waiter's loud instructions, his assistants were already scurrying round clearing the table, barging into each other and making everything disappear, as in a transformation scene when the chief scene-shifter blows his whistle. The ladies and gentlemen would be returning to the drawing-room after their coffee.

'Hell, it's not so warm in here', said Gaga, giving a tiny shiver as she went into the dining-room.

Its window had been left open. The table was lit by a couple of lamps; the coffee was being served with liqueurs. As there were no chairs, the guests drank standing up; next door the waiters were making an even greater din. Nana was nowhere to be seen, but nobody paid any attention to that; she wasn't needed, they were all serving themselves, rummaging in the drawers of the sideboard to find the coffee spoons, which had been overlooked. People had gathered into little groups; some who'd been separated at table were now able to talk together; the guests were exchanging glances and knowing laughs, reviewing various happenings.

'Auguste, don't you agree that Monsieur Fauchery must

come and have lunch with us one of these days?'

Mignon was playing with his watch-chain; he let his eye rest sternly for a second on the journalist. Rose was crazy. In his capacity as an efficient manager he'd put a stop to this sort of wasteful exercise. OK for just an article; after that, nothing doing. However, knowing how pig-headed his wife could be and that he'd made it a fatherly rule to allow her one stupid act, if need be, he made an effort to be pleasant and replied:

'Of course, I'll be delighted . . . Why not tomorrow, Monsieur Fauchery?'

Busy talking with Steiner and Blanche, Lucy overheard this invitation. She raised her voice and said to the banker:

'It's a mania with all those women. One of them even stole my dog . . . Come now, is it my fault if you're dropping her, my dear man?'

Rose looked round. She was sipping her coffee slowly and staring at Steiner, very pale; for a brief moment her pent-up anger at his desertion flared up in her eyes. She was more clear-sighted than Mignon; it was stupid to hope to bring off the Jonquier trick again, that sort of thing never worked twice. Never mind! She'd have Fauchery, to whom she'd taken a strong fancy at the supper; and if Mignon didn't like it, that would teach him a lesson.

'You're not going to have a fight?' Vandeuvres asked Lucy.

'No, don't worry. Only she'd better keep quiet or I'll give her a piece of my mind.'

With a haughty wave of her hand, she called to Fauchery:

'I've got your slippers at my place, young fellow. I'll have them sent round to your porter tomorrow.'

He tried to laugh it off. She stalked away like a queen. Clarisse was leaning back against a wall, quietly sipping a glass of kirsch. She shrugged her shoulders. What a lot of fuss about a man! Whenever two women were together in the company of their lovers, wasn't their very first thought to try to nab the other woman's man? It was a rule of the game. She'd have torn Gaga's eyes out if she'd felt like it. But hell! She didn't give a damn. As la Faloise was passing, she merely said to him:

'I say, you do like oldies, don't you? I don't just mean ripe, but actually going soft, isn't that right?'

La Faloise looked very annoyed. He was still worried. When he saw that Clarisse was poking fun at him, his suspicions fell on her:

'Come on, come clean', he said. 'You've stolen my handkerchief, give it back.'

'What a bore you are with your silly old hanky!' she exclaimed. 'What on earth should I want it for, you loon?'

'Well', he said warily, 'to send to my family so as to compromise me.'

Meanwhile Foucarmont was punishing the liqueurs. He was still looking scornfully towards Labordette, who was drinking his coffee surrounded by ladies, and kept spluttering little comments: the son of a horse-dealer, some people said the illegitimate son of a countess; no visible source of income, but never short of five hundred francs; a guy who acted as a flunkey for tarts and never went to bed with any of them.

'No, never! Never!' he was saying again and again, losing his temper. 'I've got to punch his nose, that's the only thing to do!'

He gulped down a little glass of Chartreuse. Chartreuse never did him any harm, not even as much as that, he said, flipping his thumb-nail against his teeth. But all at once, as he was walking towards Labordette, he turned ghastly pale and went down like a pole-axed ox in front of the sideboard. He'd passed out. Louise Violaine was upset. She'd said that's what would happen; now she was going to have to look after him for the rest of the night. Gaga was running her experienced eye over the naval officer and was able to reassure her: there was no harm done, the gentleman would sleep like that for the next twelve to fifteen hours and he'd be all right. Foucarmont was carted away.

'Good Heavens, where's Nana?' enquired Vandeuvres.

Where indeed? She'd slipped away immediately on leaving the table. People were becoming aware of her absence and calling out for her. Steiner was growing uneasy and questioned Vandeuvres about the old gentleman, who'd also disappeared. The count reassured him: a foreign VIP, no point in mentioning names, rolling in money and only too happy just subsidizing supper parties. Then, as people were again starting to forget Nana, Vandeuvres caught sight of

Daguenet poking his head through a doorway and making signs to him. Vandeuvres went in and saw Nana, tense and pale, sitting on her bed. Daguenet and Georges were standing watching her in consternation.

'What on earth's the matter?' he enquired in surprise. She made no reply, and continued to stare in the other direction. He repeated his question.

'The matter is that I won't have people making a fool of me!' she cried in the end.

And she started to pour out everything that came to her lips. Oh, she wasn't all that stupid, she could see all right. All through the meal, they'd been saying horrible things to show how much they despised her. A bunch of dirty bitches who weren't fit to clean her shoes! It'd be a long time before she took all that trouble again, just so people could pull her to pieces afterwards! She didn't know why she didn't kick the whole bloody lot out on their arses! She was choking with anger and her voice was breaking into sobs.

'Oh come on, little girl, you're tight', said Vandeuvres, speaking to her like a child. 'You must pull yourself together.'

No, she refused to listen, she was going to stay where she was.

'OK, perhaps I am tight but I insist on being respected.'

Daguenet and Georges had spent the last quarter of an hour vainly trying to persuade her to come back into the dining-room. She stubbornly refused; the guests could do what they damn-well liked; she despised them too much to go back and see them . . . Never! She'd sooner be boiled in oil than leave her bedroom.

'I should have known', she went on, 'it's that bitch Rose who ganged up against me. For example, I was expecting to have a nice respectable woman friend come this evening. I bet she's been put off by Rose.'

The 'nice respectable woman' was Madame Robert. Vandeuvres gave his word that Madame Robert had refused of her own accord. He was accustomed to such scenes, and was listening to her and arguing without laughing; he knew how to deal with women when they were in that sort of state. But as soon as he tried to catch hold of her hands to pull her up and drag her out of the room, she struggled and became even angrier. And nobody would ever convince her, for example, that Fauchery hadn't persuaded Count Muffat not to come. Fauchery was a real snake in the grass, an envious bastard who would stop at nothing to pursue a woman and wreck her happiness. She knew very well that the count had fallen for her. She could have had him.

'Count Muffat, my dear girl?' exclaimed Vandeuvres, laughing in spite of himself. 'That's impossible!'

'Why impossible?' she asked, sobering up a little.

'Because he's priest-ridden, and if he ever so much as laid a finger on you he'd rush off to his confessor the next day. Take some good advice. Don't let the other one get away.'

For a moment she sat in silence, thinking. Then she stood up and went to bathe her eyes. However, when they tried to get her to go back into the dining-room she again furiously yelled 'No!' With a smile, Vandeuvres left the room without trying to persuade her further. As soon as he'd gone, in a sudden burst of affection, she flung herself into Daguenet's arms, crying:

'Oh, Mimi darling, you're the only man I love! Oh, how I love you! . . . How wonderful it would be if we could be together always! Oh God, aren't women unlucky!'

Then, noticing that Georges had gone very red in the face as he watched them kissing, she kissed him too. Mimi couldn't possibly be jealous of a baby . . . She wanted Paul and Georges to be good friends always, because it would be so lovely for them to be like that, all three, all the time, knowing that they all loved each other. But they were disturbed by a peculiar sound; someone was snoring in the bedroom. They searched around and found Bordenave, who must have settled himself in there cosily after finishing his coffee. He was sleeping on two chairs, with his leg stretched out and his head resting against the bed. He looked so funny with his mouth open and his nose twitching each time he snored that Nana went into a wild fit of laughter. She left the room, followed by Daguenet and Georges, and went through the dining-room into the drawing-room, laughing more loudly than ever.

'Oh, my dear!' she exclaimed, almost throwing herself into Rose's arms, 'you can't imagine, just come and take a look!'

All the ladies had to go with her, she was coaxing them,

catching hold of their hands and forcing them to come along with her with such an uncontrollable explosion of delight that they were all laughing in anticipation. The whole lot of them trooped off and in a minute returned, having observed, with bated breath, Bordenave stretched out in all his glory on his two chairs. They were roaring with laughter, and when one of them asked for silence they could hear Bordenave snoring away in the distance.

It was nearly four o'clock. In the dining-room a card-table had been set up and Vandeuvres, Steiner, Mignon, and Labordette were sitting there while Lucy and Caroline stood behind them making bets; but Blanche, not having enjoyed her night, was drowsily asking Vandeuvres every five minutes if they couldn't go home soon. In the drawing-room they were trying to dance. Daguenet was at the piano, the 'chest-of-drawers' as Nana called it; she didn't want an 'ivory tickler', Mimi could play waltzes and polkas till the cows came home. But the dancing was hardly going with a swing; their ladyships were chatting amongst themselves, slumped half-asleep on settees. There was a sudden uproar. Eleven young men had arrived in a gang and were larking about in the entrance hall, trying to force their way towards the door of the drawing-room. They had come from the Interior Minister's ball and were wearing white ties, tails, and an assortment of unknown decorations. Annoyed by this boisterous intrusion, Nana called to the waiters in the kitchen to turn the gentlemen out; she swore she'd never set eyes on them before. Fauchery, Daguenet, Labordette, and the other men went over to make them show proper respect to the lady of the house. Abuse was flying around, threatening gestures were made, and for a moment a wholesale brawl seemed imminent. However, a blond young man, rather sickly-looking, kept saying:

'But look here, Nana, the other night at Peters',* in his large red room . . . Don't you remember? You gave us an invitation.'

The other night, at Peters'? She didn't remember a thing! And to start with, what night was it? And when the fair-headed young man had spelt out the day, Wednesday, she did recall having had supper at Peters' on Wednesday; but she hadn't issued any invitations, she felt pretty sure of that.

'All the same, my girl, if you did in fact invite them . . .', muttered Labordette, who was beginning to have doubts. 'Perhaps you were a bit merry.'

This made Nana laugh. Well, it was possible, she couldn't remember. Anyway, since the gentlemen were there they could come in. Everything sorted itself out, several of the new arrivals found friends in the drawing-room, and the squabble ended in handshakes all round. The unhealthy-looking blond young man bore the name of a great French family. They also announced that there were more people on their way, and in fact every second the door kept opening and men in official dress and white gloves kept appearing, all from the Ministry ball. Fauchery asked jokingly if the Minister wouldn't be coming himself. This annoyed Nana, who retorted that the Minister certainly frequented people who weren't as good as she was. What she didn't say was that she'd suddenly had the hope of seeing Count Muffat coming through the door amongst this stream of people. He might have changed his mind. As she chatted with Rose she kept a close eye on the door.

The clock struck five. The dancing had stopped. Only the card-players were still hard at it. Labordette had relinquished his chair; the women had returned to the drawing-room. The lamp-wicks had burned down low in their globes, and in their reddish, hazy glow there was the heavy, drowsy feeling of a party which had gone on for a long, long time. The ladies had reached that wistful stage when they feel the need to talk about their past. Blanche de Sivry was speaking of her grandfather the general, while Clarisse was inventing a romance, a duke who'd seduced her at her uncle's home where he used to come and shoot wild boar; and the pair of them were sitting back-to-back, shrugging their shoulders and asking how anyone could possibly tell such cock-and-bull stories. As for Lucy Stewart, she calmly admitted her origins and talked freely of her girlhood when her father, a greaser at the Gare du Nord, would give her an apple turnover as a Sunday treat.

'Oh, I must tell you!' exclaimed little Maria Blond suddenly. 'Opposite me there lives a gentleman, a Russian, or anyway a very wealthy man. And yesterday, what do you think happens? I get a basket of fruit and what fruit it was!—huge peaches, grapes as big as that, anyway, amazing things for this time of year . . . And tucked away inside, six thousand-franc notes! . . . It was from the Russian gentleman. Of course, I sent it all back . . . But I did feel a bit sad, because of all that lovely fruit!'

The ladies looked at each other with pursed lips: that little Maria was too cheeky by half for her age! And think of that kind of thing happening to little sluts like that! They felt only deep contempt for each other; they were particularly jealous of Lucy and her three princes. Ever since she'd started riding in the Bois de Boulogne every morning, a stunt which had launched her on her career, they'd all taken it up enthusiastically.

Dawn was breaking. Nana had given up hope and stopped watching the door. Everyone was bored stiff. Rose Mignon had refused to sing 'The Slipper' and was lying curled up on a settee having a whispered conversation with Fauchery and waiting for Mignon, who was already busily picking up a thousand francs or so from Vandeuvres. A solemn gentleman, wearing his decoration, had indeed recited a poem about Abraham's sacrifice of Isaac in Alsatian dialect in which every time God swore, he said, 'Me Almighty!', and Isaac always replied, 'Yes, Daddy!' But as nobody saw the point, the recitation fell completely flat. Nobody could think of anything really lively to finish off the evening in style, crazily. Labordette tried to start something by whispering a woman's name in la Faloise's ear, who would then crawl about trying to find out if she'd got his handkerchief round her neck. As there were still a few bottles of champagne on the sideboard, the young men had started drinking again. They were shouting and egging each other on, but the drawing-room was collapsing into hopeless alcoholic depression and stupidity. Then the blond young man bearing the name of one of the great French families, desperate to find something funny to do and unable to think of anything better, took his bottle of champagne and emptied it into the piano. The other young men all found this excruciatingly amusing.

'Good Lord!' exclaimed Tatan Néné in surprise. 'What on earth is he pouring bubbly into the piano for?'

'What, didn't you know, my dear?' replied Labordette solemnly. 'There's nothing like champagne for pianos. It improves their tone.'

'Oh!' sighed Tatan, reassured.

And as people started laughing, she became cross. How could she know? They were always having her on!

Things were definitely going sour. The evening was in danger of ending nastily. Maria Blond was having a row in a corner with Léa de Horn, accusing her of going to bed with men who hadn't got enough money, and they were starting to trade insults concerning their looks. Lucy, who was ugly, made them shut up. The face wasn't important, it was the figure that counted. Beyond them an Embassy attaché was sitting on a settee with his arm round Simonne's waist and trying to kiss her neck; fagged out and fed up, she was fending him off by rapping him sharply on the face each time with her fan, telling him not to be a bore. The women all wanted to be left alone: did the men take them for tarts? However, Gaga had managed to corner la Faloise again and got him almost sitting on her lap, while Clarisse, hidden between two men, was giving nervous giggles like a woman being tickled. The little game round the piano was continuing; a stupid throng of men were crazily jostling each other to tip the dregs of their bottles into it. It was simple, innocent fun.

Nana had her back turned and couldn't see them. She was deciding definitely to make do with the portly Steiner sitting beside her. It couldn't be helped! It was the fault of that man Muffat for not being willing to play! The friendly little tart, pale and slightly drunk, with rings round her eyes, in her white foulard dress, as flimsy and crumpled as a chemise, was quietly saying, 'OK, take me!' The roses in her chignon and on her bosom had lost their petals; only their stalks were left. But Steiner had hastily to remove his hand from her skirts, where he'd just made contact with the pins which Georges had put there; they had drawn blood, and a drop of it fell on her dress, leaving a stain.

'Now we've signed a pact', Nana said solemnly.

Outside it was growing lighter. A sinister gleam, unbelievably sad, was filtering in through the windows.

People were beginning to leave; it was a disorderly, uneasy retreat, full of ill temper. Fed up at having wasted her night, Caroline said it was high time to go if you weren't anxious to see some queer things happen. Rose gave her a black look, like a woman caught in an embarrassing situation: these young tarts were always like that, they never knew how to behave, they were just plain disgusting when they were starting their careers. And as Mignon had cleaned Vandeuvres out, the couple left without worrying about Steiner, after repeating their invitation to Fauchery for the following day. Hearing this, Lucy refused to let the journalist take her home, telling him to go back to his stage hack. At that Rose swung round and hissed: 'Dirty whore!' between her teeth. But with his experience of women's quarrels, Mignon, never at a loss, was exerting his fatherly authority to shepherd her out through the door, telling her to cut it out. Lucy went down the stairs behind them, by herself, with all the dignity of a queen. Then Gaga had to take la Faloise off, queasy and sobbing like a child, calling for Clarisse who'd slipped away with the two young gentlemen a long time ago. Simonne had disappeared too. Only Tatan, Léa, and Maria were left, all of whom Labordette obligingly agreed to look after.

'The truth is, I don't feel a bit sleepy!' Nana kept saying. 'We ought to do something.'

She was looking out of the window at the livid sky, swept by sooty clouds. It was six o'clock. Opposite, on the Boulevard Haussmann, the wet roofs of the still-sleeping houses stood out against the dawn light; on the deserted street a troop of crossing-sweepers were clumping past in their clogs. Faced by this agonizing Paris awakening, Nana's heart melted like a girl's, she felt a need for something country-like, idyllic, something white and gentle.

'Do you know what?' she said, going back to Steiner. 'You're going to take me out to the Bois de Boulogne and we'll drink some milk.'

She clapped her hands in childish delight. Without waiting for the banker to agree, which he naturally did, though secretly irritated—he had other things in mind—she ran off to fling her fur-lined coat over her shoulders. In the drawing-room, apart from Steiner, there remained only the young gentlemen who, having poured the last drops out of their glasses into the piano, were now talking of leaving when one of them ran in from the kitchen triumphantly waving one final bottle.

'Wait, don't go yet!' he cried. 'It's a bottle of Chartreuse! . . . There, it needed some Chartreuse, that'll do it good . . . And now let's be gone, chaps. We're crazy.'

In her dressing-room, Nana was having to wake up Zoé, who'd dropped off in her chair. The gas was alight. Zoé shivered as she helped her mistress to put on her hat and coat.

'Well, there you are, I've done what you wanted', said Nana, feeling expansive now that she'd taken a decision, and talking to Zoé like an old friend. 'You were right, the banker's as good as anyone else.'

The maid was feeling grumpy and not properly awake. She grunted that madam should have made her mind up that first evening. Then, following her into the bedroom, she asked what she ought to do with those two: Bordenave was still snoring away, and Georges, who'd slyly crept back and put his head down on a pillow, had ended by dropping off to sleep and was lying there breathing gently, looking cherubic. Nana said they should be left; but her heart melted again when she saw Daguenet come in; he'd been keeping watch in the kitchen, and looked very miserable.

'Oh come on, Mimi, be reasonable', she said, taking him into her arms and kissing and cuddling him. 'Nothing's changed, you know. Mimi's the only man I really, really love . . . Can't you see, I had to do it? . . . I promise you I'll be nicer than ever to you, really and truly . . . Come round tomorrow, we'll fix up some times . . . Quick, kiss me now to show how much you love me . . . No, harder than that!'

She slipped out of his arms and went back to Steiner, happily looking forward to her drink of milk. In the empty flat, the Count de Vandeuvres was left with the man wearing the decorations who'd recited *Abraham's Sacrifice*, both still rooted to the card-table, no longer realizing where they were and that it was broad daylight. In an attempt to get some sleep, Blanche had dossed down on a settee.

'Ah, Blanche must come along too!' exclaimed Nana. 'We're going to drink some milk, my dear . . . Do come,

Vandeuvres will still be here when you get back.'

Blanche lazily got to her feet. This time the banker's apoplectic face went livid with annoyance at the thought of having to take along this fat woman who was going to get in his way. But the two women had already collared him and were insisting:

'You know, we've got to see the cow actually being milked!'

Chapter 5

THE first act of the thirty-fourth performance of *The Blonde Venus* at the Variétés had just come to an end. In the green room, Simonne, dressed as the little laundry-maid, was standing in front of the mirror above the pier-table between the two corner doorways in the diagonal wall opening on to the dressing-room passage. She was alone, examining her face and running a finger along under her eyes to correct her make-up; she could feel the heat from the glare of the gas-jets set on each side of the mirror.

'Has he arrived yet?' enquired Prullière, coming in wearing his Swiss admiral's uniform with his long sword, huge boots, and immense plume.

'Has who arrived?' said Simonne impassively, watching her lips as she laughed into the mirror.

'The prince.'

'I've no idea, I'm just on my way down . . . Oh, he's bound to be coming, after all, he does come every day!'

Facing the pier-table by the fireplace, in which a coke fire was burning, there were two more flaring gas-jets. Prullière went over and looked up at the clock and the barometer standing on the left and the right beside some gilt Empire-style sphinxes. Then, stretching out in an immense wing-chair covered in green velvet now tinged a dingy yellow from being sat in by four generations of actors, he sprawled motionless, staring into space, in the wearily resigned attitude of players used to waiting to go on stage.

Old Bosc now made his appearance, coughing as he shuffled in wrapped in a coach-driver's old yellow coat, which had half slipped off one shoulder, showing the gold-spangled tunic of King Dagobert. Placing his crown on the piano, without saying a word he stood for a second grumpily stamping his feet; however, he still looked a decent sort of chap, and though his hands were shaking with the first hint of DTs, his long white beard gave a venerable touch to his fiery drunkard's face. Then, as the silence was broken by a flurry of rain lashing the panes of the large square window overlooking the courtyard, he made a gesture of disgust.

'What lousy weather!' he grunted.

Simonne and Prullière made no move. On the wall were four or five pictures, landscapes, a portrait of the actor Vernet, which were going yellow with the heat from the gas, while on top of a column a bust of Potier, one of the former glories of the Variétés, was staring into space. There was a loud bellow. It was Fontan in his second-act costume, as a smart young man dressed all in yellow, with yellow gloves.

'I say', he shouted, waving his hands about, 'do you know it's my name-day today?'

'Is it really?' said Simonne with a smile, going over to him as if attracted by the big nose and large slit of a mouth which all comedians seem to have. 'So you must be called Achille?'

'Right first time! . . . And I'm going to get Madame Bron to send up some champagne after act two.'

In the distance, a bell had just started ringing. It rang for a while, died away and then started again. When the ringing stopped, there was a shout from below which came up the stairs, went down again, and was lost in the corridors. 'On stage for act two . . . On stage for act two! . . .' The call came nearer and a wan little man went past the green-room doors, shouting at the top of his high-pitched voice, 'On stage for act two!'

'Good Lord! Bubbly!' exclaimed Prullière, apparently oblivious to the call. 'That's going some!'

'If I were you I'd get it sent up from the café', advised old Bosc in a slow voice. He had sat down on a green-plush bench-seat and was resting his head against the wall.

However, Simonne pointed out that they mustn't do Madame Bron out of her little perks. She was clapping her hands in excitement and gazing admiringly at Fontan's goat-like face, which was never still, his eyes, nose, and mouth twitching all the time.

'Oh, what a man!' she murmured. 'There's no one like Fontan, absolutely no one.'

The two green-room doors had been left wide open on to the passage leading backstage. Figures were dashing past along the yellow wall, brightly lit by an invisible gas-lamp: men in costume, half-naked women wrapped in shawls, all the second-act extras, the riff-raff for the shady dance-hall, The Black Ball; and at the end of the passage, people could be heard clattering down the five steps which led to the stage. As the tall Clarisse went running by Simonne called out to her, but she replied that she'd be back in a second and, in fact, she did reappear almost at once, shivering in her thin tunic and stole; she played Iris.

'Good Heavens, it's jolly cold!' she exclaimed. 'And I've left my fur in the dressing-room!'

Then, standing in front of the fire toasting her legs in their shimmering bright-pink tights, she went on:

'The prince has arrived.'

'Oh!' the others all exclaimed with curiosity.

'Yes, that's why I was dashing to have a look . . . He's in the first stage box on the right, the same as on Thursday. It's his third visit this week, isn't it? What a lucky girl Nana is! . . . I was betting he wouldn't come again.'

Simonne opened her mouth to say something but her words were drowned by another loud call close to the green room. The shrill tones of the call-boy echoed down the corridor as he shouted at the top of his voice:

'They've knocked!'

'That makes three times now, it's starting to look pretty good', said Simonne when she could make herself heard. 'You know he doesn't want to go to her place, he takes her off to his. And apparently it costs him the earth!'

'Of course, if you're going to town! . . .' murmured Prullière spitefully, standing up to take a quick, admiring look at his own ladykiller's face in the mirror.

'They've knocked! They've knocked!'

The call-boy's voice died away in the distance as he continued to rush along the corridors on various floors.

Then Fontan, who knew what had happened between Nana and the prince the first time, gave an account of it to the two girls, who huddled close, laughing very loudly when he bent forward to go into certain details. Showing utter indifference, old Bosc hadn't stirred. He was no longer interested in that sort of caper. He sat stroking a big ginger cat curled up smugly on the bench-seat and then picked it up lovingly in his arms, like a good-natured, doddery old king. The cat was arching its back, but after taking a good long sniff at the big white beard it went back to sleep curled up on the seat, doubtless finding the smell of glue offensive. Bosc was still solemnly pondering.

'All the same, if I were you I'd still get the champagne from the café, it's better', he said to Fontan abruptly as the latter was reaching the end of his tale.

'They've started!' the call-boy shouted in his long-drawn-out, deafening voice. 'They've started! They've started!'

The cry re-echoed for a second. There was a sound of fast-running feet. The door leading to the corridor suddenly flew open; there was a burst of music and a confused hum in the distance; then the padded door swung to with a thud.

Once again the green room subsided into its drowsy, placid mood, seemingly miles away from that auditorium where a packed house was clapping. Simonne and Clarisse were still on the subject of Nana. She certainly wasn't the sort of girl to hurry herself! Yesterday she'd again fluffed her entrance! But there was a sudden hush: a tall girl had just stuck her head in and, seeing that she'd opened the wrong door, had precipitately retreated along the corridor. It was Satin wearing a hat with a veil, giving herself airs, like a lady dropping in to pay a call. 'A proper little whore!' muttered Prullière, who'd been running into her in the Café des Variétés for the last year. Simonne explained how Nana had recognized Satin as an old schoolmate, taken a fancy to her, and was pestering Bordenave to give her a start in his theatre.

'Oh, hello! Good evening', said Fontan shaking hands with Mignon and Fauchery, who'd just come in.

Even old Bosc held out a couple of fingers, while the two women gave Mignon a kiss.

'A good house tonight?' enquired Fauchery.

'Magnificent!' replied Prullière. 'They're lapping it up!'

'I say, girls', remarked Mignon, 'it must be time for you.'

Yes, in a minute. They weren't on until scene four. Only Bosc got to his feet, with the instinctive reaction of the old stager who knows his cue is coming up. In fact, at that very moment the call-boy appeared in the doorway.

'Monsieur Bosc! Mademoiselle Simonne!' he called.

Simonne quickly flung a fur-lined coat over her shoulders and went out. Unhurriedly, Bosc walked over to pick up his crown and tipped it over his forehead; then, trailing his cloak, he went off unsteadily, grumbling, with the angry look of someone who's been disturbed.

'You gave us a very nice write-up in your last review', Fontan said to Fauchery. 'But why did you describe actors as vain?'

'Yes, young man, why did you do that?' exclaimed Mignon, giving the journalist's puny shoulders a thump with his massive hand. Fauchery reeled under the shock.

Prullière and Simonne tittered. For some time now, the whole cast had been amused by a comedy being played in the wings. Furious at his wife's sudden infatuation, and annoyed that the only benefit they were getting from the fellow was a questionable amount of publicity, Mignon had worked out a scheme to get his own back by killing Fauchery with kindness: every night when he met him on stage he'd pummel him about as if unable to restrain his affection, and the fragile Fauchery had to put up with such treatment from this giant of a man with a wan smile in order not to fall out with Rose's husband.

'Ah, my dear fellow, you're insulting Fontan!' continued Mignon, elaborating on the joke. 'On guard! One, two, three, and biff!'

He lunged and struck the young man with such force that he went pale, with all the breath knocked out of him. But Clarisse had given the others a quick wink to draw their attention to Rose Mignon standing in the doorway. She had seen what had happened. As if unaware of her husband's presence, she walked straight up to the journalist and, bare-armed in her baby dress, stood on tiptoe, putting up her forehead like a wheedling little girl.

'Good evening, baby', said Fauchery jauntily, giving her a kiss.

This sort of thing provided his compensation. Mignon didn't even seem to notice the kiss; in the theatre everybody kissed his wife. But he gave a laugh and a sharp little glance in the journalist's direction; Fauchery would certainly be paying dearly for Rose's act of defiance.

The padded door leading to the corridor opened and shut again, letting gusts of wild applause into the green room. It was Simonne, returning after her scene.

'Oh, old Bosc put on such a good show!' she cried. 'The prince was rolling with laughter and clapping as loudly as all the others, as if he'd been paid to! . . . And by the way, do you know who the tall gent is sitting beside the prince in the stage box? Very good-looking and dignified, with gorgeous whiskers.'

'That's Count Muffat', Fontan replied. 'I know that the day before yesterday, at the Empress's, the prince invited him to dine with him this evening. He's led him off the straight and narrow after the dinner.'

'Oh, Count Muffat. We know his father-in-law, don't we Auguste?' Rose said to her husband. 'You know, the Marquis de Chouard, where I went to sing? . . . In fact, he's in the house too, I caught sight of him at the back of a box. There's an old man who . . .'

But Prullière, who had just put on his immense plume, turned towards her:

'Come along Rose, we must be going.'

She ran after him, leaving her sentence unfinished. At that moment the theatre door-keeper, Madame Bron, went past the doorway carrying a huge bunch of flowers. Simonne jokingly inquired if they were for her, but without replying the door-keeper jerked her chin towards Nana's dressing-room at the end of the corridor. That girl Nana was being absolutely smothered in flowers! Then, on her way back, Madame Bron handed Clarisse a letter. She swore under her breath: la Faloise again; what a bloody bore he was! He just wouldn't take no for an answer! When she was told that the gentleman was waiting for her downstairs, she shouted:

'Tell him I'll be down at the end of the act . . . I can't wait to slap his face!'

Fontan rushed over to the door-keeper:

'Listen, Madame Bron . . . Please Madame Bron . . . can you bring up half-a-dozen bottles of champagne in the interval?'

But the call-boy was now back again, panting and out of breath:

'Everybody on stage! . . . You're on, Monsieur Fontan!

Hurry up, please.'

'OK, OK old man, we're on our way!' Fontan was flustered and dashed after Madame Bron, shouting:

'Will that be all right? Six bottles of champagne in the green room in the interval . . . It's my name-day, I'm standing treat . . .'

Simonne and Clarisse had already gone out with a great swishing of skirts, and they were all swallowed up in the distance. When the door had closed behind them with a thud and silence had once again descended on the green room, another squall of rain suddenly lashed the window. The call-boy Barillot, a pale-faced old man who'd been doing this sort of job in the theatre for the last thirty years, held out his snuff-box for Mignon to take a pinch. This was his way of giving himself a breather in his constant rush upstairs and downstairs round the dressing-room corridors. True, there was still Madame Nana, as he called her; but she was a law unto herself and didn't give a damn about being fined; when she wanted to fluff her entry, she just did so. Then he stood still in surprise and muttered:

'Good Lord, she's ready, here she comes . . . She must know the prince is here.'

Indeed, Nana now appeared in the passageway, dressed as the fishwife, with her arms and face all white apart from two patches of pink under her eyes. She didn't come in but merely nodded to Mignon and Fauchery.

'Hullo there, how's things?'

She held out her hand, which only Mignon took. And she proceeded on her royal course pursued by her dresser, who was walking at her heels, bending down to arrange the pleats in her skirt. Completing her retinue came Satin, trying to look lady-like and already bored to tears.

'How about Steiner?' Mignon asked suddenly.

'Monsieur Steiner left for the Loiret* yesterday', said Barillot, already on his way back to the wings. 'I think he's going to buy a country property down there.'

'Yes, I know, a property for Nana.'

Mignon was looking stern: earlier on, that man Steiner had been promising Rose a town-house! Ah well, he mustn't quarrel with anyone, it'd be a possibility to look into later on.

Pacing to and fro between the fireplace and the pier-table, in full control of the situation as always, Mignon was pondering. He and Fauchery were now alone in the green room. The tired journalist was stretched out quietly in the big armchair, with eyes half-closed; the other man was looking at him as he went by. When they were by themselves Mignon didn't bother about thumping him; what was the point when there was no one to enjoy the scene? He wasn't sufficiently interested to find his mischievous tomfoolery funny himself. Grateful for the few minutes' respite, Fauchery had drowsily stretched his feet out towards the fire and was letting his gaze wander idly from the barometer to the clock. Mignon interrupted his walk to stop in front of the bust of Potier, stared at it without seeing it, and then went back to the window facing out on to the gloomy depths of the courtyard. It had stopped raining and the stillness was made even more oppressive by the stifling heat from the coke fire and the flaring gas-jets. Backstage not a sound was to be heard; the staircase and the corridors were as silent as the grave. It was the sort of muffled peace you have at the end of an act, when the whole cast is on stage bringing off some deafening finale while the abandoned green room goes to sleep in a low, asphyxiating murmur.

'Oh, the little sluts!' This husky roar came from Bordenave who had only just arrived and was already exploding because of two extras who'd nearly fallen flat on their faces on stage as a result of fooling around. Seeing Mignon and Fauchery, he called them over to show them something: the prince had just asked to come and present his congratulations to Nana in her dressing-room during the interval. As he was taking them down to the auditorium, the stage-manager went past.

'Fine those two little bitches Fernande and Maria', Bordenave told him angrily.

Then, cooling down, he mopped his face with a handkerchief and, assuming his patriarchal image, added with all the dignity he could muster:

'I shall now welcome His Royal Highness!'

The curtain was coming down amid thunderous applause. Immediately, in the semi-darkness on stage, no longer lit by the footlights, a wild scramble ensued; actors and extras hurried back to their dressing-rooms while the stage-hands quickly started changing the set. However, Simonne and Clarisse stayed backstage, whispering together. During the act, in the course of a break in their parts, they'd come to an agreement: on due consideration, Clarisse thought it better not to see la Faloise, who was finding it impossible to make up his mind whether to leave her and set up with Gaga. Simonne was merely to go and point out to him that you couldn't keep on pestering a woman like that. In a word, she'd see him off.

So, still wearing her comic-opera laundry-maid costume under the fur slung over her shoulders, Simonne went off down the narrow, corkscrew staircase, with its slippery steps and damp walls, which led to the door-keeper's lodge. This was situated between the artistes' and the management's staircases, closed off each side by large glass partitions, and looking like a big transparent lantern in which two flaring gas-jets were burning. There were pigeon-holes stuffed with letters and newspapers. On the table, bunches of flowers were lying next to dirty plates that hadn't been cleared away and an old bodice whose buttonholes were being mended by the door-keeper. In the middle of this mess, reminiscent of some cluttered-up store-room, there were four ancient cane-bottomed chairs, occupied by smartly dressed men-about-town wearing gloves and sitting with patient, cowed expressions, who turned their heads sharply towards Madame Bron each time she brought down her messages from the theatre. She had, in fact, just handed a note to a young man who hurriedly tore it open under the gas-jet in the entrance hall and went slightly pale as he read the classic words, so common in this situation: 'Can't make it tonight, darling, I'm not free.' La Faloise was sitting on a chair at the end, between the table and the stove; though he seemed determined to stay there for the rest of the evening, he looked worried, with his legs drawn back to keep clear of a litter of kittens bent on annoying him, while their mother sat on her hindquarters staring at him through yellow eyes.

'Oh hello, Simonne', the door-keeper said. 'What can I do for you?'

Simonne asked her to send la Faloise over to her, but Madame Bron had to keep her waiting for a minute; she ran a bar in a sort of deep cubby under the stairs where the extras would slip down and have a drink during the intervals, and as she had at the moment five or six young fellows there, still dressed as The Black Ball toughs, who were short of time and panting for a drink, she was finding it difficult to cope. In the cubby, in the glare of a gas-jet, you could see a table covered with a tin sheet and shelves containing opened bottles. When you penetrated into this coal-hole you were met by a blast of alcohol blended with the smell of burnt fat and the pungent scent of the flowers on the table from the lodge.

'Well', the door-keeper said, after serving the extras, 'so it's the dark-haired young man over there you want, is it?'

'Don't be silly!' exclaimed Simonne. 'It's that beanpole next to the stove whose trousers are being sniffed by the cat.'

She took la Faloise away into the entrance hall while the other men, choking for breath and with sore throats, settled down again resignedly and the young toughs made off upstairs, drinking and exchanging boisterous punches and loud jokes in raucous, drink-sodden voices.

Upstairs, Bordenave was on stage angrily telling off the stage-hands, who were taking their time clearing away the set. They were doing it on purpose, the prince would find a piece of the set landing on his head!

'Tug away! Tug away!' the head stage-hand was shouting.

Finally, the backdrop went up and the stage was clear. Mignon had his eye on Fauchery and seized the opportunity of taking it out on him again. He grasped him in his big arms, shouting:

'Do look out! That pole nearly crushed you!'

And he lifted him bodily out of the way, giving him a good shake before putting him down. The scene-shifters burst into extravagant laughter. Fauchery went pale; his lips were quivering, and he was on the point of rebelling; meanwhile Mignon was being very jovial and friendly, clapping him affectionately on the shoulder in a way liable to give him a slipped disc, and saying:

'It's just that I'm so concerned for your health! . . . Hell, I'd be in a pretty mess if anything happened to you!'

A murmur went round: 'The prince! The prince!' and everybody turned their eyes towards the little door leading to the auditorium. As yet, all that could be seen was Bordenave's bent back and butcher's neck, as he bowed and scraped in a series of obsequious gestures. Then the prince himself came into view; tall and strong, with a blond beard and pink skin, he had the appearance of a well-bred, dedicated hedonist, whose sturdy limbs were recognizable under his immaculately cut frock-coat. Behind him came Count Muffat and the Marquis de Chouard. The lighting was dim in this corner of the theatre, and the group was swallowed up in the shifting shadows. To address this son of a queen and heir to the throne, Bordenave had put on a voice quivering with emotion, like a man showing off a tame bear. He kept saying:

'If Your Royal Highness would be good enough to follow me . . . Perhaps Your Royal Highness could be so kind as to step this way . . . Your Royal Highness must take care . . .'

The prince was showing great interest, quite unhurried, and in fact lingering to watch the stage-shifters' operations. They had just let down some stage-lights, whose bright lamps, hanging in their iron mesh, threw a broad beam of light over the stage. Muffat had never been backstage in a theatre and was feeling particularly surprised and uneasy, full of vague repugnance not unmixed with fear. He was gazing up towards the rigging-loft, where there were other stage-lights with their jets dimmed looking like constellations of tiny bluish stars amid the wild confusion of the grid, with its cables of every possible thickness, flying bridges, and backcloths floating in the air like huge sheets of linen hung up to dry.

'Let go!' the head stage-hand called out suddenly.

The prince himself had to warn the count. They were letting down a backcloth to set the scene for the third act, the grotto on Mount Etna. Men were sticking poles in the cuts and others were picking up the flats against the walls of the stage and fastening them securely to the framework. At the back, to produce the glow from Vulcan's forge, a lamp-trimmer had fixed up another framework, to which were attached gas-jets provided with red glass shades and which he was now lighting. Although every move was carefully worked out, everybody was scurrying around in apparent confusion. Amidst all the hustle and bustle the prompter was taking a quick turn round the stage to stretch his legs.

'Your Royal Highness is too gracious', Bordenave was saying between bows. 'Our theatre's not large, we try to do as well as we can. Now, if Your Highness would do me the honour of following me . . .'

Count Muffat was already making his way towards the passage leading to the dressing-rooms. He had been surprised at the relatively steep slope of the stage and his worried look came in great part from feeling the floor moving under his feet; through the open cuts, gas-jets could be seen burning below stage, an underground world like a cellar, full of deep shadows, draughts, and voices. As he was walking upstage he saw something which brought him to a halt: two young women, dressed for the third act, were talking to each other in front of the peephole in the curtains. One of them was bending forward with her backside stuck out, holding the hole open with her fingers in order to get a better look into the auditorium.

'Oh, I can see him', she exclaimed suddenly. 'Christ, what an ugly mug!'

Bordenave was so shocked that he nearly booted her behind, but the prince was smiling and excited by what he heard and looking fondly at this young woman who didn't give a damn for His Royal Highness. She was laughing saucily. Meanwhile Bordenave persuaded the prince to follow him. Count Muffat, who still had his hat on, had broken into a sweat; in particular, he was feeling stifled by the heavy, overheated, backstage atmosphere, with its strong underlying stench of gas, stage-set glue, squalid dark corners, and the smell of the female extras' unwashed underwear. The passageway was even more suffocating; from time to time the sharp scent of toilet-water and soap drifting down from the dressing-rooms blended with the pestilential odour of human breath. As he went by, the count raised his eyes and glanced up the stair-well, startled by the sudden burst of heat and light which struck the back of his neck from above. Upstairs there was a sound of wash-basins, laughter, shouts, and banging doors releasing female smells in which the musky odour of make-up mingled with the harsh animal scent of hair. He kept on walking, almost running away, his skin still tingling from this torrid view on to a world unknown.

'Queer thing, a theatre, isn't it?' the marquis remarked, with the delighted look of someone who finds himself back on familiar ground.

But Bordenave had at last reached Nana's dressing-room at the end of the corridor. He calmly turned the handle and stood on one side.

'If Your Highness will have the kindness to enter . . .'

They heard a startled female shriek and saw Nana, naked to the waist, hastily taking cover behind a curtain, while her dresser, who was drying her, was left holding the towel.

'It's silly to burst in like that!' exclaimed Nana, still hiding. 'Don't come in, you can see very well that you can't come in!'

Bordenave looked displeased.

'Don't go away, my dear girl, it doesn't matter', he said. 'It's His Royal Highness. Come along now, don't be childish!'

And when she persisted in refusing, still rather shocked but already beginning to laugh, he added in a bluff, fatherly voice:

'Goodness me, these gentlemen know quite well what a woman looks like. They're not going to eat you.'

'But that's not a promise', the prince added wittily.

His remark was greeted with loud, obsequious laughter. How very Parisian, as Bordenave was quick to point out. Nana had stopped talking, the curtain was waving about, no doubt she was making up her mind. With flushed cheeks, Count Muffat was examining the dressing-room. It was square, with a very low ceiling and hung entirely in a light brown material; a curtain of the same material on a brass rod closed off an area at the far end. Two large windows opened on to the courtyard, not much more than three yards away from a peeling wall on which, in the darkness outside, they were casting square patches of yellow light.

Facing a tall cheval-glass stood a white marble-topped dressing-table cluttered with cut-glass containers and bottles holding creams, perfumes, and face-powders. The count went over to the mirror and saw that his face was very red, with tiny beads of perspiration on his forehead; he lowered his eyes, walked over to the dressing-table, and seemed for a moment to be absorbed in the wash-basin full of soapy water, the scattered little ivory implements, and wet sponges. Once again he was feeling overcome by the dizziness which had overtaken him the first time he'd called on Nana in the Boulevard Haussmann. He could feel the thick dressing-room carpet giving way under his feet, and the flames of the gas-jets on the dressing-table and by the cheval-glass were making a hissing noise round his temples. For a second he was scared that this time these women's smells, aggravated by the heat and the low ceiling, would make him faint, and he sat down on the upholstered divan between the two windows. But he immediately got up again, went back to the dressing-table, and stood staring blankly, not looking at anything but thinking of a bunch of withered tuberoses he'd once had in his bedroom which had nearly made him die. Decomposing tuberoses smell like human bodies.

'Come along, buck up!' whispered Bordenave, putting his head round the curtain.

The prince was in any case trying to help by listening to the Marquis de Chouard, who'd picked up a hare's paw and was explaining how you used it to spread on grease-paint. In one corner Satin, with her pure, girlish face, was staring at the gentlemen while Madame Jules, the dresser, was getting ready Venus's tights and tunic. Madame Jules was ageless with a parchment-like skin and the stony features of old maids who've never been young. She had dried up in the sweltering heat of theatre dressing-rooms, surrounded by the most celebrated breasts and thighs Paris had to offer. She wore an everlasting faded black dress, and on her sexless, flat bosom, in the place of her heart, a thicket of pins.

'Please forgive me, gentlemen', said Nana, pulling the curtain aside. 'I was taken by surprise.'

They all spun round. She hadn't put on any more clothes but merely buttoned up a little cotton cambric bodice which half concealed her bust. When she'd had to take cover, she had just started quickly slipping off her fishwife's costume, and a tag of her shift could still be seen sticking out of her trousers. With bare arms, bare shoulders, and the tips of her breasts uncovered, an adorable young, plump blonde, she was still holding on to the curtain with one hand as if ready to close it again if she began to feel at all scared.

'Yes, I was taken by surprise, I'll never dare . . .' she faltered, pretending to be flustered, with embarrassed smiles and a pink flush on her neck.

'Oh, come on, we all think you're wonderful!' exclaimed Bordenave.

Nana was determined to push her ingénue act to the limit; wriggling as if she was being tickled, she simpered:

'His Highness is being too kind, I do beg His Highness's pardon for welcoming him like this . . .'

'It's my fault for insisting on visiting you here', the prince replied. 'But I couldn't resist the opportunity of offering you my congratulations.'

They stepped aside, and calmly, still in her trousers, she walked through the group of men to her dressing-table. The trousers clung tightly to the curves of her broad, round hips, and as she thrust her breasts forward once again she gave her sly, welcoming smile. Suddenly she seemed to become aware of Count Muffat. With a friendly gesture she held out her hand and complained that he'd not come to her supper party. The prince playfully made fun of Muffat, who could only stammer a few words in reply, still quivering with emotion at the touch of her tiny hand, so cool and scented, on his own, which was burning. The count had dined very well with the prince, who was a great lover of wine and good food; they were both even a trifle tipsy, though their behaviour was irreproachable. To cover his confusion, the only thing Muffat could think of was to comment on the heat.

'My goodness, it's hot here', he said. 'How do you manage to survive in such a temperature, madame?'

The conversation was just about to be launched on this topic when loud voices were heard outside the dressing-room door. Bordenave pushed back the little panel covering the grille of the spyhole, the sort you find in convents. It was Fontan, accompanied by Prullière and Bosc, all three with bottles under their arms and glasses in their hands. He was pounding on the door and shouting that it was his name-day and he was treating them to champagne. Nana glanced inquiringly at the prince. Of course His Highness wouldn't object, he'd be only too glad. But Fontan was already walking in without waiting for anyone's leave. He was talking baby language:

'Me no meany, me pay champers.'

Suddenly he caught sight of the prince; he hadn't known he was there. He came to a standstill and, with an air of mock solemnity, said:

'King Dagobert is in the corridor and craves the honour of drinking a toast with His Royal Highness.'

Once the prince had smiled, Fontan's action was considered charming. However, the dressing-room was too small to accommodate all these people and they were forced to pack in tightly, with Satin and Madame Jules at the far end by the curtain and the men clustered round the half-naked Nana. The three actors were still in their second-act costumes. Prullière had to remove his Swiss admiral's hat, whose huge plume would have been too tall for the ceiling; Bosc steadied himself on his drunken legs and greeted the prince like a monarch welcoming the son of a powerful neighbour. The glasses had been filled; they clinked them.

'I drink to Your Royal Highness!' old Bosc said in a regal voice.

'To the armed forces!' added Prullière.

'And to Venus!' shouted Fontan.

The prince stood amiably waiting with his glass poised, and then raised it three times, murmuring:

'Madame . . . Admiral . . . Sire . . .'

He downed it in a gulp.

Count Muffat and the Marquis de Chouard followed suit. It was no longer just a joke; they were courtiers. In the hazy heat of the gas-jets, this world of the theatre was continuing the real world in a solemn farce. Forgetting that she was in trousers with her shift showing, Nana was acting the great lady, Queen Venus opening up her private apartments to persons of note in her state. Every one of her sentences contained a 'Royal Highness', she was curtseying enthusiastically, and treating the old rogues Bosc and Prullière like a sovereign attended by her ministers. And nobody was smiling at this strange mixture, this real prince, heir to a crown, who was drinking champagne as a guest of a second-rate actor, completely at ease in this celestial carnival, this royal masquerade, surrounded by a vulgar entourage of dressers, tarts, stage hacks, showmen, and exhibitors of women. Excited by such a setting and such a cast, Bordenave was reflecting on what his box-office takings would be if His Highness agreed to appear like that in the second act of *The Blonde Venus*.

'I say', he exclaimed, forgetting his formality, 'let me bring some of my girls down here.'

Nana said no; but she too was beginning to let herself go. Attracted by Fontan and his grotesquely made-up face, she was snuggling up against him and looking at him like a pregnant woman who has a craving for something horrible to eat. She suddenly started to treat him like an old friend:

'Come on, you old stupid, how about a spot more bubbly?'

Fontan replenished the glasses and they all drank the same toasts.

'To His Highness!'

'To the armed forces!'

'To Venus!'

But Nana signalled to everybody to be quiet. She raised her glass high in the air and cried:

'No, to Fontan! . . . It's Fontan's party! To Fontan!'

So they clapped loudly and drank the third toast. The prince, who had observed that Nana had taken a great fancy to the comedian, raised his glass:

'Monsieur Fontan', he said with exquisite politeness, 'I drink to your continued success.'

Meanwhile, His Highness's coat-tails were wiping the marble top of the dressing-table. It was like being in a bedroom alcove or a tiny bathroom, with the steam from the wash-basin and the sponges, the powerful fragrance of the various oils blending with the sharp intoxicating little whiff of champagne. Nana was wedged between the prince and Muffat, and when the men made the slightest movement they had to hold their hands up high to avoid brushing against her hips or her breasts. And Madame Jules stood there stiffly waiting, with not a single bead of perspiration, while Satin, surprised despite all her experience of vice, to see a prince and gentlemen in evening dress pursuing, together with people in costume, a naked woman, was thinking to herself that these smart people weren't really very nice.

But old Barillot could be heard coming down the corridor ringing his bell. When he appeared in the doorway he stood stunned to see the three actors still in their second-act costumes.

'Please, gentlemen', he faltered, 'please do hurry up . . . The foyer bell has started ringing.'

'So what?' retorted Bordenave calmly. 'The audience'll have to wait.'

Nevertheless, as the bottles were empty, the actors bowed their way out and went upstairs to get changed. Bosc's venerable beard had got soaked in champagne and he had to take it off, thereby revealing his ravaged purple face, a drunken old actor sinking into alcoholism. At the foot of the staircase he was heard to remark to Fontan in his drink-sodden voice, referring to the prince:

'Well, I properly bowled him over, didn't I?'

In Nana's dressing-room, only His Royal Highness, the count, and the marquis were left. Bordenave had gone off with Barillot, warning him not to give the three knocks without warning Nana.

'I must ask you to forgive me, gentlemen', said Nana, starting to make up her face and arms with particular care for her nude appearance in the third act.

The prince sat down on the divan beside the Marquis de Chouard. Only Count Muffat remained on his feet. In the stifling heat of this room, their two glasses of champagne had made them tipsier than ever. Seeing the gentlemen alone with her friend, Satin had discreetly retreated behind the curtain and sat waiting on a trunk, bored at having to hang about; Madame Jules was quietly coming and going without a word or a glance.

'You sang that roundelay wonderfully', said the prince.

The conversation now got under way, but in short spurts punctuated by pauses, since Nana was not always in a position to reply. After smearing cold cream on her arms and face with her hand, she was now applying the white grease-paint with the corner of a towel. She stopped for a moment to look at herself in the mirror and smiled as the threw a quick glance towards the prince, while still applying the grease-paint.

'His Highness is trying to spoil me', she murmured.

It was a very complicated operation, which the Marquis de Chouard was following with a look of blissful enjoyment on his face. He now entered the conversation:

'Couldn't the orchestra accompany you rather more quietly? It's drowning your voice, which is an unforgivable crime.'

This time Nana didn't turn round. She had picked up the hare's paw and was lightly stroking it over her skin with great concentration, arching her body over the dressing-table so that her white trousers stretched tightly over her plump round bottom with the little tag of her shift showing above. She did however try to express her appreciation of the old man's compliment by wiggling her hips.

There was a pause. Madame Jules had spotted a tear in the right leg of the trousers. She took a pin from the array on her bodice and knelt down for a moment beside Nana's thigh while the young woman, apparently not noticing what she was doing went on covering herself with rice-powder, taking care not to put any on her cheek-bones. But when the prince said that if she were to come and sing in London the whole of England would go to applaud her, she gave a friendly laugh and turned round for a second in a cloud of powder, with her left cheek very white. Then her face suddenly took on a very earnest expression: she was about to apply her rouge. Once again, holding her face close to the mirror, she began dipping her finger in a jar and rubbing on the rouge under her eyes, spreading it gently along to her temples. The gentlemen maintained a respectful silence.

Count Muffat had not yet uttered a word. He was assailed by uncontrollable memories of his youth. His nursery had been dreadfully cold. Later on, at the age of 16, every evening when he kissed his mother goodnight, her icy kiss would pursue him even during his sleep. One day he'd caught a passing glimpse through a half-open door of one of the maids having a wash; that was his only disturbing recollection from his puberty till his marriage. Then he'd found himself with a wife conscientiously fulfilling her marital obligations while he himself experienced a sort of pious disgust. He had grown up and now was growing old ignorant of the pleasures of sex, submitting to strict religious observances, letting his life be ruled by laws and precepts. Now suddenly he'd been thrown into this actress's dressing-room, facing this naked tart. He'd never seen Countess Muffat even putting on her garters, and now he was witnessing the intimate details of a woman's toilet, amid a clutter of jars and basins, in this air heavy with soft, rich perfumes. His whole being was in revolt, he was terrified to see how Nana had slowly been taking possession of him recently, in a way that reminded him of the pious texts and fears of possession by the Devil fed to him in his childhood. He believed in Satan, and in his bewildered mind Nana, with her laughter, her breasts, the curves of her buttocks, was the Devil incarnate, vicious to the core. But he swore to himself that he'd be steadfast and resist.

'So it's agreed', the prince was saying, very much at his ease on the divan. 'Next year you'll come to London and we'll give you a welcome you'll never forget, and you'll never want to go back to France . . . Ah, my dear count, the truth of the matter is that you don't appreciate your pretty women enough. We'll take them all away from you.'

'That won't worry him much', murmured the Marquis de Chouard mischievously, who was not averse to being indiscreet in private. 'The count is virtue personified.'

Hearing this reference to his strict morality, Nana looked at the count so oddly that at first Muffat felt extremely annoyed, and then surprised and angry with himself for feeling annoyed: why should the thought of being so moral make him feel uncomfortable in the presence of this tart? He could have thrashed her! Then Nana bent down to pick up a brush which she had dropped and he quickly stooped to help her; their breaths mingled, Venus's loose hair tumbled over their hands. He felt a moment of extreme joy mixed with remorse, the joy familiar to Roman Catholics whose sinful pleasures are whetted by their fear of eternal damnation.

At that moment Barillot's voice was heard outside:

'May I give the knocks, ma'am? The audience are getting restless.'

'In a moment', Nana replied calmly.

She had dipped the brush in a jar of mascara and, with her nose pressed hard against the mirror, closing her left eye, she stroked it delicately between her lashes. Muffat was standing behind her, watching. He could see her in the mirror with her plump shoulders and her breasts bathed in pink shadows.

And despite all his efforts, he couldn't take his eyes off this face, so provocative with its dimples and one closed eye making her seem overcome by desire. When she closed her right eye and again passed the brush over it, he knew that the die was cast: she had him in her power.

'They're stamping, ma'am, and they'll finish by breaking up the seats, ma'am', the call-boy called breathlessly. 'May I knock?'

'Drat it!' exclaimed Nana impatiently. 'OK, knock away, I don't give a damn! If I'm not ready, they'll just have to wait!'

Then she calmed down and, turning to look at the gentlemen, she added with a smile:

'It's quite true, one can't get a minute for a chat.'

She'd completed her face and arms. With her finger she now added two broad streaks of rouge on her lips. Count Muffat felt more agitated than ever by these bewitching, vicious face-powders and rouge, by his unbridled desire for this painted young woman with her outrageous scarlet gash of a mouth set in her extravagantly white face, her glowing eyes looking even larger in their dark rings, as though after a night of love.

Meanwhile Nana had gone back behind the curtain for a second to take her trousers off and slip on her tights. Then, completely unabashed, she calmly unbuttoned her little cambric bodice and held her arms out for Madame Jules to slip on her short-sleeved tunic.

'Quick, they're beginning to turn nasty!' she muttered.

With eyes half-closed, the prince was letting his gaze wander over the curves of her breasts while the Marquis de Chouard couldn't resist giving an approving nod. To avoid having to see anything more, Count Muffat looked down at the carpet. With nothing more than a piece of gauze covering her shoulders, Venus was now ready. Madame Jules was fussing round her like a little old wooden figure with bright empty eyes, swiftly pulling pins out of the inexhaustible store over her heart to fix up the tunic, brushing her desiccated hands over Venus's plump young flesh with complete unconcern as to her sex or her past.

'There we are!' the young woman said, casting a final glance at herself in the mirror.

Bordenave came in looking worried to say that the third act had begun.

'OK, I'm on my way', she replied. 'What a fuss! Other people always keep me waiting.'

The gentlemen left the dressing-room; the prince had expressed the wish to watch the third act from the wings and they would join Nana again later. Left by herself, Nana ran her eyes round the room with a look of surprise.

'Where on earth can she be?' she asked.

She was looking for Satin. When she discovered her behind the curtain, sitting on a trunk, Satin said calmly:

'Of course I wasn't going to get in your way, with all those men around!'

She added that she was now going to leave. Nana wouldn't let her. How stupid could she be! After all, Bordenave was willing to take her on! They'd fix it all up definitely after the show. Satin hesitated. There were too many gadgets and contraptions, it wasn't her sort of world. However, she didn't leave.

As the prince was going down the wooden staircase, a strange sound of scuffling and swearing came from the other side of the theatre. Something very odd was happening; the actors waiting to go on stage were watching in dismay. Mignon had just been getting at Fauchery again with his affectionate digs and nudges. His latest little trick was giving him light taps on the nose, claiming it was to keep off the flies. Naturally the cast was highly amused. Then all of a sudden, excited by his success, he let his imagination take over and he gave the journalist not just a tap but a really hard punch. This time he'd gone too far. In front of so many people Fauchery couldn't laugh off a blow like that. Dropping their mask, the two men, livid, their faces contorted with rage and hatred, had flung themselves at each other's throats. They were rolling about on the ground behind the framework of a flat, calling each other pimps.

'Monsieur Bordenave! Monsieur Bordenave!' The agitated stage-manager rushed over to the manager. Apologizing to the prince, Bordenave went to see what was wrong. When he recognized Fauchery and Mignon on the ground he didn't hide his annoyance: they really had picked the right moment, with His Highness on the other side of the stage and the whole audience within earshot! To crown it all Rose, who was due on stage, was just coming along, out of breath: Vulcan had already spoken her cue. She stood dumbfounded at the sight of her husband and her lover tumbling round at her feet, tearing each other's hair out, kicking and throttling each other, their frock-coats white with dust. They were blocking her way, and a stage-hand had only just managed to catch Fauchery's hat to prevent it from shooting out on to the stage. Meanwhile Vulcan, who'd been busily gagging, once again gave Rose her cue. She was standing frozen to the spot, staring at the two men.

'Don't look at them!' hissed Bordenave furiously, coming up behind her. 'Get out on stage! On you go! . . . It's no business of yours! You're fluffing your cue!'

He gave her a shove and, stepping over the two bodies, Rose found herself on stage facing the audience in the glare of the footlights. She hadn't any idea why the two men were on the ground fighting each other. Trembling, with a buzzing in her ears, but still Diana in love, she produced a radiant smile, went towards the footlights, and burst into the first bars of her love duet in such a vibrant voice that she was greeted with an ovation. Behind the scenes she could hear the dull thud of the exchange of blows. They had rolled over right up to the proscenium arch. Fortunately the orchestra was covering the noise made by their feet kicking against the flats.

'For Christ's sake!' exclaimed Bordenave, having finally succeeded in separating the two men. 'Can't you do your fighting at home? You know very well that I can't stand that sort of thing . . . Mignon, you'll oblige me by staying here on the prompt side, and as for you Fauchery, I'll kick you straight out of the theatre if you leave the side opposite the prompter. Understand? So PS and OP,* or I'll forbid Rose to leave the theatre with either of you.'

When he went back to the prince, His Royal Highness asked what had happened.

'Oh, nothing at all', he replied nonchalantly.

Nana was standing in her fur coat chatting to the gentlemen and waiting for her cue. As Count Muffat was moving across to take a quick look at the stage between two pieces of scenery, the stage-manager signalled to him to walk quietly. A soothing warmth was coming down from the rigging-loft. In the wings, chequered in vivid patches of light, a few people stood talking before tiptoeing away. The gasman was at his post beside his complicated array of taps; a fireman was leaning against a flat, craning his neck to watch; and at the very top, the curtain-raiser was sitting resignedly on his bench, knowing nothing about the performance, just waiting for the bell before operating his ropes. In the middle of this suffocating atmosphere, full of whispers and the trampling of feet, you could hear the voices of the actors on stage, odd, muffled voices, strangely distorted. In the distance, beyond the confused sound of the orchestra, there was the vast, slow murmur of the auditorium, a sighing breath which now and again swelled to a roar of laughter or applause. Even when they were silent you could sense the presence of the audience.

'They must have left something open', said Nana suddenly, huddling into her fur coat. 'Go and take a look, Barillot. I bet someone's just opened a window . . . You could catch your death here!'

Barillot swore blind he'd shut everything up himself. Perhaps there were some broken panes. Show-people were always complaining of draughts. In the oppressive heat from the gas, there were sudden gusts of cold air, a real breeding-ground for pneumonia, Fontan used to say.

'I'd like to see you wearing a low-cut dress', muttered Nana, who was getting annoyed.

'Sh!' said Bordenave.

On stage Rose was singing a line of her duet with such sensitive phrasing that the applause was drowning the orchestra. Nana stopped talking, and her eyes took on a flinty look. Meanwhile, as the count was venturing into one of the slips, Barillot stopped him, explaining that it opened on to the stage. He could see the set from the rear and the side, the backs of the flats plastered together with a thick layer of old posters, and then a corner of the stage, the cave on Mount Etna hollowed out as a silver mine with Vulcan's forge at the back. The stage-lights had been let down and were making the large coloured spangles glitter. Bits of blue and red glass were fixed to frames to create the effect of a glowing fire, and on the floor in the background there were rows of gas-jets picking out a line of black rocks. And here, sitting half asleep on a gently sloping practicable,* blinded by all these lights which looked like lanterns placed in the grass for a public holiday, was old Madame Drouard who took the part of Juno, waiting for her cue.

There was a stir. Simonne, who was listening to some story of Clarisse's, suddenly exclaimed:

'Look, there's Tricon!'

It was indeed Tricon, with her ringlets and looking, as always, like a countess with a weakness for lawyers. She marched straight up to Nana. They exchanged a few words.

'No', said Nana. 'Not at the moment.'

The old lady looked solemn. Prullière, who was passing, shook hands with her. Two little female extras were watching her, thrilled. For a second she seemed to be hesitating. Then she made a sign to Simonne and again had a rapid exchange of words.

'Yes', said Simonne finally. 'In half-an-hour's time.'

But then, as she was on her way up to her dressing-room, Madame Bron, who was once again delivering notes, handed her one. Bordenave was furiously telling the door-keeper off in an undertone for letting Tricon in; that woman, tonight of all nights! What on earth would His Highness think? Madame Bron, who'd spent the last thirty years of her life in the theatre, replied sourly: how could she have known? Tricon did business with all these ladies; the manager had encountered her a score of times without saying anything. And while Bordenave was cursing and spluttering, Tricon was calmly and carefully looking the prince over like a woman who can size up a man at a glance. Her sallow face lit up with a smile. Then she went slowly off under the respectful gaze of Bordenave's 'little women'.

'So, straight away, right?' she said, looking back at Simonne.

Simonne was looking extremely annoyed: the note was from a young man whom she'd promised to see that night. She scribbled a note and handed it to Madame Bron: 'Can't make it tonight, darling, I'm not free.' But she was worried that the young man might still go on waiting for her all the same, so as she didn't appear in the third act she was anxious to leave at once. She asked Clarisse, who didn't have to go on till near the end of the act, to go and have a look for her. Clarisse went off downstairs while Simonne slipped up for a moment to the dressing-room which they shared.

In Madame Bron's bar downstairs there was one solitary drinker, an extra who took the part of Pluto, draped in a voluminous red gown sparkling with gold. The door-keeper's little business must have been flourishing, because the cellar-like hole under the stairs was all wet from spilt drinks. Clarisse gathered up her Iris's tunic which was trailing on the sticky steps. As a precaution, she stopped and craned her neck round the bend in the staircase to take a quick look into the lodge. Her instinct was right: who was still waiting there but that idiot la Faloise, sitting on the same chair between the table and the stove! While Simonne was there he'd pretended to leave, only to sneak back. The lodge was in any case still full of correctly dressed gentlemen, wearing gloves and looking patient and docile. They were all waiting solemnly, watching each other. On the table only the dirty plates now remained, Madame Bron having just delivered the last bunches of flowers; one single withered rose had fallen down beside the black cat curled up on the floor while the kittens were scampering wildly around, making savage swoops between the men's legs. For a moment Clarisse was tempted to kick la Faloise out. The cretin couldn't stand animals: that was him all over! He was holding his elbows in close to his sides, to avoid touching the cat.

'Look out, he'll nab you!' said Pluto, who was a wag, as he made his way upstairs, wiping his mouth with the back of his hand.

Clarisse abandoned the idea of having a row with la Faloise. She had seen Madame Bron hand the letter over to Simonne's young man who went away to read it under the gas-jet in the entrance hall. 'Can't make it tonight, darling, I'm not free.' And he'd gone off, without any fuss, no doubt used to receiving that message. At least there was one man who knew how to behave like a gentleman! Not like those others who were sitting doggedly on Madame Bron's run-down, cane-seated chairs in the large, glassed-in, sweltering lantern of a room which smelt none-too wholesome. Those men must really be panting for it! Clarisse went off upstairs full of disgust; she crossed the stage and scampered up the three flights of the dressing-room staircase to give Simonne her reply.

In the theatre the prince had taken Nana aside and was talking to her, gazing at her admiringly through half-closed lids, never taking his eyes off her. Nana was smiling and nodding agreement, without looking at him. Suddenly, overcome by an irresistible urge of his whole being, Count Muffat walked away from Bordenave, who was giving a detailed description of the working of the various drums and winches, and went over to interrupt their conversation. Nana looked up and smiled at him, just as she had been smiling at the prince. But she was listening hard to make sure she wouldn't miss her cue.

'The third act's the shortest, I'm told', the prince was saying, embarrassed by the count's presence.

She made no reply; her expression changed, the actress took over. Quickly slipping her fur off her shoulders into Madame Jules's safe keeping as she stood waiting behind her, Nana raised her hands to her head, as though checking that her hair was properly in order and went on stage, naked.

'Sh! Sh!' whispered Bordenave.

The count and the prince had been taken unawares. Suddenly complete silence had fallen, succeeded by a great sighing sound rising up like the distant murmur of a crowd; every night as Venus, the naked goddess, made her entrance, she'd created the same effect. Muffat had put his eye to a hole to look at the stage. Beyond the dazzling arc of the footlights the auditorium seemed dark, as if filled with a reddish brown smoke, and against this neutral background and the pale blur of the rows of faces, Nana stood out in white, larger than life, blocking out the boxes from the dress circle right up to the very top tier. Muffat was watching her from behind, with her back arched and arms outspread while, level with her feet, the head of the prompter, the head of an old man, poor but honest, was resting on the floor looking as if it had been severed from the body. Certain passages of her first song seemed to set off a wave motion which started at her neck, passed down through her waist and died away at the bottom of her trailing tunic. As the last note faded away and she bowed to acknowledge the storm of applause, her long hair fell down below her waist and her tunic floated in the air around her. Seeing the plump curves of her hips, made even plumper by her attitude, moving backwards towards the hole through which he was peering, the count straightened up, as white as a sheet. The stage vanished from his sight and he could see only the back of the scenery, the garish old posters stuck on higgledy-piggledy. On the practicable, amid the rows of gas-jets, all the inhabitants of Olympus had joined the drowsing Madame Drouard. They were waiting for the end of the act, Bosc and Fontan sitting on the floor, resting their chins on their knees, and Prullière stretching and yawning before going on stage, all of them fagged out and red-eyed, anxious to get to bed.

At that moment Fauchery, who, ever since Bordenave had forbidden him to go to the other side, had been prowling round the prompt side, attached himself to the count and in an attempt to save face offered to show him the dressing-rooms. Muffat, who was feeling increasingly apathetic and weak-willed, looked round for the Marquis de Chouard but he had disappeared. Muffat agreed to follow the journalist and, with a feeling of relief not unmixed with apprehension, left the wings where he could still hear Nana singing.

Fauchery was already going ahead up the stairs which, on the first and second floors, were closed off by revolving wooden doors. It was the sort of staircase you meet with in disreputable houses such as Muffat had seen when going the rounds as a member of his charity committee, rickety and bare, with yellow distemper, its treads worn by years of use and its iron banister rubbed smooth by contact with many hands. On each landing, at ground level, there was a low, recessed, square aperture for a ventilator shaft. The whole desolate scene was lit by the harsh light of gas-lamps attached to the walls, and their heat was rising up and collecting in the narrow corkscrew stairway.

As he reached the foot of the stairs the count had again felt a fiery gust of air striking the back of his neck and bringing down the smell of women from the dressing-rooms in a wave of noise and light. Now with every step upwards he could feel the musky perfume of powder and the vinegary tartness of toiletries making him hotter and hotter and increasingly bewildered. Leading off the first floor were two crooked corridors with yellow doors bearing large white numbers, like a shady lodging-house; and as the old building had subsided the tiles had lifted, making the floor uneven. The count ventured into the passage, cast a glance through a half-open door, and saw the sort of barber's booth you find in working-class slums, furnished with a couple of chairs, a mirror, and a tray with a shelf encrusted with the black grime of greasy combs. In the room a young man, sturdy and sweating, with steam rising from his shoulders, was changing his underclothes. In a similar room next door a woman was putting on her gloves, about to leave; with her damp, lank hair she looked as if she'd just had a bath. But Fauchery called out and the count was hurrying to catch up when an angry shout of 'Oh shit!' came from the corridor on the right: Mathilde, a little slut who played ingénue parts, had broken her wash-basin and a flood of soapy water was pouring out over the landing. A dressing-room door slammed violently. Two women in their corsets leapt across the passage. Another woman appeared holding the top of her shift between her teeth and scuttled away. There was laughter, a squabble; someone started singing and stopped abruptly. Along the passage, through the cracks, there were little glimpses of bare flesh, white skin, pale underwear. Two very lively girls were showing each other their birthmarks; one of them, barely more than a child, had lifted her petticoats up above her knees to mend her knickers. Seeing the two men, the dressers drew the curtains to, for the sake of propriety. The final scramble was taking place, everybody cleaning off all the rouge and grease-paint, putting on their clothes, in a cloud of rice-powder, with the doors puffing out even more musky gusts of perfume as they slammed.

On the third floor Muffat abandoned himself to his overpowering feeling of intoxication. Up here were the extras' dressing-rooms: twenty women on top of each other, a crazy clutter of bars of soap and bottles of lavender-water, rather like the room shared by the women of a cheap brothel.

Behind a closed door there came the sound of a wild gush of water, a storm in a wash-basin. On his way up to the top floor, he was impelled by curiosity to risk one more quick look through an open spy-hole: the room was empty, its floor littered with skirts, in the midst of which the glare of the gaslight revealed a chamber-pot left by someone. With this final vision in his eyes he continued on his way up. On the fourth floor, he found it hardly possible to breathe: every smell, every scrap of heat, was concentrated at the top: the yellow of the ceiling seemed to have been baked on, a lamp was burning in a reddish haze. For a second he had to hold tightly on to the iron banister, which felt warm to the touch like a living creature. He shut his eyes and inhaled a breath in which the whole sexuality of women was distilled, something which he had never before met and which struck him full in the face.

'Do come along!' shouted Fauchery, who had vanished for a moment. 'You're wanted!'

He was in Clarisse's and Simonne's dressing-room at the end of the passageway. It was an oblong room, badly designed and constructed, with cut-off corners and receding walls. Daylight came through two deep apertures in the ceiling, but at night the room was lit by gas. The shabby, cheap-looking wallpaper depicted pink flowers twined round a green trellis. The dressing-table consisted of two boards placed side by side, covered in a piece of oilcloth and stained black from spilt water; underneath were battered zinc pots, pails full of slops, and crude yellow earthenware jugs. The toilet articles were cheap and shoddy, the horn combs had lost many of their teeth: the sort of shambles you'd expect from two busy, easy-going young women washing and undressing together in a place where they never spent long and who had stopped worrying about squalor.

'Do come along', repeated Fauchery in the offhand way men speak to each other when in the company of tarts. 'Clarisse wants to give you a kiss.'

Muffat finally went in and to his surprise saw the Marquis de Chouard installed on a chair between the two dressing-tables, where he'd taken refuge. He was keeping his feet apart to avoid a puddle of whitish liquid caused by a leaking pail.

He obviously felt at home here, like a man who knows all the best places to go, a man reinvigorated in this steamy bathroom atmosphere of easy-going, shameless women which seemed entirely appropriate to, and was even enhanced by, the sordid surroundings.

'Do you go with the old man?' whispered Simonne into Clarisse's ear.

'Not very often these days', she replied out loud.

The dresser, a very ugly and pert girl who was helping Simonne into her coat, collapsed in laughter. All three were nudging each other and spluttering words that made them laugh even more.

'Come on now, Clarisse, kiss the gentleman', said Fauchery again. 'You know he's got pots of money.'

And turning to the count:

'You'll see what a nice girl she is, she's going to give you a kiss.'

But Clarisse was fed up with men and launched into a diatribe against those bastards waiting downstairs in the door-keeper's lodge. Anyway, she was in a hurry to get back on stage, they'd make her late for her last scene. Then as Fauchery was barring the way, she gave Muffat two pecks on his whiskers, saying:

'Anyway, they're not for you, they're for Fauchery who won't leave me alone!'

She dashed away. The count went bright red, embarrassed by the presence of his father-in-law. In Nana's dressing-room, with its luxurious draperies and mirrors, he hadn't felt the sharp thrill of excitement he experienced amid the sluttish neglect of this sordid, poverty-stricken garret. Meanwhile the marquis had left the room in pursuit of Simonne, who was also rushing off; he was whispering in her ear while she kept shaking her head. Fauchery went after them, laughing. The count found himself alone with the dresser, who was rinsing out the wash-basins. He too left, trembling at the knees as he went down the stairs, once again flushing out women in petticoats and hearing doors slam as he went by. But amongst all these girls scrambling around on each of the four floors, the only thing he saw clearly was a cat, the fat ginger cat sliding away down the steps of this oven of a staircase which reeked of musk, rubbing its back against the banister rails with its tail erect.

'Good Lord', a woman was saying in a husky voice, 'I thought they'd never let us go tonight! What a bore they are with all their curtain-calls!'

The curtain had gone down for the last time. There was a wild stampede in the stair-well, with everybody exclaiming as they frantically rushed off to get dressed and leave. As Count Muffat reached the bottom step he saw Nana going slowly along the passage with the prince. The young woman stopped and said with a smile, in a low voice:

'All right. I shan't be long.'

The prince returned to the stage where Bordenave was waiting for him. Left alone with Nana, Muffat gave way to a sudden impulse of anger and desire. He ran after her and just as she was going into her dressing-room kissed her roughly in the nape of her neck, on the little blonde curls which grew right down between her shoulders. It was rather as if he was returning the kiss he'd just been given upstairs. Nana spun round angrily, raising her hand, but when she saw the count she smiled and simply said:

'Oh, you did give me such a fright!'

It was an adorable smile, embarrassed and deferential, as if she had given up hoping for this kiss and was glad to get it. But tonight was impossible and tomorrow too. He'd have to wait. Even if it had been possible, she wouldn't have wanted to appear too eager. Her eyes showed all this running through her mind. She went on:

'Did you know I'm a landowner? I'm buying a house in the country, near Orléans, close to where you sometimes go and stay. Baby told me about it, that's little Georges Hugon, do you know him? . . . Do come and call on me there.'

Frightened and ashamed at his uncouth behaviour, the result of his own timidity, the count gave a very polite bow and promised to accept her invitation. He walked away in a dream.

On his way to rejoin the prince, passing by the foyer, he heard Satin shouting:

'You're a dirty old man! Leave me alone, will you?'

It was the Marquis de Chouard, who was falling back on to

Satin; but she had had just about enough of all these smart folk. Nana had just introduced her to Bordenave. However, she'd been bored stiff standing there with lips sealed for fear of blurting out something stupid and now wanted to make up for lost time, particularly as she'd just run across an old flame of hers, the extra who was taking the part of Pluto, a pastry-cook who had once spent a whole week making love to her and bashing her up. She was waiting for him and was irritated because the marquis was addressing her as if she was one of those theatrical ladies. So finally, putting on her most respectable look, she launched a stinging retort:

'You just wait and see what happens when my hubby comes out!'

Meanwhile the tired-looking actors in their overcoats were leaving one by one; groups of men and women were coming down the spiral staircase; in the shadows, you could see the outlines of battered hats, tatty scarves, the pallor and ugliness of actors without their grease-paint. On the stage the battens and set-piece lights were being extinguished, and the prince was listening to one of Bordenave's anecdotes while waiting for Nana. When she finally arrived, the stage was in darkness and the duty fireman was completing his rounds, lamp in hand. To save His Highness from having to go out through the Passage des Panoramas, Bordenave had arranged to open the passage leading from the door-keeper's lodge to the lobby. His 'girls' immediately started scuttling away through it, glad to be able to avoid the men waiting for them in the passageway. They were huddled together, jostling each other, looking back over their shoulders, hardly daring to breathe until they were outside; Bosc and Prullière on the other hand made their way out slowly, laughing when they saw the men earnestly pacing up and down the Variétés Arcade while the young women dashed off along the boulevard with their fancy men. Clarisse was particularly crafty; she didn't trust la Faloise. And in fact he was still in the lodge with the others, all doggedly waiting, on the alert, on Madame Bron's chairs. She shot past like a streak of lightning, hiding behind a friend. The men blinked, bewildered by this sudden rush of swirling skirts at the foot of the staircase and miserable at having waited so long only to see them make their get-away without being able to recognize a single one of them. The litter of black kittens had gone to sleep on the oilcloth tucked against the belly of their mother, lying blissfully with her paws outspread; meanwhile the fat ginger cat was sitting with outstretched tail on the other end of the table watching the women make their escape through his yellow eyes.

'If Your Royal Highness would care to go out this way', said Bordenave at the bottom of the stairs, pointing to the passageway.

A few female extras were still elbowing each other on their way out. The prince was following Nana, with Muffat and the marquis bringing up the rear. There was a long alley-way between the theatre and the neighbouring houses, a sort of narrow lane under a penthouse roof with skylights. The walls were oozing with damp. Their steps echoed hollowly on the flagstones. The passage was full of storehouse litter: a workbench where the porter could plane odd bits of scenery, a pile of wooden barriers used to control the queues at night. There was a street standpipe with a dripping tap; Nana had to pick up her dress as she went by the flooded pavement. At the entrance they all went their separate ways. Once on his own, Bordenave summed up his view of the prince with a philosophical and contemptuous shrug of his shoulders:

'A bit of a bounder, all the same', he said, without further enlightening Fauchery, who was now carted off along with her husband by Rose Mignon, for a reconciliation scene in the conjugal home.

Muffat was left standing by himself on the pavement. His Highness had nonchalantly shown Nana into his carriage. The marquis had dashed off in hot pursuit of Satin and her extra, anxious to catch up with the vicious couple in the vague hope of receiving some special privilege. Muffat, in a fever of excitement, decided to go home on foot. He'd given up the struggle. Forty years of principles and beliefs were being swept away in a flood-tide of new life. As he strode along the boulevards, the deafening rumble of the last carriages on the streets seemed to be calling one single word: 'Nana!' The gas-jets set nude figures dancing before his eyes, the nimble arms and white shoulders of Nana; and he knew that he belonged to her, that he would have abandoned everything, sold all he had, to possess her for one single hour, that very night. His youth was stirring from its sleep; inside this earnest, middle-aged man, this austere Roman Catholic, a passionate adolescent was greedily awakening to the pleasures of sex.

Chapter 6

COUNT Muffat had arrived at Les Fondettes the previous day with his wife and daughter to spend a week at the invitation of Madame Hugon, who was in residence there alone with her son Georges. The late-seventeenth-century house, a simple, austere building, stood in the middle of a vast, square close; but the garden offered superb shade, a series of ponds and artificial waterways supplied by springs, a profusion of greenery, a mass of trees along the Paris–Orléans road breaking the monotony of the flat countryside of arable land which stretched out beyond the horizon.

At eleven o'clock, the second luncheon bell brought the whole party together. Giving her kind, motherly smile, Madame Hugon planted two big kisses on Sabine's cheeks.

'You know, I always do that when I'm in the country . . . I feel twenty years younger seeing you here . . . Did you sleep well in your old bedroom?'

Without waiting for a reply, she turned to Estelle:

'And this little one slept right through, too? Give me a kiss, my dear.'

They were in the immense dining-room which overlooked the park, sitting at one end of the table in order to be closer together. Sabine was very lively and talked of her childhood memories which Madame Hugon had just recalled: the months she spent at Les Fondettes, her long walks, falling into the fountain one summer evening, discovering an old knightly romance on top of a cupboard one winter and reading it in front of a blazing fire of vine-shoots. Georges hadn't seen the countess for a few months and was finding her strange, her face somehow changed; that beanpole Estelle, on the other hand, seemed more reserved than ever, awkward and uncommunicative.

They were having a very simple meal of boiled eggs and cutlets and Madame Hugon was complaining of housekeeping problems: butchers were becoming impossible; she bought everything in Orléans and they never delivered the joints she'd ordered. Anyway, if her guests weren't eating very well, it was their own fault, they'd come too late in the season.

'It's ridiculous', she said. 'I've been expecting you since the middle of June and here we are halfway through September . . . So, as you can see, things aren't at their best.'

And she pointed to the trees in the lawn which were beginning to turn yellow. It was cloudy, and in the distance everything was bathed in a soft, peaceful, melancholy blue haze.

'Oh, I'm expecting guests', she went on. 'That will make things livelier . . . First of all, Georges has invited two friends, Monsieur Fauchery and Monsieur Daguenet, you know them both, I think? . . . Then Monsieur de Vandeuvres, who's been promising to come for the last five years. Perhaps this year he'll finally take the plunge . . .'

'Ah well,' said the countess with a laugh, 'if we can manage to get Monsieur de Vandeuvres . . . He's too busy.'

'What about Philippe?' inquired Muffat.

'Philippe has asked for leave', the old lady replied, 'but I doubt if you'll still be here when he comes.'

Coffee was being served. The conversation had come round to Paris and someone mentioned Steiner. Madame Hugon uttered a little cry as she heard the name.

'Isn't Monsieur Steiner that stout gentleman I met one evening in your house, a banker, isn't he? What a nasty man . . .' she said. 'And now he's bought a property for some actress, on the other side of the Choue, in the direction of Gumières, about a couple of miles from here! Everybody round here thinks it's scandalous! Had you heard anything about that, my dear count?'

'Not a word', replied Muffat. 'So Steiner's bought a country house in the district!'

When he heard his mother broach the subject Georges had started staring into his coffee cup, but now he looked up and stared at the count in amazement. Why was he telling such a blatant lie? Noticing the young man's look, the count threw him a suspicious glance. Madame Hugon was proceeding to give the details: the estate was called La Mignotte; you had to follow the course of the Choue as far as Gumières to cross over a bridge and that added more than a mile to the distance, otherwise you'd get your feet wet and run the risk of a ducking.

'And what's the actress's name?' asked the countess.

'Ah, they did mention it', murmured the old lady. 'You were there this morning, Georges, when the gardener was talking to us . . .'

Georges pretended to be searching his memory while Muffat waited, twirling his spoon in his fingers. Then the countess turned to her husband:

'Isn't Steiner in with that Nana woman who's singing at the Variétés?'

'Yes, that's it, that horrible woman Nana!' exclaimed Madame Hugon heatedly. 'And she's expected to be staying at La Mignotte. I know all this through the gardener . . . That's right, isn't it, Georges? The gardener was saying she's expected this evening.'

The count gave a slight start of surprise. But Georges replied sharply:

'Oh, the gardener didn't know what he was talking about, Mummy. Earlier today, the coachman was saying something quite different, that no one was expected at La Mignotte before the day after tomorrow.'

He was trying to speak in a natural tone of voice, checking the count's reaction out of the corner of his eye. The latter started twirling his spoon again, as if reassured. With the shadow of a smile round her lips, the countess was gazing vacantly out into the distant blue haze of the park and seemed to have lost interest in the conversation, following a secret train of thought which had suddenly come into her mind. Estelle was sitting stiffly in her chair listening to what was being said about Nana without the slightest change of expression on her pale, innocent face.

'My goodness', said Madame Hugon less heatedly, recovering her good humour, 'I'm wrong to lose my temper. People have got to live as best they can . . . If we meet that lady in public, all we need do is to cut her dead . . .'

And as they were leaving table, she again tackled Countess Sabine for being so hard to get that year. The countess defended herself by putting the blame on her husband: twice when they'd packed all their bags he'd cancelled the trip the day before they were due to leave, saying that some urgent business had turned up, and then, when the visit seemed to be definitely off, he'd suddenly decided to go. The old lady said that Georges had similarly twice announced he was coming and never come, and when she'd given up all hope of seeing him he'd arrived the day before yesterday. They had gone out into the garden; the two men on either side of the ladies were bending forward and listening in silence.

'Never mind!' said Madame Hugon, giving her son a few kisses on his golden curls, 'it's very nice of Zizi to come and shut himself away in the country with his old mother . . . He's a kind boy, he doesn't forget her!'

In the course of the afternoon she had reason to be concerned over Georges. Immediately after lunch he had complained of a headache, which seemed gradually to turn into an agonizing migraine. By four o'clock, he decided that the only cure was bed; after a nice long sleep, tomorrow he'd be as fit as a fiddle. His mother insisted on seeing him into bed herself. As she was leaving the room, he jumped out of bed and locked his door, with the excuse that by shutting himself in, nobody would be able to come and disturb him. He called out, 'Goodnight, Mummy dear, see you tomorrow!' in a loving voice, promising he'd sleep right through till morning. But he didn't get back into bed; with eyes sparkling and looking extremely well, he got dressed again without making a sound and sat quietly waiting. When the dinner bell rang, he kept watch until Muffat had made his way down to the drawing-room. Ten minutes later, certain of being unobserved, he climbed nimbly out of the window and let himself down by a drainpipe. His bedroom was at the back of the house, on the first floor. He scuttled into a clump of trees, slipped out of the park, and shot off at full speed towards the Choue. His stomach felt empty, his heart was pounding with emotion. Night was falling, and it had started to drizzle.

Nana was, in fact, due to arrive at La Mignotte that evening. Ever since Steiner had bought her this house in the country in May, she'd had such a longing to settle in there that at times she'd been reduced to tears. But each time Bordenave had refused to release her before September, on the grounds that during the World Fair he couldn't possibly replace her, even for one night. By the end of August, he'd begun to talk of October. Nana was furious and declared she'd be down at La Mignotte by September the fifteenth. She even defiantly issued invitations in Bordenave's hearing. In her flat one afternoon when Muffat, whom she was craftily holding at arm's length, was frantically begging her to stop being so cruel, she finally promised to do what he wanted, not here and now, but at her country house; and she made the date for the fifteenth of September. Then, on the twelfth, she felt an urge not to delay any longer and to go off by herself with Zoé. If Bordenave had advance notice, he might perhaps find a way of stopping her from going. She sent him a doctor's certificate, delighted to be leaving him in the lurch. Once the idea of being the first to arrive at La Mignotte and spend two days there unknown to anyone had taken firm root in her mind, she hustled Zoé into packing their bags, bustled her into a cab, and then gave her a most affectionate hug and asked to be forgiven. It wasn't till they were in the station buffet that the thought occurred to her of sending a note to Steiner, asking him to wait for a couple of days before coming down to join her if he wanted to find her in good shape when he arrived. Then she suddenly had another idea and sent a letter urging her aunt to bring little Louis down straight away. It'd be so good for baby! And what fun they'd have in the woods! In the train she could talk of nothing else the whole way to Orléans, with tears in her eyes, in a sudden fit of motherly love in which flowers, birds, and her son were all jumbled together.

La Mignotte was nearly ten miles from Orléans. It took Nana an hour to find a carriage, a huge, dilapidated barouche which rumbled along, clanging and rattling. She immediately fastened upon the driver, a taciturn little man, pestering him with questions. Had he often been past La Mignotte? It was behind that hill, wasn't it? There were lots of trees, weren't there? Could you see the house a long way off? The little old man replied in grunts. Nana was bouncing up and down with impatience while Zoé, annoyed at having to leave Paris at such short notice, was sitting up stonily and sulking. The horse came to a halt. The young woman thought they'd arrived. Sticking her head out of the window, she asked:

'We're here, are we?'

The driver's reply was to whip up his horse, and they drove laboriously up a hill. Seeing the vast plain spread out under the grey sky, in which big clouds were already gathering, Nana exclaimed delightedly:

'Oh, look at all that grass, Zoé! Is that all wheat? . . . Oh my goodness, isn't it pretty!'

'Madam obviously doesn't come from the country', the maid replied after a pause. 'I got to know it all too well when I was with my dentist in Bougival.* And what's more, it's cold this evening. It's damp in these parts.'

They were driving along under trees. Nana was sniffing the smell of leaves like a puppy. Suddenly, round a bend, she caught sight of a corner of a house through some branches. Perhaps that was it? She questioned the driver, who again shook his head. Then as they were going down the other side of the hill he pointed with his whip and muttered, 'Look over there.'

She jumped to her feet and hung her whole body out of the window.

'Where is it? Where is it?' she shouted, pale-faced, not seeing where he was pointing.

Then she caught sight of part of a wall and again started bouncing up and down, uttering little shrieks like a woman unable to control her emotion.

'Zoé, I can see it, I can see it! . . . Look out the other side . . . Oh, the roof's got a brick terrace on it! And there's a greenhouse over there! Isn't it huge! . . . Oh, I'm so happy! Look over there, Zoé, do look!'

The carriage had stopped in front of an iron gate. A tall, lean man came out of a small door, hat in hand. It was the gardener. Nana tried to control her excitement because the driver seemed to be laughing to himself behind his tightly shut lips. She made an effort not to rush away on her own, and listened to the gardener who, unlike the driver, was very loquacious; madam must please overlook the untidiness because he'd only got her letter that morning; but try as she might, her feet were twinkling over the ground and she was walking so fast that Zoé couldn't keep up with her. At the end of the avenue Nana stopped for a second to take in the whole building. It was a large, vaguely Italian sort of villa with another, smaller building set beside it; it had been built by a rich Englishman who'd spent two years in Naples, and who had then taken an immediate dislike to it.

'Let me show madam over the house', the gardener said.

But she'd gone on ahead, shouting that he needn't bother, she'd sooner go over it by herself. And without stopping to take off her hat, she rushed through the various rooms, telling Zoé to follow, tossing comments over her shoulder as she ran along the corridors and making this empty house, which had been unoccupied for many months, echo with her laughter and her exclamations. First it was the entrance hall: a trifle damp, what did it matter, nobody would be sleeping there! The drawing-room: very smart, with windows looking out over a lawn; only the red material of the furniture was dreadful, she'd be changing all that. And as for the dining-room, well, how about that now, wasn't it magnificent! And think of all the wonderful parties you'd be able to give if you had a dining-room that size in Paris! As she was going up to the first floor, she remembered she hadn't looked at the kitchen, so she ran down again. There were further exclamations; Zoé had to be duly impressed by the beautiful sink and the huge fireplace where you could have roasted a sheep. When she went upstairs again, Nana was particularly excited by her bedroom with its delicate, pink, Louis XVI cretonne hangings from an Orléans upholsterer. Well, you'd certainly enjoy sleeping there! A real cosy schoolgirl's den! Then came four or five guest-rooms and magnificent attics, very handy for trunks. Zoé was lagging behind, fed up and not showing much enthusiasm as she viewed each room. She watched her mistress disappear up the steep ladder leading to the attic. She'd no wish to break her leg, thanks very much! However, she could hear the distant sound of a voice, muffled as if coming down a chimney.

'Zoé, where are you? Come on up! Oh, you can't imagine, it's like a fairy tale!'

Zoé clambered up, grumbling. She found her mistress on the roof, leaning against the brick parapet and looking over the little valley spread out underneath, an immense view, almost hidden by grey mist and a driving drizzle. It was blowing half a gale and Nana was having to hold her hat on with both hands. Her skirt was flapping like a flag.

'Oh no, not for me!' exclaimed Zoé, beating a hasty retreat. 'Madam will be blown away . . . What lousy weather!'

Her mistress wasn't listening; she was bending forward, looking down over the grounds below, some seven or eight acres, completely walled in. The next thing to excite her interest was the vegetable garden. She rushed downstairs, brushing past Zoé and stammering:

'It's full of cabbages! . . . Cabbages as big as that! And lettuces and sorrel and onions, the lot! Come on!'

The rain was coming down faster. She opened her white silk sunshade and ran along the avenues.

'Madam will catch her death!' exclaimed Zoé, taking good care not to move beyond the terrace porch.

But madam was determined to take a look. Each new discovery produced fresh exclamations.

'Zoé, there's some spinach! . . . Do come . . . And artichokes! Aren't they funny? So artichokes have flowers . . . Good Lord, what on earth's that? I don't know what that is. Come along Zoé, perhaps you'll be able to recognize it.'

The maid didn't stir. Madam must be crazy. The rain was now coming down in torrents, the little white silk parasol was already black all over and it wasn't covering madam, her skirt was streaming wet. It didn't seem to bother her. In the pouring rain she continued to inspect the kitchen garden and the orchard, stopping at every tree, bending down to examine each vegetable plot. Then she ran over to take a look down the well, lifted up a frame to see what was underneath and became lost in contemplation of a giant pumpkin. She felt a need to explore all these avenues, to take immediate possession of these things which she used to dream about when she was slopping around the streets of Paris in her working-girl's clogs. It was raining harder than ever but she didn't notice; her only regret was that it was growing dark. She could no longer see things clearly, she had to feel them to discover what they were. Suddenly, in the dim light, she caught sight of some strawberries. She became a child again.

'Strawberries, strawberries!' she exploded. 'They've got

strawberries, I can feel them! . . . Zoé, bring a plate. Come and help me pick strawberries.'

Nana dropped her sunshade and squatted down in the mud, letting the rain soak her. She started picking strawberries, groping under the leaves with her wet hands. But Zoé hadn't brought the plate. As she got up, she had a sudden shock: she thought she'd glimpsed a shadowy figure moving about nearby.

'It's an animal!' she shouted.

Then she stood paralysed in the middle of the avenue. It was a man and it was someone she knew.

'My goodness, it's Baby! What are you doing here, Baby?'

'Why shouldn't I be here?' retorted Georges. 'I just came, that's all!'

She was still in a daze.

'So the gardener told you I was coming? . . . Oh, what a boy! And you're wet through, too!'

'Well, let me explain . . . The rain came on while I was on my way here, I didn't want to go as far as Gumières and as I was crossing the Choue, I slipped into a damned hole!'

Nana immediately forgot all about her strawberries. She was quivering and full of sympathy. Poor Zizi falling into a hole in the river! She started dragging him along back to the house; they'd light a great big fire.

'You know', he whispered, making her stop for a moment in the shadow, 'I was hiding because I was afraid you'd tell me off, like you do in Paris when I come and see you without letting you know in advance.'

Her only reply was a laugh and a kiss on the forehead. Up to now she'd been treating him as a little boy, never taking his protestations of love seriously and making fun of him as just a whipper-snapper. Making him comfortable was quite a business. She insisted on having a fire lit in her own bedroom; they'd be better off there. Zoé hadn't been surprised to see Georges, she was used to every sort of rendezvous; but when the gardener brought up the logs, he was dumbfounded to see the young gentleman streaming with water; he certainly had never let him in himself. They told him he could go, he wasn't needed anymore. A lamp had been lit and the fire was blazing cheerfully.

'He'll never get dry, he's going to catch cold', said Nana seeing Georges give a shiver.

And there were no men's trousers! She was just about to send for the gardener again when a thought struck her. Zoé, who was unpacking the trunks in the dressing-room, brought in some underwear for her mistress to change into, a night-gown, some petticoats, and a dressing-gown.

'But that's ideal', the young woman cried. 'Zizi can put my things on. You've no objection to me, have you? . . . And once your clothes are dry you can put them on again and go back home quickly, so that your mummy isn't cross with you . . . Be quick, I'm going to get changed as well in the dressing-room.'

When she came back ten minutes later in her dressing-gown, she clasped her hands in delight.

'Oh, the darling, how sweet he looks dressed up as a girl!'

He'd merely slipped on a large night-gown with lace inserts, a pair of long, embroidered knickers, and a dressing-gown, a long cambric one trimmed with lace. In it, with his fair skin, bare arms, and tawny hair still wet and wavy down the back of his neck, the boy looked just like a girl.

'And he's as slim as me!' said Nana, catching hold of him round the waist. 'Zoé, come here and see how well it fits . . . It looks as if it had been made for him, doesn't it? The bodice is a bit too big though . . . He's not got as much there as I have, poor little Zizi.'

'Well, yes, I'm a bit lacking up there', Georges said with a smile.

They all laughed. Nana had started buttoning the dressing-gown all the way down, for decency's sake. She turned him round like a doll, giving him little taps, making the skirt flare out at the back. She asked him if that was all right, if he was warm enough. My goodness, wasn't he just! There was nothing warmer than a woman's night-gown, he'd always wanted to wear one if he could. And he wriggled about inside it, enjoying the fine feel of the material; it was loose, it smelt good, and still seemed to have kept something of Nana's living warmth.

Meanwhile Zoé had taken his wet clothes down to the kitchen to get them dried as soon as possible in front of a fire of vine-shoots. Georges was sprawling in an armchair. He wanted to confess something:

'I say, aren't you going to have anything to eat tonight? I'm starving, I missed my dinner!'

Nana was cross. What a silly boy, to run away from mummy like that on an empty tummy and then tip himself into a hole in the river! But she was famished herself. Of course they'd get something to eat! But it would have to be anything they could find. So they moved a little occasional table in front of the fire and improvised the oddest meal. Zoé dashed off to find the gardener who'd cooked a cabbage soup in case madam hadn't had dinner in Orléans before coming on; madam had failed to tell him in her letter what he ought to prepare. Fortunately the cellar was well stocked. So they had some cabbage soup with a bit of fat bacon. Then Nana rummaged in her bag and brought out all sorts of stuff which she'd put in for an emergency: a lump of foie gras, a bag of sweets, and some oranges. They both wolfed everything in sight like a couple of 20-year-old pals who didn't stand on ceremony. Nana had started calling Georges 'my dear girl', it was more fun, it sounded friendly and affectionate. To avoid disturbing Zoé, they took it in turns to use the same spoon for their dessert, a jar of jam discovered on top of a wardrobe, which they knocked off together.

'Well, my dear girl', said Nana, pushing the table aside, 'I haven't had such a good meal for ten years!'

However, as it was getting late, she wanted to send Georges home so that he wouldn't get into trouble, while he kept saying there was plenty of time. Anyway his clothes weren't drying very fast; Zoé said they'd need at least another hour, and as she was tired out by the journey and dropping with sleep, she was sent off to bed. They were on their own in the silent house.

It was a mild, still evening. The fire had by now been reduced to glowing embers and it was a trifle stuffy in the large blue bedroom where Zoé had made up the bed before going upstairs. Nana was feeling too hot and got up to open the window for a second. She gave a little cry:

'My goodness, isn't it lovely! Come and take a look, you dear girl.'

Georges ran over and, slipping his arm round her waist, as if the window-sill was too narrow, he rested his head on Nana's shoulder. The weather had suddenly changed, a deep clear sky was unfolding above and, below, the countryside was bathed in the silvery rays of a full moon. Peace reigned over the little valley which opened out into the vast plain where the trees formed little islands of shadow in the bright, unruffled lake of light. Nana felt her heart melting; memories of childhood came flooding back. Certainly, she had dreamed of such nights in a period of her life which she could no longer recall. Everything that had happened to her since she had got out of the train, this immense landscape, the powerful scent of all these plants, the house, the vegetables, everything was so bewildering that she felt that she'd left Paris twenty years ago. Her previous life seemed far away; she was experiencing emotions she'd never known before. Meanwhile Georges was depositing gentle little kisses on her neck which tickled and flustered her even more. Timidly, she pushed him away, like an over-affectionate child, insisting that he must go now. All right, he didn't object; he'd be off in a minute.

A bird sang and then stopped. It was a robin redbreast in an elder bush under the window.

'Wait', whispered Georges, 'it's scared by the light. I'll turn the lamp out.'

And when he came back, slipping his arm round her waist again, he added:

'We'll light it again in a minute.'

As she listened to the robin and the boy snuggled up to her, Nana was thinking: yes, she'd seen this sort of thing happening in romances. In the old days, she'd have given her heart to have all this, the moon, robins, and a young fellow full of love. Heavens, wasn't everything so nice, so good! She could have cried. Obviously she was born to live a sensible, respectable life. Georges was growing bolder and she was holding him off.

'No, leave me alone, I don't want to, it'd be very wrong at your age . . . Look, I want to be just a mother to you, that's all . . .'

She was blushing with embarrassment and modesty. Yet no one could see her; behind her the night was flooding into the bedroom while outside the deserted countryside was full of stillness and silence. Never before had she felt bashful like this. Little by little, in spite of her embarrassment and reluctance, she was beginning to weaken. She was still finding the disguise, the dressing-gown and woman's night-gown, rather funny. It was as if she was being pestered by a girl-friend.

'Oh, it's not right, it's not right', she faltered.

It was her final effort; surrounded by the beauty of the night, she fell into the boy's arms; she felt like a girl losing her virginity. The house still slept.

When the lunchbell rang at Les Fondettes next day, the table was no longer too big. The first carriage had brought Fauchery with Daguenet and, following them on the next train, the Count de Vandeuvres had just arrived. Georges was the last one down to lunch, looking rather pale, with dark rings round his eyes. He said he was feeling much better but that it had been such a bad attack that he still felt under the weather. Madame Hugon was watching him closely with a worried smile; she smoothed back his hair, which seemed badly combed that morning. He shrank back as if embarrassed by her caress. At table she affectionately teased Vandeuvres, saying that they'd been expecting him for the last five years.

'Well, here you are at last. How did you manage it?'

Vandeuvres turned it into a joke: last night he'd lost an enormous amount gambling at his club, so he'd left Paris and was going to end his days in the country.

'Certainly if you can produce a rich local heiress. Goodness me, there must be some delightful women living round here!'

The old lady was just proceeding to thank Daguenet and Fauchery as well for accepting her son's invitation when she received a most pleasant surprise, as the Marquis de Chouard came into the room; he'd been in a third carriage to arrive at Les Fondettes that morning.

'Well now', she exclaimed, 'it must be a conspiracy amongst you all to meet here this morning, isn't it? What's in the wind? I've been trying to get you all together unsuccessfully for ages and now you're all here at once . . . Oh, I'm not complaining.'

They laid another place. Fauchery was sitting next to Countess Sabine and finding her remarkably lively and cheerful, in contrast to her listlessness in her austere drawing-room in the Rue Miromesnil. Daguenet, on the other hand, on Estelle's left seemed uneasy at sitting so close to this taciturn girl, and was finding her angular elbows uncomfortable. Muffat and Chouard had exchanged a furtive glance. Vandeuvres meanwhile was enlarging on his joke with regard to his impending marriage.

'Talking of ladies', remarked Madame Hugon eventually, 'I've acquired a new neighbour whom you must know.'

She mentioned Nana. Vandeuvres pretended to be greatly surprised.

'Really? Nana's property is near here?'

Fauchery and Daguenet also exclaimed in surprise. The marquis was eating a piece of chicken suprême and didn't seem to understand. None of the men had smiled.

'Yes indeed', the old lady continued, 'and the person in question even arrived at La Mignotte last night, as I was saying. My gardener told me so this morning.'

This time the gentlemen were genuinely surprised and couldn't help showing it. They all looked up. Good Lord! Nana had already arrived? But they weren't expecting her until the next day and thought they'd arrived before her! Only Georges sat gazing at his glass through half-closed eyes with a tired look on his face. Ever since the beginning of lunch he'd seemed to be asleep with his eyes open, vaguely smiling.

'Are you still feeling not very well, Zizi?' asked his mother, watching him closely.

He gave a start, and blushed as he replied that he was feeling fine now. He still had his dreamy look of a girl who's been dancing too long but is greedy to go on.

'What's that on your neck?' asked Madame Hugon in a startled voice. 'It's all red.'

He looked confused and lost for words. He didn't know, there wasn't anything wrong with his neck. He pulled his shirt-collar up.

'Oh yes, something bit me.'

The Marquis de Chouard cast a sidelong glance at the little red mark. Muffat was also looking at Georges. Luncheon was coming to an end and they were making plans for excursions. Fauchery was finding Countess Sabine's laugh increasingly exciting. As he was passing her a plate their hands touched, and for a second she gave him such a dark, piercing glance that once again his mind went back to that secret he'd been told one drunken night. And she was different too, certain things were becoming more marked; her grey silk foulard dress hanging softly over her shoulders added a touch of wantonness to her finely strung elegance.

When they rose from table, Daguenet remained behind with Fauchery, making rude remarks about that funny beanpole of a girl who was going to be pushed into some poor man's arms. But when the journalist told him the size of her dowry—four-hundred thousand francs—he stopped joking.

'And how about the mother, eh?' asked Fauchery. 'Smart, isn't she?'

'Certainly, as far as she's concerned, any time and as often as she likes . . . But not a hope, old man!'

'Rubbish, you can never tell! . . . You'd have to explore . . .'

Nobody was going out that day; it was still showery. Georges had quickly taken himself off to his bedroom and locked himself in. The gentlemen avoided any discussion of their business at Les Fondettes, though they knew well enough why they were all down here together. Vandeuvres, who was in dire straits because of his gambling, really did have thoughts of putting himself out to grass and was relying on having a girl-friend handy should he get too bored. Fauchery was taking advantage of leave of absence from Rose, who was extremely busy at the moment, and he planned to negotiate with Nana on the subject of another article about her, in the hope that the country air would lead to greater warmth in their relationship. Daguenet, who'd been on bad terms with Nana ever since the Steiner episode, was thinking of making it up with her and picking up a few favours should luck smile his way. As for the marquis, he was biding his time. But among all these men pursuing this blonde Venus before she'd even had time to remove all her grease-paint, the keenest of all was Muffat, and the most tormented by the unfamiliar feelings of lust, fear, and anger which were tearing him apart. She had given him her solemn promise and was expecting him. Then why had she left two days early? He determined to go over to La Mignotte after dinner that very night.

That same evening, as the count was leaving the park, Georges slipped away after him, watched him go off along the Gumières road, scrambled across the Choue, and reached Nana's house out of breath, very angry, and with tears in his eyes. Oh, he knew what was happening, that old man was on his way to a rendezvous with her! Flabbergasted by this display of jealousy and upset by the turn things were taking, Nana took him into her arms and comforted him as well as she could. It wasn't true, he was quite wrong, she wasn't expecting anybody. If that man was on his way there it wasn't her fault. What a silly billy he was to get into such a state for no reason at all! She solemnly swore, on her son's head, that she didn't love anybody but her little Zizi. Then she kissed him and wiped away his tears.

'Listen, I'll prove to you I've not got anything left for anyone else', she said when he had calmed down. 'Steiner's here, he's upstairs. And you know that I can't show him the door, don't you, my darling?'

'Yes, I know, I'm not talking about him', the boy muttered.

'Well, I've stuck him away in a bedroom at the back, explaining that I'm not feeling very well. He's unpacking now. So, since nobody saw you come, go upstairs quickly, hide in my bedroom . . . and wait for me.'

Georges flung his arms round her neck. So it was really true? She did love him a bit? So it would be the same as yesterday? They'd turn out the light and stay together in the dark till morning? A bell rang and he quickly made his way upstairs. In the bedroom he slipped off his shoes straight away to avoid making any noise, hid behind a curtain, and lay there obediently waiting on the floor.

When she greeted Count Muffat, Nana was still shaken and rather embarrassed. She'd given him her word and would even have been glad to keep it, because this man seemed earnest and reliable. But who could really have foreseen what had happened yesterday, the journey, the unfamiliar house, the boy who'd turned up wet through; and how nice it had all seemed and how nice it would be to keep on like that! It was just the count's bad luck! She'd been keeping him on tenterhooks for the last three months, pretending to be very proper in order to whet his appetite. Well, he'd have to go on waiting, that's all, and if he didn't like it, he'd have to lump it! She'd sooner give up everything rather than let Georges down.

The count had sat down, like a man making a polite, neighbourly call. Only his hands were trembling. Nana's skilful tactics of breathing hot and cold were finally proving devastating for this chaste, full-blooded man; the dignified chamberlain who would walk solemnly through the state-rooms of the Tuileries Palace during the day, at night would sob and chew his pillow in wild frustration, obsessed by one single erotic vision. This time, however, he was determined to put an end to all that. On his way here, in the deep peace of twilight, he had toyed with thoughts of violence, and after the first few words he attempted to seize hold of Nana with both hands.

'Oh no, oh no, take it gently', she said very calmly.

He grasped her, grinding his teeth, and when she struggled he reminded her crudely, without mincing his words, that he'd come to go to bed with her. Still smiling but embarrassed, she held on to his hands, and to soften her refusal said in a gentle, friendly voice:

'Darling, look, please calm down, please, please, I can't now, Steiner's upstairs.'

But he was out of his mind; never had she seen a man in such a state. She was becoming scared. She put her fingers in front of his mouth to stifle the cries that he was unable to control and lowering her voice pleaded with him to keep quiet and let go of her. Steiner was coming down. He really was being stupid! When Steiner came in he heard Nana saying nonchalantly, as she sprawled in her deep armchair:

'I do adore the country.'

She turned her head and broke off:

'Darling, Count Muffat's here. He was out walking when he saw a light and he's come to say hello to his new neighbours.'

The two men shook hands. Muffat stood in silence for a moment with his face in shadow. Steiner seemed grumpy. They talked about Paris; business was slack, dreadful things had been happening on the Stock Exchange. After a quarter of an hour Muffat left, and as Nana was seeing him out he asked for a rendezvous the following night, but without success. Steiner went up to bed almost immediately afterwards, grumbling about the way women always had something wrong with them. Well, she'd got rid of those two old men at last! When she came upstairs to find Georges, he was still crouching behind his curtain like a good little boy. The bedroom was dark. He pulled her down on to the floor beside him and they started fooling about, rolling round together, stopping and stifling their laughter with kisses each time their bare feet kicked against a piece of furniture. Far away on the Gumières road, Count Muffat was walking along slowly, hat in hand, cooling his burning head in the silence of the night.

For the next few days her life was idyllic. In the boy's arms Nana felt like a 15-year-old girl again. She was used to being with men, who disgusted her; but now love was rekindled by the caresses of a child. She would suddenly blush, shivers would run down her back; she felt a need to laugh and cry, an uneasy, new-born innocence and bursts of sensuality which left her ashamed. Never had she had such feelings before. Country life was flooding her heart with love. As a little girl she had longed to live in a meadow with a nanny goat, because one day on an embankment of the fortifications* she had seen a goat tethered to a stake, bleating. Now this estate, all this land which was hers was making her feelings overflow, for reality had gone so far beyond her wildest ambitions. She was like a little girl discovering emotions she had never felt before; and when at night she went upstairs to find her Zizi hiding behind his curtain, dazed from her day spent in the open, intoxicated by the scent of leaves, she felt like a schoolgirl on holiday having a madcap adventure with a young cousin whom she loved and was going to marry, trembling at the slightest sound, terrified her parents might hear, enjoying the fumbling delights and scary thrills of losing your virginity.

She fell into sentimental, childish fancies. She'd watch the moon for hours on end. One night when the house had gone to sleep she decided to go down into the garden with Georges, and they walked about under the trees with their arms round each other's waists, and lay down in the grass, damp with dew. On another occasion, when they were lying silently in her bedroom, she hid her head in the boy's neck, sobbing and blubbering that she was afraid of dying. She would often sing under her breath one of Madame Lerat's sentimental drawing-room ballads, full of birds and flowers, shedding tears of emotion until she broke off to give Georges a passionate hug and made him promise to love her for ever and ever. In a word, she was being stupid, as she herself recognized when, having recovered their calm, they would sit together like two old friends on the edge of the bed, smoking and tapping their heels against its wooden sides.

But it was the arrival of her little Louis which finally turned her heart into jelly. Her maternal love became hysterical. She would carry her son out on to the lawn to watch him wriggling about in the sun and roll about with him in the grass, after first dressing him up like a little prince. She insisted at once that he must sleep nearby, in the adjoining bedroom, where Madame Lerat, much impressed by life in the country, used to start snoring as soon as she was on her back. But Zizi didn't suffer as a result, quite the opposite, for she said she now had two children to look after and her spontaneous affection included both of them, indiscriminately. A dozen times a night she'd leave Zizi to go and see if Louiset was breathing properly, and when she came back she'd smother her Zizi with all the motherly hugs and kisses she had to spare; she was his mummy too and the boy shamelessly delighted in being cuddled by this big young woman, like a baby being lulled to sleep. It was so charming an existence that she seriously suggested to him never going back to town; they'd send everybody packing and live all by themselves, he and she and her son. And they would work out hundreds of plans until day broke, never hearing Madame Lerat snoring away, sound asleep, tired out from picking wild flowers.

This wonderful life lasted nearly a whole week. Count Muffat made his appearance every evening and went off again with his hands burning and his features congested with blood. One evening he wasn't even allowed in; Steiner had had to go up to Paris and the count was informed that the mistress was not very well. Every day Nana was feeling more and more appalled at the thought of being unfaithful to Georges. Such an innocent little boy who trusted her! She'd have considered herself the lowest of the low! And anyway, she'd have found it disgusting . . . Zoé was watching the progress of this affair with quiet contempt; she thought her mistress must be going off her head.

Suddenly, on the sixth day, a band of visitors burst in on this idyllic scene. Nana had issued invitations to all sorts of people, assuming that they wouldn't come, so she was flabbergasted as well as upset when she saw a busload of people pull up outside La Mignotte's front gate one evening.

'Here we are!' shouted Mignon as he got out first, dragging his sons Henri and Charles after him.

Next Labordette appeared, offering his hand to an endless succession of ladies: Lucy Stewart, Caroline Héquet, Tatan Néné, and Maria Blond. Nana was hoping that was the lot when down jumped la Faloise from the running-board and caught Gaga and her daughter Amélie in his shaky arms. That made eleven in all, and finding accommodation for them wasn't easy. La Mignotte had five guest-rooms, one of which was already occupied by Madame Lerat and Louiset. The largest was allocated to the la Faloise–Gaga set-up, with Amélie sleeping on a camp-bed in the adjacent dressing-room; Mignon and his two sons were put in the third bedroom, and Labordette in the fourth. The remaining room was turned into a dormitory with beds for Lucy, Caroline, Tatan, and Maria. As for Steiner, he could doss down on the divan in the drawing-room. It took an hour to settle everybody in; after being furious to begin with, Nana was now enjoying her role as lady of the manor. The ladies were very complimentary about La Mignotte: what a smashing place, my dear! And they brought with them a whiff of Paris air, last week's gossip, all talking together, laughing, exclaiming, and giving little taps. And by the way, what about Bordenave? How had he reacted to her unceremonious departure? Not very violently, really. After yelling that he'd get the police to fetch her back, he'd merely brought in a replacement that same evening; and this understudy, little Violaine, was even proving quite successful as the blonde Venus. Hearing this, Nana looked pensive.

It was only four o'clock. A tour of inspection was suggested.

'As a matter of fact', said Nana, 'I was just going out to lift some potatoes when you arrived.'

So without even bothering to change, they all trooped out to lift potatoes. Let's make a party of it! The gardener was already in the potato patch at the rear of the property, together with a couple of assistants. Their ladyships went down on their knees, rummaging in the earth with their bejewelled fingers and screaming loudly each time they came upon an outsize potato. What fun it was! Néné was in her element; in her youth she'd lifted so many that she forgot where she was and started offering advice to the others, describing them as stupid. The gentlemen were more lackadaisical. Mignon was good-naturedly taking advantage of this trip in the country to further his sons' education, and was telling them all about Parmentier.*

Dinner that night was a festive and furious occasion. They were all busily stuffing themselves while Nana gabbled away exuberantly, nearly coming to blows with her butler, who'd been in service with the bishop of Orléans. Over coffee, the ladies smoked. An ear-splitting din was escaping through the windows and fading away into the distant peace of the countryside. The yokels lingering between their hedgerows turned to look at the house ablaze with light.

'How annoying that you've got to go back the day after tomorrow', said Nana. 'Anyway, we'll manage to organize something.'

They decided that tomorrow, which was a Sunday, they'd go on a trip to the ruins of the former abbey of Chamont, no more than five miles away. Five carriages would come out from Orléans and pick them all up after lunch, bringing them back to dinner at La Mignotte at about seven o'clock. It'd be charming.

When Count Muffat came up the hill as usual that evening, he was surprised by the blaze of light from the windows and the sound of loud laughter. Hearing Mignon's voice, he realized what had happened and went away again, infuriated at this new obstacle, his patience exhausted, and determined to take drastic action. Georges had the key to a side-door; he crept along the wall of the house and quietly slipped upstairs. However, he found he had to wait till after midnight. When Nana appeared she was very tipsy and even more motherly than on earlier nights. When she'd been drinking she became so amorous that she clung like a leech, and she now insisted that he must come along with her to the abbey of Chamont. He tried to get out of it by pointing out that he was afraid of being seen, and if anyone were to catch sight of him in her carriage there'd be hell to pay. She burst into tears of despair and loudly proclaimed that she was being victimized; to comfort her, he promised he would come on the excursion.

'So you really are fond of me?' she sobbed. 'Tell me that you really are . . . If I died, darling, you would be very unhappy, wouldn't you?'

Having Nana as a neighbour was causing a great to-do at Les Fondettes. Every morning over lunch, in spite of herself, Madame Hugon would come back to the subject and repeat what she had been told by her gardener, with the sort of obsessive fascination that the most respectable women feel towards ladies of easy virtue. Tolerant though she was, she felt exasperated and repelled, with a vague premonition of impending disaster; at night she felt scared, as if some wild beast had escaped from a zoo and was prowling round the district. She took all her guests to task, suspecting them of lurking round La Mignotte. Count de Vandeuvres had been seen on the main road laughing in the company of a woman *not wearing a hat*; but he stood up for himself and denied being with Nana; the truth was that it was Lucy who'd been with him, telling him how she'd just sent her third prince packing. The Marquis de Chouard also went out every day, but he explained that it was on doctor's orders. Madame Hugon was being unfair to Daguenet and Fauchery. The former in particular, having given up his plan of taking up with Nana again, never went out of Les Fondettes and was paying marked and respectful attention to Estelle. Fauchery similarly was spending a great deal of time with the Muffat ladies. Only on one occasion had he met Mignon in a country lane, carrying an armful of wild flowers and giving his sons a botany lesson. The two men had shaken hands and exchanged news of Rose; she was very well; they had each received a letter from her that morning, urging them to continue to benefit from the good country air for a little while longer. So, amongst all her guests only Count Muffat and Georges escaped scot-free; the count, who claimed to have serious business to attend to in Orléans, was certainly not a man to be chasing any bits of skirt, and as for Georges, she was beginning to be seriously worried about him because of his dreadful attacks of migraine every evening which were forcing him to stay in bed during the day.

Meanwhile Fauchery had become a faithful attendant on Countess Sabine when the count had to go off and leave her every afternoon. As they walked to the end of the park, he would carry her folding chair and her sunshade. She was amused by his quirky, shallow journalist's wit, and he was establishing with her one of those easy, casual relationships sanctioned by country customs. She appeared to have accepted this without hesitation; this young man's boisterous jokes could surely never compromise her, and in his company she had regained her youth; now and again, when they happened to be alone for a second, hidden by a bush, in the middle of their laughter, they would suddenly break off and exchange a deep, earnest look, as if they had had a flash of insight and understanding.

At lunch on the Friday there was a new face at table. Monsieur Venot had arrived; Madame Hugon recalled having invited him last winter at the Muffats'. His humble stoop, the image he offered of a good-natured man of no consequence, gave the impression that he was unaware of the uneasy deference surrounding him. Having retreated into the background, as he nibbled little lumps of sugar over dessert, he examined Daguenet who was passing some strawberries to Estelle and listened to one of Fauchery's stories, which was making the countess laugh. As soon as people looked at him, he gave a quiet smile. When they left table, he took Muffat's arm and led him off into the park. It was notorious that he still exercised great influence over the count since his mother's death. There were queer stories going round concerning this ex-solicitor's domination of the family. Fauchery, no doubt embarrassed by his arrival, explained to Georges and Daguenet the origins of his wealth, a big lawsuit in which he had acted for the Jesuits some time ago. According to Fauchery, this fellow with his meek, unctuous manner was a dreadful man who had a finger in every underhand intrigue of the dog-collar brigade. The two young men treated it as a joke, because they thought the old fellow looked a bit of an idiot and the idea of a secret Venot, a super-Venot working hand-in-glove with the clergy, seemed an amusing fancy. But when Count Muffat, still holding the old man's arm, came back red-eyed as if he'd been crying, they fell silent.

'They'll certainly have been having a little chat about hell', muttered Fauchery facetiously.

Countess Sabine overheard this remark and slowly turned to look at him. Their eyes met and lingered, still warily sounding each other out before taking the plunge.

After lunch, they all usually made their way to a terrace overlooking the plain at the far end of the flower garden. On Sunday, the afternoon was delightfully mild. At about ten o'clock there had been a threat of rain but now, although not completely clear, the sky seemed to have melted into a pearly mist, a hazy light shot through with golden sunlight. Madame Hugon suggested going out through the little terrace gate and walking towards Gumières as far as the Choue; she was fond of walking and still very nimble for all her sixty years. In any case, they all agreed that they didn't need a carriage. In this way they arrived in scattered groups at the wooden bridge over the river. Fauchery and Daguenet were leading the way with the Muffat ladies, followed by the count and the marquis accompanying Madame Hugon; Vandeuvres brought up the rear, looking very dapper and bored on this main road; he was smoking a cigar. Monsieur Venot was darting from one group to the other, altering his pace as required, seemingly anxious not to miss anything.

'And poor Georges is in Orléans', Madame Hugon was telling them again. 'He wanted to consult old Doctor Tavernier about his sick headaches. He has his surgery at home these days. Yes, you weren't up, he left before seven. It gives him something to do.'

She broke off and said:

'Goodness me, why have they all stopped?'

The ladies, Daguenet, and Fauchery were standing by the

end of the bridge, looking uncertain, as if something was blocking the way. Yet the road seemed clear.

'Keep going', the count called.

They still didn't move; they were watching something approaching which the others couldn't yet see; there was a bend in the road lined by a closely planted row of poplars. Meanwhile they could hear a dull rumble slowly growing louder, a clatter of wheels mingled with laughter and the cracking of whips. Suddenly five carriages appeared in line, weighed down to the axles with people and blazing with a flashy assortment of gorgeous pale blue and pink dresses.

'What's that?' exclaimed Madame Hugon in surprise.

Then she had an intuition and understood; she was revolted by such an invasion of her road.

'Oh, it's that woman', she muttered. 'Just keep on walking, keep on walking, pretend you don't . . .'

But it was too late. The five carriages taking Nana and her guests to the ruins of Chamont were starting to cross the little wooden bridge. Fauchery, Daguenet, and the Muffat ladies had to step backwards while Madame Hugon and the others, spread out at intervals along the road, also came to a halt. It was a splendid procession. The laughter had stopped and the occupants of the carriages were looking out with curiosity. People stared at each other in silence; the only sound was the steady trot of the horses. In the first carriage Maria Blond and Tatan Néné were lolling back like duchesses, with their skirts fluttering out over the wheels, looking down their noses at these respectable women on foot. Next came Gaga occupying one whole seat and swamping la Faloise, who was sitting beside her with only his worried nose peeping out. Then followed Caroline Héquet with Labordette, Lucy Stewart with Mignon and his sons, and last of all an open victoria* containing Nana accompanied by Steiner and opposite, sitting on a tip-up seat with his knees thrust between hers, was poor darling Zizi.

'She's the last one, isn't she?' the countess asked Fauchery calmly, as if she failed to recognize Nana.

The wheel of the victoria almost brushed against her; she didn't step back an inch. The two women exchanged a searching look, very brief but which sums a person up completely, once and for all. The men behaved impeccably. Fauchery and Daguenet froze and acknowledged no one. Fearing that the ladies might play some funny trick, the marquis nervously broke off a piece of grass which he twiddled between his fingers. Only Vandeuvres, standing somewhat apart from the others, raised an eyelid to Lucy when she smiled at him driving past.

'Take care', muttered Monsieur Venot, standing behind Count Muffat.

The count was gazing in utter bewilderment at this spectacle of Nana careering past under his eyes. His wife had turned her head and was watching him closely. He looked down at the ground as if trying to ignore these swiftly trotting horses snatching away any hope of satisfying his body or his heart, for seeing Georges half-hidden in Nana's skirts, he had suddenly understood. He could have screamed out with pain. A child! He was shattered that she should have preferred a child to him. Steiner he could accept . . . but that little boy!

At first Madame Hugon hadn't noticed Georges, who was thinking of throwing himself into the river while they were crossing the bridge but was held tight between Nana's knees. White as a sheet, he froze and sat motionless staring ahead; perhaps he wouldn't be seen.

'Good heavens!' the old lady exclaimed suddenly. 'That's Georges in there with her!'

The carriages proceeded on their way; the atmosphere was tense; people who were acquainted had refused to recognize each other. The awkward encounter had lasted a few seconds, which had seemed an eternity. However, enlivened by the fresh air, the carriage-loads of young women now became jollier than ever as the wheels clattered away through the golden landscape; vivid flecks of dresses fluttered in the breeze as they started laughing and joking again, turning to look over their shoulders at these prim and proper people standing by the roadside, terribly put out. Looking back Nana saw the walkers hesitate and then retrace their steps, not crossing the bridge. Madame Hugon was leaning on Count Muffat's arm, saying nothing, and with such a sad expression that nobody had the heart to try to comfort her.

'I say, my dear', Nana called to Lucy, who was leaning out

of the next carriage, 'did you see Fauchery? What a nasty look he gave me! I'll get even with him for that . . . And Paul, who I've been so kind to! Not even a nod! . . . Talk about manners!'

And she flared up when Steiner expressed the view that the gentlemen had behaved very correctly. So they weren't even good enough to take your hat off to? They could let any lout insult them? Thanks very much! He was a shit too! That just about put the lid on it! You ought always to take your hat off to a lady.

'Who's the tall one?' called Lucy abruptly, above the rumble of the wheels.

'Countess Muffat', replied Steiner.

'Ah, I suspected as much', said Nana. 'Well, my dear man, she may be a countess but she's not much cop . . . She's a tramp. I can use my eyes, you know, and I know her now as well as if I'd known her all my life, that countess of yours . . . Would you like to bet she goes to bed with that snake-in-the-grass Fauchery? . . . Well, I'm telling you she does! Women have got a nose for that sort of thing!'

Steiner shrugged his shoulders. Ever since yesterday, he'd been growing more and more disgruntled. He'd received letters which meant that he'd got to go back to Paris tomorrow morning; anyway it wasn't much fun making a trip into the country and then having to sleep on the divan in the drawing-room.

'Oh, you poor baby!' exclaimed Nana sympathetically, having suddenly noticed how pale Georges was, still stunned by shock and hardly able to breathe.

'Do you think Mummy recognized me?' he faltered eventually.

'Oh yes, she must have, she gave a cry . . . And it's all my fault too, he didn't want to come and I forced him to! Look, Zizi, would you like me to write to your mum? She looks a very respectable lady, I'll tell her that I'd never seen you before, that it was Steiner who brought you along for the first time today.'

'Oh no, please don't write', said Georges in a very worried voice. 'I'll fix it myself . . . And anyway, if they make a fuss, I'll not go home.'

But he remained pensive, trying to work out what lies he could tell that evening. The five carriages were bowling along over the plain on a straight road lined with fine trees, that went on and on. The countryside was bathed in an airy, silvery grey light. Their ladyships continued to call out to each other from their carriages behind the backs of their drivers, who were laughing at this strange bunch of customers; from time to time one of them would stand up to take a look and then persist in remaining on her feet, leaning on her neighbour's shoulders until a jolt flung her back into her seat. Meanwhile Caroline Héquet was deep in conversation with Labordette; both were agreed that in less than three months from now Nana would be disposing of her property, and Caroline was asking Labordette to buy it on her behalf, surreptitiously, for a song. In front of them, the highly amorous la Faloise, unable to reach the back of Gaga's apoplectic neck, was kissing one of her vertebrae through her dress, which seemed on the point of splitting, while Amélie sat stiffly on the edge of her tip-up seat, urging them to stop it, thoroughly annoyed at having to sit with her legs dangling and watch her mother being kissed. In the other carriage Mignon was trying to impress Lucy by getting his sons to recite one of La Fontaine's fables; Henri in particular was a star performer, he could do it for you straight off without a single mistake. In the front carriage, however, Maria Blond was bored stiff, having finally become tired of pulling that twerp Tatan Néné's leg; she'd been telling her that in Paris they manufactured eggs out of saffron and glue . . . The trip was lasting too long, wouldn't they ever get there? Her question was passed back from one carriage to the next until it reached Nana who, after enquiring from her driver, stood up and shouted:

'Only a quarter of an hour longer. Can you see that church over there, behind the trees? . . .'

And she added:

'You'll never guess, it appears that the woman who owns the Château de Chamont is a veteran tart from the time of Napoleon . . . And she really lived it up, according to Joseph, who's got it from the servants at the bishop's palace . . . You know, really wild, they don't make them like that anymore.

Now she's got priests all over her.'

'What's her name?' asked Lucy.

'Madame d'Anglars.'

'Irma d'Anglars? I knew her once!' exclaimed Gaga.

There was a chorus of exclamations from the other carriages, which subsided as the drivers whipped up their horses. The girls were craning their necks to look at Gaga; Maria Blond and Tatan Néné knelt upon their seats to see better, holding on to the open hood. Everybody was firing questions, and though some of their comments were hardly kind it was obvious that they were secretly admiring Gaga who had once known Madame d'Anglars. This remote past deserved great respect.

'Well, naturally I was very young', Gaga continued. 'All the same, I can recollect her, I saw her going by . . . People said that in her home she was disgusting, but in her carriage you can't imagine how smart she looked! And there were all sorts of amazing stories about dirty tricks and swindles that would make you die with laughing . . . I'm not surprised she's got a château. She'd clean a man out in two shakes of a lamb's tail . . . So Irma's still alive! Well, duckies, she must be getting on for 90!'

The ladies looked suddenly earnest. Ninety! As Lucy exclaimed, there wasn't one of them likely to live that long. Old crocks, that's what they were, the lot of them! Nana said that she didn't want to make old bones anyway, it was nicer to have fun.

They were nearing their destination and their conversation was cut short by the crack of the drivers' whips as they speeded up their horses. However, in the middle of all this noise Lucy changed the subject and started urging Nana to leave with the rest of the gang tomorrow. The World Fair would be closing down and the ladies had to go back to Paris, where the season was fulfilling their wildest expectations. Nana wasn't keen; Paris was loathsome, it'd be a long time before she set foot there again . . .

'That's right, isn't it, darling? We'll stay on here, shan't we?' she said, ignoring Steiner's presence and squeezing Georges' knees between her own.

Suddenly the carriages all stopped, and as the surprised

passengers clambered out, they saw that they were in a deserted spot at the foot of a little hill. One of the drivers had to point out with his whip the ruins of the old abbey of Chamont tucked away amongst trees. There was great disappointment. Their ladyships thought it ridiculous: just a few heaps of old stones covered in brambles and a half-tumbledown tower! It certainly wasn't worth driving all that way! The driver then pointed out the château, whose park adjoined the abbey, and recommended them to follow a little path along the walls; they could go all the way round on foot while the carriages would drive on and wait for them in the village square. It was a charming walk. The girls agreed.

'Gosh, Irma's done herself proud!' said Gaga, stopping in front of an iron gate by the roadside on the corner of the park. They all looked in silence at the huge thicket blocking the gateway. Then they followed the little path alongside the park wall, looking admiringly up at the overhanging branches of the tall trees which formed a thick green canopy above. Three minutes later they came to another gate; this one gave a view on to a large lawn shaded by two widespreading ancient oaks. Then, after another three minutes, yet another gate gave a vista on to an immense avenue, a shady tunnel at the end of which the sun was gleaming like a star. At first they were dumb with surprise but then they started chattering excitedly, trying to joke about it but with a touch of envy. They were obviously impressed: what a super woman that Irma must have been! That sort of thing showed you what a woman was capable of! The trees went on and on, and all the time they kept seeing ivy-clad walls with lodge-roofs peeping up above them, and thick clumps of elms and aspens followed by screens of poplars. Wouldn't they ever come to an end? Tired of following the curving track and never getting an open view of anything except thick greenery, the ladies were longing for a glimpse of the house. They grasped the iron bars with both hands, pressing their noses hard against them; they were beginning to be overcome by a sense of awe at being kept at such a distance; it was turning into a sort of fairy-tale château, hidden away in a vast domain. And as they were unused to walking, they soon began to feel tired. Yet still the wall went on and on; at each bend in the little deserted track there was the same long line of grey stone. Despairing of ever reaching the end, some of them were suggesting turning back; but the more exhausted they felt, the more respectful they became. Every step made the quiet grandeur of the park seem more majestic and more royal.

'We're being idiotic', exclaimed Caroline Héquet, gritting her teeth.

Nana silenced her with a shrug of her shoulders. For the last few minutes she hadn't spoken. She looked pale and very earnest. At the last bend, as they came out on to the village square, the wall suddenly ended and the château appeared at the back of the great forecourt. They all stopped, staggered by the size and splendour of the broad terraces, the façade with its twenty windows, the three extensive wings built in brick with string-courses of stone. Henri IV had lived in this historic château, and they had preserved his bedroom with his big bed draped in Genoa velvet. Nana gave a breathless little gasp, like a child.

'Hell's bells!' she said quietly, under her breath.

There was another shock: Gaga suddenly exclaimed that it was Irma herself over there in front of the church. She recognized her perfectly: as straight-backed as ever and still that look in her eyes when she put on her grand air. They were coming out of Vespers. Madame Irma stood for a second under the porch. In her sober silk dress she looked very tall and neat, with the venerable aspect of some old marchioness who had survived the horrors of the Revolution. Carrying a large, glossy prayer-book in her right hand, she walked slowly across the square followed by a liveried footman fifteen steps behind. People were coming out of church; all the inhabitants of Chamont were bowing deeply to her and an old man kissed her hand, while a woman almost knelt down at her feet. She was like a queen, full of years and honours and power. She went up on to the terrace of the château and vanished inside.

'That's what you can achieve if you're organized', said Mignon solemnly, looking at his two sons to point the moral.

They all added their comments. Labordette thought she was wonderfully well preserved; Maria Blond made an indecent remark which annoyed Lucy, who said that old age should command respect. In general, the ladies all thought she was fantastic. They got into their carriages. The whole way back to La Mignotte, Nana didn't open her mouth. Twice she turned round to look back at the château. Lulled by the sound of the wheels, she didn't even feel Steiner sitting beside her or see Georges sitting opposite; in the evening twilight she was watching a vision, she could still see the lady of the château going by, majestic and queenly, full of years and honours and power.

That night Georges went back to Les Fondettes for dinner. Nana, who seemed increasingly absent-minded and peculiar, had insisted on his going home to apologize to his mother; it was only right and proper, she said sternly, showing a sudden burst of respect for family life. She even made him promise not to come back to spend the night; she was tired, and the least he could do was to obey. Georges went off to see his mother, heavy-hearted and crestfallen, extremely annoyed by her sermon. Fortunately his brother Philippe, a tall, very lively young officer, had arrived, which cut short the scene he'd been dreading. Madame Hugon merely looked at him tearfully, and when Philippe was informed of his escapade he threatened to go over and drag him back by the ear if he ever went near that woman's place again. Georges was greatly relieved and started slyly calculating how he might slip away tomorrow at about two o'clock and fix the times when he could call on Nana.

However, the atmosphere amongst the guests at Les Fondettes that night at dinner was strained. Vandeuvres had announced his departure; he was hoping to take Lucy back to Paris, thinking it would be fun to make off with this young woman, whom he'd been seeing for the last ten years without once wanting to go to bed with her. The Marquis de Chouard was contemplating his plate and thinking of Gaga's daughter; he could recall dandling Lili on his knees; how children did shoot up! And the little girl was filling out nicely, too . . . Count Muffat in particular was very silent and lost in thought; his face was flushed. He had given Georges a long look. On rising from table, he went off and shut himself up in his room, complaining of feeling a trifle feverish. Monsieur Venot hurried after him and there was a scene between them upstairs; the count had collapsed on his bed, nervously sobbing into his pillow while Venot, addressing him as 'my brother in Christ', called on him to throw himself on God's infinite mercy. The count was gasping and whimpering and didn't hear him. Suddenly, he sprang up from the bed and stammered:

'I'm going to see her . . . I can't bear it any longer!'

'Very well', the old man replied. 'I'll come with you.'

As they were leaving the park, two shadowy figures disappeared into the depths of a dark avenue. Every evening Fauchery and Countess Sabine were now letting Daguenet help Estelle to see to the tea after dinner. When he reached the main road, the count walked so fast that his companion had to trot to keep up with him, but his breathlessness did not prevent the old man from producing a stream of the strongest arguments against the temptations of the flesh. The other man pressed on through the night, not saying a word. When he came to La Mignotte he said simply:

'I can't go on like this. Go away.'

'Then God's will be done,' said Monsieur Venot in a gentle voice. 'He works in many mysterious ways to conquer evil . . . Your sinfulness will be one of them.'

During the meal at La Mignotte, there had been squabbles. Nana had got a letter from Bordenave advising her to take a rest, apparently quite unconcerned what she would do; little Violaine was getting two curtain-calls every night. And when Mignon urged her to leave with them tomorrow, Nana flared up and said she didn't need advice from anybody. Moreover, at table she'd been ridiculously prim. When Madame Lerat used a coarse expression she had said that she didn't allow anyone, not even her aunt, to talk obscenely in her house, for Christ's sake! Then she got on everybody's nerves with her moralizing and her sudden cult of respectability, which included thoughts of providing Louiset with a religious education and adopting a whole programme of good behaviour for herself. When people laughed she became very earnest, wagging her finger like a paragon of middle-class morality and explaining that the only way to succeed in life was to be orderly; *she* didn't want to die in the workhouse. Their ladyships were irritated and exclaimed: 'It's not possible!

That's not our Nana!' But she sat very still, lost in visions, dreaming of a Nana very rich and revered.

As they were going to bed, Muffat arrived. It was Labordette who sighted him in the garden, realized what was afoot, helped him by keeping Steiner out of the way, and led him by the hand along a dark passageway up to Nana's bedroom. In such matters, Labordette had the perfect touch: discreet, shrewd, and, as it were, utterly delighted at making other people happy. Although she was annoyed, Nana showed no surprise at seeing Muffat pursuing her so passionately. Life was real and life was earnest, wasn't it? Love was stupid, it got you nowhere. And she did have qualms about Zizi because he was so young; she really had behaved badly there. Ah well, she was going to get back on to the right track, she'd go for an old man . . .

'When you get up tomorrow, Zoé, pack our bags, we're going back to Paris', she said to her maid, who was thrilled at the thought of getting away from the country.

And without enjoyment, she went to bed with Muffat.

Chapter 7

ONE December evening three months later, Count Muffat was walking through the Passage des Panoramas. It was a very mild night and there had just been a shower; people had crowded into the narrow arcade for shelter and were slowly and laboriously threading their way between the shop-fronts. The glass roof was gleaming with bright reflections and the passage was ablaze with light from the white globes, the red lamps, the blue transparencies, and banks of flaring gas-jets depicting giant watches and fans flickering in the air; and behind the clear plate-glass shop-windows, the gaudy displays, the gold of the jewellers, the crystal ware of the confectioners were all glittering in the glare of the reflectors; amidst the motley collection of garish shop-signs, a huge purple glove seemed from afar like a bleeding severed hand held on by a yellow cuff.

Count Muffat strolled up to the boulevard, glanced out into the street, and came slowly back, keeping close to the shop-fronts. In the narrow arcade the steamy air was producing a luminous haze. The only sound along the passage was the constant echo of footsteps on the flagstones, wet from dripping umbrellas. He was being constantly elbowed by these silent, scurrying passers-by, who gazed in curiosity at this tight-lipped man whose face was livid in the light of the gas. To escape their inquisitive stare, the count took up his stand in front of a stationer's shop and studied with close attention a display of round, glass paperweights in which flowers and landscapes were floating.

But he didn't see them; he was thinking of Nana. Why had she once again lied to him? That morning she'd written telling him not to bother to come round that evening because Louiset wasn't well, and she'd be spending the night at her aunt's looking after him. Being suspicious, he had gone round to her house where the portress had told him that madame had just left to go round to her theatre. This surprised him, for she wasn't in the latest show. Why had she lied and what could she be doing at the Variétés that night?

A passer-by bumped against him, and without realizing it the count left the paperweights and found himself standing absent-mindedly in front of a cheap gift shop displaying notebooks and cigar-holders, all marked with the same blue swallow in a corner. Certainly, Nana was not the same; in the early days, when they'd come back from the country, she would make him crazy with lust as she kissed him all over his face and whiskers, stroking and fondling him, calling him her darling honey-bunch, and swearing he was the only man for her. He now had no fear of Georges, whose mother was keeping him under strict watch at Les Fondettes. There was still old Steiner, whom he thought he'd eliminated, though this was something he was not anxious to pry too closely into. He did know that Steiner was once again in an appalling financial tangle, close to being hammered on the Stock Exchange and pinning his hopes on the Landes Saltpans Co., out of whose shareholders he was desperately squeezing the last penny. Whenever he met him at Nana's, she explained, reasonably enough, that she couldn't just throw him away like a worn-out glove after all the money he'd spent on her. In any case, for the last three months Muffat had been living in such a daze of sensual pleasure that he had no clear ideas at all apart from his need to go to bed with her. The joys of the flesh had been revealed to him late in life, and like a greedy little boy he had no room for vanity or jealousy. There was only one precise impression which was causing him alarm: Nana was not being as kind as she had been, she'd stopped kissing him on his beard . . . He was worried, and being a man who knew nothing about women he was wondering what he'd done wrong. Yet surely he was doing everything possible to please her? And he kept coming back to the letter he'd got that morning, to this additional puzzle of her lying merely to be able to spend the evening at her theatre. The crowd had by now shifted him further along and he'd finally reached the far end of the passage, still wrestling with his problem in front of the entrance to a restaurant, where he was standing staring at the plucked larks and large salmon displayed in the window.

Finally managing to tear himself away from these objects,

he shook himself, looked up, and realized that it was nearly nine o'clock. Nana would be coming out, he'd demand to know the truth. He walked on, recalling previous evenings he'd spent here when he used to pick her up at the stage-door. He knew all the shops, and in the air full of gas fumes he could recognize the smells, the tang of Russian leather, the scent of vanilla coming from the basement of a chocolate shop, the gusts of musk through the open door of the perfumeries. So now he didn't dare stop in front of the pale lady-assistants at the counter placidly looking at him, as a face familiar to them. For a second he seemed to be examining the row of little round windows above the shops, as though he were seeing them for the first time in the jumble of shop-signs. Then he again walked up as far as the boulevard and remained standing there for a minute. The rain had turned into gentle drizzle, cooling his hands and calming him down. He'd started thinking of his wife, who was staying in a château near Mâcon* where her friend Madame de Chezelles had been in very poor health since the autumn; on the roadway, carriages were splashing through a river of mud; in such horrible weather the country must be dreadful. Then, feeling suddenly worried, he went back into the stuffy arcade and walked quickly through the throng of passers-by: the thought had just occurred to him that if Nana was suspicious, she'd slip out through the Galerie Montmartre.

The count decided that from now on he'd keep watch on the stage-door. He didn't like waiting in this part of the passage, where he was afraid of being recognized. It was at the corner of the Galerie des Variétés and the Galerie Saint-Marc, a seedy sort of place with gloomy shops, a cobbler permanently without customers, dusty furniture-stores, a smoky, dozy, reading-room whose lamps gleamed with a tired green light at night, under their cowls; and the only people ever seen in this corner were patient, well-dressed gentlemen, prowling round the fauna cluttering up the stage-door entrance, drunken stage-hands and slatternly extras. To light up the entrance there was only one gas-jet in a frosted globe. For a moment Muffat toyed with the idea of questioning Madame Bron; then he was afraid that, if forewarned, Nana might make her escape along the boulevard. He resumed his patrol, determined to wait until told to leave when they closed the gates, something which had already happened twice; the thought of going home alone was excruciating. Whenever hatless young women or scruffy-looking men came out and stared at him, he went back and stood in front of the reading-room, between two posters stuck on the window where he saw the same sight as before: a little old man sitting all alone at the huge table, in a patch of green light, with green hands, reading a green newspaper. But a few minutes before ten another gentleman, a tall, good-looking man with fair hair and wearing tight-fitting gloves, came up in front of the theatre as well. Each time they passed, they gave each other a furtive glance, with a look of distrust. The count walked along as far as the corner of the two arcades, adorned with a tall panel of mirror-glass; when he saw himself looking so dignified and solemn, he felt a mixture of shame and fear.

It struck ten. Muffat suddenly realized that it was very easy for him to discover if Nana was in her dressing-room. He went up the three steps, crossed the tiny, yellow distempered entrance hall, and slipped out into the yard through a latched door. At this time of night the narrow courtyard, as damp as the bottom of a well, with its stinking toilets, its water tap, the kitchen oven, and the clutter of plants left there by the caretaker, was hidden in a murky haze; but the two high walls were ablaze with lighted windows: down below, the props room and the firemen's duty room; on the left the manager's office, and on the right and above, the dressing-rooms, giving the impression, all the way up this sort of pit-face, of oven-doors opening out on to the gloom. The count had seen straight away that the windows of the dressing-rooms on the first floor were all lit up. Happy and relieved, still looking up, he relaxed, amidst the stale stench and sticky mud of this backyard of an old Paris house. From a broken gutter large drops of water were dripping, while a stray beam of light from Madame Bron's window cast a yellow patch on to a few mossy cobbles, the foot of the wall eaten away by water from a sink, a real rubbish tip cluttered with old pails and cracked earthenware pots and pans; a limp euonymus provided a touch of green. The count heard the scraping of a window-latch and made himself scarce.

Nana would certainly be coming down. He went back to look at the reading-room; in the sleepy half-light the little old man hadn't stirred; his tired profile was still poring over the newspaper in the dim glimmer of the lamp. Muffat set off again, going further afield, walking through the large arcade and the Galerie des Variétés up to the Feydeau Arcade, cold and deserted and sunk in lugubrious gloom; he retraced his steps, passed in front of the theatre, went round the corner of the Galerie Saint-Marc, and ventured as far as the Galerie Montmartre where he watched with interest sugar being sawn up into pieces in a grocer's shop. But the third time round, afraid that Nana might give him the slip while he wasn't looking, he stopped being concerned about what people might say and stationed himself beside the fair-haired gentleman directly in front of the theatre; they exchanged a brotherly look of humiliation, with a glint of lingering distrust as to possible rivalry. Some stage-hands who'd come out to smoke their pipes during the interval barged into them without either of them daring to protest. Three tall, unkempt young women in dirty dresses were standing in the doorway crunching apples and spitting out the pips; and the two men had to put up with their impudent stares and foul language, keeping their eyes fixed on the ground as the little sluts bespattered and made fun of them, amusing themselves by pushing each other so that they lurched into the two men.

At that very moment, Nana made her way down the three steps. Seeing Muffat, she went very pale.

'Oh, it's you', she faltered.

Recognizing her, the extras who'd been jeering became scared and froze to attention, looking very earnest, like servants caught fooling around by their mistress. The tall, fair-haired man had moved off, looking mournful but reassured.

'Well, give me your arm', added Nana impatiently.

They walked quietly away. The count had planned what to ask her but was unable to find anything to say. It was left to her quickly to blurt out her story: she'd been at her aunt's till eight o'clock, then, seeing that Louiset was much better, she'd thought she might drop in at the theatre.

'Anything important?'

'Yes, a new play', she answered, after a moment's hesitation. 'They wanted my opinion.'

He saw she was lying. But the warmth of her arm pressing heavily on his own left him weak and defenceless. He no longer felt angry or resentful at being made to wait so long; his only concern was not to let her go now she was there. He'd wait till tomorrow to try to find out what she'd been doing in her dressing-room.

Still looking evasive, and obviously trying to regain her composure, when they'd turned into the Variétés Arcade Nana stopped in front of a fan-maker.

'I say', she murmured, 'that mother-of-pearl decoration with the feather trimming is pretty!'

Then unconcernedly:

'So you'll be coming home with me, will you?'

'Of course', he replied in a surprised voice. 'Now that your son's better . . .'

She was sorry she'd told that story. Perhaps little Louis had had a relapse; she talked of going back to Batignolles. When he volunteered to go back with her she didn't pursue the matter, and for a second experienced the blind fury of a woman who feels trapped but has to appear amiable. In the end she decided to play for time and accept the situation; as long as she could get rid of him around midnight, everything would be all right.

'Yes, of course, you're a bachelor tonight', she murmured. 'Sabine won't be back until tomorrow morning, will she?'

'No', replied Muffat, rather embarrassed at hearing her refer to the countess in such familiar terms.

But she persisted, wanting to know the time of the train and enquiring whether he'd be going to meet it. She'd started loitering again, apparently greatly interested in the shops.

'Just look at that odd bracelet!' she exclaimed stopping in front of another jeweller's shop.

She adored the Passage des Panoramas, a survival of her childhood passion for flashy fancy goods, dress jewellery, fake leather, and rolled gold. Whenever she went through there, she could never tear herself away from the various displays, just like the down-at-heel little chit of a girl who used to stand dreamily staring at the sweets in a confectioner's, listening to a barrel-organ playing in a nearby shop; she had a special weakness for cheap and gaudy knick-knacks, vanity cases made of nutshells, rag-and-bone men's baskets in which to stuff toothpicks, or thermometers in the shape of Vendôme columns and obelisks.* But tonight she was too upset, she was just staring blankly. What a pest it was not to be free! And her secret resentment was beginning to give her a wild urge to do something stupid. What advantage was there in going for respectable lovers? She'd just cleaned out the prince and Steiner on childish spending-sprees and couldn't think where the money had gone. Her flat in the Boulevard Haussmann wasn't even completely furnished; only the drawing-room, all in red satin, which struck quite a false note by being too ornate and too crowded. Yet she was now being dunned by creditors, more than in the old days when she hadn't a penny; she felt continually baffled by this because she considered herself a model of frugality. For the last month that shark Steiner had been having the greatest difficulty in raking together a thousand francs when she'd threatened to kick him out if he didn't cough up. As for Muffat, he was an idiot who didn't know how much a man was supposed to give a girl, and she couldn't feel cross with him for his meanness. Oh, how she'd have loved to get away from all these people, if she hadn't told herself a dozen times a day that she must behave properly! Every morning Zoé told her that she must be sensible, and she herself still kept that pious memory, the ever-present vision of the Queen of Chamont, who became grander every time she thought of her. This was why she hung submissively on to the count's arm, quivering with suppressed rage as she went from one shop-window to the next through the bustle of passers-by, now thinning out. Outside the road was drying and a cool wind swirled through the arcade, sweeping the hot air away from the glass roof, flustering the coloured lanterns, the banks of gas-jets, and the fan flaring like a giant firework display. A waiter was putting out the light in the globe outside the restaurant while in the brilliantly lit, deserted shops the lady-assistants were standing motionless as if they'd fallen asleep with their eyes open.

'Oh, the pet!' exclaimed Nana in front of the end shop-window, retracing her steps to look fondly at a greyhound made out of biscuit, holding up a paw beside a nest hidden in roses.

They finally left the arcade; she refused to take a cab. The weather was very nice, she said; anyway, there was no rush, it'd be charming to go home on foot. Then as they passed the Café Anglais,* she said she fancied something, a few oysters perhaps; she'd not had a bite to eat since that morning because of Louiset's illness. Muffat didn't dare to object. As he still preferred not to appear with her in public, he asked for a private room. He walked quickly along the corridor, while she followed like a woman on familiar territory; a waiter opened the door and just as they were about to go in, a man dashed out of an adjoining room from which great bursts of laughter and shouting were proceeding. It was Daguenet.

'Good Lord, Nana!' he exclaimed.

The count quickly dived into his room, leaving the door ajar. But as his stooping figure disappeared, Daguenet gave a wink and added jocularly:

'Christ, you're doing yourself proud, aren't you! You're picking them up in the Tuileries now!'

Nana gave a smile, holding her finger to her lips to warn him to be quiet. Though he was obviously pretty tight, she was still glad to see him. True, he had played a dirty trick on her by refusing to recognize her when he'd been with those respectable ladies, but she still had a soft spot for him.

'How goes it with you?' she enquired amiably.

'I'm going to settle down. No, I'm not joking, I'm thinking of getting married.'

She shrugged her shoulders with a look of pity. But he went on to explain that it was no sort of life, playing the Stock Exchange and earning barely enough to provide bunches of flowers for the ladies, at any rate, if he wanted to keep his hands clean. His three-hundred thousand francs had lasted just eighteen months. He wanted to be practical, he'd marry a big dowry and finish up as a prefect, like his father. Nana was still smiling incredulously. She nodded towards the room he'd just come from:

'Who's with you in there?'

'Oh, a whole gang of people', he blurted out drunkenly, forgetting all about his schemes. 'Just imagine, Léa's giving us an account of her trip to Egypt. It's hilarious! She's got a story about something that happened in a Turkish bath . . .'

He told Nana the story. She listened obligingly. By now they were leaning against the wall, facing each other across the corridor. Gas-jets were flaring under the low ceiling and vague kitchen smells lingered in the folds of the hangings. Now and again, in order to hear each other when the noise from the next room became too deafening, they were forced to put their faces closer together. Every twenty seconds a waiter carrying dishes would have to disturb them to make his way through. Without breaking off, they drew back against the wall, jostled by the waiters, and went on chatting against the noisy background provided by the supper-party as quietly as if they were talking in their own homes.

'Look at that', whispered the young man, pointing to the door of the private room into which Muffat had vanished.

They both looked. The door was moving slightly, as if quivering in a draught. Finally it closed, extremely slowly, without making the slightest sound. The pair exchanged a silent laugh. The count must be looking pretty silly all alone in there.

'By the way', she asked, 'did you read Fauchery's article on me?'

'Oh yes, "The Golden Fly"', Daguenet replied. 'I didn't mention it because I thought it might be a rather painful subject.'

'Painful? Why should it be? It's a very long article.'

She was flattered to receive any attention from the *Figaro*. Her hairdresser Francis had brought the article along, and without his explanations she wouldn't have realized that it was about her. Daguenet was watching her furtively, tongue in cheek, with a grin on his face. Well, if she was happy, why shouldn't everybody be.

'Excuse me!' shouted a waiter, coming between them holding a bombe glacée in both hands.

Nana took a step towards the private room where Muffat was waiting.

'Ah well, goodnight then', said Daguenet. 'Off you go to your friend the cuckold . . .'

She stopped:

'Why do you call him that?'

'Because he is one, for goodness sake!'

She came back and leant against the wall, greatly intrigued.

'Oh!' she said simply.

'Good Lord, didn't you know? His wife goes to bed with Fauchery, my dear girl . . . It must have started while they were in the country . . . Fauchery left our party just a short time ago and I suspect he'll be waiting for her at his flat tonight. I think they've pretended she's gone away on a visit.'

Nana was speechless with surprise.

'I thought he might be!' she exclaimed eventually, slapping her thighs. 'I guessed it that time, just by seeing him walking along the road with her . . . What do you know, a respectable married woman deceiving her husband with a bastard like Fauchery! He'll be teaching her some fine tricks!'

'Oh, she's not a beginner', murmured Daguenet spitefully. 'I expect she's as good at that sort of thing as he is.'

She exclaimed indignantly:

'Really? . . . What a fine lot they are! It's too disgusting for words!'

'Excuse me!' bawled a waiter laden with bottles, pushing his way between them.

Daguenet caught hold of her hand for a second, drawing her closer. He'd put on his silvery voice, like the sound of a glass harmonica, which women found so irresistible.

'Goodnight, darling . . . You know, I still love you.'

With a smile she pulled herself free, and speaking through the barrage of shouts and cheers which were making the door of the room beside them shake:

'You're a silly boy . . . It's all over and done with . . . But never mind. Come up and see me sometime. We'll have a little chat.'

Then, looking very earnest again, like a respectable married woman, she said indignantly:

'So his wife's deceiving him . . . Well, you know, my dear, that's embarrassing. I've never been able to stand cuckolds.'

When she at last rejoined Muffat, he was sitting resignedly on a narrow divan, white in the face; his hands were twitching.

He made no attempt to complain. She was still very disturbed and torn between pity and contempt. Poor man, humiliated and deceived by his horrible wife! She felt an impulse to fling her arms round his neck to comfort him. All the same, it served him right, he was stupid where women were concerned; that'd teach him a lesson. However, pity won the day. After having her oysters, she didn't leave him, as she had promised herself to do. They spent barely fifteen minutes in the Café Anglais before going back to the Boulevard Haussmann. It was eleven o'clock; there'd be ample time to get rid of him gently before midnight.

As Zoé was letting them in, Nana took the precaution of giving her whispered instructions:

'Keep an eye open and warn him not to make any noise if the other man's still here.'

'But where shall I put him, madam?'

'Keep him in the kitchen. It's safer.'

In the bedroom, Muffat was already removing his frock-coat. There was a big fire. There had been no change in the bedroom, still with its rosewood furniture, its draperies, and chairs in figured damask with large blue flowers on a grey background. Nana had twice thought of redoing it, the first time all in black velvet, the second in white satin with pink bows; then, as soon as Steiner had agreed, she'd demanded the necessary funds which she'd promptly frittered away. She had, however, satisfied her whim for a tiger-skin hearth-rug and a cut-glass night-light hanging from the ceiling.

'I'm not sleepy', she said when they were by themselves. 'I shan't go to bed yet.'

Now he was no longer in danger of being seen, the count was prepared to agree to anything; his only concern was not to annoy her.

'Do whatever you like', he said gently.

However, he still took off his boots before sitting down in front of the fire. Nana enjoyed undressing in front of her wardrobe so that she could see her whole body in the mirror. She took off everything, even her chemise, and stood there naked, lost in contemplation of herself. She adored her own body, her satin-smooth skin, the flowing curves of her waist and she would stand there sunk in thought, completely absorbed in her self-adoration. Her hairdresser would often find her like that and she wouldn't even look round. Then she was surprised when Muffat got cross. What was he fussing about? It was for herself, not for anybody else.

Tonight, anxious to take a better look, she lit the six bracket candle-lights. But as she was slipping out of her last garment she stopped; she had something on her mind.

'Have you read the *Figaro* article? The paper's on the table.'

She remembered how Daguenet had laughed and she didn't quite know what to think. If that man Fauchery had been taking the mickey out of her, she'd make him pay for it . . .

'People are saying it's about me', she said in a casual voice. 'Have a look, darling, see what you think.'

And she let her slip fall to the ground and stood there naked waiting for Muffat to read through the article. He read it slowly.

Entitled 'The Golden Fly', Fauchery's piece was about a tart, the offspring of four or five generations of alcoholics, her blood tainted by a long heredity of deep poverty and drink, which in her case had taken the form of unhinging the nervous balance of her sexuality. She'd been brought up on the streets in a working-class Paris slum and now, a tall and lovely girl with a magnificently sensual body, like a plant flourishing on a dung-heap, she was avenging the poor, underprivileged wretches from whom she'd sprung. While the people were left to rot in degrading circumstances, she would carry this pollution upwards to contaminate the aristocracy. She was turning into a force of nature and, without any intention on her part, a ferment of destruction; between her plump white thighs, Paris was being corrupted and thrown into chaos; she was making it rot in the same way as, every month, women make milk go sour. At the end of the article came the comparison with the fly; a golden fly, the colour of sunshine, escaping from its dung-heap and bringing with it the deadly germs of the carrion allowed to fester by the roadside; dancing and buzzing, as dazzling as a precious stone, it would slip through the windows of palaces and poison the men inside merely by settling on them.

Muffat raised his head and sat staring into the fire.

'Well?' asked Nana.

He made no reply. He seemed to be about to reread the article. He could feel an icy sensation running from the top of his skull down to his shoulders. It was a poorly written piece, in jerky phrases, full of queer, extravagant words and outlandish comparisons. All the same, he was struck by it because it had suddenly made him aware of something which he'd been refusing to face for months.

He looked up. Nana was lost in blissful contemplation of herself. Craning her neck, she was examining in the mirror a little brown birthmark above her right hip, touching it with the tip of her finger and making it stick up by leaning backwards, no doubt thinking it looked funny as well as pretty in that particular spot. Then, falling back into the vicious habits of her childhood, she amused herself by studying other parts of her body. She was always curious to find something new whenever she looked at herself; she had the intrigued and fascinated expression of a girl who discovers she's turning into a woman.

Slowly she opened her arms to bring out the full, plump beauty of her Venus-like torso, bending at the waist, examining herself back and front, lingering over the curves of her breasts and her round thighs tapering towards the knees. Finally, she decided to indulge in a peculiar exercise: standing with her knees apart, she swayed to and fro rolling her hips in the continuous circular motion of Egyptian belly-dancers.

Muffat watched her. She frightened him. The newspaper had slipped out of his hands. He'd had a sudden vision and he despised himself; yes, it was quite true, in the space of three months she'd corrupted him, he already felt rotten to the core with all the filth he would never have suspected. Now he was going to sink into utter degradation. For a brief second he realized the disastrous effects of evil, he saw the disorder caused by this festering wound, he himself would be poisoned, his family destroyed, a whole section of society would break up and collapse. Unable to look away, he stared at her, trying to fill himself with disgust at her nakedness.

Nana was now standing motionless. With her hands clasped behind her neck, she was bending her head backwards, with her elbows apart. He had a foreshortened view of her half-closed eyes and half-open mouth; a voluptuous laugh was spreading over her face; her tawny hair was hanging loosely down her back like a lion's mane. She was bending at the waist, forcing her hip sideways; with her firm buttocks and breasts, she was like some female warrior, her muscles rippling under her satiny skin. A delicate line, barely broken by her shoulder and hip, ran from one of her elbows down to her foot. Muffat followed this soft outline, this sweep of pale flesh glowing into a lustrous gold, these curves shimmering like silk in the flickering candles. He was thinking of his earlier horror of women, of the biblical monster, like some lascivious wild beast. And there was indeed something bestial in her fleshy rump, like a brood-mare's, her sturdy thighs, and in the full curves and deep creases behind which lurked the disturbing slit of her genitals. Nana was very hairy, her body covered all over in the velvety down of a redhead. She was the Golden Beast, a mindless force whose very scent could poison the world. Muffat was continuing to look, obsessed and possessed to such an extent that when he closed his eyes to stop watching, the beast loomed up again still larger out of the darkness, terrifying and even more menacing. And now he would see this beast in his mind and feel it in his flesh for ever.

Now Nana was hugging herself; her limbs seemed to be quivering in a fit of tenderness. With eyes full of tears, she was trying to make herself as small as possible in order to feel herself better. Unclasping her hands, she slid them down her body as far as her breasts and squeezed them convulsively. Then, melting as though her whole body was being caressed, she flung out her chest and rubbed her cheeks tenderly to and fro over her shoulders. Her greedy lips were breathing desire over herself; she pursed them and placed a long kiss beside her armpit, laughing at the other Nana who was also kissing herself in the mirror.

Muffat drew a deep breath. This self-abuse was exasperating him. Suddenly, something broke inside him, he was caught up as if by a gale. He seized Nana round the waist and flung her brutally down on to the rug.

'Leave me alone!' she cried. 'You're hurting me!'

He realized he was beaten; he knew she was stupid,

obscene, and a liar but he wanted her, poisonous as she was.

'God, that's crazy!' she exclaimed angrily when he'd let her get up.

Then she calmed down. He'd be going now. Putting on a lace night-dress, she came and sat down in front of the fire, her favourite spot. When she once again questioned Muffat about Fauchery's article, in order to avoid a scene he gave evasive replies. In any case, she said, Fauchery was a pain in the neck. A long pause ensued. Nana was wondering how best to get rid of the count. She'd have liked to do it in a friendly way because she was a good-natured girl who didn't like hurting people, the more so as his wife was being unfaithful, which had finally made her feel sorry for him.

'So you're expecting your wife back tomorrow morning', she enquired eventually.

Muffat was stretched out in the armchair, looking sleepy; his arms and legs felt tired. He nodded in agreement. Nana was watching him earnestly; a hidden thought was running through her mind. She was sitting on one thigh, her lacy night-dress slightly crumpled all around her. She was holding one of her feet in her hands, twisting and turning it mechanically.

'Have you been married long?' she asked.

'Nineteen years', the count replied.

'Oh! And is your wife nice? Do you get on well together?'

He didn't reply. Then, with an embarrassed look:

'You know that I've asked you not to talk about that sort of thing.'

'Well, why not?' she exclaimed, beginning to feel irritated. 'I shan't be doing your wife any harm by talking about her . . . Ah, my dear man, all women are the same.'

Then she stopped, afraid she might say too much. However, she assumed a condescending air, because she felt she was being very considerate. Poor chap, he'd have to be handled gently. Anyway, an amusing thought had just struck her and she was smiling about it. She went on:

'I say, I didn't tell you a story that Fauchery has been spreading about you. What a rat that chap is! I don't bear him any grudge, because there may be something in his article. But he's still a dirty rat!'

She started laughing more loudly, and letting go of her foot she crawled over and pressed her breasts against the count's knee.

'Just imagine, he swears you'd never had a woman before marrying your wife . . . Never had a woman, eh? Is it true?'

She was peering into his face and had put her hands on his shoulders, shaking him to make him own up.

'I suppose so', he replied solemnly in the end.

Hearing that, she fell back again at his feet, in a fit of uncontrollable laughter, giving him little taps.

'Oh no, that's too good to be true!' she spluttered. 'That could only be you, you're unreal . . . But, my poor pet, you must have been so stupid! When a man doesn't know what to do, it's so funny! Gosh, how I would've loved to be a fly on the wall! And did it go off all right? Do tell me about it, please do!'

She pestered him with questions, insisted on hearing the exact details. And she laughed so much, in sudden bursts that made her rock from side to side, with her night-gown slipping off her shoulders and working up over her thighs, glowing golden in the firelight, that he gradually told her about his wedding night. He no longer felt embarrassed, he was even beginning to find it amusing to explain, in the well-worn phrase, 'how he'd lost it'. However, with a few remaining shreds of modesty, he chose his terms with care. Now in full swing, the young woman started questioning him about the countess. She had a wonderful figure but was like a block of ice; and on a sudden cowardly impulse he added:

'No need to worry, you've no cause to be jealous.'

Nana had stopped laughing. She went back to her place on the rug with her back to the fire, clasping her hands round her legs and resting her chin on her knees. Looking solemn, she declared:

'My dear, it's a bad thing to look like a clumsy idiot with your wife the first time.'

'Why?' the count asked in surprise

'Just because', she replied slowly in a judicious voice.

She condescended to explain herself more plainly.

'Well, I know what happens . . . You see, my dear man, women don't like men to be stupid in that sort of way . . . They won't say anything because they feel coy, you understand . . . But you can bet your boots they think a lot and sooner or later, if you haven't managed to do it properly, they'll go off and find someone who can . . . That's how it is, my pet.'

He didn't seem to grasp her meaning, so she spelt it out, becoming all motherly; she was letting him in on the secret, as a friend, out of the kindness of her heart. Ever since she'd heard that his wife was deceiving him this secret had been weighing on her mind, and she felt a tremendous urge to talk to him about it.

'My goodness, I'm talking about things that aren't any concern of mine . . . but I mention it because I think everybody has a right to be happy . . . We're just having a little chat together, aren't we? Look, you must tell me honestly . . .'

She broke off to change her position.

'It's jolly hot, isn't it? My back's scorching . . . half a mo, I'm just going to toast my tummy a bit . . . That's good for any aches and pains.'

She turned round and presented her breasts to the fire, squatting down on her thighs.

'Well now, you've stopped going to bed with your wife, haven't you?'

'Yes, I promise you I have', said Muffat.

'And you reckon she's like a log of wood?'

He dropped his chin and gave a nod.

'And that's why you love me? . . . Come on, out with it, I won't be cross.'

He nodded again.

'Ah!' she exclaimed, 'I thought so. Oh, you poor pet! . . . You know my Aunty Lerat? Next time you meet her, get her to tell you about the greengrocer who lives opposite her . . . Can you believe it, this greengrocer . . . Hell, this fire's hot, I've got to turn round. I'll toast my left side . . .'

As she turned her hip towards the fire, a funny thought struck her and she started joking about herself, like a silly, cheerful girl delighted to see how pink and fat she looked in the glow from the hearth.

'I look a bit like a goose, don't I . . . yes, that's what it is, a goose on a spit . . . I just keep on turning. I'm really cooking in my own juice.'

She burst out laughing. Suddenly there came the sound of loud voices and slamming doors. In surprise, Muffat looked at her questioningly. She became earnest again and seemed worried. Oh, that must be Zoé's cat, the damned thing kept breaking everything. Half-past twelve! Why on earth had she had the idea of cheering this cuckold up! Now the other man was there, she'd have to get rid of Muffat, double quick.

'What were you saying?' the count asked, humouring her and delighted to see her in such a good mood.

But she was now keen to get him out of the house; her mood changed and she started to speak bluntly, not bothering to spare his feelings.

'Oh yes, the greengrocer and his wife. Well, my dear, they never laid hands on each other, not once! . . . She wanted it very much, you understand. And he was such a silly ass that he didn't realize it . . . So, thinking she was a block of ice, he went elsewhere, to all sorts of sluts who taught him all kinds of disgusting tricks, while she did exactly the same thing herself with young men who were smarter than her clot of a husband . . . And that's how it always turns out if people don't understand each other. I know all about it!'

Finally realizing what she was getting at, Muffat went pale and tried to make her stop, but by now she'd got the bit between her teeth.

'No, just be quiet, will you? . . . If you weren't all such a nasty lot, you'd be as nice to your wives as you are to us, and if your wives weren't so stupid they'd take as much trouble to keep you as we do to get you . . . It's a lot of humbug . . . So there you are, old boy, put that in your pipe and smoke it!'

'Don't talk about respectable women', he said harshly. 'You don't know any!'

Nana knelt up with a jerk.

'I don't know any? . . . But they're not even clean, your respectable women! No, not clean! I defy you to find one who'd dare to show herself as I'm doing! . . . God, you make me laugh with your respectable women! Don't push me too far, you'll make me say things I might be sorry for later on!'

The count's only reply was a muttered insult. It was Nana's

turn to go white. For several seconds she looked at him without replying. Then she said bluntly:

'What would you do if your wife was being unfaithful to you?'

He made a threatening gesture.

'Well, suppose I was unfaithful to you?'

'Oh, you!' he muttered, shrugging his shoulders.

Nana wasn't at all an unkind girl, from the start she'd been resisting the temptation to fling his wife's conduct in his face. She'd have liked to get the truth out of him, without any fuss. Now, however, she was becoming infuriated; she felt it was time to put an end to the matter.

'In that case, old boy', she rejoined, 'I don't know what on earth you're doing here . . . You've been getting on my nerves for the last couple of hours . . . Why not go along and look up your wife who's busy having it off with Fauchery. Yes, that's right, in the Rue Taitbout, on the corner of the Rue de Provence . . . You see, I'm letting you have the address.'

Then, seeing Muffat get to his feet, staggering like a stunned ox, she added gloatingly:

'Well, if respectable married women are going to compete with us and take away our lovers, they're not doing too badly, these respectable wives!'

She got no further. Making a terrifying lunge at her, Muffat flung her flat on to the floor and lifted his foot, ready to smash her head under his heel to make her keep quiet. For a second she was panic-stricken. Then he started lurching blindly round the room like a madman, gasping for breath, unable to speak; and seeing his appalling inner turmoil, Nana felt desperately sorry for him. Huddling up in front of the fire to toast her right side, she set about consoling him:

'I thought you knew, I swear I did, darling. Of course, I wouldn't have said anything otherwise . . . And anyway, it may not be true. I can't say for sure, someone told me so and people are talking about it. But what does that prove? Oh, come on, you're wrong to take it so much to heart. If I was a man, I'd not give a damn about women! You see, women are all the same, whatever class they come from. Out for a good time, the whole lot of them!'

And ignoring her own interests in order to try to soften the blow, she started running down women. But he wasn't listening and didn't hear her. Stumbling, he pulled on his boots and put on his frock-coat. For a second or two he continued to prowl round the room. In the end, as if he'd finally realized where the door was, he rushed out. Nana was very irritated.

'Well, I hope you have a nice trip!' she said, talking to herself out loud. 'What manners the man's got when he's being spoken to! . . . And there was I doing my very best to be helpful! I was the first to take back what I'd said, I reckon I apologized enough! . . . And anyway, he was getting on my nerves here.'

But she wasn't happy and sat scratching her legs with both hands. Then she stopped worrying about it.

'To hell with him! It's not my fault if he's a cuckold!'

And feeling nicely toasted on all sides, she tucked herself cosily into bed, all warm and snug, and rang for Zoé to show in the other man who was waiting in the kitchen.

Outside, Muffat was striding violently along the Boulevard Haussmann. There had been another shower and he was slipping on the wet cobbles. Without thinking, he looked up at the sky; sooty clouds were shooting raggedly across the moon. At this time of night there were not many people left on the streets. He passed along beside the Opéra building-site,* keeping in the shadow, babbling incoherently. That whore had been lying. She'd made it all up because she was stupid and cruel. He should have smashed her head in when he'd got it under his heel. No, the whole thing was too shameful to bear, if he ever saw or touched her again he'd be an utter coward. He took a deep breath, feeling like a man who's suddenly been relieved of a great burden. Oh, that stupid, naked fiend of a woman, roasting herself like a goose, dragging all he'd held holy for the last forty years through the mud! The moon had emerged from the clouds and the street was bathed in light; he felt afraid and in sudden despair burst out sobbing, terrified, as if he'd fallen into an immense void.

'Oh God!' he faltered. 'It's the end, there's nothing left for me, nothing!'

Some belated pedestrians were hurrying by; he made an effort to calm himself. In his feverish mind, this whore's story kept coming back to him, he was attempting to work out, rationally, the facts of the case. The countess was supposed to be returning from Madame de Chezelle's château that morning. In fact, there was nothing to prevent her from coming back to Paris yesterday evening and spending the night with that man. He found himself recalling certain details of their stay at Les Fondettes. One evening he'd come upon Sabine unexpectedly in the wood, in such an emotional state that she'd not been able to reply to him. That man had been there. Why shouldn't she be at his place now? The more he thought about it, the more likely it seemed. In the end, he came to see it as something perfectly natural and inevitable. As he was taking his frock-coat off in the company of that slut, his wife was stripping in her lover's bedroom; nothing could be simpler or more logical. As he reasoned, he was making an effort to remain calm. He had the sensation of being flung into a world of orgy growing larger and larger until it took over everything around him. He was pursued by indecent images. Nana's nakedness suddenly conjured up the image of Sabine naked. This vision of the two women together, equally shameless and breath-takingly desirable, made him lose his footing and a passing cab nearly ran him over. Women coming out of a café were jostling and laughing at him. Again overcome by tears, despite his efforts, but ashamed to break down in public, he took flight into a dark, empty side-street, the Rue Rossini, where he walked along beside the silent houses, sobbing like a child.

'It's the end', he muttered dully to himself. 'I've got nothing left, nothing!'

He was sobbing so violently that he had to lean against a railing, holding his head in his wet hands. The sound of footsteps made him move on. Frightened and ashamed, he felt he must keep running away from everyone, like some restless night-prowler. Whenever passers-by came towards him he tried to look casual, afraid he might give himself away by his quivering shoulders. He'd gone along the Rue de la Grange-Batelière as far as the Rue du Faubourg-Montmartre. Upset by the glaring lights, he now retraced his steps, and for more than an hour he roamed round the district in this way, picking the darkest corners. No doubt there was a goal to which his steps were leading him, patiently, of their own accord, even if it was by a complicated, roundabout route. Finally, at a bend in the street, he looked up: he had arrived. It was the corner of the Rue Taitbout and the Rue de Provence. With the terrible throbbing in his brain, it had taken him an hour to reach the spot which he could have got to in five minutes. He recalled that last month he'd gone up to Fauchery's flat to thank him for his article on a ball in the Tuileries in which his name had received special mention. His flat was on the mezzanine floor, with tiny square windows half-hidden behind a colossal shop-sign. The last window on the left was showing a bright slit of light from a lamp shining through the half-closed curtains. He stood there absorbed, staring up at this beam of light, waiting.

The moon had vanished into an inky-black sky which was letting fall an icy drizzle. The Trinité church-clock struck two. The Rue de Provence and the Rue Taitbout retreated into the distance, with the bright specks of light from the gas-jets being swallowed up into a yellow mist. Muffat didn't stir. That was the bedroom: he could remember it as being draped in turkey-red cotton, with a Louis XIII bed at the back. The lamp must be on the right, on the mantelshelf. He supposed they were in bed because there were no shadows; the beam of light was as steady as the glimmer of a night-light. He stood there still looking up, working out a plan: he'd ring the doorbell, run upstairs, ignoring the porter's calls, batter down the door with his shoulder, and pounce on them in bed before they'd time to spring apart. He hesitated for a second, remembering that he was unarmed; then he decided he'd throttle them. He went over his plan again, perfecting the details, still waiting for a definite clue, some firm evidence. Had a woman's shadow appeared at that moment he would have rung, but he was paralysed by the thought that he might be mistaken. What would he say? His doubts returned: his wife couldn't be with that man, it was a monstrous idea, quite impossible. However, he stood there, slowly growing numb, unnerved by his long wait which, as he stared up at the window, was turning into an hallucination.

There was a sudden shower. Two policemen were coming along and he had to move out of the doorway where he'd taken shelter. When they had disappeared from view along the Rue de Provence, he came back, wet and shivering. The shaft of light was still shining through the window. This time he was just about to go away when he saw a shadow. It happened so quickly that he thought he'd been mistaken. But then there was a quick succession of dark patches; the whole bedroom sprang into restless activity. Once again he was riveted to the spot, this time with an agonizing cramp in his stomach as he tried to figure out what was happening. There was a flurry of shadowy arms and legs; a huge hand moved across, holding the silhouette of a jug. He couldn't make anything out clearly, although he thought he recognized a woman's chignon. He debated with himself: it was somewhat like Sabine's hair-style but the back of her neck was too thick. He felt incapable of thinking or doing anything. In his dreadful agony of uncertainty, his stomach cramp was so acute that he had to hang on to the door for relief; he was shivering like a tramp. Then, as he still couldn't tear his eyes away from that window, his anger took a moralizing turn: he imagined himself as a deputy speaking in front of some assembly, thundering against debauchery and prophesying doom, reproducing Fauchery's ideas about the poisonous fly and taking the stage himself as he declaimed that society was falling apart, that modern depravity was reminiscent of the most decadent period of the Roman Empire. After that, he felt better. Now the shadows had disappeared: he supposed they'd gone back to bed. He continued to watch and wait.

It struck three o'clock and then four. He couldn't bring himself to leave. Each time there was a shower, he cowered back into the doorway, with the rain spattering his legs. The street was now completely deserted. From time to time his eyes closed, as though burning from the beam of light which he was still watching intently, with idiotic persistence. Twice again shadows flitted across the window, with the same gestures and the same giant silhouette of a moving jug; and twice calm returned. The night-light continued to cast its discreet, gentle glow. These shadows increased his doubts. Anyway, he was feeling much calmer; he'd been struck by a sudden thought which provided him with an excuse to delay any action for the time being: all that was required was to wait for his wife to come out. He'd certainly recognize Sabine. Nothing simpler, no scandal, and he'd know for certain. He only had to wait where he was. His earlier agitation had been reduced to one idea: a need to know. But he was dropping off to sleep with boredom in this doorway; as a distraction, he tried to calculate how long he'd have to wait. Sabine would have to be at the station at about nine o'clock. That gave him nearly four and a half hours. He felt full of patience, he wouldn't budge, finding a certain charm in imagining that his night vigil would last for an eternity.

Suddenly the ray of light vanished. This very simple fact struck him as something disturbing, annoying, a disaster. Obviously they'd turned the lamp out, they were going to sleep. At this time of night it was a reasonable thing to do, but he was irritated by it because now this dark window had ceased to interest him. He watched it for another quarter of an hour and then got tired of doing so and strolled up and down on the pavement. He continued to walk to and fro till five o'clock, occasionally looking up. The window showed no sign of life; now and again he wondered whether he'd imagined the shadows up there on those panes of glass. He was being overcome by a feeling of immense tiredness, falling into a daze which made him forget why he was waiting on this corner, stumbling over the cobble-stones, jerking into life with an icy shiver, like a man unable to realize where he is. Nothing was worth bothering about. Since those people were asleep, they ought to be left undisturbed. What was the point of interfering? It was very dark, nobody would ever know anything about it. And so he let everything slide, even his curiosity; he had only one wish, to be rid of the whole business, to find some sort of relief, somewhere. It was growing colder, he was beginning to find the street unbearable; twice he moved off and shuffled back before leaving for good. That was that, there was nothing more to do. He walked down to the boulevard and this time didn't come back.

He wandered dismally round the streets. He was walking slowly and steadily, hugging the walls. He heard his heels tapping on the pavement; all he could see was his own shadow revolving, getting larger and smaller as he passed under each gas-lamp. This mechanical occupation had a soothing effect.

Later, he never knew where he'd walked; it seemed to him as if he'd kept walking on and on for hours, round and round, as if in a circus. Only one memory remained in his mind, very plainly. Without realizing how, he found himself with his face pressing against the gates of the Passage des Panoramas, clutching the iron bars with both hands. He wasn't shaking them, merely trying to look into the arcade, his heart suddenly full of emotion. But he couldn't distinguish anything, the arcade was deserted and in deep shadow; and the wind sweeping in from the Rue Saint-Marc felt damp on his face, like the air in a cellar. And still he persisted. Then, awakening out of his dream, he felt amazed and asked himself what he was doing at that hour of night, huddled so passionately against the gate that its bars were digging into his face. Then, in the depths of deepest despair, he set off again, feeling betrayed and deserted for ever in this utter gloom.

Finally dawn came, that squalid dawn so desperately sad in Paris's wintry, muddy, cobbled streets. Muffat had once again come back to the new wide roads under construction round the Opéra building-site. Flooding rain and cart-tracks had reduced the chalky soil to a lake of slush. He kept on walking, slithering about and recovering, not looking where he was putting his feet. As Paris awoke and the light grew brighter, the gangs of road-sweepers and the teams of early workers added to his bewilderment. They watched him in surprise, covered in mud and frightened, with his hat dripping wet. He took refuge for a long time under the scaffolding against the fencing. In his utter annihilation, he realized one thing: he was desperately miserable.

A thought came to him: there was God. This sudden idea of divine help, of comfort from above, took him by surprise, it was unexpected and strange, it brought to mind Monsieur Venot with his little fat face and rotten teeth. Certainly Monsieur Venot, to whom he'd been causing considerable distress for months by refusing to call on him, would be only too happy were he to knock on his door and fall crying into his arms. Previously God had never refused him His mercy; at the slightest affliction he would go into church, kneel down, and humble himself, a poor miserable sinner, before the power of Almighty God; and he came out strengthened by prayer, ready to give up all worldly things, concerned only with his eternal salvation. But nowadays he went to church only in fits and starts, whenever his fear of hell revived; his moral fibre had been undermined, Nana was coming between him and his religious duties. Now this thought of God surprised him: why hadn't he thought of Him straight away when faced by this appalling crisis in which his human weakness was shaken and collapsing?

Meanwhile, as he continued to trudge miserably on, he looked out for a church. He couldn't remember properly, he couldn't recognize the streets, it was too early in the morning. Then, turning a corner in the Rue de la Chaussée-d'Antin, he caught sight of La Trinité at the end, its tower dimly melting into the fog. The white statues dominating the leafless garden seemed like chilly Venuses amid the yellow leaves of a park. In the porch, tired by climbing the steps of the broad terrace, he stopped to take breath. The church was very cold; its stove had been out since the night before and its high vaulting was filled with a fine mist which had filtered through the stained glass. The transepts were bathed in shadow, there was not a soul to be seen, and the only sound was a verger shuffling around grumbling at having had to get up. However, after banging into a clutter of chairs, bewildered and crushed, on the verge of tears, Muffat had fallen on his knees against the entrance to a little chapel next to the font. He'd clasped his hands and was trying to find words to pray, urging himself on with everything in his power to surrender to God's will and lift his soul to heaven. But the faltering words were coming only from his lips, his thoughts kept escaping elsewhere, going back outside, walking the streets, never stopping, as if spurred on by an inexorable fate. He kept repeating: 'Dear God, please help me! Dear God, don't desert Thy creature who is surrendering himself to Thy justice! Dear God, I adore Thee, willst Thou suffer me to perish under the blows of Thine enemies?' There was no reply. The murky cold pressed down on his shoulders, and in this deserted church, which had not yet even been swept out that morning before being warmed up a little in time for the early Masses, the only sound, a continual, irritating, distant shuffle of feet, prevented him from praying. As he grasped a chair and helped himself to his feet, his knees cracked. God was not yet present in this church. And why should he go and sob in Monsieur Venot's arms? There was nothing that man could do to help him.

So, like a robot, he went back to Nana's flat. Outside, his foot slipped and he felt tears come to his eyes, not through anger at his misfortune but because he felt weak and ill. No, he really was too tired, the cold and rain were too much for him and the thought of going home to his gloomy mansion in the Rue Miromesnil was even more chilling. The door of Nana's block was closed and he had to wait for the porter to come and open up. As he went upstairs he was smiling in anticipation of the cosy warmth of this little love nest where he could lie down and sleep.

When she saw who was at the door, Zoé was completely taken aback. Madam had had a dreadful sick headache and hadn't slept a wink; well, she could just go and see if she'd gone to sleep yet. She slipped away into the bedroom while Muffat collapsed into an armchair in the drawing-room. However, Nana appeared almost at once. She'd just got out of bed, barely stopping to slip on a petticoat, with her hair dishevelled, her night-dress crumpled and torn, still in disarray from a night of love.

'Good God, it's you again!' she cried, red in the face.

And she made a dash towards him to kick him out herself, fuming with rage. But seeing him looking so pathetic, so utterly done in, she felt a final burst of compassion.

'Well, you are in a mess, my poor pet!' she went on more gently. 'What's the matter? You've been watching them, have you? You're upset?'

He made no reply; he looked like a broken-down animal. However, she guessed that he still lacked proof and tried to cheer him up:

'You see, I was wrong. Your wife's a good woman, I promise you. Now, my dear boy, you must go home. You need some sleep.'

He didn't stir.

'Come along, off you go. I can't keep you here. You're not expecting to stay here at this time of day, are you?'

'Yes, let's go to bed', he faltered.

Her patience was running out; she was thinking of using violence. Was he going out of his mind?

'Come along, off you go', she said again.

'No.'

Her anger and disgust boiled over. She burst out:

'You really are revolting! Can't you get it into your thick head that I'm fed up with you? Fed up to the teeth! Why not go and find your wife who's going to bed with someone else? Yes, you're a cuckold, this time it's me who's telling you! So there you are! Is there anything more you want? Now will you leave me alone?'

Muffat's eyes filled with tears. He clasped his hands.

'Let's go to bed.'

Nana almost choked with fury, herself almost speechless with hysterical tears. He really was trying to take advantage of her! Was all this any concern of hers? She'd certainly done everything possible to spare his feelings, out of kindness to let him learn the truth gently. And now she was supposed to carry the can! It really was too much! She might be kind-hearted but not as kind-hearted as that!

'Bloody hell! I've just about had all I can take!' she screamed, banging a piece of furniture with her fist. 'Yes, here I was doing everything I could, wanting to be faithful . . . But I could be a rich woman tomorrow, my dear man, I've only to say the word!'

He looked up in surprise. He'd never thought about money. If she was suggesting she wanted something, he'd make sure she got it. Everything he possessed was at her disposal.

'No, it's too late now', she retorted violently. 'I like men who give without waiting to be asked. You see, if someone offered me a million francs for just one go, I'd refuse . . . No, it's all over, I've got something else in mind now. Off you go or I won't answer for the consequences. I'll do something desperate.'

She advanced towards him threateningly. And in the middle of her exasperation, the exasperation of a good-hearted tart whose patience is exhausted, who is certain she's in the right and convinced of her superiority over these fine gentlemen who are driving her crazy, suddenly the door opened and in came Steiner. It was the last straw. She gave a blood-curdling scream.

'Oh no! And here comes the other one!'

Bewildered by the sound of her yelling, Steiner came to a halt. He was also upset to see Muffat, because he was afraid the truth might come out, something he'd been trying to prevent for the last three months. He blinked and shuffled uneasily from one foot to another, avoiding Muffat's eyes. He was breathing heavily with the red face and disconcerted expression of a man who's been scouring the streets of Paris to bring good news and feels he's landed up in disaster.

'Well, what do *you* want?' asked Nana truculently, not worried about making her intimate relationship with Steiner obvious to the count.

'I . . . I . . .' he faltered, 'I want to let you have what you've been expecting.'

'And what's that?'

He hesitated. The day before, she'd given him to understand that if he didn't come up with a thousand francs for her to pay a debt, she'd stop seeing him. He'd finally managed to collect the whole amount that very morning.

'The thousand francs', he said eventually, pulling an envelope out of his pocket.

Nana had forgotten.

'The thousand francs!' she cried. 'Do you think I'm asking you for charity? Here, that's what I think of your thousand francs!'

And she snatched the envelope and flung it in his face; it fell on the floor and, being a sensible Jew, he laboriously bent down and retrieved it. He was looking at the young woman as if dazed. Muffat exchanged a despairing glance with him while, putting her hands on her hips, Nana shouted even louder.

'Well, have you both finished insulting me now? . . . I'm glad you've come along, too, my dear man, because it gives me the chance to make a clean sweep. So, out you go, the pair of you!'

Then, as they seemed paralysed and reluctant to leave:

'Well? You think I'm being stupid? Maybe. But you've both been getting on my nerves too much . . . And then, hell,

I'm tired of being smart. If I come to a bad end, that's my choice.'

They both tried to calm her down and begged her to think again.

'One, two . . . you're refusing to leave? . . . Well, take a look here. I've got company.'

And she suddenly flung the bedroom door wide open. On the rumpled bed, the two men saw Fontan. He wasn't expecting to be shown off like this; his legs were exposed, his nightshirt was flapping loose, and with his swarthy skin, sprawling in the middle of the crumpled lace, he looked like a goat. However, used to coping with surprises on stage, he remained unperturbed. After the initial shock he took the whole thing triumphantly in his stride, putting on a funny face and producing what he used to call his 'bunny look' by sticking out his lips, wrinkling his nose and wiggling the whole front of his face. He looked vicious to the core, a real gutter faun. It was Fontan whom Nana had been picking up from the Variétés for the last week, carried away by the sudden mad infatuation which makes young women fall for comic actors with grinning, ugly faces.

'So now you know!' she said, with a dramatic gesture worthy of a tragic actress.

For Muffat, who till now had been uncomplainingly submissive, this last humiliation was too insulting to bear.

'You whore!' he stammered.

Nana, who had already gone into the bedroom, came back, determined to have the last word:

'Did you say whore? And what about your wife?'

And she went back, slamming the door behind her and loudly pushed the bolt. Left to themselves, the two men looked at each other in silence. Zoé had just come in. She made no attempt to hurry them out but chatted to them very reasonably; as a sensible woman, her view was that her mistress was being rather stupid. All the same, she stood up for her: that business with the ham actor wouldn't last, you had to let that sort of craziness take its course. The two men left. They hadn't spoken a word. On the pavement, they silently shook hands, with a feeling of being brothers in adversity; and turning their backs on each other, they shuffled off in opposite directions.

When the count finally went into his house in the Rue Miromesnil, his wife had just come home. They met on the huge staircase, under its gloomy, chilling walls. They both raised their eyes and saw each other. Muffat was still wearing his muddy clothes, his face was pale and distraught, like a man returning from some debauch. The countess seemed to be asleep on her feet, as though exhausted by a night in the train, with her hair flying loose and dark blue rings round her eyes.

Chapter 8

NANA and Fontan had invited a few friends up to their cramped living-quarters on the fourth floor of a house in the Rue Véron, in Montmartre, for a Twelfth Night party; it was going to be a house-warming, as they'd moved in only three days ago.

It had all taken place unexpectedly, in the first flush of their honeymoon, without any previous thought of setting up together. The day after her superb show-down, when she'd so unceremoniously kicked out both the banker and the count, Nana had felt everything falling apart round her. She summed up her position in a glance: her creditors were going to cram into her entrance hall, interfere in her love affairs, and talk of selling up everything unless she was sensible; there'd be endless wrangles and problems in trying to save her few sticks of furniture from their clutches. She preferred to throw in the towel and clear out. Anyway, the flat in the Boulevard Haussmann was getting on her nerves. Those huge, gilt rooms were stupid. In her infatuation for Fontan she had visions of a bright, pretty little bedroom—a relic of her earlier ideals when she was a flower-girl, when she could never imagine anything nicer than a rosewood wardrobe with a mirror and a bed draped in blue repp. It took her only two days to sell off anything she could salvage, her knick-knacks and jewels, and then vanish into thin air with about ten thousand francs, without informing her caretaker; a quick flit, up sticks and away without leaving a single trace. In that way none of the men would be able to come and sniff around her skirts. Fontan was very nice, raising no objection and letting her go ahead. He even showed what a good pal he was, though people were always accusing him of being stingy, by agreeing to add nearly seven thousand of his own to the kitty. It seemed to both of them a sound foundation to set up on and they went ahead on that basis, drawing on their joint savings to rent and furnish the two rooms in the Rue Véron, sharing everything with each other, like old friends. In the beginning, it was pure bliss.

For the Twelfth Night feast, Madame Lerat was the first to arrive with little Louis. As Fontan hadn't yet come home, she timidly expressed her misgivings: she felt anxious because her niece was giving up her lucrative career.

'Oh, I love him so much, Aunty!' cried Nana, charmingly clasping her hands in front of her chest.

These words had an extraordinary effect on Madame Lerat. Her eyes filled with tears.

'Yes, that's true', she said. 'Love's the only important thing!'

And she exclaimed how nice the rooms were. Nana showed her round the bedroom, the dining-room, even the kitchen. Of course it wasn't palatial, but they'd done the paint up and changed the wallpaper and it was cheerful and sunny.

Madame Lerat detained Nana in the bedroom while Louiset made himself comfortable in the kitchen watching the daily help roasting a chicken. If she was taking the liberty of making a comment it was because Zoé had just called on her. Zoé was staying on, staunchly holding the fort out of loyalty to her mistress; madam would be able to pay her later on, she wasn't worried. And in the break-up of the Boulevard Haussmann flat she was fighting an impressive rearguard action, holding off the creditors, salvaging whatever she could from the wreckage, explaining that madam was away on a trip but always refusing to give her address. For fear of being shadowed, she had even deprived herself of the pleasure of calling on her mistress. But that morning she had dashed round to Madame Lerat's because something new had transpired. The previous day, the creditors had all turned up, the paper-hanger, the coal-merchant, the linen-maid, offering madam time to pay and even to loan her a large sum if she was prepared to come back to the flat and behave sensibly. Her aunt quoted Zoé's own words. No doubt there was a gentleman behind it all.

'Never!' Nana exclaimed in disgust. 'What a lousy lot those tradesmen are! Do they think I'm going to sell myself just to settle their accounts? . . . I tell you, I'd sooner starve than be unfaithful to Fontan!'

'Exactly what I told them', replied Madame Lerat. 'My niece is too soft-hearted.'

However, Nana was very annoyed when she heard that La Mignotte was being sold and Labordette was buying it for a song, for Caroline Héquet. It made her furious with the whole bunch of them, proper sluts in spite of their pretence. One thing was certain: she was worth the whole lot of them put together!

'They can go on talking through their hats', she said finally, 'money will never make them really happy. And you see, Aunty, I really find it hard to imagine such people exist. I'm just too happy!'

At that very moment Madame Maloir came in wearing one of those queer hats that were her own speciality. It was lovely to be seeing each other again! Madame Maloir explained that she felt intimidated by anything terribly grand, so now she'd again be dropping in for her game of bezique. They did another tour of the flat, and in the kitchen, where the daily help was basting the chicken, Nana talked about saving money and said that a maid would have cost too much and she was going to look after her home herself. Louiset was blissfully watching the chicken on the spit.

There was a clamour of voices: it was Fontan with Bosc and Prullière. They could start eating. The soup was already on the table but Nana showed off the flat for the third time.

'Won't you be cosy here!' Bosc was saying, merely to be agreeable to his friends who were offering him a free dinner, because basically this question of a 'love nest', as he described it, left him quite indifferent.

In the bedroom he made an even greater fuss. Normally he referred to women as cows and in the cynical, drunken haze through which he viewed the world the only thing capable of arousing his indignation was the thought of a man lumbering himself with one of the beastly breed.

'Ah, the crafty blighters', he went on with a wink. 'They did it on the sly . . . Ah well, you did the right thing. It'll be wonderful and we'll all be calling on you, you just see!'

Louiset came in riding on a broomstick. Prullière gave a spiteful laugh:

'Good Lord, you've got one already!'

Everybody thought it a funny remark. Madame Lerat and Madame Maloir nearly collapsed with laughter. Far from being annoyed, Nana laughed and went misty-eyed. Unfortunately not, she wished they had, for the boy's sake and her own; but perhaps one might come along . . . Fontan put on a kind uncle act and playfully picked the little boy up in his arms, dropping into baby-talk:

'Diddums den, still likey daddykins? Call me Daddy, you little scamp, you!'

'Dadda, Dadda', the little boy babbled.

Everybody gushed over him. Fed up, Bosc suggested they might start eating; after all, that was the main thing in life. Nana asked to have Louiset next to her. The dinner was very lively, though Bosc was put out by having the boy beside him as he kept making raids on his plate. He was embarrassed by Madame Lerat too. She was becoming maudlin, whispering all sorts of cryptic remarks, telling him stories of well-to-do, respectable gentlemen who were still after her; and twice he had to move his knee away because she was encroaching on him with melting eyes. Prullière was behaving boorishly to Madame Maloir, never once bothering to pass her anything; he was concentrating his whole attention on Nana, peeved at seeing her with Fontan. Anyway, the little love-birds were becoming tedious; they couldn't stop kissing each other. They'd broken all the rules by insisting on sitting beside each other.

'Keep eating, for God's sake! You'll have plenty of time for all that!' Bosc kept saying, with his mouth full. 'Can't you wait till we've gone?'

But Nana couldn't restrain herself. She was ecstatic, all pink like a little girl, laughing, with her eyes oozing affection, staring at her man and smothering him in endearments, 'my pet', 'my honey-bunch', 'my sweetie-pie,' and whenever he passed her the salt or the water she'd bend forward and snatch a kiss on his lips, his nose, or an ear; and when she was told off for doing it, she'd look coy, wriggle about like a cat who's been slapped, and cunningly change her tactics, slyly reaching for his hand and holding it so as to kiss it again. She couldn't keep her hands off him. Fontan was accepting all this adulation with smug condescension. His big nose was twitching in sheer sensual pleasure. His freakish, comical face, like some ugly satyr's, was basking in this adoration from this well-rounded young woman with such a wonderful white skin. Occasionally, he'd return one of her kisses, like a man full of his own pleasure but prepared to be charitable.

'I can't stand this any more!' shouted Prullière in the end. 'Out you get!'

And he made Fontan give up his seat to him. There was a burst of applause, exclamations, and a number of very strong words. Fontan put on his comical pantomime of Vulcan desperately mourning his lost Venus. Prullière at once started to make up to Nana, but when he tried to play footsie under the table she gave him a slap and told him to keep himself to himself. No, she certainly wouldn't go to bed with him. The previous month she had started to fancy him because of his good looks, but now she couldn't bear him, and if he pinched her just once more while pretending to pick up his serviette she'd throw her glass in his face.

Nevertheless, the evening went off well. The conversation had naturally come round to the Variétés. Wouldn't that swine Bordenave ever kick the bucket? His foul diseases were breaking out again, putting him in such pain that he was like a bear with a sore head. During the previous day's rehearsal he'd been bawling Simonne out all the time. Certainly, none of the cast would ever be sorry to see him go! Nana stated that if he were to offer her a part, she'd tell him what to do with it; anyway, she was talking about giving it up, theatre life wasn't a patch on home. Fontan, who wasn't in the current show or the one in rehearsal, also elaborated on the delights of being completely free, warming his feet by the fire and spending his evenings with his little chickabiddy. The others exclaimed how lucky they were and pretended to be envious of them.

They served the Twelfth-cake,* and the bean went to Madame Lerat who popped it into Bosc's glass. Everybody shouted playfully: 'The King drinks! The King drinks!' Nana took advantage of this noisy diversion to put her arm round Fontan's neck and kiss him, whispering something into his ear. But the good-looking young Prullière exclaimed petulantly that that wasn't fair. Louiset was asleep on a couple of chairs. The party didn't break up till nearly one o'clock; as the guests went off downstairs, everybody shouted goodnight.

And for three weeks, the 'love-birds' really did have a very pleasant life. Nana felt as though she'd gone back to her early days when she'd been so happy at getting her first silk dress. She hardly went out at all, playing at being the simple, secluded housewife. She used to do her own shopping, and while on her way early one morning to buy some fish at the La Rochefoucauld market, she was quite taken aback to run into her former hairdresser Francis. He was, as always, perfectly turned out, with an immaculate frock-coat over an impeccable shirt, and she felt ashamed to be seen in the street in her dressing-gown with her hair not properly done and down-at-heel. Full of tact, he was more polite than ever. He refrained from asking questions and pretended to believe that madam was travelling. Ah, what a lot of people madam had made quite miserable by deciding to go away on that trip! It was everybody's loss. As the young woman's curiosity got the better of her embarrassment, she finally started questioning him. They were being jostled by the crowd, so she pushed him into a doorway and faced him with her little basket in her hand. What were people saying about her escapade? Well, dear me, some of the ladies he went to said one thing, others said something else; all in all, it had caused a big stir and was a great success. And how about Steiner? Monsieur Steiner was in a bad way; if he couldn't float a new enterprise he was going to land up in Queer Street. And what about Daguenet? Oh, he was doing very well, Monsieur Daguenet was organizing himself very nicely. Nana was growing excited at these memories of her past, and was about to ask him more questions but was embarrassed at the thought of mentioning Muffat. Francis forestalled her with a smile: as for the Count Muffat, he'd suffered dreadfully when madam had gone off; he'd behaved like a lost soul, people kept seeing him in all the spots where he might meet madam. In the end, Monsieur Mignon had noticed him and taken him off to his own house. This piece of information made Nana laugh, but it was a forced laugh.

'Oh, so he's with Rose now', she said. 'Well, Francis, you know I don't give a damn . . . Just look at that pious hypocrite! You give him a taste for it and he can't do without it for even a week! And there he was, swearing he'd never touch another woman after me!'

Inwardly she was seething.

'It's my left-overs', she went on. 'What a nasty bit of work she's got her hands on there! Oh, I realize she wanted to get her own back because I took that beast Steiner away from her . . . Very clever of her to pick up someone I'd kicked out.'

'That's not the way Monsieur Mignon's putting it', said the hairdresser. 'According to him, it was the count who got rid of you . . . And roughly too. He says that he literally kicked you out—gave you a kick up the backside.'

Nana went as white as a sheet.

'What did you say?' she cried. 'A kick up the backside? Oh, that's really going too far! But, my dear Francis, I'm telling you it was me who actually kicked the cuckold downstairs! You do know he's a cuckold, don't you? His countess is sleeping around with everybody, even that dirty skunk Fauchery . . . And that fellow Mignon who goes about pimping for his frightful wife whom nobody wants because she's so skinny . . . They're all stinkers, they really are!'

She was gasping for breath, but recovered and went on:

'Well, so that's what they're saying . . . Well, Francis my boy, I'll pay a call on them . . . Shall we go together, straight away? Yes, I'll go and we'll see if they've still got the nerve to talk about kicks up the backside . . . I've never let any man lay a hand on me and I'd never let anyone beat me up because if anybody tried, I'd scratch his eyes out!'

Then she calmed down. After all, they could say what they liked, for her they were less than the mud on her shoes . . . They were too dirty to worry about. Her conscience was clear. Seeing her showing herself in public like this, in her everyday dressing-gown, as he was saying goodbye Francis took the liberty of offering her some friendly advice: she was wrong to sacrifice everything for a passing infatuation; infatuations were bad things. As he stood addressing her with a concerned look, like an expert in such matters sorry to see such a lovely young girl making a mess of her life in this way, she hung her head. But when he'd finished, she said:

'That's my business. But thanks all the same, Francis.'

She shook his hand, always a trifle clammy in spite of his

impeccable turn-out, and went off to buy the fish. During the day this story of the kick up the behind preyed on her mind. She even mentioned it to Fontan, once again putting on her tough woman act, someone who wouldn't stand for the slightest show of violence. Speaking in the tone of a man who's seen it all, Fontan explained that all the upper classes were rotten and beneath contempt, reinforcing Nana's feeling of scorn.

It so happened that they went to the Bouffes that evening to see the debut of a little actress, known to Fontan, who had only about ten lines to speak. By the time they had walked back up to Montmartre, it was nearly one o'clock. They'd bought a mocha cake in the Rue de la Chaussée-d'Antin and ate it in bed because the flat was rather chilly and it wasn't worth bothering to light a fire. They were sitting side by side with the blanket drawn up over their legs and pillows stacked behind their backs, talking about the little actress while they had their supper. Nana thought she was plain and dowdy. Fontan was lying on the outside of the bed and handing her the slices of cake, which were on the edge of the bedside table between the candle and the matches. They started to bicker.

'Well, what else can one say!' Nana exclaimed. 'She's got beady eyes and mousy hair.'

'Oh, do be quiet!' Fontan retorted. 'Her hair's magnificent and she's got really fiery eyes. Isn't it funny, you women always try and run each other down!'

He was looking cross.

'Oh, come on, that's enough of that!' he said eventually. 'You know I don't like being rubbed up the wrong way . . . Let's go to sleep before there's trouble.'

He blew out the candle. Nana was furious and kept on talking: she refused to be spoken to like that, she was used to being treated with respect. As he didn't reply, she was reduced to silence. But she couldn't get to sleep and kept twisting and turning.

'Hell's bells, can't you keep still?' he suddenly shouted, sitting up with a jerk.

'It's not my fault if we've got crumbs', she snapped.

There were indeed crumbs in the bed. She could feel them under her thighs, she was itching all over; it only needed one single crumb rubbing her to make her scratch herself till she bled. Anyway, when someone eats a cake, doesn't he always shake the blanket afterwards? Inwardly seething, Fontan re-lit the candle. They both got out of bed and in their night-wear uncovered it and swept the crumbs off with their hands. He went back to bed shivering and when she told him to make sure he wiped his feet properly, told her to go to hell. Finally she got into bed as well but still couldn't settle down. There were still some crumbs.

'That was bound to happen', she said, wriggling about. 'You brought them back in on your feet . . . I can't bear it, I tell you, I just can't!'

And she was just about to scramble out over him when, unable to bear it any longer, Fontan landed her such a savage slap in the face that she ended up flat on her back with her head lying on the pillow. She lay there dazed.

'Oh!' she said simply, with a big gasp like a child.

He enquired if she'd finished wriggling, threatening to box her ears again. Then blowing out the candle, he settled himself comfortably on his back and immediately started snoring. She was sobbing gently into her pillow. It was cowardly to take advantage of your strength. But she had been really scared by the terrible look on Fontan's funny face. Her anger evaporated as if the slap had calmed her down. She felt respect for him and squeezed close up against the wall to leave him plenty of room. She even finally dropped off to sleep, with her cheek burning and her eyes full of tears, feeling so delightfully meek and mild and so prostrate with exhaustion that she stopped noticing the crumbs. When she woke up in the morning she was hugging Fontan hard against her breasts in her naked arms: he'd never do anything like that again, would he? Never ever! She loved him so much! It was even nice being slapped, by him.

So a new sort of life began. For no reason at all Fontan would hit her, and she got used to it and put up with it. Sometimes she would yell and threaten him, but he would shove her up against the wall and tell her he'd strangle her. Most often she'd collapse on to a chair and sob for five minutes. Then she'd forget everything and become very cheerful, laughing and singing and filling the flat with the swirl of her skirts as she dashed around. The worst thing was that Fontan had taken to staying out all day long and never coming home till midnight; he'd spend his time in cafés with his cronies. Nana remained loving and apprehensive, prepared to put up with everything, scared only that if she complained he might never come home. But some days when she had neither Madame Maloir nor her aunt with Louiset, she was dreadfully bored, so that once when she was at the La Rochefoucauld market, haggling over some pigeons, she was delighted to meet Satin who was buying a bunch of radishes. They hadn't seen each other since the night when the Prince had accepted a glass of Fontan's champagne.

'Good Lord, it's you! Do you live round here?' said Satin, amazed at seeing her wearing slippers in the street at that time of day. 'Oh, you poor dear, has something gone wrong?'

Nana gave her a frown to tell her to be quiet, because there were other women there, with their hair hanging loose and covered in fluff, still not dressed under their dressing-gowns; in the morning all the tarts in the neighbourhood, as soon as they'd got rid of the man they'd spent the night with, would come and do their shopping, bleary-eyed and down-at-heel, in a foul temper and tired out from the various hassles of the previous night. They would all pour in from every street leading to the square, looking very pale, some still young and charming and high-spirited, others blowsy old hags exposing their flabby flesh to all and sundry, completely unconcerned at being seen like that outside working hours. On the pavement the passers-by kept turning to look at them, while none of them deigned even to smile, like busy, scornful housewives for whom men had momentarily ceased to exist. And indeed, when a young office worker called out 'Hello, ducks!' as he went by, late for work, Satin, who was paying for her bunch of radishes, drew herself up disapprovingly like an offended queen and said:

'Who does that pig think he is?'

Then she thought she recognized him: three days ago, as she was going up the boulevard by herself, round midnight, she'd spent half an hour with him on the corner of the Rue La Bruyère trying to get him to make up his mind. But that only made her even more indignant.

'What rotten pigs they are to shout things like that in broad daylight', she exclaimed. 'When people are going about their business, they reckon to be respected.'

Nana had finally bought the pigeons, though she had some doubts as to their freshness. Then Satin wanted to show her where she lived, close by in the Rue La Rochefoucauld. As soon as they were by themselves, Nana told Satin how crazy she was about Fontan. Having reached her block, Satin stood there with her radishes under her arm, all excited by Nana's last detail, when she gave her equally false version of the way Muffat and she had parted: she'd booted him up the backside, several times.

'Oh, that's wonderful, absolutely fantastic!' exclaimed Satin. 'So you really kicked him hard? And he didn't say a word, I bet! . . . Oh, I wish I could have seen his face! Nana my dear, you're right! And bugger the cost! When I've got a crush on someone, I'm ready to starve for him . . . Anyway, you must promise to come and see me. It's the door on the left, knock three times, because there are a lot of arseholes around . . .'

After this, whenever Nana was too bored she dropped in on Satin, always certain of finding her in because she never went out till six. Satin had two rooms which a pharmacist had furnished for her to save her from the police; but in less than thirteen months she'd broken the furniture, smashed the chairs, and made the curtains filthy with her irresistible urge to live in chaos and squalor, so that her lodging looked as if it was occupied by a swarm of crazy cats. When the squalor became too great even for her, she'd set about trying to clean up; in her fight against filth, she'd find chair-rails and bits of drapery coming off in her hands. On such days the squalor was even greater, and no one could get in because the doorway was blocked by things having fallen down in front of it. She'd finally given up trying to cope. By lamplight, the wardrobe with its mirror, the clock, and what was left of the curtains were still able to hide the truth from her men. Anyway her landlord had been threatening to evict her for the last six months, so why should she worry about the future? To help the landlord perhaps? Not bloody likely! And on the days when she got out of bed in a good mood, she'd shout 'Gee up,

Neddy!' and kick the sides of her wardrobe and her chest-of-drawers until they rattled under the shock.

Whenever Nana came, Satin was almost always in bed. Even if she'd gone out shopping, when she came back home she was so tired that she'd fling herself down on the edge of the bed and go to sleep again. During the day she'd loaf around, dozing on chairs and coming out of her torpor only when evening came and the street-lamps were lit. Nana felt very cosy in her flat, sitting doing nothing, facing the unmade bed, with basins lying around on the floor and last night's dirty petticoats leaving mud-stains on the armchairs. She would gossip away, confiding all sorts of secrets while Satin sprawled in her slip with her feet above the level of her head smoking cigarettes as she listened. Sometimes, on those afternoons when they had problems, they'd treat themselves to some absinthe, to help them forget, they said; without going downstairs or even bothering to slip on a petticoat, Satin would go outside and call down over the banisters to the caretaker's daughter, a pert little 10-year-old, who would cast furtive glances at the lady's legs when she brought in the glass of absinthe. Their talks always ended with the conclusion that men were beasts. Nana's conversation was incredibly tedious: she couldn't utter ten consecutive sentences without harping on the subject of Fontan, the things he did and said. But Satin was a good sort and wasn't bored by her everlasting tales of how she would stand watching out of the window, how they'd quarrel over burning a bit of stew, and how, after sulking for hours in silence, they'd make it up in bed. In her need to talk about it, Nana had reached the point of giving her a blow-by-blow account of each of his attacks: last week, he'd given her a swollen eye; as recently as last night, being unable to find his slippers, he'd knocked her into the bedside table; the other girl would puff away at her cigarette, showing no surprise and interrupting only to comment that, personally, she always ducked, which made the man miss and go sprawling. They'd both settle down to exchange tales of how they'd been bashed about, in a euphoric daze from endlessly repeating silly details, wallowing in the tired, warm feelings induced by being knocked about so outrageously. It was this pleasure of going over Fontan's brutality, explaining

Fontan in minute detail, even down to the way he took off his boots, that brought Nana back to Satin's rooms regularly every day, and even more willingly when Satin responded in similar vein, quoting examples of even more outrageous behaviour, a pastry-cook who'd lay her out flat on the floor and whom she still loved. Then there were the days when Nana was in tears and saying that things couldn't go on like this. Satin would go along with her to her door and wait down in the street for an hour to make sure he wasn't doing her in. And next day the two young women would be in raptures over the reconciliation, preferring, though unwilling to admit it, the days when there were thrashings in the air, because that was more exciting.

They became inseparable. However, Satin never went up to Nana's because Fontan had said bluntly that he wouldn't have any whores in his house. They used to go out together, and this is how one day Satin took her friend along with her to the house of a certain woman, in fact of that very same Madame Robert who'd been intriguing Nana and arousing a certain respect in her ever since she'd refused the invitation to her supper party. Madame Robert lived in the Rue Mosnier, a quiet new street, without any shops, in the Europe district,* full of fine houses containing exiguous little flats occupied by single ladies. It was five o'clock; in the peaceful, aristocratic atmosphere of the tall white houses, stockbrokers' and business men's barouches were parked alongside the pavements, deserted except for a few men who were rushing through with their eyes peering up towards the windows, where women seemed to be waiting in their peignoirs. At first Nana was unwilling to come up, saying primly that she didn't know the lady. But Satin insisted; after all, you were always allowed to bring a friend along, it was only a courtesy call on Madame Robert, whom she'd met in a restaurant the day before, who'd been extremely friendly and made her promise to drop in on her. Nana finally agreed. Upstairs a drowsy little maid told them that madam hadn't come home yet. However, she showed them into the drawing-room, where she left them.

'Hell, isn't it smart!' muttered Satin.

It was furnished austerely and hung in some dark material, suggesting the middle-class gentility of a moderately prosperous, retired Paris shopkeeper. Nana was impressed and made a mischievous comment. But Satin was cross: she could guarantee Madame Robert wasn't that sort of woman; in public, she was always escorted by older, highly respectable men. At the moment she had a retired chocolate-shop proprietor, a very staid person. Whenever he came to visit her he was so charmed by the decorum of her establishment that he would insist on being announced, and used to address her as 'my dear child'.

'But take a look, that's her!' exclaimed Satin pointing to a photograph standing in front of the clock.

Nana scrutinized the portrait for a second. It was of a very dark-haired woman with a long face, tight-lipped and smiling discreetly. She looked the epitome of a society lady, but rather more reserved.

'It's funny', she said, 'I swear I've seen that face somewhere, I've forgotten where, but it won't have been anywhere very nice. Oh no, certainly nowhere nice.'

She turned to her friend and added:

'So she made you promise to come and see her. What does she want you for?'

'What does she want me for? Good heavens, I expect to have a chat, pass the time of day with her . . . she's just being polite.'

Nana was watching Satin closely; she clicked her tongue. Ah well, it was all the same to her; but as the lady in question was keeping them waiting, she wouldn't stay any longer. They both left.

Next day, as Fontan had warned Nana that he wouldn't be home for dinner, she went down early to find Satin and offered to take her out for a meal in a restaurant. The big question was: where? Satin suggested going to a brasserie, which Nana thought revolting. Finally, Satin persuaded her to eat at Laure's, a restaurant with a fixed-price menu in the Rue des Martyrs. Dinner cost three francs.

They arrived early at Laure's, and not wanting to hang around outside on the pavement, they went upstairs twenty minutes before the restaurant was due to open. It consisted of three rooms, all empty. They took their seats at a table in the room where Laure Piédefer was presiding on a high bench behind the counter. Laure was 50 years old, a lady of exuberant curves tightly strapped up in belts and corsets. Women were arriving in quick succession, leaning familiarly across over the saucers and placing on her mouth tender kisses which the monster herself, misty-eyed, was trying to dole out evenly in an endeavour not to arouse any jealous feelings. The waitress serving these ladies was, on the other hand, a tall, gaunt woman with ravaged features, black eyelids, and darkly glowing eyes. The three rooms quickly filled up; there must have been about a hundred female customers spread out at the tables, most of them verging on 40, huge women bloated with fat, with flabby, vicious, thick lips; and amidst these bulging busts and bellies, you could see a few thin, pretty girls, still innocent-looking in spite of their saucy demeanour, novices who'd been picked up in some cheap dance-hall and brought along to Laure's restaurant by a female customer, where the herd of fat women, unsettled by the smell of their young flesh, were competing with each other for their favours like anxious old bachelors by offering them tasty little titbits. There were also a few men—ten or fifteen at the most—lying very low in this invading wave of skirts, apart from four lively young sparks making themselves very much at home, who'd come to watch and were cracking jokes.

'The grub's not bad, is it?' Satin remarked.

Nana nodded her agreement. It was the standard solid fare of country hotels: sweetbread-and-mushroom vols-au-vent, chicken and rice, French beans, caramel cream. Their ladyships were tucking into the chicken and rice with particular gusto, bursting out of their bodices as they slowly lifted their hands to wipe their lips. At first Nana had been scared of seeing some of her former girl-friends, who'd have asked her silly questions, but she felt reassured when she could see no one she knew in this very mixed crowd, where faded dresses and tatty hats mingled with expensive finery, worn by women drawn together by the same perverted tastes. Her attention was caught for a second by an insolent-looking young man who was captivating a whole tableful of grossly obese young women, reacting to his slightest whim. The young man laughed; his chest bulged out. Nana uttered a little cry.

'Good lord, it's a woman!'

Satin, who was stuffing herself with chicken, looked up and said quietly:

'Yes, I know her . . . Isn't she smart! Everybody's after her!'

Nana pursed her lips disgustedly. She still couldn't understand that sort of thing. However, in her sensible way, she said there was no accounting for tastes and you could never know what you might come to like one day. So she went on eating her caramel cream philosophically, noticing that Satin's big, innocent blue eyes were clearly creating havoc at the tables around them. Above all there was a stout, friendly blonde very close to Satin who was positively on fire and kept edging towards her. Nana was on the point of intervening.

At that moment, however, the door opened and Nana was surprised to see Madame Robert come in, looking like a pretty brown mouse. She nodded familiarly to the tall, gaunt waitress, went over to the counter, leaned forward and exchanged a lingering kiss with Laure. Nana found this very odd in such a distinguished lady, the more so as Madame Robert had abandoned her normal modest demeanour for one which was quite the reverse. She kept casting glances into the room and talking in a low voice. Laure resumed her seat, settling herself with all the majesty of an old idol dedicated to vice, its face worn and polished by the kisses of the faithful; dominating the heaped plates, she sat in state over her bloated female customers, herself an outsize monster vying with the fattest, lording it over them, secure in the wealth earned by forty years of running her restaurant.

Madame Robert had caught sight of Satin. She left Laure and dashed over, exuding charm, saying how sorry she was not to have been at home when they called the day before. Satin was overcome by her charm and tried to persuade her to squeeze in beside her, but Madame Robert said that she'd already eaten and had only come to 'take a look around'. She was standing behind her new friend, leaning on her shoulders, smiling and wheedling.

'Now, you must tell me when we can see each other. If you're going to be free . . .'

Unfortunately Nana couldn't hear the rest of the sentence,

but she was extremely annoyed and bursting to tell this respectable woman a few home truths. Suddenly she was transfixed by the entry of a group of elegant women in evening dress, dripping with diamonds and obviously intending to have a party at Laure's. They all greeted Laure like a close personal friend, drawn here as though by a magnet by their perverted tastes, flaunting hundreds of thousands of francs-worth of jewellery on their bare flesh while partaking of a three-franc dinner under the amazed and envious eyes of the poor little draggle-tailed tarts.

Their raucous voices and loud hoots of laughter on arrival had been like a sudden ray of light from outside; but Nana was upset to see that among the newcomers were Lucy Stewart and Maria Blond and, hastily turning away, for the next four or five minutes she kept her eyes fixed on the table-cloth, busily pretending to be rolling her breadcrumbs into little balls while the ladies chatted with Laure before going through into the next room. When she was finally able to look up, she was amazed to see that the chair next to her was empty. Satin had vanished into thin air.

'Where on earth can she be?' she exclaimed out loud.

Seeing her annoyance, the stout blonde who'd been so attentive to Satin gave a little laugh, and when Nana appeared irritated and looked threateningly in her direction, she said in a soft drawl:

'No, of course it's not me, it's that other woman who's snaffled her.'

Realizing that she could make herself look ridiculous, Nana kept quiet. Not wishing to show how angry she was, she even remained in her seat for a minute or two. At the back of the room next door, she could hear Lucy Stewart creating a great rumpus; she was standing treat to a tableful of girls who'd come down from the dance-halls of Montmartre and La Chapelle.* It was very, very warm in the restaurant, and as the waitress removed the stacks of dirty plates there was a strong smell of chicken and rice. The four men had reached the stage of filling the glasses of half-a-dozen couples with one of the restaurant's better wines in the hope of making them tipsy and hearing lots of lurid details. The thing which infuriated Nana was having to pay for Satin. What a tramp she was to stuff herself at someone else's expense and then go off with the first ugly bitch that asked her, without so much as a thank you! Of course, it was only three francs, but all the same it seemed callous, the way she'd done it was really lousy. However, she paid up, plonking down her six francs in front of Laure who at that moment, in her eyes, was the lowest of the low.

In the Rue des Martyrs, Nana could feel her resentment growing. Naturally, there was no question of her chasing after that little rat Satin who wasn't fit to be touched by a barge-pole! But her evening had been spoiled and she walked slowly back to Montmartre feeling particularly angry with Madame Robert. The cheek of that bloody woman, pretending to be so distinguished, oh yes, she was distinguished all right, a distinguished bit of garbage! She now felt certain she'd met her in Le Papillon, a revolting dive in the Rue des Poissonniers where men could pick her up for a couple of francs. And that slut was bamboozling heads of departments, putting on her prim and proper act, and turning down supper invitations that people were kind enough to make just to appear respectable! What fun it'd be to kick a bit of respectability into her up her backside, it really would! It's prudes like that who get themselves stuffed till they're silly in filthy dumps that decent people didn't know existed.

While turning these thoughts over in her mind, Nana had arrived at the Rue Véron and was shaken to see a light on in the flat. Fontan had also been left to his own devices by the friend who'd paid for his dinner, and he was in a foul mood. He listened frigidly to Nana's explanations. Taken by surprise at finding him home so early and afraid of getting her face slapped, Nana lied about her evening, admitting she'd spent six francs but saying she'd been with Madame Maloir. Still unbending, Fontan handed her a letter addressed to her which he'd unblushingly opened himself. It was a letter from Georges, still shut away in Les Fondettes and letting off steam by writing passionate letters to Nana. She adored getting letters, especially when they were full of grand expressions of love, complete with solemn vows. She used to read them out loud to everybody. Fontan knew Georges's style and admired it; but that night she was so afraid of a row that she pretended to be unconcerned, skipping rapidly through it and immediately discarding it. Fontan was drumming on the window, bored at having to go to bed so early and not knowing how to spend the evening. He suddenly swung round:

'How about answering that kid's letter straight away?'

It was usually he who did this; he was happy to compete with Georges in stylish turns of phrase and was delighted when, as he read out his efforts, Nana expressed her enthusiastic admiration by kissing him and telling him he was the most wonderful letter-writer she knew. One thing would lead to another, and they'd both end up very excited and full of mutual adoration.

'If you feel like doing it', she replied, 'I'll make some tea and then we'll go to bed together . . .'

Fontan carefully assembled pen, paper, and ink and settled himself at the table. He stuck out his chin, with his hand poised:

'"My dearest heart"', he began, speaking out loud.

And he kept hard at it for more than an hour, sometimes turning a sentence over in his mind, clasping his head in his hands, adding little touches, chuckling to himself when he'd found a particularly affectionate turn of phrase. Meanwhile Nana, without uttering a word, drank two cups of tea. Finally he read out the epistle in the way actors read on the stage, in a toneless voice, with a few gestures. In it, over five pages, he expatiated on 'the delightful hours we spent together at La Mignotte, the memory of which lingers on like a haunting fragrance'; he swore 'never to be false to this springtime of love'; and finally declared that his only wish was 'to renew our happiness, if happiness can ever be renewed'.

'You know', he explained, 'all this is just a formality, a way of being polite, it's all just a joke really, isn't it? But it's got a lovely touch, don't you think?'

He was full of himself, but Nana was still on her guard and tactlessly failed to fling her arms round his neck in ecstatic delight. She thought it was a good letter, no more, no less. He was extremely put out. If she didn't like his letter, she could write a better one herself, and instead of kissing as they normally did after indulging in a little billing and cooing, they sat glaring at each other across the table. However, she poured him out a cup of tea.

'What on earth's this dog's piss?' he yelled when he sipped it. 'You've put salt in it!'

Unfortunately for herself, Nana shrugged her shoulders. He became enraged.

'Oh, I can see we're heading for trouble tonight!'

And the row began; it was only ten o'clock and it was one way of killing time. He was whipping himself up into a fury, covering Nana in a flood of abuse and hurling all sorts of accusations at her, one after another, not giving her any chance of defending herself. She was a dirty, stupid slut who'd been to bed with everybody. He fastened on to the question of money. When *he* had dinner out, did he spend six francs? He got someone to pay for him, otherwise he'd have his bit of stew at home. And for that old flesh-peddler Maloir, too, an old shrew whom he'd kick out tomorrow! Well, it was a bright prospect for the two of them together, wasn't it, if each of them chucked six francs out of the window every day!

'And let's start by having a look at some accounts, shall we?' he shouted. 'Come on, come clean, what's the position?'

His sordid stinginess was coming to the fore. Utterly intimidated, Nana hurried over to the secretaire to fetch their money and lay it out on the table in front of him. Up to now, they'd left the key in their cash-box so that they could each help themselves as they required.

'What's happened?' he shouted after he'd counted out the money. 'There's barely seven thousand left out of the seventeen we started with and we've been together only three months. It can't be true!'

He dashed over himself, wrenched open the secretaire, and brought the drawer over to rummage in under the light. There was no doubt that there were only six thousand eight hundred or so francs. The storm broke.

'Ten thousand francs in three months!' he screamed. 'Bloody hell! What have you done with them, eh? Tell me! It's all going to that arsehole of an aunt of yours, isn't it? Or you're treating yourself to a few fancy boys, that's obvious! . . . Are you going to answer me?'

'Well, if you're going to lose your temper!' retorted Nana. 'It's easy to work out . . . You haven't reckoned in all the furniture and I've had to buy some linen. It runs away quickly when you're setting up house!'

Having insisted on an explanation, he was now refusing to listen to it.

'Yes, it's running away too quickly for my liking', he went on more calmly. 'And let me tell you, my little girl, I've had enough of sharing our household expenses . . . These seven thousand francs are mine, you know. Well, as they're here, I'm going to hang on to them . . . Now I know that you're incompetent, I don't want to be ruined by you, for Christ's sake! Fair shares all round! This lot's mine!'

And with a lordly gesture, he stuffed the money into his pocket while Nana watched dumbfounded. He continued smugly:

'You must realize I'm not so stupid as to support other people's aunts and children . . . You chose to spend your money, that's your business, but my money's sacrosanct . . . When you cook a leg of lamb, I'll pay half. We'll settle up every night, that's all.'

This was more than Nana could stand.

'Look, it's you who've got through my ten thousand francs!' she cried angrily. 'That's a shit's trick!'

He didn't bother to pursue the discussion. Leaning over the table, he gave her a tremendous swipe across the face, and said:

'Just say that again!'

Despite the blow, Nana did say it again, and he set about her with kicks and punches, soon reducing her to such a state that, as usual, she undressed and went to bed in tears. He was panting. As he was getting into bed himself, he noticed the letter he'd written to Georges lying on the table. He carefully folded it up and turning towards the bed, said threateningly:

'This letter's very good, I'll post it myself because I just can't stand people who put on airs and graces. And stop bloody whining, you're getting on my wick!'

Nana held her breath to quieten her little sobs and when Fontan joined her in bed, she flung herself choking and in tears on to his chest. Their fights always ended like this; she was desperately afraid of losing him, and in spite of everything she needed to know he belonged to her. Twice he pushed her away with a majestic gesture, but the cosy embrace of this woman cowardly begging for mercy, like a faithful hound with large, tearful eyes, excited him and he relented, though not condescending to make any advances himself, letting her stroke and fondle him and take him by force, like a man whose forgiveness is worth working for. Afterwards he felt uneasy, afraid that Nana might be putting on an act to get back the key of the cash-box. The candle had been put out; he felt the need to assert his authority:

'I'm in deadly earnest you know, my girl. I'm hanging on to that money.'

Snuggling into his neck, Nana was dropping off to sleep; she produced an awe-inspiring reply:

'Don't worry, my dearest! . . . I'll go out to work!'

But after that evening, their life together grew increasingly stormy. From one week's end to the next, there was a constant sound of slaps, regulating their lives like the ticking of a clock. Nana got so many thrashings that she became as soft as fine linen, her skin delicate, her complexion pure peaches-and-cream, so tender to the touch and so radiant that she looked even lovelier. As a result, Prullière was always after her, calling when Fontan wasn't at home and pushing her into corners to steal a kiss. She would immediately start struggling, blushing with shame and indignation; she thought it was disgusting to try to betray a friend. Prullière would get annoyed and sneer: what a silly little girl she was turning into! How could she feel attached to such a monkey of a man! After all, Fontan really was like a monkey, with his huge twitching snout. What an ugly mug he'd got! And he kept beating her up, too!

'That's as maybe, but I love him as he is', she replied one day, soberly, like a woman confessing to having a perverse taste.

Bosc was quite content just to come to dinner as often as he could. Behind Prullière's back, he'd shrug his shoulders and say: a pretty young fellow, but flighty. He'd witnessed their domestic rows on a number of occasions; when Fontan was slapping Nana's face, he'd solemnly go on munching, seeing such things as quite natural. His form of singing for his supper was to go into constant raptures over how happy Nana and Fontan were. He claimed he was a philosopher and had given up everything, even fame. When, after a meal, Prullière and Fontan sometimes tilted back on their chairs and let themselves go, retailing stories of past successes till two in the morning, shouting and waving their hands about as if they were still on stage, Bosc would sit back meditatively knocking off the last of the brandy, with an occasional snort of scorn. What was left of Talma* now? Not the slightest trace, so please leave him alone, it was all too stupid!

One night he found Nana in tears. She took off her slip to show him her back and arms which were black and blue. He gazed at her skin without being tempted to take advantage of the situation, as that idiot Prullière would have done. Then, sententiously:

'My dear girl, where there's women, there's whacks! I think it was Napoleon who said that . . . Wash yourself in salt water. Wonderful stuff for that sort of damage, salt water. You'll be getting more of that yet, believe you me, and as long as you don't get any broken bones, don't complain . . . D'you know, I think I saw a bit of leg of lamb, I'm going to invite myself to dinner.'

But Madame Lerat wasn't so philosophical and vented her indignation every time she saw a fresh bruise on her white flesh. Her niece was being killed, that sort of thing couldn't go on . . . In fact, Fontan had shown Madame Lerat the door, saying that he didn't want to see her face again in his house; and ever since, whenever he came home and she was there she had to slip away through the kitchen, which she found extremely humiliating. As a result she never stopped attacking him: he was a lout. Her principal criticism was his vulgarity, which she expressed in a very lady-like way, to emphasize the fact that she herself was impeccably well bred.

'Oh, it's obvious straight away', she'd say to Nana, 'he hasn't got the faintest idea of what's right and proper or not. His mother must have been a common lot, no, it's no good protesting, there's no mistaking that sort of thing! . . . I'm not talking for myself, although someone of my age has the right to some respect, but how can you possibly put up with his bad manners, because, without wanting to flatter myself, I've always taught you how to behave and given you the very best advice. We were all well brought up in our family, weren't we?'

Nana was listening with downcast eyes; she didn't protest.

'And you never knew any but the very best society . . . We were only talking about that yesterday evening with Zoé, at my place. She can't understand you either. "How on earth", she said, "can madam, who'd got the count, such a perfect gentleman, eating out of her hand—because between you and I, he was downright crazy about her—how can madam allow herself to be decimated by that big-nosed freak?" Well, I said to her, one can put up with being knocked about but never would I stand not being respected . . . In fact, there's nothing one can say in his favour, I'd never let him into my house, not in a month of Sundays, I can't bear the sight of him. And here you are, ruining yourself for a real bad lot like that, yes, my darling, you're ruining yourself, you're nearly at the end of your tether, when there are so many others as rich as they come and bigwigs in the government, too. Well, I've said enough, it's not my job to tell you what to do, but the first time he does the dirty on you I'd dump him just like that, with a "Who do you think I am", you know, very grand-like, I've seen you do it before, and leave him high and dry.'

Then Nana burst into tears and said brokenly:

'But I love him, Aunty!'

The truth was that Madame Lerat was worried to see how difficult her niece was finding it to provide her, at infrequent intervals, with the odd franc or two for little Louis's keep. Of course, she was prepared to accept the sacrifice and go on looking after the little lad, hoping for better times. But the thought that Fontan was preventing her, the boy, and his mother, from rolling in money was so infuriating that she didn't want any truck with love. She concluded the conversation with some stern words:

'Listen to me, my dear. One day when he's flayed you alive, you'll come knocking at my door and I'll let you in!'

Money soon became Nana's major concern. Fontan had spirited away the seven thousand francs and no doubt put them in a safe place; she would never dare to raise any questions about the matter because she shrank from speaking freely to that 'bad lot', as her aunt described him; she was terrified he might think she was fond of him because he had a little money. He had certainly promised to contribute to the household expenses, and for the first few days he did give her three francs every morning. But he was determined to get a lot for his money: butter, meat, out-of-season vegetables; and if she gently tried to point out that three francs wasn't enough to buy up the whole market, he'd fly into a temper, call her a good-for-nothing, a stupid, wasteful, bloody fool letting herself be diddled by stall-keepers; and he wasn't slow to hint that he might take his own custom elsewhere. Then, after a month, on some mornings he forgot to leave the three francs on the chest-of-drawers. She timidly, in a roundabout way, tried to remind him, but this gave rise to such squabbles and he made her life so disagreeable on the slightest pretext that she preferred not to have to rely on him. On the other hand, on the days when he hadn't left any money and still found something on the table in the evening, he was as pleased as a dog with two tails, flirtatious, kissing her and dancing round the room with a chair. This made her so happy that she reached the point of wanting not to find the three francs on the chest-of-drawers, in spite of her difficulty in making ends meet. One day she even gave him back the money, telling him some story about still having something left over from the day before. As he hadn't given her any money the day before, he had a moment's hesitation, afraid she might be trying to teach him a lesson. But she was looking at him so lovingly and kissing him, putting herself so completely at his mercy, that he put the coins back into his pocket with the little convulsive quiver of a miser getting back money which he feared he'd lost. From that time on he stopped worrying, never enquired where the cash was coming from, looked sour when there were only potatoes to eat, and laughed delightedly when he saw turkey or a leg of lamb; which didn't prevent him from administering the odd slap, even when he was pleased, just to keep his hand in.

Nana had found a means of providing everything. Some days the house was positively overflowing with food. Twice a week, Bosc would turn up to give himself indigestion. One night when Madame Lerat was taking herself off in a fury, having seen a big dinner being cooked which she herself wouldn't be enjoying, she couldn't resist asking Nana bluntly where the money was coming from. Taken unawares, Nana looked foolish and burst into tears.

'Well, I never did! That's a fine thing, I must say!' exclaimed her aunt, realizing the situation.

Nana had given in for the sake of a quiet life. Anyway, Tricon was to blame. Nana had met her in the Rue de Laval one day when Fontan had stormed out because she'd served up some cod. So she'd said yes to Ma Tricon, who happened at the time to be in some difficulty herself. As Fontan never came back before six she had her afternoons free, and she could bring home forty or sixty francs, sometimes more. If she'd been able to maintain her earlier position she'd have been able to think in terms of two or three hundred, but as it was she was very glad to earn enough to keep the pot boiling. And in the evening, as Bosc sat stuffing himself, she would forget everything when Fontan, with his elbows on the table, allowed her to kiss him on the eyes with the lordly air of a man who is loved for himself alone.

So, still adoring her darling man, her pet lamb, with a passion all the blinder now that it was she who was paying, Nana fell back into the gutter where she had started, prowling around the streets as she had when, as a down-at-heel little slut, she'd been glad to lay hands on a five-franc piece.

One Sunday, at the La Rochefoucauld market, after meeting Satin and furiously telling her off because of Madame Robert, Nana had made it up with her. Satin's only comment had been that if you didn't like doing something yourself, that was no reason to stop anyone else enjoying themselves. And acting on the philosophical principle that you never knew what you might end up doing yourself, Nana had broad-mindedly forgiven her. She even began to feel curious herself about certain odd little secret corners of vice and questioned her on them, amazed at all the things she had to learn at her age, over and above what she already knew; and she laughed, uttering little exclamations and finding it funny, even if a little off-putting, because at heart she was deeply conventional in any matter that didn't form part of her own habits. As a result, when Fontan wasn't going to be dining at home, she went back to eat at Laure's. She was intrigued by the love affairs and jealouses and other happenings which aroused the emotions of Laure's female customers without in any way impairing their appetites. All the same, she wasn't one of them, yet, as she put it. Massive and motherly, Laure kept issuing affectionate invitations for her to spend a few days in her villa at Asnières,* a country house with seven bedrooms for lady guests. Nana was scared and refused. But when Satin assured her that she'd got it wrong, and that she'd find gentlemen from Paris there who'd play pigs-in-clover with you and push your swing for you, she promised she'd go later, when she could get away.

For the moment, Nana was far too worried and distressed to be in the mood for fun of any sort; what she needed was money. When Tricon couldn't use her, which was all too often, Nana was at a loss what to do with her body. When this happened she'd launch out with Satin into wild expeditions on the Paris streets, lurking in muddy little back-streets, offering sex on the cheap. She went back to the sleazy dance-halls on the outskirts of Paris where she'd hopped around in her grubby petticoats in earlier days; she hung around the dark corners of the boulevards in the outer suburbs and the stone posts she'd sat on when she was 15, being kissed by men while her father was trying to find her to tan her backside. The pair of them would hustle around, trying out the dance-halls and cafés of a district, climbing up stairs wet with spittle and spilt beer; or else saunter up streets to take up their post in carriage gateways. Satin had started her career in the Latin Quarter and took Nana down there to Bullier* and the brasseries of the Boulevard Saint-Michel. But the holidays were due to start and the area had a strong smell of lack of cash.

They'd always find their way back to the main boulevards, as still offering them the best chance. In this way, they combed the whole city, from the heights of Montmartre to the plain of the Observatoire, on rainy nights in their down-at-heel bootees, on warm nights when their bodices clung to their skin, hanging around for hours or walking endlessly, jostled and covered in abuse, the parting obscenities of some man picked up on the street and taken to a squalid hotel, as he goes off swearing down the slimy stairs.

Summer was coming to an end, a summer of storms and burning-hot nights. They'd set off together after dinner, around nine o'clock. Along each pavement of the Rue de Notre-Dame-de-la-Lorette, a line of women, slipping along close to the shop-fronts without ever giving them a single glance, would busily scuttle down to the boulevards. It was the Bréda district, hungrily launching its raid as the gas-lights were beginning to come on. Nana and Satin would go down past the church, always following the Rue Le Peletier. Then, a hundred yards short of the Café Riche, as they approached their field of operations, they released the tails of their skirts which they'd been carefully holding up and, letting them sweep the pavement regardless of the dust, they would saunter along, rolling their hips, slowing down when they came into the glare of some large café. Laughing noisily as they swaggered along, glancing back over their shoulders as the men turned to look at them, they were in their element. In the shadow, their whitened faces with the red smudges of their lips and the black patches of their eyelids evoked the disturbing charm of a cheap Oriental bazaar, openly on offer on the public highway. Until eleven o'clock they would remain lively and in good spirits amid the jostling throng on the boulevards, restricting themselves to calling out 'rotten bastard!' after the retreating backs of clumsy men who'd torn off part of a flounce by treading on it; and they'd exchange friendly greetings with café waiters, stop for a chat at a table, accept a drink, which they'd sip slowly, like people glad to be able to sit down, meanwhile waiting for the theatre audiences to emerge. But as the night wore on, if they hadn't made a trip or two up to the room in the Rue de la Rochefoucauld, they'd begin to turn nasty and their pursuit grew grimmer. Under the trees along the boulevards, now darkened and slowly emptying, there'd be ferocious bargainings, abuse and blows would be exchanged, while respectable families, mother, father, and daughters would walk quietly and sedately by, accustomed to witnessing such encounters. Then, after walking a good dozen times from the Opéra to the Gymnase Theatre, seeing that the men were definitely losing interest and making off more quickly as it grew darker and darker, Nana and Satin kept to the pavements of the Rue du Faubourg-Montmartre.* There the restaurants, brasseries, and delicatessens would still be blazing with light till two o'clock in the morning, and a swarm of persistent women would collect round the café entrances; it was the last corner of Paris which stayed alive and full of light at night, the last market-place still open to strike a bargain for the night, where trade was conducted in groups, crudely, along the whole street, as in the public corridor of a brothel. And on those nights when they went back empty-handed, they would squabble with each other. The Rue Notre-Dame-de-la-Lorette stretched out dark and deserted; shadowy female figures were still lurking around; men were coming home late; prostitutes, miserable and exasperated at not having had a single client all night but unwilling to give up, were still arguing in husky voices with some stray drunk whom they'd managed to corner by the Rue Bréda or the Rue Fontaine.

All the same, there were odd windfalls: twenty francs collected from respectable, middle-class gentlemen who slipped the decoration out of their buttonhole into their pocket as they made their way upstairs—Satin in particular had a good nose for this sort of man. On wet nights, when Paris had the stale, damp smell of a bedroom not properly cleaned, she knew that this gamy, musty odour made men crazy for a woman. And she'd keep a look-out for the best-dressed ones; she could recognize them by their pale eyes. It was as if a wave of wild randiness was sweeping over the city. True, she was a little scared because it was the most prim and proper who were the dirtiest; all their veneer vanished, they became like animals, insisting on the most revolting practices and every possible refinement of perversion. This was why the little floozy was no respecter of persons, letting fly when she saw people sitting in their carriages looking all dignified; their coachmen were nicer, because they respected women and didn't want filthy, unnatural, freaky things which did for a girl. Even Nana, who had certain preconceptions which Satin was busily demolishing, was surprised that smart people could sink so low. So there's no decency left any more, she'd say, when she was in a serious mood: people were lying to each other, from the top to the bottom. Well, a fine sight that must be in Paris from nine in the evening to three o'clock in the morning! And she laughed out loud and exclaimed that you'd see some funny things if you could look into every bedroom, with ordinary people having it off with each other like mad and quite a few grand people as well, here and there, with their snouts in the trough, even dirtier than the others. Her education was being completed.

One night when coming to pick up Satin, she recognized the Marquis de Chouard tottering downstairs, white-faced and clutching the banister. She pretended to be blowing her nose. When she got upstairs, seeing the dreadful squalor in which Satin lived, with everything neglected from one week's end to the next, she expressed surprise that Satin knew the marquis. Oh yes, she knew him all right, and what a bore he'd been for her and her pastry-cook boyfriend when they'd been together! Now he came back occasionally but he got on her nerves, he used to stick his nose in every little dirty corner, even sniffing her slippers.

'Yes, my dear, my slippers! . . . Oh, he's a really disgusting old man! He's always asking you to do all sorts of things! . . .'

The thing which bothered Nana most was the genuineness of this disgusting debauchery. She remembered how, at the time of her theatrical success, she would pretend to be enjoying such things, whereas now she found herself surrounded by tarts who every day were gradually succumbing to their way of life. What was worse was that Satin had made her scared stiff of the police. She had a whole stock of stories on the subject. She'd previously been going to bed with a member of the vice squad so as to be left in peace; he'd twice been able to help her to avoid having to register as a prostitute,* and she was terrified that if they nabbed her once more, she'd be sunk . . . And that wasn't all! To qualify for a bonus, police officers would arrest as many women as possible; they'd haul in everyone, and if you made a fuss they'd shut you up with a slap in the face, certain of being backed up by the authorities and rewarded, even if they hauled in a respectable girl. In the summer, groups of twelve to fifteen of them would operate round-ups on the boulevards; they would close off a stretch of pavement and pick up as many as thirty women in one night. But Satin knew the spots they worked in, and as soon as she caught sight of a policeman she'd make herself scarce among the panic-stricken women in long skirts trying to slip away in the crowd.

The women were so terrified of the power of the law and the dreaded central police headquarters that some of them would stand rooted to the spot outside the cafés as the police swept ruthlessly up the street. But Satin was even more scared of being framed; her pastry cook had been such a bastard as to threaten to turn her in after she'd left him: yes, there were men who used that trick to live off their girl-friend's earnings, quite apart from bloody-minded women who might very well put the police on to you behind your back, just because you were prettier than they were. As she listened to these tales, Nana became more and more frightened. She'd always had a fear of the law, that unknown power by which men could wreak vengeance on her and eliminate her without anyone being able to defend her. She saw Saint-Lazare* as a pit, a dark hole in which women were buried alive after having their hair cut off. She told herself that of course she only needed to dump Fontan in order to get protection. Satin had told her about lists of women's names, with their photos, which the police had to consult; and they had been told not to molest any women on the lists. But Nana was still apprehensive; she could see herself being hustled and dragged away and next day having to submit to a medical examination, and the thought of lying exposed on the doctor's chair shocked and distressed her, even though she'd done far more indecent things dozens of times before.

One evening towards the end of September, when she was walking with Satin along the Boulevard Poissonnière, her friend suddenly took to her heels and when Nana asked what was up, she hissed:

'The cops! Get cracking!'

Everyone was joining in a wild stampede through the crowd. Skirts were swirling and getting torn; people were shouting, blows were being struck. A woman fell over. The crowd laughed as they watched the relentless thrust of the police rapidly closing in on their prey. Meanwhile Nana had lost sight of Satin. Her legs had turned to jelly, and she would certainly have been caught if a man hadn't grasped her by the arm and led her away under the nose of the furious police officers. It was Prullière, who had caught sight of her in the crowd. Without saying a word he took her into the Rue

Rougemont, which was deserted and where she was able to get her breath back. She was almost fainting and he had to support her. She didn't even thank him.

'Come along now', he said, 'you must pull yourself together . . . Come up to my room.'

He lived just round the corner, in the Rue Bergère. She immediately reacted.

'No, I don't want to!'

He became crude:

'It happens all the time, doesn't it? Why don't you want to?'

'Because.'

In her view, that was sufficient explanation: she was too fond of Fontan to betray him with one of his friends. The others didn't count as long as she got no pleasure out of it and she did it out of necessity. Faced by such stupid pigheadedness, which offended his vanity—he was good-looking enough, wasn't he?—young Prullière turned nasty:

'OK, please yourself, my dear girl, but I'm afraid I'm not going your way . . . You'll have to fend for yourself . . .'

And he left her standing there, once again terrified. She took an enormously roundabout route to get back to Montmartre, scurrying along close to the shop-windows as fast as she could, going pale with fright each time she saw a man coming towards her.

Next day, still shaken by her terrifying experience, Nana was on her way to her aunt's when she ran into Labordette in a lonely side-street hidden away in Batignolles. At first, they both looked embarrassed. Always anxious to oblige people, he was on an errand which concerned matters he wanted to keep secret. He was the first to recover, exclaiming how nice it was to see her. Really, everyone had been quite flabbergasted at her complete disappearance. People were calling for her return, her old friends were positively pining away without her. He started lecturing her in a fatherly tone of voice:

'Between you, me, and the gatepost, my dear, it's a bit farcical. We can all understand a passing fancy, but to let it go so far, getting swindled and then bashed about as a reward . . . Are you hoping to get a prize for good conduct?'

She was looking embarrassed. But when he mentioned how

cock-a-hoop Rose was at having got her claws into Muffat, her eyes blazed and she muttered:

'Ah, if I wanted to . . .'

Obliging as ever, he immediately said he'd be only too happy to offer his services, as a friend . . . She refused. He then tackled her from another angle, telling her that Bordenave was putting on a play by Fauchery in which there was a superb part for her.

'Did you say a play with a part for me?' she exclaimed, unable to believe her ears. 'But he's in it and didn't tell me a thing about it!'

She didn't mention Fontan's name and quickly regained her composure. She'd no intention of ever going back to the stage. But Labordette must have remained unconvinced because he persisted, with a smile:

'You know, with me there's nothing to fear, I'll soften up Muffat for you. You go back on to the stage and I'll see he's returned to you meek as a lamb.'

'No!' she retorted vigorously.

And she went on her way, filled with self-pity for her heroic conduct. No male bastard would have sacrificed himself like that without proclaiming it from the house-tops. But one thing did strike her: Labordette had just given her the same advice as Francis. When Fontan came home that night, she questioned him about Fauchery's play. He himself had gone back to acting at the Variétés two months ago. Why hadn't he told her about that part?

'What part?' he replied in his boorish way. 'You don't mean the part of the duchess, do you? God, you really do fancy yourself, don't you! But you'd be a complete and utter flop in that sort of part. You really are a joke!'

She was deeply offended. For the rest of the evening he pulled her leg, addressing her as Mademoiselle Mars.* And the more he ridiculed her, the more she gritted her teeth, taking a bitter enjoyment in her crazy, heroic infatuation which made her, in her eyes, a very noble woman, capable of great love. Ever since she'd been going with other men in order to provide for Fontan, she loved him all the more because of the disgust and hardships she suffered for his sake. He was her private vice which she couldn't do without and for which she was prepared to pay the price; his thrashings added zest. Seeing how stupidly good-natured she was, in the end Fontan started to take advantage. She was getting on his nerves and a savage hatred was growing inside him, even blinding him to his own interests. Any comments by Bosc would make him fly into a rage for no apparent reason; he'd shout that he didn't give a damn for her or her wonderful meals, that he'd kick her out just for the pleasure of offering his seven thousand francs to some other woman. And that was how their relationship eventually broke up.

Coming home one night at eleven o'clock, Nana found the door bolted. She knocked once without reply; she knocked again; still no reply. However, she could see light under the door, and inside the room Fontan was making no attempt to keep quiet. She kept on knocking and calling out to him; she was beginning to lose her temper. Eventually, she heard him say something in his deliberate, gruff voice: just two words:

'Get stuffed!'

She struck the door with her fists.

'Get stuffed!'

She pounded on the door even harder, almost splitting it:

'Get stuffed!'

And for the next fifteen minutes he flung the same crude insult at her as a sort of jeering echo to each of her knocks. Then, seeing that she wasn't going to give up, he suddenly whipped open the door and stood with his arms crossed firmly barring the way and said in the same cold, brutal voice:

'Christ all-bloody-mighty! Can't you take a hint? What the bloody hell do you want? We're trying to go to sleep! Can't you see I've got a visitor?'

And, indeed, he was not alone. Nana caught a glimpse of the little woman from the Bouffes, already half-undressed, with her faded blonde hair and gimlet eyes, thoroughly enjoying the situation in the comfort of the furniture that Nana had bought with her own money. However, Fontan had a terrible look in his eyes, his thick fingers were clawing at the air. He took a step forward:

'Now fuck off or I'll wring your bloody neck!'

Breaking into hysterical sobs, Nana took fright and fled. This time, it really was she who was being kicked out. In her rage, suddenly the memory of Muffat crossed her mind; but it wasn't fair for Fontan to have returned the compliment.

Outside on the pavement, her first thought was to seek refuge for the night with Satin, unless she had someone with her. But she met her in front of her house; she'd also just been turned out by her landlord who'd put a padlock on her door, a thing he'd absolutely no right to do, it was her furniture. She was cursing and swearing and threatening to put the police on to him. In the meantime, as it was striking twelve, they had to do something about finding a bed for the night. In the end, thinking it wiser not to involve the police in her affairs, Satin took Nana round to a little lodging-house run by a lady she knew in the Rue de Laval. She gave them a tiny room on the first floor overlooking the courtyard.

'I'd have gone to Madame Robert', Satin was saying, 'she's always able to squeeze me in somewhere. But it wouldn't have been possible with you there . . . She's becoming ridiculously jealous . . . She walloped me the other night.'

As soon as the door was closed behind them, Nana, who'd been holding herself in, burst into tears and told Satin over and over again about Fontan's disgusting behaviour. Each time Satin listened sympathetically and tried to comfort her, growing more and more indignant as she pitched into the male sex:

'Oh, they're pigs, just dirty pigs! We don't want anything more to do with pigs like that!'

She helped Nana undress, fussing round her like a dutiful little wife and coaxing her to come to bed.

'We'll be better there, my pet. Let's go to bed straight away. Oh, you're stupid to get so het up! They're all shits, I'm telling you! Stop thinking about them . . . I'm very very fond of you, so please stop crying for the sake of your darling little Satin!'

Once they were in bed, she immediately started cuddling Nana and soothing her. She didn't want to hear Fontan's name ever again; every time Nana said it, she cut her off with a pretty little pout of indignation and a kiss on her lips; her hair was hanging loose and she looked like a charming affectionate little girl. Cuddling in her soft arms, Nana gradually dried her tears. Feeling affectionate herself, she started kissing and hugging Satin, too. When the clock struck two, the candle still hadn't been put out; they were both billing and cooing and stifling their giggles.

Suddenly, Satin heard a noise on the ground-floor; half-naked, she shot upright in bed and listened.

'The cops!' she cried, white in the face. 'Oh hell, what rotten luck! Now we are in the shit!'

She'd often talked about police-raids on hotels, yet for once, on that very night when they'd taken shelter in the Rue de Laval, they'd both been caught napping. Hearing that it was the police, Nana lost her head, sprang out of bed, ran across the room, and opened the window with the distraught, mad look of someone preparing to throw herself out. But fortunately the little courtyard had a glass roof and there was a protective iron grating level with the window. She didn't hesitate: with her slip flapping round her, she lifted her bare thigh over the window-sill and disappeared into the dark night air.

'Oh, stay here!' Satin kept saying in a scared voice. 'You'll kill yourself!'

Then, hearing banging on their door, like the nice girl she was, she ran over, pulled the window to, and bundled her friend's clothes into a cupboard. She'd already accepted the inevitable, telling herself that, after all, if they did register her she'd no longer have this stupid fear hanging over her any more. She pretended to be fast asleep, yawned, argued, and finally opened up to a tall, burly young fellow with a dirty beard who said to her:

'Let's see your hands. No sign of needle-pricks there, you can't have a job. Come on, get your clothes on!'

'But my job's burnishing, not dressmaking', said Satin cheekily.

However she got dressed without making any fuss, knowing that there was no point in protesting. Shouting could be heard in the hotel; one of the tarts was hanging on to the doorpost and refusing to go quietly; another one, in bed with her lover who was vouching for her, pretended to be outraged, she was a decent girl, and she talked of suing the chief police commissioner. For more than an hour heavy boots could be heard tramping up and down the stairs, fists banging on doors, shrill protests ending in stifled sobs, the swish of skirts against walls; a whole herd of frightened women was being suddenly woken up and brutally carted off by three police officers under the command of an extremely polite little blond-haired police superintendent. Finally deep silence again descended on the little hotel.

Nobody had given her away; Nana was safe. Shivering and half dead with fright, she groped her way back into the room. Her feet were bleeding, gashed by the sharp grating. For a long time she sat on the bed, listening. Towards morning, however, she dropped off to sleep. When she woke up at eight o'clock, she quickly slipped out of the hotel and hurried round to her aunt's. Madame Lerat happened to be taking her breakfast cup of coffee with Zoé, and when she saw her at this early hour of the morning, looking so bedraggled and distraught, she realized immediately what had happened.

'Well, that's that, isn't it?' She exclaimed. 'I told you he'd flay you alive, didn't I? Come in, dear, you know I'll never turn you away.'

Zoé had stood up and in a friendly, respectful voice said quietly:

'Madam's come home to us at last. I've been waiting for madam to come.'

But Madame Lerat wanted Nana to go and give little Louis a kiss straight away because, she said, his mother's good sense would be the nicest possible present she could give him. Louiset was still asleep. He looked a sickly, anaemic little boy; when Nana bent over his white, scrofulous face, all the trials and tribulations of the past few months welled up inside her, choking her.

'Oh, my poor little boy!' she stammered, breaking into sobs for the last time. 'Oh, my poor, dear little boy!'

Chapter 9

THEY were rehearsing *The Little Duchess* at the Variétés, and having worked over the first act were about to start on the second. On the proscenium, Fauchery and Bordenave were sitting in a couple of old armchairs having a discussion while Cossard, the prompter, an aged hunchback, sat on a rush-seated chair with a pencil held between his teeth, thumbing through the script.

'Well, what's everybody waiting for?' shouted Bordenave suddenly, furiously thumping the floor with his big stick. 'Why aren't we starting, Barillot?'

'It's Monsieur Bosc. He's disappeared', replied Barillot, who functioned as assistant stage-manager.

All hell broke loose. Everyone began calling for Bosc. Bordenave was blaspheming.

'Christ Almighty, it's always the same old story. You give them a warning bell and they're always somewhere else. And then they bellyache like mad if they're kept after four o'clock.'

However, Bosc now appeared, completely unruffled.

'What's the fuss? What do you want me for? Ah, I see, it's my turn. You should have let me know . . . OK, Simonne gives her cue, "Here come the guests", and on I come . . . Where do I come on from?'

'Through the door, of course', said Fauchery irritably.

'OK, but where is the door?'

This time Bordenave jumped on Barillot, swearing and again banging the floor with his stick.

'Christ Almighty, I said put a chair there to represent the door. The scenery's got to be set up on stage every day. Barillot? Where the devil's he gone? . . . Here we go again. They're never there when they're needed!'

Bowing to the storm, without saying a word, Barillot himself went over and put the chair in place. The rehearsal resumed. Wearing a hat and her voluminous fur coat,

Simonne went through the motions of a maid arranging the furniture, but stopping to say:

'It's jolly cold, you know. I'm going to keep my hands in my muff.'

Then, with a change of voice, she greeted Bosc with a little cry:

'Well, if it isn't the count himself! You're the first to arrive, sir, and madam will be very pleased.'

Bosc had on muddy trousers and a large yellow overcoat with an enormous muffler wrapped round the collar. Hands in pockets, wearing an old hat and making no attempt to act he drawled in a toneless voice:

'Don't disturb your mistress, Isabelle. I want to take her by surprise.'

The rehearsal proceeded. Bordenave was slumped in his armchair listening with a tired expression on his scowling face. Fauchery kept nervously fidgeting, constantly itching to interrupt but restraining himself. Then, behind him in the dark, empty auditorium, he heard whispering.

'Has she arrived?' he asked, bending towards Bordenave.

The latter nodded. Before accepting the part of Géraldine which he was offering her, Nana had wanted to see the play because she was dubious about accepting yet another part as a tart; she had dreams of finally getting a role as a respectable woman. She had secreted herself in a dark, empty stage box with Labordette, who was actively concerning himself on her behalf with Bordenave. Fauchery glanced over to see where she was and then went back to watching the rehearsal.

Only the apron was lit, by a tiny auxiliary light connected to the gas-pipe which supplied the footlights. It had a yellow reflector that lit only the foreground, and in the semi-darkness it cast a sinister glare like a large, sad, yellow eye. In order to see properly, Cossard was holding the script close to the stem of this little lamp, directly under the light which emphasized the hump on his back. Beyond him, Bordenave and Fauchery were already half-engulfed in the gloom. In the middle of this vast auditorium this tiny lamp was like a railway lantern hanging on a post; it illuminated an area only a few yards wide in which the actors and their dancing shadows behind them were like eerie visions in a nightmare. The rest of the stage was covered in the sort of haze found on demolition sites, a church nave gutted and cluttered with ladders, frames, and stage-sets whose dingy paint made them look like piles of rubble; and the backdrops suspended in the air looked like ragged pieces of cloth hanging down from the beams of some huge fabric warehouse. At the very top, a bright ray of sun shining down through a window cut a golden beam of light through the gloom of the rigging-loft.

Meanwhile, at the back of the stage, actors were chatting together waiting for their cues. Their voices were gradually becoming louder.

'Look, can't you shut up?' yelled Bordenave, jerking upright in his chair. 'I can't hear a word . . . If you want to talk, you can go outside. We're working in here . . . Barillot, if anyone talks again, I'll fine the whole lot.'

For a second, they kept quiet. They formed a little group sitting on a bench and rustic chairs in the corner of a garden, the first scene of the evening performance which was all ready to set up. Fontan and Prullière were listening to Rose Mignon: she'd just been offered a magnificent contract by the manager of the Folies Dramatiques. A voice shouted:

'The Duchess! . . . Saint-Firmin! . . . Come along, the duchess and Saint-Firmin!'

It wasn't until they called him a second time that Prullière remembered he was Saint-Firmin. Rose, who was the duchess Hélène, was already waiting for their entrance. Dragging his feet over the empty, hollow-sounding boards, old Bosc slowly came back to take a seat. Clarisse offered him half her bench.

'What's he bawling like that for?' she said, referring to Bordenave. 'It's going to be really wonderful later on . . . We can't put on a new show now without him having kittens!'

Bosc gave a shrug. He was above all these squalls. Fontan muttered:

'He can scent a flop. This play looks idiotic to me.'

Then, returning to the subject of Rose:

'Do you believe that offer from the Folies? Three hundred francs a night for a hundred performances? . . . Why not throw in a place in the country as well? If they gave his wife three hundred francs, Mignon would drop Bordenave pronto!'

Clarisse did believe in the three hundred francs. Fontan

was always running down his colleagues! But Simonne broke in. She was shivering. Everyone was buttoned and muffled up to their necks, watching the ray of sun which was shining in at the top without ever penetrating as far as the cold, gloomy stage. Outside, with a clear November sky, it was freezing.

'And they haven't lit a fire in the fireplace!' Simonne continued. 'It's disgusting, he's getting so stingy! . . . As for me, I'm tempted to go off. I don't want to catch anything nasty.'

For a few minutes there was nothing to be heard but the confused murmur of the actors speaking their lines. They were scarcely bothering to make any gestures, but when they wanted to make a special point they would throw a sudden glance into the auditorium which opened up in front of them, a gaping hole of vague shadows, like a tall, window-less hay-loft full of fine dust. The body of the theatre was gloomy, lit only by the half-light from the stage: it seemed sunk in an alarming, dreary slumber. The ceiling paintings were in complete darkness. Hanging down over the stage boxes on both sides were enormous grey canvas strips to protect the curtains, and there were further covers all round the edge of the velvet-covered handrails of the balconies, a sort of double shroud matching the overall gloom. In this pervading ghostly light, the only things which stood out were the darker recesses of the boxes picking out the carcass of each floor-level, while their plush armchairs showed up as red patches, veering towards black. The chandelier had been completely lowered, filling the orchestra stalls with its crystals, leaving the impression of someone moving house, as if the public was going away on a trip and not intending to come back.

At that moment, Rose Mignon, who was playing the part of the little duchess who'd found her way by mistake into the house of a tart, walked towards the footlights, held out her hands, and pouted adorably at this dark, empty auditorium, as gloomy as a house of mourning.

'Goodness me, what a queer bunch of people', she said pointedly, certain of the effect she would create.

Wrapped in a large shawl Nana was listening to the play, hidden at the back of a ground-floor box; she was watching Rose intently. Turning towards Labordette, she asked him in an undertone:

'You're positive he's coming?'

'Absolutely positive. I imagine he'll be with Mignon, to give him an excuse for coming . . . As soon as he appears, you must go up to Mathilde's dressing-room. I'll show you the way.'

They were referring to Count Muffat. Labordette had arranged an interview on neutral territory. He'd had a serious talk with Bordenave, whose financial situation had been badly shaken recently by two failures in succession, and as a result he'd been more than ready to offer a part to Nana in one of his plays, thereby hoping to oblige the count and get a loan out of him.

'What's your view of the Géraldine part?' Labordette continued.

Nana sat still and didn't reply. After the first act, which showed the Duc de Beaurivage deceiving his wife with the blonde Géraldine, an operetta star, in the second act the Duchess Hélène goes to a masked ball in the singer's house to discover by what magic such ladies bewitched and held on to other women's husbands. She is taken along by the handsome Oscar de Saint-Firmin who hopes to seduce her himself. The first lesson she learns comes when, to her great surprise, she hears Géraldine abusing the duke like a fishwife while he laps it up delightedly, leading her to exclaim: 'Well, if that's the way you need to talk to men! . . .' This was practically Géraldine's only scene in the whole act. As for the duchess, it didn't take long before she was punished for her curiosity: mistaking her for a tart, an old buck, the Baron de Tardiveau, becomes very pressing while on a couch on the other side of the stage Beaurivage makes his peace with Géraldine by giving her a kiss. As the part hadn't yet been allotted to anybody old Cossard had gone over to read it and, in spite of himself, was interpreting it, acting it out in Bosc's arms. They'd just reached that part of the scene and the rehearsal was dragging miserably on, when suddenly Fauchery shot out of his chair. Till now he'd been able to restrain himself but his nerves could stand it no longer.

'That's not the way to do it!' he shouted.

The actors stopped and stood undecided, their hands dangling. With his usual air of not giving a damn, Fontan stuck his nose in the air and enquired stiffly:

'What's not the way to do what?'

'Everybody's got it wrong, quite wrong!' retorted Fauchery, waving his arms about; and marching up and down, he started to mime the scene himself. 'Look, Fontan, you must convey how excited and eager Tardiveau is, you've got to lean over like this and catch hold of the duchess . . . And Rose, that's when you do a quick little turn like this, but not too soon, wait until you hear the kiss . . .'

He broke off and in the heat of the moment, called out to Cossard:

'Géraldine, now you give him that kiss . . . A loud one, so it can be heard.'

Old Cossard turned towards Bosc and vigorously smacked his lips.

'Good, that's OK for the kiss', continued Fauchery triumphantly. 'Let's have it once more . . . Now Rose, you see I've had time to turn and come back and I utter a little cry: "Oh, she's kissed him!" But to do that, Tardiveau must be a little more upstage. D'you get that, Fontan, you move upstage . . . Right, now try that all together.'

The actors repeated the scene, but Fontan was making so little effort that it didn't work at all. Twice Fauchery had to repeat his instructions, each time miming more heatedly. They listened bleakly, exchanged a brief glance as if they were being asked to walk on their hands, and tried it out so clumsily that they came to a full stop, looking as stiff as marionettes whose strings had broken.

'No, it's beyond me, I can't understand', said Fontan eventually, in his insolent way.

Bordenave was keeping quiet; he'd slid right down into his chair with his hat pulled down over his eyes, leaving only its top visible in the dim light of the tiny gas-jet. He'd let go of his stick, which was lying across his stomach. He suddenly jerked upright.

'My dear boy, it's idiotic', he said to Fauchery, calmly.

'What do you mean, idiotic?' the author said, going very pale. 'Idiotic yourself, my dear man.'

Bordenave was annoyed. He repeated the word 'idiotic' and then, looking for something more forceful, produced 'imbecilic' and 'cretinous'. It would be booed, they'd never get to the end of the act. In exasperation, although not unduly put out by this exchange of amenities, which were a regular feature with every new show, Fauchery now bluntly called him a pig, whereupon Bordenave flew off the handle, waving his stick about, puffing like a bull and shouting:

'Christ Almighty! For God's sake, why don't you bugger off? We've wasted a quarter of an hour on this crap . . . yes, sheer bloody crap. It's utter rubbish. Yet it's as simple as falling off a log! Fontan, you stay quite still. Rose, you make a little movement, you see, like this, no more, and come downstage . . . OK and this time make it work. Cossard, let's have your kiss.'

Everyone was confused; the scene still didn't go any better. Bordenave himself started miming with all the grace of a bull elephant, while Fauchery shrugged his shoulders and sneered pityingly. Fontan now decided to take a hand himself, and even Bosc felt free to offer advice. Rose had sat down exhausted on the chair which represented the doorway. Nobody knew exactly what was happening. To complete the confusion, thinking she'd heard her cue, Simonne made her entrance too soon, which so enraged Bordenave that, brandishing his stick, he gave her an enormous wallop on her backside; at rehearsals he often whacked women he'd been to bed with. She scuttled off as he shouted furiously after her:

'That'll teach you and by Christ, if there's any more fart-arsing about, I'll close the whole show down!'

Fauchery had pulled his hat down over his ears and looked as if he was intending to leave the theatre. However, he stayed on at the back of the stage and when he saw Bordenave resume his seat, sweating heavily, he himself came back and sat down again. For a moment, they both sat motionless, side by side. A deep hush fell over the dark auditorium. The actors were waiting, feeling as exhausted as if they'd just done some very hard work. Two minutes went by.

'Well, let's move on', said Bordenave finally, in his normal voice, perfectly calm.

'Yes, let's do that', echoed Fauchery. 'We'll straighten that scene out tomorrow.'

They stretched out in their chairs and the rehearsal proceeded on its bored and apathetic course. During the set-to between the manager and the author, Fontan and the others had been listening delightedly at the back of the stage, on the bench and the rustic chairs, giggling and grumbling, with a few savage comments. But when Simonne came back blubbing with her whacked backside, feelings rose: if it had been them, they'd have throttled that swine. She dried her tears, nodding agreement: that was the end for her, she was going to ditch him, the more so as yesterday Steiner had offered to back her. Clarisse expressed surprise: the banker was flat broke; but Prullière gave a laugh and reminded them of his previous 'kike's trick' when he'd flaunted himself with Rose to establish his credibility on the Stock Exchange at the time he was floating his Landes Saltpan venture. And in fact he was just launching a new project, a tunnel under the Bosphorus.

Simonne was listening with great interest. As for Clarisse, she'd been livid all that week: just think, that beast la Faloise, whom she'd dumped by tipping him into the venerable clutches of Gaga, was about to inherit from a very wealthy uncle! And that bastard Bordenave had once again given her a bit part, only fifty lines, as if she couldn't have played the role of Géraldine! She was longing to get that part, in the hope that Nana would turn it down.

'Well, what about me?' said Prullière glumly. 'I've got less than two hundred lines. I was tempted not to accept . . . It's scandalous to make me play that wimp Saint-Firmin. And Fauchery's style! . . . You know, we've got a lead balloon on our hands, my dears!'

Simonne, who'd been chatting with Barillot, now hurried back breathlessly.

'By the way, Nana's here.'

'Where is she?' asked Clarisse sharply, jumping to her feet.

The news spread like wildfire. They were all craning their necks. For a second, the rehearsal seemed to have come to a standstill. Then, suddenly emerging from his lethargy, Bordenave shouted:

'What's going on? Come on, let's get this act finished . . . And stop talking over there, we can't hear a word!'

In her ground-floor box Nana was continuing to follow the

play. Twice Labordette tried to speak to her, but she dug him impatiently in the ribs to warn him to keep quiet. The second act was coming to an end when two shadowy figures appeared at the back of the theatre. As they tiptoed noiselessly towards the stage, Nana recognized Mignon and Count Muffat; they silently shook hands with Bordenave.

'Ah, there they are', she muttered with a sigh of relief.

Rose Mignon spoke her last line. Bordenave said they'd have to go over the second act again before starting on the third, and left the rehearsal to welcome the count with exaggerated politeness while Fauchery acted as if he was interested only in the cast which had gathered round him. Mignon was whistling gently with his hands behind his back, not taking his eyes off his wife, who appeared nervous.

'Well, shall we go up?' Labordette asked Nana. 'I'll take you up to the dressing-room and then come back and fetch him.'

Nana left the box straight away. She had to grope her way along the orchestra-stalls corridor, but as she was slipping quickly away Bordenave glimpsed her in the darkness and caught up with her at the end of the passageway which ran behind the stage, a narrow tunnel, gas-lit day and night. Wanting to clinch the matter on the spot, he started enthusing about the part of Géraldine.

'What a part, eh? Absolutely smashing, just right for you! Why not come along and start rehearsing tomorrow?'

Nana seemed unimpressed. She'd like to hear something about the third act.

'The third act? A real snorter! . . . The duchess starts playing the tart in her own house and this disgusts Beaurivage, who becomes a reformed character. And it includes a very funny scene where Tardiveau comes along under the mistaken impression he's at a dancer's house.'

'And what's Géraldine doing all this time?'

'Géraldine?' repeated Bordenave, a trifle embarrassed. 'She's got one scene, not terribly long but very effective. Just the thing for you, I'm telling you! Will you sign on?'

She was watching him closely. Finally she replied:

'Let's talk about it a bit later.'

And she caught up with Labordette waiting for her at the

staircase. The whole cast had recognized her; people were whispering together. Prullière was scandalized to see her back, Clarisse very worried about her part. As for Fontan, he pretended to be unconcerned and unmoved; it wasn't for him to run down a woman he'd loved, although at heart, now that his recent infatuation for her had turned into hatred, he was still nursing a savage resentment towards her because of the devotion she'd shown him, her beauty, and their life together which he'd thrown away through his revolting conduct.

Meanwhile, when Labordette reappeared and went over to the count, Rose Mignon, alerted by Nana's presence, suddenly realized what was afoot. Muffat bored her stiff, but the thought of being dropped in this way infuriated her. Normally reticent about such matters with her husband, she burst out harshly:

'You see what's happening? If she tries the same trick she did with Steiner, I swear I'll scratch her eyes out!'

Quite unmoved, Mignon majestically shrugged his shoulders with the air of a man who knows all the answers.

'Be quiet, will you?' he muttered. 'Just do me the favour of keeping your mouth shut!'

He knew where he stood. He'd squeezed Muffat dry and he knew that one sign from Nana would be enough to make the count lie down and let her wipe her feet on him. You can't fight that sort of passion. So, knowing what men are like, his only concern was to extract the greatest benefit possible out of the situation. He'd just have to wait and see.

'On stage, Rose!' called Bordenave. 'We're starting the second act again.'

'Come along, off you go', said Mignon. 'Just leave it all to me.'

And unable to resist his little joke, he mockingly congratulated Fauchery on his play. An excellent play—but why had he made the aristocratic lady so respectable? Hardly true to life, was it? And he asked with a grin who'd been the model for Beaurivage, Géraldine's twerp of a lover. Far from showing annoyance, Fauchery gave a smile. But Mignon was disturbed to see Bordenave casting a glance in Muffat's direction and appearing put out. His facetiousness evaporated.

'Let's get cracking, for Christ's sake!' yelled Bordenave.

'Come along, Barillot . . . What's that? Bosc's not here? Is he trying to completely bugger up the whole show?'

However, Bosc now appeared, unperturbed as ever. The rehearsal started again, just as Labordette left with the count, who was quivering at the thought of seeing Nana again. After their breakup his life had seemed completely empty and, quite at a loss, he'd let himself be taken along to Rose, imagining that it was the change in his habits that was causing him such distress. In any case, in his bewildered state he wanted to draw a veil over everything, rejecting any thought of approaching Nana and shying away from any confrontation with the countess, feeling that this was the only dignified thing to do. But hidden forces were at work inside him, and slowly Nana was winning him back through his memories, his inability to resist her sex-appeal, and by a new feeling of almost fatherly tenderness focused entirely on her. The memory of that horrible scene was fading; Fontan had disappeared from sight, and he'd forgotten Nana's dreadful words when she'd turned him out and flung his wife's adultery in his face, nothing but mere words that had vanished into thin air leaving him with his heart gripped by a feeling of tenderness so painful that he felt suffocated. He was acting like a child, accusing himself and imagining she would never have betrayed him had he loved her properly. His distress was becoming unbearable and he was very unhappy. It wasn't like his earlier blind lust, when he was ready to accept anything for the sake of immediate gratification, but more the sharp ache of an old wound; his desire had turned into a jealous passion, an obsessive desire for her alone, her hair, her mouth, her body. When he recalled the sound of her voice, a shiver would run through every limb. His love for her was infinitely tender, as desperately tenacious as a miser's, so overpowering and so painful that when Labordette, that prince of wheelers and dealers, came and offered to arrange a meeting with Nana he couldn't resist flinging himself into his arms, feeling ashamed afterwards at having let himself go and acting so ridiculously for a man in his position. But Labordette saw everything and said nothing. He gave a further proof of his tact when he left the count at the foot of the stairway, saying discreetly:

'Second floor, right-hand passage, the door's not closed.'

Muffat was alone in this silent corner of the building. As he'd passed by the green room, he'd seen through the open doors how run-down this huge room was, how deplorably filthy and decrepit in the full light of day. But as he moved out of the darkness and commotion of the stage, he was struck by the brightness and stillness of the stairs where one night he'd met gas-fumes and which had been resounding with pounding women's feet as they scampered away on the various floors. He could sense the deserted dressing-rooms and empty corridors, not one single sound, not a single soul, while the pale November sun shone through the square windows set at floor-level, casting patches of yellow light dancing with dust, and a death-like peace descended from above. He was glad of this silence and calm as he went slowly up, recovering his breath; his heart was pounding and he was afraid he might start gasping and crying and behaving like a child, so on the first floor he leaned back against the wall, sure of not being observed. Holding his handkerchief to his mouth, he stood looking at the uneven stair-treads, the flaking distemper, the banister worn smooth by the rubbing of many hands, the whole brothel squalor cruelly exposed in this wan, afternoon light, the time when prostitutes are asleep. However, when he reached the second floor he had to step over a large ginger cat curled up on the stairs. With eyes half-closed, drowsy from the smells left behind every night by the women and which were now cold and fuggy, this cat was the only caretaker for the house.

The door of the dressing-room in the right-hand passage was, as Labordette had said, only pushed to. Nana was waiting. Mathilde, a little slut of a girl who favoured ingénue parts, kept her dressing-room in a revolting state, with a clutter of chipped pots and jars, a greasy wash-stand, and a chair with red stains that looked like blood on its rush seat. The paper on the walls and ceiling had been splashed up to the top with soapy water. There was such a foul smell, like lavender-water which had gone off, that Nana had opened the window, resting her elbows on the sill for a moment to breathe the outside air and leaning forward to look down at Madame Bron, who could be heard frantically brushing away at the slimy green flagstones of the courtyard shrouded in shadow. In a cage hanging from a shutter, a canary was producing high-pitched trills. Any sound of traffic from the neighbouring streets and boulevard was inaudible; it was a broad, spacious, countrified sort of feeling, under a drowsy sun. Raising her eyes she could see the low buildings and gleaming glass roofs of the arcade galleries, and beyond them, opposite, the tall backs of the houses in the Rue Vivienne, silent and empty-looking. There were tiers of roof-terraces; on one, a photographer had perched a large blue glass cage. It was a very cheerful scene, and Nana was lost in contemplation of it when suddenly she thought she heard a knock on the door. She turned round and called:

'Come in!'

When she saw the count, she closed the window; it was rather chilly and there was no need to let that nosy Madame Bron hear what was happening. They eyed each other with a serious look. Then, as he seemed very tense and unable to speak, she gave a laugh:

'Well, there you are, you silly billy!'

He was in such a state of emotion that he seemed paralysed. When he spoke he was very formal, saying how glad he was to see her again. Trying to break down his reserve, she addressed him even more familiarly:

'Oh, come off it, don't get on your high horse! You wanted to see me, didn't you? Well, it can't have been because you wanted us to stare at each other like stuck pigs! . . . We both did some silly things. Well, I'm ready to forgive you!'

And it was understood that they'd never talk about that again. He was nodding his agreement and becoming calmer but words were welling up inside him too tumultuously to be uttered. Surprised at his coldness, she played her big card.

'OK, you're being sensible', she went on with a coy smile. 'Now we've made peace, let's shake hands and remain good friends.'

'What do you mean, good friends?' he muttered, suddenly uneasy.

'Yes, it may seem idiotic of me but I wanted you to have a good opinion of me . . . Now we've sorted everything out between us, at least if we meet, we shan't glare at each other like two village idiots . . .'

He made a gesture to interrupt her.

'No, let me finish . . . There's not one single man, you realize, who can say I ever treated him shabbily . . . Well, I'd have felt annoyed if you were going to be the first . . . We've all got our sense of honour, my dear.'

'But that's not the point!' he exclaimed violently. 'Sit down and listen to me.'

And he pushed her down on to the only chair as if he was afraid she might attempt to leave. As he strode up and down, he was becoming more and more agitated. The tiny closed room was peaceful and sunny, with a gentle, damp, cosy warmth, untroubled by any outside noise. Apart from their voices, the only sound was the shrill song of the canary, like the trill of a distant flute.

'Listen', he said, stopping in front of her. 'I've come to take you back . . . I want to start all over again. You know very well I do, why are you talking to me as you are? . . . Well, do you agree?'

She was looking down, picking with her nail at the bleeding wound on the rush seat of her chair. She'd seen his anxiety and was in no hurry to speak. Finally, with a solemn expression, she raised her face and her lovely eyes into which she'd managed to inject a touch of wistfulness.

'Oh no, that's not possible, my dear. I'll never go back to you.'

His face contracted in an agonizing spasm of pain.

'Why not?' he faltered.

'Why not? . . . Just because . . . It's not possible, that's all. I don't want to.'

He looked at her for a few seconds longer, feverishly. Then his legs gave way and he collapsed on the floor. She said in a bored voice:

'Oh, don't start behaving like a child!'

But he was already doing so. He'd fallen at her feet and seized her round the waist, hugging her tightly and pressing his face hard into her flesh between her knees. When he felt her body, when he recognized her velvety thighs through her thin dress, a convulsive shudder ran through his body and he started desperately shivering as if in a fever, pressing his face harder and harder against her legs as though wanting to force his way into her, between her thighs. The old chair was creaking. He was moaning with lust; the sound rose up to the low ceiling to be smothered in the sour reek of stale scent.

'Well, where do we go from here?' Nana said, making no attempt to stop him. 'It's not getting you anywhere, you know. Seeing that it's impossible . . . My goodness, what a child you are!'

He calmed down but still stayed on the floor holding on to her. He said brokenly:

'At least you can listen to what I've come to offer you . . . I've already found a lovely town-house near the Parc Monceau.* I'll make all your dreams come true. I'd give everything I have to keep you all for myself, just for myself . . . That would be the only condition, I don't want to share you with anyone else, do you understand? And if you agreed to be just mine, nobody else's, oh, I'd want to see you become the loveliest, richest woman in Paris, with carriages, diamonds, beautiful clothes . . .'

She greeted each offer with a proud shake of her head. Then, as he still persisted and talked of settling money on her, at a loss to discover what else to propose, she seemed to lose patience.

'Look, can you stop pawing me about? I'm a good-natured sort of girl, I'm quite ready to let you do a bit of it, because you're in such a state, but I think that's enough, isn't it? . . . Let me get up, you're making me tired.'

She pulled herself free. When she was on her feet:

'My answer's no, no, and again no! I don't want to!'

He picked himself up laboriously and fell exhausted on to the chair, resting his chin on its back and holding his head in his hands. It was Nana's turn to start walking up and down. For a moment she gazed at the stained wallpaper, the greasy wash-stand, this filthy hole bathed in pale sunlight. Then, standing squarely in front of him, she said calmly:

'It's funny, rich men think they can get everything they want with money . . . Well, supposing I don't want to? . . . I don't give a damn for your presents. If you offered me Paris, I'd still say no, always . . . As you can see, it's pretty grubby here, well, if I felt like living here with you, I'd find it very pleasant, while living in your grand house, if my heart wasn't in it, would be like a living death. Money! My poor pet, you know where you can put your money! You see, I despise it, it makes me want to puke!'

She wrinkled her nose in disgust. Then she put on a sentimental look and said in a melancholy voice:

'There's something better than money . . . Oh, if only you could give me what I really want . . .'

He slowly looked up, with a glint of hope in his eyes.

'Oh, *you* can't give it to me!' she said. 'It doesn't depend on you and that's why I can mention it to you . . . Anyway, we're only having a little chat, aren't we? Well, I'd like to have the part of the lady, the respectable married woman, in Bordenave's show.'

He looked surprised.

'What lady's that?'

'That Duchess Hélène, of course! If they think I'm going to play Géraldine, they've got another think coming! It's a potty little part, only one scene and not much of that! . . . Anyway, that's not the point. I'm fed up with tarts. Nothing but tarts, you'd think that was the only thing I'm capable of playing. It's become really irritating because it's obvious they seem to think I'm common . . . Well, old boy, they're barking up the wrong tree! When I want to be, I can be as distinguished as anyone . . . Take a look at this.'

She went over to the window and then came swaggering back, carefully measuring each stride, like a wary, fat hen anxious not to get her feet dirty. He followed her with his eyes still full of tears, bewildered by this stage act suddenly breaking into his grief. She walked around for a minute to show off her whole range, smiling daintily, blinking her eyes, and swirling her skirts. Then she came back and stood in front of him.

'Well, how about that? Spot-on, isn't it?'

'Oh, yes, absolutely', he faltered, still choking and tearful.

'I told you, I've got the respectable lady to a T! I've been practising at home, there's no one else who's got that special little touch of a duchess who doesn't give a damn for men like I have! Didn't you notice it as I went past you, giving you a look? That's the sort of look you're born with, it's in your blood. Anyway, I want to play the part of a respectable lady, that's my dream and it's making me very unhappy, I've got to have it, do you understand?'

She'd become very serious, her voice was harsh and full of emotion, her silly ambition was making her really distressed. Still cowed by seeing her turn down all his offers, Muffat sat waiting, not understanding what she was driving at. There was complete silence; in the empty house you could have heard a pin drop.

'I tell you what', she went on bluntly, 'you've got to get me the part.'

He was flabbergasted. He made a despairing gesture:

'That's out of the question! You said yourself that it doesn't depend on me.'

She interrupted him with a shrug.

'You must go downstairs and tell Bordenave that you want the part . . . Don't be so naive! Bordenave needs cash. You've got bags of it, so you can lend him some.'

And seeing that he was still reluctant, she lost her temper.

'OK, I understand, you're afraid of annoying Rose . . . I didn't mention her while you were lying about on the floor crying, there'd've been too much to say . . . Oh no, when you've sworn to love a woman forever, you don't just make a bee-line for any old woman who turns up next day. Oh, I've not forgotten how much you hurt me. Anyway, my dear man, the Mignon's left-overs aren't exactly appetizing! Before behaving like a silly child on my lap, wouldn't it have been better to part company with a lousy bunch like them?'

He started protesting and finally got her to listen to him.

'But I don't care about Rose, I'm intending to leave her straight away.'

This seemed to satisfy Nana. She went on:

'Well, in that case, what's holding you back? Bordenave's the boss . . . Perhaps you'll say that there's Fauchery to be considered as well?'

She was speaking more slowly now; she was coming to the tricky part of the deal. Muffat was looking down at the floor and saying nothing. He'd deliberately chosen to remain ignorant of Fauchery's constant attentions towards the countess, and had eventually managed to set his mind at rest, hoping he had been mistaken during that dreadful night he'd spent lurking in the doorway in the Rue Taitbout. But he still harboured a secret resentment and repugnance for the man.

'Surely Fauchery's not as bad as all that?' Nana said, feeling her way and trying to find out how matters stood between the husband and the lover. 'We can handle Fauchery. Basically, I promise you, he's quite a decent chap. What do you think? OK, you'll tell him it's for me.'

The count was revolted at the thought of taking such a step.

'No, I couldn't possibly do that', he cried.

She waited. She was tempted to say, 'But he can hardly refuse you', but she felt that might be pushing him too far; she merely gave a little smile which made the words superfluous. Muffat, who'd raised his eyes to look at her, dropped them, embarrassed and pale.

'Ah, you're not very obliging', she muttered.

'But I just can't do that!' he said, deeply distressed. 'Anything else you want, my love, but not that, oh, I beg you . . .'

She wasted no time in arguing. Seizing his head between her two little hands, she tipped it back, bent forward, and pressing her lips against his, gave him a long, deep kiss. His body jerked convulsively, his eyes closed and he started trembling all over. She pulled him to his feet and said simply:

'Now off you go.'

He didn't argue and walked towards the door, but as he was going out she again took him into her arms, lifting her face and rubbing her chin kittenishly against his waistcoat, with a humble, coaxing look.

'Where's the house you mentioned?' she asked in a very quiet whisper, with the cheerful, embarrassed expression of a little girl who's coming back to ask for something nice she's previously refused.

'In the Avenue de Villiers.'

'And there are carriages there?'

'Yes.'

'Diamonds? Lots of lovely lace?'

'Yes.'

'Oh, what a kind man you are, my pet! You know, I said what I did a moment ago because I was jealous . . . And this time won't be like last time, because now you understand what a woman needs. You're going to give me everything, aren't you, so I shan't need anyone else . . . Oh, from now on, this is all for you . . . And this and this and this!'

And with a shower of kisses on his face and hands, she set his whole body tingling, before pushing him through the doorway. Then she took a deep breath. Heavens, what a dreadful smell there was in that slut Mathilde's dressing-room! It was cosy enough, like the gentle warmth of sunny Provençal bedrooms in winter, but there really was too strong a smell of sour lavender-water and other unsavoury things. She opened the window and leaned on the sill again, trying to curb her impatience by examining the glass roofs.

Muffat stumbled down the stairs; he had a buzzing in his head. What was he to say? How could he broach this matter, which was really none of his business? As he reached the stage, he heard bickering. They were coming to the end of the second act and Prullière was cross because Fauchery wanted to cut out some of his lines.

'Why not scrap the whole part, then?' he was shouting. 'I'd sooner you do that! When you think I've only got two hundred lines and you want to get rid of some of them . . . No, enough's enough, you can take your miserable part back!'

He pulled a crumpled little notebook out of his pocket and stood twisting it feverishly in his hands, making as if to throw it in Cossard's lap. Tight-lipped, with bloodshot eyes, his pale face was convulsed with wounded vanity, unable to hide his inner exasperation: Prullière, the idol of the public, playing a two-hundred-line part!

'Why not just use me to bring letters in on a tray?' he went on bitterly.

'Oh, come on, Prullière, be a good fellow', said Bordenave, who humoured him because of his effect on the ladies in the boxes. 'Don't keep going on . . . We'll find something special for you. That's right, Fauchery, isn't it? We arrange something special for Prullière? We might even lengthen a scene in the third act.'

'In that case', the actor declared, 'I want the curtain speech. You owe me that at least.'

Fauchery's silence seemed to give consent and Prullière put

his part back into his pocket, still alarmed and not entirely satisfied. During this altercation, Bosc and Fontan had assumed an attitude of complete indifference; it was a free-for-all, it didn't concern them, they weren't in the least interested. And all the actors now gathered round Fauchery, questioning him and wanting to be praised, while Mignon listened to Prullière's final grumbles with his eyes fixed on Count Muffat; he had been waiting for him to come back.

The count had stopped at the back of the dark stage, reluctant to arrive in the middle of a squabble. But Bordenave had spied him and hurried over.

'What a bunch, eh?' he muttered. 'You'd never credit, Count, the trouble I have with that lot. Each of them vainer than the next and on the look-out to diddle you as well, a thoroughly nasty crowd, always up to some dirty trick or other, they'd be pleased as Punch if I came unstuck . . . Sorry, I'm getting carried away.'

He stopped; there was a pause. Muffat was trying to find a way to broach the subject, without success. Finally, he plunged in and said bluntly:

'Nana wants the part of the duchess.'

Bordenave gave a start and exclaimed:

'Oh, come on, that's absolutely crazy!'

Then noticing how upset and pale the count was, he immediately calmed down.

'Good God!' he said simply.

There was another pause. Basically, he didn't care one way or the other; it might even be funny to see that buxom girl in the part of the duchess. In any case, such a deal would certainly put Muffat firmly in his power. He didn't hesitate for long. Turning round, he called:

'Fauchery!'

The count made a move to stop him; Fauchery hadn't heard. Cornered against the proscenium arch by Fontan, he was having to submit to an analysis of how the actor conceived his role as Tardiveau. Fontan saw him as a man from Marseilles, complete with the accent, which he imitated. He was spouting line after line: was that how it ought to go? He seemed to be merely putting forward ideas which he wasn't certain about himself; but when Fauchery looked unimpressed and started raising objections, he at once took offence. All right, then, if his idea of the part was wrong, it'd be better for all concerned if he didn't take it.

'Fauchery!' Bordenave shouted again.

The young man quickly made himself scarce, glad to get away from the actor, who was offended by his hurried departure.

'Let's go somewhere else', said Bordenave. 'Come along with me, gentlemen.'

To be safe from eavesdroppers, he took them behind the stage into the props-room. Mignon watched them disappear with surprise. They went down a few steps into a square, low-ceilinged room dimly lit by two grimy windows from the cellar-like yard outside. It was cluttered with racks containing all sorts of odds and ends, clearance-sale junk from a Rue de Lappe* second-hand dealer who'd gone out of business, an indescribable litter of plates, gilt cardboard champagne glasses, old red brollies, Italian jugs, clocks in every possible style, trays, inkwells, firearms, and syringes, all covered in a layer of dust an inch thick, chipped, broken, piled up together and unrecognizable. And from this heap of debris from all the shows put on over the last fifty years there rose an unbearable smell of old iron, rags, and wet cardboard boxes.

'Come on in', Bordenave said. 'We won't be disturbed here anyway.'

Full of embarrassment, the count took a few steps up and down the room, leaving the manager to put his tricky proposal forward first. Fauchery was looking surprised.

'Well, what's this all about?' he asked.

'Well', said Bordenave, after a moment's hesitation, 'it's like this: We've had an idea . . . But please don't be too hasty, it's meant very seriously . . . What would be your view of Nana taking the part of the duchess?'

The author was completely taken by surprise. Then he exploded:

'You don't really mean it, do you? It's just a joke, isn't it? People would think it too laughable for words.'

'Well, it's not a bad thing to make people laugh! . . . Give it thought, my dear man. The count likes the idea very much.'

To hide his embarrassment, Muffat had just picked up

from a dusty shelf an object which he didn't seem to recognize. It was a plaster egg-cup which had had its base repaired. Without realizing what he was doing, he kept hold of it as he came forward and mumbled:

'Yes, it would be a very good idea.'

Fauchery swung round and looked at him impatiently; the count had nothing to do with his play. He said firmly:

'No! Nana will make a good tart, of course, but as a society lady it's just not on, it's out of the question!'

'I assure you you're wrong', Muffat persisted, gaining in confidence. 'In fact, it so happens she's just shown me what she can do in the part of a respectable woman.'

'Where was that?' asked Fauchery, increasingly surprised.

'In a dressing-room upstairs. And it was absolutely right. She really did look distinguished. And the way she gave you a glance as she walked past, you know, rather like this . . .'

And still clutching his egg-cup, in his passionate eagerness to convince the two men he tried to imitate Nana, completely oblivious of the impression he was making. Fauchery watched him, dumbfounded. He'd sized up the situation and was no longer annoyed. Suddenly becoming aware that the other man was looking at him with a mixture of pity and mockery, the count blushed slightly and stopped.

'Well, yes, it's possible', he murmured, trying to be friendly. 'She might perhaps be very good . . . Only that part's been allocated. We can't take it away from Rose.'

'Oh, if that's the only objection', said Bordenave, 'I can undertake to square that.'

But seeing that both men were ganging up against him, and realizing that Bordenave had a hidden interest in the deal, Fauchery felt he shouldn't give in so tamely and suddenly flared up even more vigorously. To put an end to the discussion, he exclaimed angrily:

'No, I won't do it, I absolutely refuse! Even if the part were free, I'd never let her have it! . . . Am I making myself clear? Just leave me alone, I don't want to kill my play dead!'

There was an embarrassed silence. Feeling his presence was superfluous, Bordenave moved away. The count was looking down at the floor; then, with an effort he raised his eyes and said uncertainly:

'Suppose I asked you as a special favour, my dear fellow?'

Fauchery was still not prepared to give way.

'No, I can't, I just can't!' he repeated.

Muffat's voice took on a harder note.

'I'm asking you to do it . . . I must insist!'

He was staring him squarely in the eyes. Seeing his grim look, and sensing the hidden threat, the young man became flustered and suddenly caved in.

'Oh, all right, do it if you want to, I don't give a damn', he stammered. 'But you're taking advantage of me. You'll see, you'll see! . . .'

The atmosphere became even more tense. Fauchery was leaning against a rack, nervously tapping the floor. Muffat seemed to be closely inspecting the egg-cup which he was still twisting in his hands.

'It's an egg-cup', said Bordenave helpfully.

'Goodness me, yes, so it is', the count replied.

'I'm sorry, you've got covered in dust', the manager went on, replacing the object on a shelf. 'If we had to dust everything off every day, we'd never finish the job, you understand . . . So it's all rather dirty. What a clutter, eh? Well, you may not believe this, but it's still worth something. Have a look at all this.'

And threading his way between the racks in the pale green light coming from the courtyard, he took Muffat round, telling him the names of various utensils, trying to make this inventory of his junk shop sound interesting as he laughingly itemized it. Then when they'd come back to where Fauchery was standing, he said brightly:

'Well now, since we've all reached agreement, let's settle the matter, shall we? . . . And look, there's Mignon himself.'

In fact, Mignon had been lurking in the corridor for some while. As soon as Bordenave mentioned altering their contract, Mignon blew up: it was an outright scandal, they were trying to ruin his wife's career, he'd take them to court. Very calmly, Bordenave explained his reasons: the role didn't seem quite good enough for Rose, he'd prefer to keep her in reserve for an operetta he was putting on after *The Little Duchess*. But when Mignon went on shouting, he abruptly offered to cancel the contract and mentioned the offers being made to the singer by the Folies Dramatiques. Temporarily put off his stride, Mignon, while not denying these offers, professed to spurn the money; his wife had been engaged to play the part of the Duchess Hélène and she would do so even if he, Mignon, thereby incurred financial ruin; it was a question of honour and self-respect. Once embarked on this course, the argument went on and on. The manager kept reverting to his reasoning: since the Folies were offering his wife three hundred francs a night for a run of a hundred nights while she was getting only a hundred and fifty francs from him, if he released her she'd be earning an extra fifteen thousand francs. Her husband repeated his argument concerning the professional aspect of the matter: what would people say if they saw his wife losing her part? That she wasn't up to it, that she'd had to be replaced, and this would cause her considerable harm, a bad loss of face. No, he'd never agree to that! Fame was more important than money! Then, suddenly, he produced a compromise: under the terms of her contract Rose would have to pay a penalty if she withdrew; well, let her have her ten thousand francs and she'd go over to the Folies Dramatiques. Bordenave was dumbfounded, while Mignon, whose eyes had not once left the count, stood waiting patiently.

'Then everything's all right', murmured Muffat in relief. 'Agreement can be reached.'

'No, it can't be!' shouted Bordenave, his business instincts suddenly getting the better of him. 'It'd be too stupid for words! Ten thousand francs to let Rose go! Everyone would be laughing at me!'

But the count was looking at him and nodding, making it quite plain that Bordenave had to agree to the deal, so finally, with much grumbling, extremely unhappy at losing ten thousand francs even though they weren't going to come out of his own pocket, he said roughly:

'Ah well, I'm prepared to accept. At least I'll be rid of you!'

Extremely intrigued, Fontan had gone down into the courtyard where he'd been eavesdropping for the last quarter of an hour. Realizing what had happened, he hurried upstairs to savour the pleasure of passing the news on to Rose. Well, well, what a great fuss was going on about her, she was for the chop . . . Rose rushed down to the props-room. Silence fell. She looked at the four men. Muffat looked down at the floor, Fauchery answered her questioning glance with a disconsolate shrug of his shoulders, while Mignon was discussing the terms of the contract with Bordenave.

'What's happening?' she asked curtly.

'Nothing's happening', her husband replied. 'It's just that Bordenave is paying us ten thousand francs to get your part back.'

She clenched her little fists, quivering and very pale. For a split second this woman who, in business matters normally deferred meekly to her husband and let him sign her contracts with her managers and her lovers, glared at him, almost speechless, before flinging these words into his face like a whiplash:

'So that's it! What a coward you are!'

She spun on her heels and left. Flabbergasted at the violence of her reaction, Mignon hurried after her. What was the matter? Had she taken leave of her senses? In an undertone, he explained that ten thousand francs from one party and fifteen from the other added up to twenty-five thousand francs. What a windfall! Moreover, Muffat would be leaving her in the lurch whatever happened; it was a splendid achievement to have squeezed the last drop of juice out of that orange! But seeing that Rose was too infuriated to reply, Mignon scornfully let her get on with her feminine sulks on her own. When Bordenave came back on to the stage with Fauchery, Mignon said to him:

'We'll sign tomorrow morning. Don't forget to bring the money.'

At that very moment, Nana, who'd been informed by Labordette, came in exultantly. She was putting on her respectable lady act, full of genteel airs and graces to impress her colleagues and prove to those clots that when she wanted to, no one could be as classy as she was. But she nearly gave herself away. When Rose caught sight of her, she rushed towards her, choking and spluttering:

'I'll get you! We're going to have a show-down, do you understand?'

Faced by this sudden attack, Nana nearly forgot her role

and was on the point of putting her hands on her hips and calling Rose a slut. However, she controlled herself; exaggerating her flute-like tone of voice, she made a gesture like a marchioness wishing to avoid stepping on an orange peel.

'What's that? What's that?' she intoned. 'My dear, you must be out of your mind!'

And she continued her spiel while Rose went off, followed by Mignon who still couldn't understand what had got into his wife. Clarisse was delighted at getting the part of Géraldine. Fauchery was shifting from one foot to another, looking very glum and unable to make up his mind whether to stay or leave: his play was a dead loss and he was wondering how he might salvage it. But then Nana came up to him and, catching hold of his wrists, pulled him close to her and asked if he really found her so dreadful. She wasn't going to muck up his play for him. He couldn't help laughing. She also hinted that he'd be very unwise to quarrel with her in view of his situation with the Muffats. Anyway, if her memory let her down, there was always the prompter to help her out. They'd pack the house with supporters. And in any case, he'd got it all wrong, he'd see that she'd bring the house down. It was agreed that the author would slightly rewrite the duchess's part to give a bit more to Prullière. He was delighted. In this cheerful atmosphere that Nana had a natural gift for inspiring, only Fontan remained aloof. He was sprawling in a deliberately nonchalant attitude in the yellow beam of the tiny lamp, which picked out the sharp bony profile of his faun-like face. Nana calmly went over and shook his hand.

'How are you?'

'Not too bad, thanks. How about you?'

'I'm very well, thank you.'

That was all. You would have thought they'd left each other at the stage-door the night before. Meanwhile the actors were waiting, but Bordenave said they wouldn't be starting on the third act. Old Bosc went off grumbling: for once he'd been on time and so had been hanging around for nothing; they were being made to waste whole afternoons. Everybody left. Outside on the pavement they blinked, blinded and bewildered by the light of day, like people who'd spent the last three hours, under continuous nervous stress, squabbling in a cellar. Numbed and aching in every limb, Muffat went off with Nana while Labordette took Fauchery away with him, trying to offer consolation.

One month later, the first performance of *The Little Duchess* was a catastrophe for Nana. She was appalling; her pretentious efforts at high comedy aroused roars of laughter; the audience was too amused even to boo. In her stage box, Rose Mignon greeted her rival with a shrill peal of laughter each time she came on stage, which sparked off the whole house. Her vengeance was beginning. So in the evening, when Nana was at home alone with the count, who was very distressed, she said to him in a fury:

'They're ganging up on me! It's sheer jealousy! If they only knew how little I care! Do I need any of them now? . . . Well, I bet five hundred francs I'll have all those people who were laughing at me coming to lick my boots! . . . I'm going to teach that Paris of yours what a great lady is like!'

Chapter 10

So Nana became the toast of Paris, the queen of first-class tarts, battening on the stupidity and beastliness of males. In the smart world of amorous intrigue, a world of reckless extravagance and brazen exploitation of beauty, her rise to fame was meteoric; and she immediately joined the ranks of the most expensive. Her photo was on display in every shop-window; her name featured in the newspapers. When she drove along the boulevards in her carriage, everyone turned to look and breathed her name like subjects greeting their monarch while she, in her loose dress with her tiny blonde curls tumbling down over her blue-rimmed eyes, would sprawl back giving a cheerful, friendly smile with her red, painted lips. And miraculously, this big, sturdy girl, so awkward on the stage and so ludicrous when she tried to play the part of a respectable woman, became, off-stage, an effortless public charmer, looking as lithe as a snake in her skilfully low-cut dresses, exquisitely elegant, which offered, as though by accident, revealing glimpses of her body, as refined and supple as a pedigree cat. She represented the aristocracy of vice, magnificent and untamed, holding Paris to ransom under her all-powerful heel. She set the fashion; great ladies copied her.

She lived in a mansion in the Avenue de Villiers, on the corner of the Rue Cardinet, in that luxurious district being developed in the middle of the wastelands of what used to be the plain of Monceau. The house had been built by a young painter in the first flush of his success, and he'd been forced to sell it almost before the plaster was dry. It was a palatial, Renaissance-style building with a fantastic interior arrangement of rooms and furniture, modern comfort in a setting of rather studied originality. Count Muffat had bought it complete with all the furnishings, a ragbag of knick-knacks, of wonderful Oriental hangings, antique sideboards, and huge Louis XIII armchairs; Nana had found herself surrounded by a mass of expertly chosen artistic furniture, a jumble of various periods. However, as the studio occupying the centre of the house was of no use to her, she'd reorganized the various floors, leaving a conservatory, a large drawing-room, and the dining-room on the ground floor and putting a small drawing-room on the first floor, next to her bedroom and dressing-room. She surprised the architect with her ideas; brought up in the streets of Paris but having an instinctive feel for elegance of every sort, she suddenly became aware of the possibilities of luxury and refinement. In the end, she didn't spoil the house too much and even added to the opulence of the furniture, apart from a few silly, sentimental touches and a bit of gaudy magnificence recalling the tastes of the flower-girl who once used to stand day-dreaming in front of the shops in the arcade.

The steps under the grand glass awning in the courtyard leading up to the front terrace were carpeted, and once in the vestibule you were assailed by a scent of violets in the warm air trapped between the heavy wall-hangings. The staircase was wide and lit through a pink-and-yellow stained-glass window which cast a pale, flesh-coloured golden light. At its foot, a carved wooden blackamoor stood holding out a silver tray full of visiting-cards; there were four candelabra, each supported by a bare-breasted marble female, while the vestibule and landings were furnished and decorated with bronze figures, Chinese cloisonné vases full of flowers, divans draped with antique Persian rugs, and armchairs covered in old tapestry, forming a sort of entrance hall on the first floor where men's hats and overcoats were always to be seen lying around. Sounds were muffled by the materials; the atmosphere was solemn and meditative; you might have imagined you were entering a chapel pervaded by a feeling of piety and hiding its mysteries behind the silence of its closed doors.

Nana opened up her large, over-opulent Louis XVI drawing-room only on very special occasions, when entertaining people from the Tuileries or foreign VIPs. Normally she'd come downstairs only for meals, feeling rather lost when lunching by herself in the very high-ceilinged dining-room hung with Gobelin tapestries and having a monumental buffet graced by antique faience-ware and wonderful old silver. She'd quickly make her way back to her living quarters, three rooms on the first floor, a bedroom, dressing-room, and small drawing-room. She'd already had the bedroom done up twice, first in mauve satin and then in blue silk with lace appliqué; but she still wasn't satisfied: it was insipid, and she was now looking for something else without knowing quite what, and was unable to find it. There was twenty-thousand-francs worth of Venetian lace on the upholstery of the low, divan-like bed. The furniture was in blue-and-white lacquer, with silver lines, and there were so many bearskin rugs scattered round the room that they completely covered the carpet; this represented one of Nana's quirky little affectations, for she couldn't break herself of the habit of sitting on the floor to take off her stockings. Leading off the bedroom was the small drawing-room, an amusing hotchpotch of exquisitely crafted objects of every style and every country—Italian cabinets, Spanish and Portuguese chests, Chinese pagodas, a superb, richly finished Japanese screen—set against a background of pale silk hangings of faded Turkish pink embroidered in gold thread, not forgetting more faience-ware, bronzes, embroidered silk, and petit-point tapestries. Armchairs as wide as any bed and settees as deep as alcoves set the mood of *dolce far niente*, the drowsy existence of a harem. The room had an atmosphere of old gold and melting greens and reds, with nothing too conspicuously tartish apart from the voluptuous armchairs; the only blot on the room to betray her native stupidity was provided by two terracotta figurines representing a woman catching her fleas and a completely naked woman walking on her hands with her legs in the air. Through a door, which was usually left open, there was a glimpse of the dressing-room, all in marble and mirrors, with a white bath, silver jars and basins, and fittings of ivory and cut-glass. The curtain was drawn, admitting a pale, sleepy-looking white daylight, drowsy from the scent of violets, that heady scent of Nana's which pervaded the whole house from the courtyard upwards.

The important thing was to get domestic staff. Nana had, of course, the ever-faithful Zoé, firmly attached to her star and who'd been waiting for months to see her mistress's meteoric rise, quietly confident in her flair. Zoé was now exultantly taking charge of the household, feathering her own nest while serving her mistress as honestly as possible. But a chambermaid was no longer adequate; a butler, a coachman, a caretaker, and a cook were obvious necessities. And the stables needed organizing, too. Labordette proved invaluable, running errands that the count found boring. He haggled over the price of the horses, went the rounds of the coach-builders, and helped the young woman to make her choice; she could be seen taking his arm as they called on the various suppliers. Labordette even recruited the servants: a tall, sturdy young fellow by the name of Charles as the coachman, who'd been in service with the Duke of Corbreuse; a smiling, curly-headed little butler called Jules; and a married couple, the wife Victorine as cook and the husband François as caretaker and footman. The latter, in breeches, with powdered hair and wearing Nana's livery of pale blue, silver-laced, received callers in the vestibule. The whole style and get-up were princely.

It took her less than two months to set up house. It had cost more than three-hundred thousand francs. There were eight horses in the stables and four carriages in the coach-house, including a landau with silver fittings which for a while was the talk of Paris. And amid all this wealth, Nana was organizing her life and carving out a niche for herself. She'd abandoned the stage after the third performance of *The Little Duchess*, leaving Bordenave struggling under the threat of bankruptcy despite the money put up by the count. All the same, she felt embittered by her lack of success. That was something to be added to what she'd learned from Fontan, a dirty trick for which she held all males responsible. So now, she told herself, she'd be very tough and immune to passing fancies. But scatter-brained as she was, any idea of vengeance was short-lived. What did remain very much alive, apart from her occasional bursts of temper, was her wild extravagance, a natural contempt for the sucker who was stumping up, her constant urge to indulge in reckless consumption, and her pride in ruining her lovers.

The first thing Nana did was to tell the count where he stood and lay down a clear programme for their relationship.

He was to provide twelve hundred francs a month, apart from presents, and in return could expect her to be completely faithful, which she promised to be. But she demanded to be shown every consideration, absolute control in her own house, and complete compliance with her wishes. So she would have her friends to call every day; he would come only at fixed times; in a word, he would have to show blind trust in her at all times. And when he seemed hesitant, troubled by jealousy, she got on her high horse and either threatened to hand back everything or else gave her solemn word of honour, on the head of her little son Louiset. That ought to satisfy him! There couldn't be love without respect; and by the end of the first month Muffat did respect her.

But she wanted and obtained more than that. She soon got round him with her cheerful good-nature; whenever he arrived looking gloomy, she'd jolly him along, and having got him to confess the cause, she'd offer him advice. Gradually she came to concern herself with his domestic problems, his wife, his daughter, the state of his finances and of his feelings, making helpful, honest suggestions. Only once did she let her emotions run away with her; this was when he confided to her that Daguenet appeared likely to ask to marry his daughter Estelle. Ever since the count had openly acknowledged his affair with Nana, Daguenet had thought it wise to break with her. He'd even described her as a tramp and promised to rescue his future father-in-law from her clutches. She now set about painting a pretty picture of the man she used to call her Mimi: a womanizer who'd squandered a fortune on nasty women; he'd got no moral sense whatsoever; he might not accept money from people, but he took advantage of their money by merely paying for the odd bunch of flowers or a dinner; and when the count seemed to be offering excuses for his shortcomings, she told him bluntly that Daguenet had had her and went into various disgusting details. Muffat turned very pale. That was the end of the young man's chances. It would teach him not to be ungrateful.

Nevertheless, even before the house was completely furnished, Count Xavier de Vandeuvres, who'd been keenly pursuing Nana with regular visits and gifts of flowers, found himself spending the night with her on the very same evening when she had repeatedly given Muffat her word of honour never to go to bed with anyone else but him. She'd given herself to him not out of a passing fancy but rather to prove to herself that she was a free woman. Any thought of gaining personal benefit came to her only the following day, when Vandeuvres helped her to settle a bill which she didn't want Muffat to know about. Xavier would certainly be good for eight or ten thousand francs a month, which would come in very handy as pin-money. Vandeuvres was feverishly getting through all that was left of his fortune. Lucy Stewart and his horses had swallowed up three farms; Nana would certainly make short work of his last château near Amiens. He seemed in a hurry to liquidate everything, even the remains of the old tower built by a forebear under Philippe Auguste,* in a desperate urge to make a clean sweep of everything; he felt it was the smart thing to do to let the last gold bezant of his coat-of-arms end up in the possession of this tart whom all Paris was itching to have. He too accepted Nana's conditions: no strings attached, love-making restricted to certain days only; and he was neither naive nor passionate enough to expect any sort of solemn promises. Muffat had no suspicions, Vandeuvres no illusions, but he kept his mouth shut and pretended to know nothing, with the gentle smile of the sceptical man-about-town who doesn't expect the impossible as long as he has his stint and all Paris knows about it.

Nana was now completely set up. Her stables and servants' hall were staffed; she had her own personal maid. Zoé supervised everything, coping with the most unforeseen complications; it was a well-oiled machine, like a theatre or the management of a large business. It functioned so perfectly that for the first few months there were no mishaps or hitches. The only trouble was that madam was making life difficult for Zoé by her fecklessness, impulsiveness, and downright foolhardiness. So much so that the chambermaid gradually started to take things more easily, having meanwhile observed that she earned more from crises, when her mistress had done something silly that had to be put right. On these occasions she was showered with presents; fishing in troubled waters was bringing rich rewards.

One morning, when Muffat was still in the bedroom, Zoé

smuggled a trembling young man into Nana's dressing-room where she was getting dressed.

'Good Lord, Zizi!' she exclaimed in amazement.

It was indeed Georges. But when he saw her in her underwear with her golden hair hanging down over her bare shoulders, he flung his arms round her neck and held her tightly, smothering her in kisses. She struggled to free herself and whispered in a scared voice:

'Stop it! He's in there! Don't be so stupid! Zoé, have you gone crazy? Take him away and keep him downstairs, I'll try and come down later on.'

Zoé had to push him along in front of her. When Nana was free to join them downstairs in the dining-room, she told both of them off. Zoé pursed her lips and went away looking offended, saying that she thought madam would have been pleased. Georges was overjoyed to see Nana again; his charming eyes filled with tears as he looked at her. Now the bad days were over; his mother thought he'd seen reason and she'd given him permission to leave Les Fondettes, so as soon as he got off the train, he'd jumped into a cab to come and kiss his lovely darling straight away. He said from now on he didn't intend to leave her, just as he'd done in the country when he used to wait for her bare-footed in her bedroom at La Mignotte. And while he was saying all this, he couldn't resist reaching out all the time to touch her with his fingers, after his cruel mother had kept him away from her for a whole year. He held her hands and then slipped his own into the wide sleeves of her dressing gown and felt his way up towards her shoulders.

'Do you still love your little baby?' he asked in his childish voice.

'Of course I do', retorted Nana, jerking herself away. 'But you've come round here without giving any warning. I'm not free, you know, so you must be a good, sensible little boy.'

Having just got straight out of the cab and still in a daze at the thought of finally satisfying his pent-up desires, Georges had paid no attention to his surroundings. Now he looked round and noticed the change in her circumstances. He examined the luxurious dining-room with its lofty decorative ceiling and sideboard resplendent with silver.

'Oh yes', he said sadly.

She emphasized that he must never come in the morning. In the afternoon, if he wanted to, from four till six; that was when she was 'at home'. Then, as he looked pleadingly at her without saying a word, she kissed him on the forehead, making a great show of kindness.

'If you're very good, I'll see what I can do', she said softly.

But the truth was that she no longer felt attracted. Georges was certainly a very nice boy, and she would have liked to have him just as a good friend and nothing more. However, when he turned up every day at four o'clock looking thoroughly miserable, she often weakened, hiding him in wardrobes and cupboards and continually letting him enjoy a few spare crumbs of her beauty. He became a sort of permanent fixture in the house, rather like the little dog Bijou, both of them being allowed to sniff round their mistress's skirts, getting a little bit of her when she was with someone else and picking up little windfalls like lumps of sugar or being fondled when she was bored and lonely.

Madame Hugon must have learned that her young son had again fallen into the clutches of that dreadful woman, for she rushed up to Paris to enlist the help of her other son, Philippe, now garrisoned in Vincennes. Georges, who'd been steering clear of his elder brother, was desperately scared that Philippe might take forceful action, and as his love for Nana left him in an excitable, garrulous state, he was unable to keep anything to himself, with the result that he was soon talking of nothing else but his big brother; he was a big fellow and no respecter of persons.

'You see', he explained, 'Mummy won't come here herself but she can send my brother. I'm sure she'll send Philippe to take me away.'

The first time she heard this, Nana was very offended. She said sharply:

'I'd like to see him try! He may be a lieutenant but François will kick him out for you double-quick, don't worry!'

Then, as the boy kept coming back to the subject of his brother, she began to pay closer attention. By the end of a week, she knew everything about him: he was very tall and strong, lively, rather outspoken; and a few more personal details as well: hairy arms, a birthmark on his shoulder. As a result, she became so intrigued by the image of this man whom she was going to have kicked out of her house that one day she exclaimed:

'I say, Zizi, your brother hasn't shown up yet . . . He must be backing down!'

Next day, when Georges was alone with Nana, François came in to ask if madam would receive Lieutenant Philippe Hugon. Georges went as white as a sheet and muttered:

'I thought so, Mummy told me this morning.'

And he pleaded with Nana to say that she wasn't at home. But she was already on her feet and saying excitedly:

'Why should I? He'd think I'm afraid. Ah, we're going to have fun . . . François, show the gentleman into the drawing-room and let him wait for a quarter of an hour before showing him up here.'

She remained on her feet, walking feverishly between the Venetian mirror hanging above an Italian cabinet and the one over the fireplace, each time taking a quick look at herself and practising a smile while Georges sat helplessly on a settee trembling at the thought of the row that was brewing. As she strode to and fro, she flung a few brief phrases over her shoulder:

'That'll dampen that young man's ardour, having to wait for a quarter of an hour . . . And if he's got the idea in his head that he's calling on a tart, this drawing-room will be a bit of an eye-opener for him! Take a good look, young man, there's nothing bogus here! That'll teach you respect for the lady of the house . . . Where men are concerned, respect's the only thing . . . Is the quarter of an hour up yet? Ah, only ten minutes. There's lots of time!'

She couldn't keep still. When the fifteen minutes were up she sent Georges away, making him promise not to eavesdrop. As he went off into the bedroom, Zizi gasped timidly:

'You know, he *is* my brother . . .'

'Don't be afraid', she said grandly. 'If he's polite, I'll be polite too.'

François showed Philippe Hugon in; he was in mufti and wearing a frock-coat. In obedience to Nana's instructions,

Georges was tiptoeing away across the room when, hearing the sound of voices, he stopped and hesitated; he was in such a state of anxiety that his knees were wobbling. In his mind's eye he could see catastrophe, slapped faces, something dreadful that would poison his relationship with Nana for ever. His curiosity got the better of him; he went back and stuck his ear to the door. It was a thick door which deadened the sound, but he could hear his brother's harsh voice, emphasizing words like 'child', 'family', 'honour'. His heart pounded and he could feel a confused buzzing in his head as he listened anxiously to hear how his darling would reply. Surely she'd let fly with 'you lout!' or 'clear out, you're in my house!' But nothing came, not even a whisper; Nana was giving absolutely no sign of life. Soon his brother's voice even seemed to become softer. Greatly puzzled, Georges was suddenly thunderstruck to hear a strange murmur coming from the next room: it was Nana sobbing. For a second he didn't know what to do. Should he run away? Confront Philippe? But at that very moment Zoé came into the bedroom and Georges moved away from the door, embarrassed at being caught listening.

Zoé said nothing, but quietly started putting linen away in a cupboard. Sick with worry, Georges stood motionless, resting his forehead against a window-pane. After a pause, she asked:

'Is that your brother with madam?'

'Yes', the boy replied, barely able to speak.

Another pause.

'And you're worried, aren't you, Monsieur Georges?'

'Yes', he whispered in the same anguished voice.

Zoé was in no hurry. She folded some lace and said slowly:

'You needn't be . . . Madam will sort things out.'

And that was all. She said nothing more but she didn't leave the room. For a good quarter of an hour she moved around, not noticing the boy's increasing exasperation. Pale with uncertainty and the strain of having to control his feelings, he kept throwing sidelong glances towards the drawing-room. What could they be doing all this time? Perhaps Nana was still crying? That brute in there must have smacked her face! When Zoé finally left, he rushed over and once more stuck his ear to the door. This time he was startled and completely at a loss, for he could hear bursts of laughter, whispered endearments, and stifled giggles, as if from a woman who's being tickled. In any case, almost immediately Nana accompanied Philippe to the top of the staircase, where they parted on the friendliest of terms.

When Georges went sheepishly back into the drawing-room, the young woman was standing looking at herself in the mirror.

'Well?' he enquired, utterly confused.

'Well what?' she retorted, without turning round.

Then in a casual voice:

'What was that story you were telling me about your brother? He's a poppet.'

'So everything's OK?'

'Of course, everything's OK. What's wrong with you? Anybody would think we were going to have a fight!'

Georges still couldn't understand. He stammered:

'I thought I heard . . . Weren't you crying?'

'Crying?' she exclaimed, looking him squarely in the eye. 'You must be dreaming! Why should I have been crying?'

And it was he who now became flustered as she told him off for disobeying her and listening at the door. Seeing that she was cross, he started playing up to her and asked meekly:

'So my brother . . . ?'

'Your brother realized straight away what sort of house he was in. You can see, I might have been some sort of tart, in which case he'd have had the right to intervene because of your age and the honour of the family. Oh, I can appreciate those sort of feelings . . . But he only needed to take one look and he behaved like a perfect gentleman. So stop worrying, it's all over and done with, he'll be able to reassure your mama.'

And she added with a laugh:

'Anyway, you'll be meeting your brother here . . . I've invited him to call again.'

'Oh, so he'll be coming back', said the boy, going pale.

Nothing more was said and Philippe wasn't mentioned again. Nana started dressing to go out, and he watched her through his big, sad eyes. Naturally he was very pleased that everything had been settled because he would rather have died than have to give her up; but deep down he still had a dull, uneasy ache that he didn't understand and which he didn't dare mention. He never discovered how Philippe managed to reassure his mother, but three days later she went back to Les Fondettes looking satisfied. That same evening at Nana's he was startled to hear François announce the lieutenant. Philippe was in high spirits, making jokes and treating the whole matter as a foolish escapade by a young rascal whom he'd stood up for because the whole thing was trivial. With his heart in his mouth, Georges didn't dare move, blushing like a schoolgirl at the slightest comment. He'd never been very close to Philippe, who was ten years older than he; he was afraid of him, in the same way that you're afraid to tell your father about your women-troubles. As a result he felt ashamed and extremely uneasy when he saw him behaving so freely with Nana, laughing very loudly, enjoying himself immensely, bursting with health. However, as his brother soon started coming every day, in the end Georges managed more or less to accept the situation. Nana was radiant. She'd made her final move into the messy world of amorous intrigue; her insolent house-warming party was everything she desired: the grand residence was bursting at the seams with men and furniture.

One afternoon when the Hugon brothers were there, Count Muffat called on Nana outside his fixed visiting-hours. When Zoé told him her mistress was entertaining friends, he didn't insist and, gentleman that he was, tactfully withdrew. When he returned that evening Nana greeted him with icy rage.

'I don't think I've given you any cause to insult me, my dear count', she said in a deeply offended voice. 'Please understand that when I'm at home, I expect you to come in like anyone else.'

The count was completely taken aback.

'But my dear Nana . . .' he started to explain.

'It was because I had visitors, was it? Yes, there were men there. What do you think I was doing with them? . . . Behaving like a discreet lover is exactly how you make a woman notorious and I don't want to be made notorious.'

He found it hard to obtain her forgiveness. At heart, he was delighted. She used such scenes to keep him reassured and docile. In the past, she'd forced him to accept Georges; such an amusing youngster, she said. She had the count to dinner with Philippe and Muffat showed himself very friendly; after dinner, he drew the young man to one side and enquired after his mother. From that time onwards, the Hugon brothers, Vandeuvres, and Muffat became a regular, acknowledged part of the household and were on the friendliest of terms. It was a more convenient arrangement. Only Muffat tactfully refrained from coming too often, continuing to stand on ceremony, as if he were just a casual caller. At night, as Nana sat taking off her stockings on her bearskin rugs, he'd talk amiably about 'those nice young men', particularly of Philippe; what a genuine, honest young fellow he was!

'You're quite right, they're very nice', agreed Nana, still on the floor, now putting on her night-gown. 'But you know, they realize who I am. One word and they'll be out on their necks!'

But in spite of being surrounded by her admirers and in spite of all her luxury, Nana was bored to death. She had men to fill every minute of her nights and money even tucked away with her brushes and combs in the drawers of her dressing-table, but still she wasn't satisfied. She felt a vacuum, a hole in her life which left her yawning. In her idle existence, time dragged on monotonously, hour after hour. She lived like a bird, with no thought of the morrow, sure of being fed and all ready to perch for the night on the most convenient branch. Safe in the knowledge of where her next meal was coming from, she loafed about all day and every day, listless and lethargic, a drowsy, acquiescent victim of her profession of tart, as cloistered as in a convent. As she always took a carriage, she was losing the use of her legs. She reverted to the ways of her childhood, kissing Bijou from morning to night, killing time in stupid pursuits, with only one thing to look forward to: some man whom she wearily submitted to, in order to oblige. In her shiftless life she retained only one concern: the care of her body, washing and scenting it all over, taking pride in being able to strip naked at all times before all and sundry without any need to blush.

Nana used to get up at ten o'clock; the little Scottie, Bijou, would wake her by licking her face and she'd play with him for five minutes, letting him scramble all over her arms and thighs, which offended Count Muffat. Bijou was the first little man to make him jealous. It wasn't decent to let a pet stick his nose under the blankets like that. Then she'd go off to her dressing-room and take her bath. At about eleven, Francis would come and put her hair up in anticipation of the elaborate hairdressing session in the afternoon. As she loathed eating alone, she usually had lunch with Madame Maloir, who would appear in the morning from some place unknown wearing one of her extraordinary hats and at night return to her mysterious existence in which no one showed the remotest interest anyway. But the worst time of the day was the two-to-three-hour gap between lunch and dressing for the evening. Normally she'd suggest a game of bezique with her old friend; sometimes she'd read the *Figaro*; she was interested in items on the theatre or society news; and now and again she'd even open a book, because she prided herself on her literary taste. Getting dressed took her up to five o'clock. Only then did she come to life, either going off in her carriage or receiving a whole host of male visitors at home, frequently going out to dinner, getting to bed very late only to wake up next morning as weary as ever to pursue the identical routine day after day.

Her great distraction was to go over to Batignolles to see her little son Louis at her aunt's. For a couple of weeks she'd forget about him; then she'd go into a frenzy, dashing up there on foot, like a simple, kind, loving mother, taking him presents like someone visiting a patient in hospital, with snuff for her aunt and oranges and biscuits for her son; or else she would arrive in the landau on her way back from the Bois de Boulogne, wearing flashy dresses that nearly caused a riot in this little backwater. Ever since her niece had been leading such a grand life, Madame Lerat had been unable to contain her vanity. She rarely came to the house in the Avenue de Villiers, professing to think that it wasn't the place for her; but in her own street she would flaunt herself and be delighted when the young woman appeared in her four- or five-thousand-franc dresses; she would spend all next day showing off her presents and quoting figures that stupefied her neighbours. Nana usually kept her Sundays free for her family visits and if Muffat invited her on those days, she would smile and decline, like a good little middle-class housewife and mother: sorry, she couldn't, she was going to see baby and have supper with her aunt. What was more, the poor little brat was always ill. Louiset was 3 and a big lad already; but he'd had eczema on the back of his neck and pus was starting to collect in his ears. There were fears of some sort of bone decay in the skull. When Nana saw him looking so pale, with his tainted blood and flabby flesh with its yellow spots, she was worried and above all surprised: what was wrong with her pet to be so sickly when she, his mother, was so healthy?

On the days when she wasn't busy with her son, Nana relapsed into her monotonous, rackety life—drives in the Bois, first nights, dining and supping at the Maison d'Or or the Café Anglais, every kind of public entertainment, all the shows that drew crowds: Mabille, music-halls, the races. And still this feeling of vacuous, stupid, idleness which gave her a kind of cramp in the stomach. Her frequent passing infatuations did little to relieve her boredom; as soon as she was left to her own devices, she'd yawn and stretch her arms in utter weariness, for being alone made her sad because she came face to face with the hollowness of her life and her own tedium. Although cheerful by nature and the demands of her profession, she'd relapse into deep gloom and between yawns would sum up her existence in one constant wail:

'Oh, aren't men a pain!'

Coming back from a concert one afternoon, Nana noticed a woman in a dirty skirt, down-at-heel and wearing a rain-sodden hat, scuttling along the pavement in the Rue Montmartre.

'Stop, Charles!' she shouted to her driver and called out: 'Satin! Satin!'

The passers-by turned round; the whole street looked. Satin came over, getting even more splashed by the carriage-wheels.

'Get in, my dear', said Nana, completely disregarding the bystanders.

And she opened the door and took her off, disgusting as she was, in her pale blue landau and her lace-trimmed pearl-grey silk dress, while the crowd grinned at the haughty coachman's dignified expression.

From then on, Nana had an absorbing passion: Satin became her vice. She took her into her house in the Avenue de Villiers, cleaned her up, got her decent clothes, and for three whole days Satin told her all about Saint-Lazare, her troubles with the hospital sisters, and the pigs of policemen who made her register as a public prostitute. Nana was indignant, comforted her, and promised faithfully to get her out of that situation even if she had to go and see the minister herself. Meanwhile there was no urgency, no one would look for her here, that was for sure. The two women started spending their afternoons together, cuddling and kissing and generally billing and cooing, interspersed with giggles. It was the same little game they'd been playing in the Rue de Laval on the night the police burst in on them. Then one evening it turned into something earnest . . . Nana, who'd been revolted at Laure's, now realized what it was all about; she was ecstatic and devastated, the more so as, on the morning of the fourth day, Satin vanished. Nobody had seen her leave. She'd felt nostalgic for her life on the streets, she needed a change of air, so she'd slipped away, wearing her new dress.

That day the atmosphere in the house was so electric that the servants walked round with a frightened look on their faces, afraid to utter a word. Nana very nearly struck François for failing to stop her leaving. Then she made an effort to restrain herself and called Satin a dirty little whore; that'd teach her to pick up that sort of slut out of the gutter. In the afternoon she shut herself away, and Zoé heard her mistress sobbing. That evening she suddenly asked for her carriage and drove round to the Rue des Martyrs, thinking she might find Satin at Laure's. She didn't want to get her back, just smack her face. In fact, Satin was sitting at a little table with Madame Robert. When she caught sight of Nana, she burst out laughing. Nana's heart suddenly melted, and far from creating a scene she was very mild and conciliatory. She ordered champagne, made half-a-dozen tables tipsy, and then made off with Satin while Madame Robert was in the lavatory. But once they were in the carriage she bit her and threatened to do her in if she did a thing like that again.

But she did do it again, constantly. A score of times or more, Nana, furious at the fickleness of that slut, set off in tragic pursuit of Satin who didn't think twice about running away when she became bored by the comfortable life in the Avenue de Villiers. Nana threatened to go and slap Madame Robert's face; she even toyed with the idea of a duel: there wasn't room for both of them. Nowadays, whenever she dined at Laure's she would wear her diamonds, sometimes taking Louise Violaine, Maria Blond, and Tatan Néné along with her, all looking glittering; and in the yellow gaslight and reek of burnt fat, these opulent ladies went slumming, delighted to be startling the little tarts of the district whom they picked up after dinner. On these days, Laure herself, all sheen and tight corsets, would kiss her customers with an even more expansively maternal air. But amidst all this commotion, Satin, with her blue eyes and schoolgirlish look, remained quite calm; bitten and beaten and torn this way and that by the two women, she simply said it was odd, they'd be much better occupied in coming to some agreement. There was no point in smacking her face; she'd like nothing better than to please everybody but she couldn't cut herself in two. In the end it was Nana who won by smothering her in affection and lots of presents. To get her own back, Madame Robert wrote abominable anonymous letters to her rival's lovers.

For some time Count Muffat had been looking very concerned. One morning, in a state of great emotion, he showed Nana an anonymous letter which began by accusing her of deceiving the count with Vandeuvres and the Hugon brothers.

'It's not true, it's not true!' she cried, stamping her foot, in a tone of extraordinary sincerity.

'You promise?' asked Muffat, already relieved.

'I swear on anything you like . . . If I'm lying, I hope my son dies!'

But it was a long letter; it went on to describe her relations with Satin in the coarsest and most revolting detail. When she'd finished, she gave a smile:

'Now I know who's written it', she said simply.

And when Muffat wanted her to deny it, she went on calmly:

'That's nothing that concerns you, my pet. How does it affect you?'

She didn't deny it. He said he found it disgusting. She shrugged her shoulders. What sort of world did he live in? It was happening everywhere. She mentioned the names of her friends and assured him that society ladies did it. According to her, there was nothing more common or more normal. A lie was a lie and he'd seen a moment ago how indignantly she'd reacted on the subject of Vandeuvres and the Hugon boys. Certainly, he'd have had every right to strangle her for anything like that. But what was the point of lying about something so unimportant? She repeated:

'Look, how can that possibly affect you?'

Then, as he refused to calm down, she abruptly cut him short:

'Anyway, my dear man, if it doesn't suit you, there's a simple remedy . . . The door's open . . . You see, you've just got to accept me as I am.'

He lowered his eyes. At heart, he was delighted to hear her protesting her innocence, while she realized the power she had over him and began to stop humouring him. From that time on, Satin became openly a member of the family, on the same footing as the three men. Vandeuvres hadn't needed the anonymous letters to realize the situation; he treated it as a joke and put on a great show of jealousy with Satin, while Philippe and Georges welcomed her into the community with hearty handshakes and lots of very rude jokes.

One evening Nana had a brief encounter. The little tramp had deserted her, and she'd gone to eat in the Rue des Martyrs but without being able to lay hands on her. As she was dining by herself, Daguenet had turned up; although he was a reformed character, his vicious tastes sometimes led him to drop in at Laure's, hoping not to be seen in such a sleazy place. Consequently he looked embarrassed at seeing Nana there; but he wasn't easily put out. He marched over to her, and with a smile requested permission to join the lady at her table. Seeing his flippant manner, Nana put on her grand, icy expression and replied drily:

'Sit where you like, my dear man, this is a public restaurant.'

Beginning on such a note, the ensuing conversation was

funny, but when they reached the dessert Nana became bored and, eager to gloat, putting her elbows on the table and resuming their former intimate tone, she said:

'Well, my pet, how are your marriage plans going?'

'Not brilliantly', confessed Daguenet.

In fact, just as he was on the point of taking the plunge, he'd gained such a frosty impression from the count that he'd prudently held back. It looked to him as if the whole affair was a non-starter. Cupping her chin in her hands, Nana was watching him through her limpid eyes with an ironic smile on her lips.

'So I'm a tart', she said slowly. 'So you want to get your future father-in-law out of my clutches . . . No, really, for an intelligent man, you've been pretty stupid! You pass on idle gossip to a man who adores me and who tells me everything people tell him . . . Listen to me, my dear boy: you'll get married if and when I say so.'

He was beginning to realize that the only possible strategy was abject surrender. However, he continued to joke; he didn't want the matter to take too serious a turn. Putting on his gloves, he asked her, in the most strictly formal terms, for the hand of Mademoiselle Estelle de Beuville. She couldn't help laughing, rather as if she'd been tickled. What a lad Mimi was! There was no way you could go on bearing him a grudge! Daguenet's trump card with the ladies was the warm quality of his voice, so pure and expressive that the tarts had given him the nickname of Velvet Lips. And they never failed to succumb to the soft layers of sound which he wrapped them in. He was aware of his power, and he now proceeded to mesmerize her with the effortless flow of his soft voice as he started telling her amusing stories. They left the restaurant arm in arm; she was flushed, her heart was throbbing: he'd won her back. As the night was very fine she dismissed her carriage, walked home with him, and went up to his flat like an automaton. Two hours later, as she was getting dressed again:

'So you're keen on this marriage, Mimi?'

'What else can I do', he muttered. 'It's still the best possible solution. You know I'm stony broke.'

She called him over to fasten her bootees. Then, after a pause:

'OK, I don't mind . . . I'll try to pull some strings for you . . . She's as thin as a lath, that girl. But if that's what everyone wants . . . Oh, I'm a kind girl, I'll fix that for you!'

Still with her breasts bare, she laughed and added:

'But do you know what you're going to do for me in exchange?'

In a sudden burst of gratitude, he'd caught hold of her and was kissing her shoulders, while she was laughing, leaning back and struggling, quivering with excitement from his caresses.

'I've got it!' she exclaimed. 'Listen to me, this is what I want as my fee . . . On your wedding night, you'll give me first go, before your wife gets you, do you understand?'

'OK, it's on!' he said, laughing even more than Nana.

The deal struck them as being very funny; it would make a really good story.

It so happened that Nana was giving a small dinner-party next day, in fact the usual dinner with Muffat, Vandeuvres, the Hugon brothers, and Satin. The count arrived early. He needed eighty thousand francs to clear two or three of Nana's overdue bills and give her a sapphire necklace which she had her eye on. As he'd already made large inroads into his capital he was looking for a loan, not daring to sell another of his properties. On the advice of Nana herself he'd approached Labordette, but the latter had felt that the transaction was too big for him and had decided to sound out Francis the hairdresser, who liked obliging his female customers. Determined to steer clear of any personal involvement in the matter, the count put himself into those two gentlemen's hands and they jointly agreed not to call on the IOU which he was prepared to sign. They apologized profusely for the twenty-five per-cent interest, loudly complaining about those money-lending sharks whom they alleged they'd had to use. When Muffat was shown into the dressing-room, Francis was putting the finishing touches to Nana's hair. Labordette was also there; people were used to see him hanging around, as a friend whom nobody bothered about. Seeing the count, he discreetly placed a thick wad of banknotes down among the powders and pomades; the IOU was signed on the marble top of the dressing-table. Nana tried to persuade Labordette to stay for dinner but he declined: he was showing a rich foreigner round Paris. However, Muffat drew him on one side and asked him to go round urgently to Becker's the jewellers and bring back the sapphire necklace which he wanted to give Nana as a surprise that very night. Labordette gladly obliged, and half-an-hour later Julien slipped Muffat the jewel-case with a conspiratorial air.

During dinner Nana was jumpy; the sight of those eighty thousand francs had unsettled her. To think of all that money going to tradesmen! It was disgusting. As soon as the soup had been served in this magnificent dining-room, resplendent with gleaming silver and cut-glass, she became sentimental and started extolling the delights of poverty. The men were wearing full evening dress and she herself was dressed in an embroidered satin gown, while Satin, more modestly, was in black silk and wearing a simple, heart-shaped gold pendant, a present from her sweetheart Nana. Standing behind the guests, Julien and François were serving, helped by Zoé: all three were looking extremely dignified.

'I certainly had more fun when I hadn't got a penny', Nana was saying.

She had put Muffat on her right and Vandeuvres on her left but she hardly spared them a glance; she had eyes only for Satin, who had the place of honour between Philippe and Georges.

'Isn't that right, darling?' she went on. 'What a lark it was in those days when we were at old Madame Josse's school in the Rue Polonceau.'

They were serving the roast. The two girls started reminiscing; they were subject to these sudden spells of gossiping when they felt the urge to go back to their squalid early years; and it was always when men were present, as though they felt the irresistible need to rub their noses in the filth of their unsavoury past. The men had gone rather pale and looked embarrassed. The Hugon brothers were trying to laugh it off, while Vandeuvres was stroking his beard and Muffat was looking more and more solemn.

'Do you remember Victor?' asked Nana. 'What a vicious little boy he was! He used to take little girls down into cellars!'

'Of course I do', replied Satin. 'I can remember very well

the big yard at your place. There was a caretaker who had a broom.'

'That was old Madame Boche. She's dead.'

'And I can still see your shop . . . Wasn't your Mum fat! And when we were playing together one evening, your father came home tight, tight as a drum!'

At this point Vandeuvres tried to interrupt these ladies' reminiscences.

'I say, my dear, I wouldn't object to a few more of your truffles. They're quite delicious. I had some yesterday at the Duc de Corbreuse's and they weren't half as good as yours.'

'Truffles, Julien', Nana said curtly.

She returned to the conversation.

'Oh yes, Daddy wasn't sensible. You should have seen how he went downhill, an utter disaster. He was stony broke . . . I tell you, you can't imagine all the things I had to put up with. It's a miracle I didn't go under, like Mummy and Daddy.'

This time Muffat, who'd been nervously playing with his knife, ventured to make a comment:

'These things you're talking about aren't very cheerful . . .'

'Did you say cheerful?' snapped Nana, giving a glare. 'Of course they're not cheerful! What we needed was for someone to offer us a crust of bread, my dear man . . . Oh, you know, I'm a straightforward sort of girl, I call a spade a spade. Mummy was a laundress, Daddy was a drunk and he died from it. That's the long and the short of it, so if you're ashamed of my family . . .'

They all hurriedly protested: what on earth was she talking about, of course they had every respect for her family. But she didn't intend to stop there.

'If you're ashamed of my family, well, there's nothing to oblige you to stay, because I'm not the sort of woman who disowns her father and mother . . . You must accept me as I am, do you understand?'

They took her as she was, they were happy to accept her Daddy and her Mummy, her own past, anything she liked. Staring hard at the table-cloth, all four were trying to make themselves as small as possible while she trampled over them in the muddy clogs she used to wear in the old days in the Rue de la Goutte d'Or, unable to resist showing her complete domination of them. And she continued to show them no mercy: no, people could offer her all the money in the world, build palaces for her, she'd still miss those days when she ate crunchy apples. All that money was just a farce: it was only fit for tradesmen. And then her outburst petered out into sentimentality, she felt a yearning for the simple life, in which everything would be honest and straight from the heart and everybody would be kind.

At that moment she noticed Julien standing with his hands idly dangling at his side.

'Well, what's the matter?' she snapped. 'What are you looking at me for like a dying duck in a thunderstorm? Just serve the champagne!'

During this whole scene the servants hadn't smiled once while their mistress was letting herself be carried away so uncontrollably; they might have been deaf, looking more dignified than ever. Without a flicker, Julien started pouring the champagne. Unfortunately, as François was offering the dessert the dish tipped and the pears, apples, and grapes tumbled over the table.

'Clumsy idiot!'

The footman made the mistake of trying to explain that the fruit had been piled up badly and Zoé had dislodged some when she took some oranges.

'In that case', said Nana, 'it's Zoé who's the clumsy idiot!'

'Oh, madam . . .' the maid murmured, offended.

At which madam sprang to her feet and with a regal gesture, in a domineering voice said curtly:

'And that's enough of that, d'you understand? . . . Get out, the lot of you . . . We don't need you any more.'

Bullying them calmed her down, and she immediately became very amiable and gentle. Dessert was charming. The men enjoyed having to serve themselves. But Satin peeled a pear and came over to her darling and leaned over her shoulder from behind to eat it, whispering things into her ear which set them both laughing very loudly. Then she wanted to share her last piece of pear with Nana by offering it in her teeth, so that they were both nibbling each other's lips. They finished off the pear with a kiss. The gentlemen made a show of protesting, jokingly; Philippe said not to mind them, just go ahead; Vandeuvres asked if the men ought to leave the room. Georges put his arm round Satin's waist and conducted her back to her seat.

'What a stupid lot you are', said Nana, 'can't you see you're making her blush, the poor little pet . . . Don't worry, my dear, just let them go ahead. Ours is just a private affair between the two of us.'

And turning towards Muffat, who was watching with his earnest expression:

'That's right, my dear, isn't it?'

'Certainly', he agreed, giving a slow nod.

There were no more protests. In the presence of these men bearing great names, of old and honourable families, these two women faced each other exchanging tender glances, imposing their will on them, calmly exploiting their sex in undisguised contempt, while the men clapped their hands to applaud them.

They went upstairs to have coffee in the small drawing-room; the pink hangings and knick-knacks in various shades of crimson and old gold glowed in the soft gleam of the two lamps. Amid the chests, bronzes, and faience-ware, at this time of night the light flickered discreetly over the silver and ivory inlay, bringing out the glint of a carved beading or the shimmer of watered silk on a panel. The afternoon fire was dying down into glowing embers, the enervating heat held in by the curtains hanging over the doors and windows was making the room very warm. And in this room full of reminders of Nana's private life, gloves scattered all round, a handkerchief left lying on the floor, an open book, she revealed herself without pretence in her easy-going, friendly untidiness, with her scent of violets, creating an atmosphere of charm in these opulent surroundings; and the wide chairs like beds, the settees as deep as alcoves, were an invitation to drowse away the hours, laughing and flirting and exchanging loving words in shadowy corners.

Satin tucked herself away in a corner of a settee near the fireplace. She was smoking a cigarette. Vandeuvres was joking with her, pretending to be madly jealous and threatening to challenge her to a duel if she didn't stop leading Nana astray. Philippe and Georges joined in, teasing her and pinching her so hard that she called out:

'Darling, do come and make them leave me alone! They won't let me be!'

'Oh, do leave her alone', said Nana seriously. 'I don't want you to keep bothering her, you know that . . . And as for you, my pet, why do you keep on hanging around them when you know they're so silly?'

Satin went quite red, stuck out her tongue, and flounced off into the dressing-room, through the wide-open door of which large areas of pale marble could be seen gleaming in the milky light of the frosted gas-lamp globes. Nana now became the charming hostess and chatted to the four men. During the day she'd read a novel that was arousing a great deal of discussion, the story of a tart; and she was saying that it was appalling and quite untrue; she also expressed her indignation and revulsion at that sort of filth that claimed to give a true picture of life. As if you could put everything into a book, as if a novel should be written for any reason but a reader's entertainment! Nana held very firm views on books and drama: novels should be full of sentiment and high principles, uplifting, something to make you dream! From here, the conversation turned to the current unrest in Paris, inflammatory articles, public meetings calling for violence, incitement to outbreaks of rioting every night. She spoke angrily of the Republicans. What did they think they were up to, those great unwashed? Weren't people all happy, hadn't the Emperor done everything possible for the lower classes? What scum they were! And forgetting how, earlier on, she'd been demanding respect for her little world of the Rue de la Goutte d'Or, she roundly condemned them, her own people, showing the disgust and fear of a woman who's made it to the top herself. That very afternoon, in fact, she'd read in the *Figaro* the report of a public meeting, a caricature of a meeting which was still making her laugh because of their slangy language and the ugly mug of the boozer who'd been kicked out.

'Oh, those dipsos!' she exclaimed, turning up her nose. 'It'd be a disaster for everybody, that Republic of theirs! May God preserve our Emperor as long as possible!'

'God will hear those words, my dear', Muffat replied solemnly. 'Don't worry, the Empire's as solid as a rock.'

He liked hearing her express such healthy sentiments; their views on politics coincided. Vandeuvres and Captain Hugon joined them in deriding those 'guttersnipes' who ran a mile at the sight of cold steel. Georges didn't join in; he was looking pale and gloomy tonight. Noticing how unsettled he seemed, Nana asked:

'What's wrong with my baby?'

'Nothing, I'm just listening', he mumbled.

But he was desperately unhappy. After leaving table, he'd noticed Philippe joking with her and now it was his brother, not he, who was sitting beside her. He could feel his chest heaving as if it was ready to burst; he couldn't bear to see them so close and he was full of horrid thoughts which were giving him such a dreadful choking sensation that he felt distressed and ashamed. He'd taken Satin as a joke, he'd been prepared to put up with Steiner, then Muffat, and then all the others, but the thought of Philippe laying hands on Nana was revolting and made him see red.

'Here you are, take Bijou', she said, trying to console him, and handed him the little dog asleep on her lap.

Georges cheered up: he was holding something of hers, all warm from lying close to her.

Mention was made of a considerable loss sustained by Vandeuvres the previous day at the Imperial Club. Muffat never gambled, and expressed his surprise. Vandeuvres merely smiled and said that his imminent ruin was already the talk of the town; but it didn't matter how you died, the main thing was to make a decent exit. For some time past Nana had noticed his taut lips and a flicker in the depths of his pale eyes which suggested that he was in a nervous state. He still maintained his haughty, aristocratic poise, the effete, elegant refinement of his family breeding, but there were times when for a few brief seconds his head, emptied by gambling and women, had started spinning: one night, lying in bed with her, he had horrified Nana with a terrifying story: he was thinking, when he'd finally got through all his money, of shutting himself up in his stables and going up in flames with all his horses. His only hope now was in a horse called Lusignan which he was training for the Prix de Paris. This horse was his lifeline; it provided the backing for his shaky credit. Whenever Nana made a fresh demand he'd put her off: she'd have to wait till June, to see if Lusignan would win.

'Pooh!' she said jokingly. 'He's quite likely to lose. After all, he's going to clean them all up at the races.'

His only reply was a gentle, enigmatic smile. Then he said casually:

'By the way, I've taken the liberty of giving your name to my outsider. It's a filly and Nana has got just the right ring about it. No objection?'

'Objection? Why should I have?' she replied, secretly delighted.

They continued to chat. As they were talking about an impending execution which Nana was very keen to attend, Satin appeared at the dressing-room door, asking her to come urgently. Nana immediately got up and left the gentlemen sprawling in their armchairs, finishing off their cigars and discussing the serious question of the extent of responsibility of a murderer who was a chronic alcoholic. In the dressing-room Zoé sat slumped in a chair crying her eyes out, while Satin was vainly trying to comfort her.

'What's the matter?' asked Nana in surprise.

'Oh, do speak to her, darling', said Satin. 'I've spent the last twenty minutes trying to make her see sense . . . She's crying because you called her a clumsy idiot.'

'Yes, madam . . . It's very hard, very hard', gulped Zoé, overcome by a fresh burst of sobbing.

At the sight of her distress, Nana's heart melted. She spoke gently to her, and when she still didn't calm down she squatted down in front of her and in a friendly, affectionate gesture put her arms round her waist.

'But I only said "clumsy idiot" like I'd have said anything, you know, you silly . . . How could I have known! I was just angry. Look, I was in the wrong. Do calm down.'

'I'm so fond of madam', faltered Zoé. 'And after all I've done for madam . . .'

Nana kissed her. Then, to show she wasn't cross, she gave her a dress she'd worn only three times. Their quarrels always ended with presents. Zoé went away with the dress over her arm, dabbing her eyes; she added that they were still miserable in the kitchen, Julien and François hadn't been able to eat a bite, they'd quite lost their appetite as madam had been so angry with them. So madam sent each of them a twenty-franc piece to show her appreciation; seeing people looking miserable around her always made her so unhappy.

As Nana was making her way back to the drawing-room, glad at having settled the squabble which had been secretly on her mind because of its possible future repercussions, Satin quickly whispered to her how upset she was about the men's teasing of her and threatened to clear out if they didn't stop it; and she told her darling Nana to kick all of them out at bedtime. That'd teach them! And it'd be so nice, just the two of them all to themselves! Nana felt worried again: no, she couldn't do that. The other girl started bullying her, just like a petulant little child trying to get its own way.

'I want you to, do you understand? . . . Get rid of them or I'll go away myself!'

And she flounced off back into the drawing-room where she snuggled down on a divan under the window, well away from them all and lay there, completely inert, silently staring at Nana through her big eyes and waiting.

The gentlemen were condemning all these new-fangled theories of criminologists: how very clever of them to have dreamed up the idea of diminished responsibility in certain pathological cases! So there weren't any criminals now, only sick people! The young woman was nodding approvingly while pondering how she might best get rid of the count. The others would in any case be leaving but Muffat would certainly dig his heels in. Indeed, when Philippe got up to go, Georges immediately followed suit; his only concern had been not to leave his brother behind. Vandeuvres stayed on a few minutes longer, feeling his ground and waiting to see if Muffat perhaps had some business which would force him to relinquish his rightful place. Once he saw him plainly set to stay the night, he didn't insist and tactfully withdrew. As he was making for the door, he caught sight of Satin staring, and no doubt realizing what was happening he was amused and went over to say goodnight to her too.

'No ill feelings, eh?' he said softly. 'Forgive me. You're the smartest of the lot and no mistake!'

Satin didn't deign to reply. Now that the count and Nana

were left alone, she was watching them like a hawk. Finally relaxing, Muffat went over to Nana, took hold of her fingers, and kissed them. Nana was trying to find some way of breaking the news. She asked if Estelle was feeling better. The day before he'd been complaining how depressed she was; he was finding it impossible to spend a day at home with any enjoyment, with his wife never there and Estelle withdrawing into an icy silence. Nana was never short of good advice concerning such domestic problems. Muffat, now relaxed in mind and body, was giving free rein to his feelings and started going over all his grievances again. Nana remembered her promise.

'Why not marry her off?' she said.

And without hesitation, she brazenly suggested Daguenet. The count looked horrified. After all she'd told him? He could never agree to that!

She pretended to be surprised and then burst out laughing. Slipping her arm round his waist:

'Surely you're not jealous? . . . You must remember that people had been saying horrid things about me and I was feeling very angry. But now, I'd feel sorry . . .'

Then she met Satin's eyes over his shoulder and nervously released him. She continued earnestly:

'My dear, this marriage must go ahead, I wouldn't like to stand in the way of your daughter's happiness . . . That young man's a very good match, you couldn't do better.'

She launched into extravagant praise of Daguenet. The count took hold of her hands: he'd think it over, they could discuss it later. He said they ought to go to bed; she lowered her eyes: unfortunately, it wasn't possible, she was indisposed; if he loved her at all, he wouldn't insist. He refused to be put off: he intended to stay. She started to weaken, but at that moment caught Satin's eye again and said firmly that there was nothing doing, it was out of the question. The count looked very upset but he got up and fetched his hat. In the doorway, he suddenly remembered the sapphire necklace still in the jewel-case in his pocket. He's been intending to hide it at the bottom of the bed so that she would feel it with her legs when she got into bed first, a sort of schoolboy surprise that he'd been looking forward to ever since dinner.

Now, bewildered and distressed at being sent away, he abruptly handed her the case.

'What's that?' she asked. 'Goodness me, it's sapphires . . . Oh yes, that necklace . . . Aren't you kind! . . . I say, darling, are you sure it's the same one? It looked grander in the window.'

That was all the thanks he got; she let him leave. He caught sight of Satin lying there and silently waiting. He looked at the two women and admitted defeat. Without further ado, he went downstairs. Before the front door had closed behind him, Satin had grasped Nana round the waist and was dancing and singing. Then she ran over to the window.

'Let's look how fed up he is in the street!'

The two women leant against the wrought-iron railing, hiding in the shadow of the curtain. It was striking one o'clock. Along the deserted Avenue de Villiers, swept by violent squalls of rain, the double row of gas-jets stretched out into the damp March night; under the murky sky, half-built houses surrounded by tall scaffolding could be seen in dark patches of wasteland. Hunching his shoulders, Muffat was trudging along, a disconsolate figure reflected in the gleaming wet pavement as he made his way over this icy, deserted plain of the new Paris. The two girls burst into uncontrollable laughter. Then Nana told Satin to be quiet:

'Look out, there's the police.'

They stifled their laughter and watched two dark figures walking in step on the other side of the avenue. They were both still secretly afraid of the police; Nana in particular, despite all her luxury, her almost royal status as a woman who dictated to everybody, had never lost her terror of them and disliked hearing them mentioned as much as she hated any mention of death. One of the police looked upwards; Nana felt anxious: you never knew with that lot, they might very well take them for prostitutes if they heard them laughing at that time of night. Satin gave a little shiver and snuggled up against Nana. But they didn't leave the window; their interest had been caught by an approaching lantern, bobbing about amidst the puddles on the roadway. It was an elderly rag-woman rummaging about in the gutter. Satin recognized her.

'Good Lord!' she exclaimed. 'It's Queen Pomaré* with her wicker scarf!'

And as a spatter of rain lashed their faces, she told her darling Nana the story of Queen Pomaré. What a super tart she'd been in the old days when she'd been the toast of Paris! And what impudence and verve, leading men by their noses like tamed animals, with men of high position in tears on her staircase! And now she'd taken to drink and her neighbours would give her absinthe to have a laugh; street urchins used to chase her, throwing stones. In a word, completely and utterly degraded, a queen ending up literally in the gutter! Nana was listening in frozen silence.

'Just watch', Satin went on.

She gave a wolf-whistle. Standing under the window in the yellow gleam of her lantern, the ragwoman looked up. From this bundle of rags wrapped in a tattered, coarse silk headscarf, her deeply seamed purple face peered out with bloodshot, ravaged eyes and toothless mouth. Confronted by this appalling old whore soaked in alcohol, in the murky background Nana had a vision of the former tart Irma d'Anglars whom she'd seen in Chamont, full of years and honours, walking up to the terrace of her manor, with the villagers bowing and scraping around her. Then, as Satin gave another whistle, still laughing at the old woman who couldn't see her:

'Please stop doing that', Nana said in an undertone, with a change of tone. 'Here come the police again. Let's go back in, my pet.'

The tramping feet were coming back. They shut the window. As she turned round, shivering, with her face wet, Nana stood for a second in amazement at the sight of her drawing-room as if she'd forgotten where she was and had been in some strange place. The air was so warm and scented that she felt surprised and very happy. This accumulation of precious objects, antique furniture, silks, gold embroideries, ivories, and bronzes lay peacefully bathed in the light of the lamps while the whole of the magnificent house was permeated by a feeling of luxury, the majestic reception-rooms, the vast, comfortable dining-room, the reverent atmosphere of the staircase, the soft rugs and chairs. It was like a sudden extension of her own personality, her need for power and pleasure, her urge to possess everything in order to destroy everything. Never before had she felt so deeply the immense force of her sexuality. Looking slowly around, she said with an earnest, philosophical air:

'Ah well, it's really jolly sensible to get what you can while you're young!'

Satin was already lying on the bearskin rugs in the bedroom, wriggling about and calling to her:

'Come on! Do come on!'

Nana undressed in the dressing-room. To save time, she took hold of her thick blonde hair in both hands and shook it over the silver wash-basin; a shower of long pins fell out, tinkling like bells on the shining metal.

Chapter 11

It was Sunday, one of the first hot days in June; the clouds threatened storms. In the afternoon, the Grand Prix de Paris was going to be run on the Bois de Boulogne racecourse. The sun had come up in a reddish haze, but round about eleven o'clock, just as the carriages were beginning to arrive at the Longchamp course, a southerly wind had dispersed the clouds and over the whole sky patches of intense blue were showing through the long, ragged, grey wisps of vapour as they were swept away. As the sun darted through the clouds, everything suddenly brightened up: the extensive public enclosure gradually filling up with carriages and people on foot or horseback; the track itself, still deserted, with its judge's box, the winning-post, the pole to display the horses' numbers on; and the five symmetrical grandstands opposite, with their brick-and-timber balconies one above the other, set in the middle of the private enclosure. Beyond all this the huge level plain lay bathed in the midday sun, with its border of little trees, stretching out until it was lost in the distance, cut off in the west by the wooded slopes of Suresne and Saint Cloud, dominated by the harsh outline of the Mont Valérien.

Nana was wildly excited, almost as if her whole prosperity depended on the Grand Prix, and had insisted on getting a place next to the barrier, beside the winning-post. She'd come very early, amongst the first arrivals, in her landau with its silver fittings, drawn by four superb greys hitched up in the Daumont style, which were a present from Count Muffat. When they had trotted in through the entrance to the course, with their two outriders on the left-hand horses and two postilions perched like statues at the back, there had been a stir amongst the spectators as if it was royalty going by. Nana was wearing an extraordinary get-up in the blue-and-white racing colours of Vandeuvres: her little bodice and tunic of blue silk, skin-tight, drawn up over her backside into a voluminous sort of pouf, clung to the curve of her thighs in a very provocative manner, for the prevailing fashion was for loose, full skirts; her dress was in white satin, with white satin sleeves and a white satin shawl worn as a sash, all embroidered in silver gimp which glinted in the sun. Finally, to add a touch of jockey, she'd perched a jaunty little blue toque with a white feather above her curly blonde hair, which was gathered in the nape of her neck and then allowed to stream down her back like an enormous red horse-tail.

It was just striking twelve; there were more than three hours to wait before the Grand Prix. Once her landau was parked beside the barrier, Nana was able to relax, completely at home. She'd had the odd idea of bringing Louiset along with her as well as Bijou, who was now lying on her lap trembling with cold in spite of the warm day, while the little boy, decked out in lace and ribbons, had a pinched, wan little face, even paler from exposure to the fresh air, and was sitting in frozen silence. Meanwhile, regardless of the people around, his mother was talking very loudly with Georges and Philippe Hugon sitting opposite her and almost covered up to the neck in a heap of bunches of flowers, white roses, and blue forget-me-nots.

'So', she was saying, 'as he was getting on my nerves, I showed him the door . . . And he's been sulking for the last two days.'

She was referring to Muffat but failed to reveal the true cause of their first quarrel. One night he'd found a man's hat in her bedroom, a stupid, passing fancy for a man she'd picked up in the street and taken back to her room out of boredom.

'You can't imagine how funny he is', she went on, enjoying the details she was giving them. 'At heart he's a sanctimonious prig, a sheer hypocrite. For example, he says his prayers every night. Yes, I'm positive. He thinks I don't notice because I get into bed first so as not to embarrass him, but I peep out of the corner of my eye, he mumbles something and makes the sign of the cross while he's stepping over me to lie down next to the wall . . .'

'Good Lord, the crafty beggar', murmured Philippe. 'So he does that before and after?'

She giggled loudly.

'That's right, before and after. As I'm going off to sleep, I can hear him mumbling away again . . . The real bore is that we can't have the slightest squabble without him having to fall back on to his priests. I've always been religious myself—yes I have, you can joke about it as much as you like, you won't stop me believing in what I believe . . . The trouble is, he's so dreadfully dull, he's always snivelling and talking about feeling guilty. The day before yesterday, for example, after we'd had our little tiff, he completely lost control of himself, it made me quite nervous . . .'

She broke off:

'Look, there are the Mignons arriving. Good Lord, they've brought their children along . . . God, look how she's got them up!'

The Mignons were in the obligatory luxurious landau, in sober colours, of the newly rich middle-class family. Rose was wearing a grey silk dress trimmed with red ruffles and bows. She was smiling happily, delighted to see Henri and Charles sitting opposite her on the front seat, all bundled up in their school tunics that were too big for them but enjoying the treat nevertheless. However, when their landau had parked close to the barrier and she caught sight of Nana in all her glory, with her flowers, her four horses and her own livery, she stiffened, pursed her lips and turned away.

'By the way', Nana continued, 'do you know a tiny old man, very neat, with bad teeth? . . . A Monsieur Venot . . . He called on me this morning.'

'Monsieur Venot!' exclaimed Georges in amazement. 'It can't have been . . . He's a Jesuit.'

'That's the man! I thought I got a whiff of that. Oh, you can't imagine our conversation, it was absolutely hilarious . . . He talked to me about the count, the breakup of the family, and begged me to let them all live happily together again . . . Extremely polite, incidentally, smiling all the time . . . So I told him there's nothing I'd like better and I undertook to see the count go back to his wife . . . I'm not joking, you know, I'd be really delighted to see them all happily together again, all of them! And in fact, it would be a relief for me because frankly there are days when I could scream for boredom!'

Her heartfelt admission revealed how desperately weary

she'd become over the last few months. What was more, the count seemed to be in considerable financial difficulties; he was looking worried, and the letter of credit he'd given Labordette seemed in danger of not being honoured.

'As a matter of fact, the countess is over there', said Georges, who'd been running his eye over the grandstands.

'Where is she?' exclaimed Nana. 'What sharp eyes you've got, baby! Take my sunshade, Philippe.'

But Georges had quickly moved to forestall his brother, delighted to hold the blue silk parasol with its silver fringe. Nana was scanning the grandstands with an enormous pair of binoculars.

'Oh yes, I can see her', she said finally. 'Next to a pillar in the right-hand grandstand, isn't she? She's in mauve with her daughter beside her, wearing white . . . Well, well! Daguenet's just going up to speak to them.'

Philippe mentioned Daguenet's impending marriage to that beanstalk Estelle. It was all arranged, the banns were going to be put up. At first the countess had been reluctant but the count, people said, had put his foot down. Nana was smiling.

'I know, I know', she murmured. 'Good luck to Paul. He's a nice boy, he deserves it.'

And leaning forward towards Louiset:

'Are you enjoying it? How serious you look!'

The little boy was gazing round at all these people without a smile. He looked like an old man saddened by what he was seeing. Bijou had been driven out of his mistress's lap by her constant fidgeting and, still trembling, had taken refuge beside Louiset.

Meanwhile the public enclosures were filling up. An unbroken stream of carriages was pouring through the Waterfall entrance-gate. There were large omnibuses, the *Pauline* laden with her fifty passengers from the Boulevard des Italiens, which parked to the right of the grandstands; dogcarts, victorias, and landaus, all superbly turned out, mingling with shabby cabs rattling along behind their scraggy horses, drivers whipping up their four-in-hands, and mail-coaches with their owners perched on the top seats, leaving their servants to look after the crates of champagne inside; buggies with their immense flashing steel wheels, and light tandems dashing along to the tinkling of bells, like delicate pieces of clockwork. From time to time a man on horseback rode by; a stream of scared pedestrians was slipping nimbly between the vehicles. Suddenly the distant rumble of traffic from the avenues of the Bois de Boulogne died down into a mere rustle, and in the enclosures the only sound was the buzz of the ever-growing crowd, calls and shouts, the crack of whips, all swept away into the air. The sun came out through the scurrying clouds, streaking the harnesses and lacquered coach-panels with gold and setting the ladies' dresses glowing, while the coach-drivers with their long whips sitting high on their boxes were gleaming in the flood of light.

Labordette was seen climbing down from the barouche in which Gaga, Clarisse, and Blanche had offered him a lift. He hurried off across the track, heading for the jockeys' enclosure, but Nana got Georges to call him back and as he came up, asked with a laugh:

'Well, what's the odds on me?'

She was referring to the filly Nana, who had run a dreadful race in the Prix de Diane and hadn't even been placed during April and May in the Prix des Cars and the big Producers' Stakes, both of which had been won by Vandeuvres' other horse, Lusignan. As a result, Lusignan was now the hot favourite and since yesterday evening he was being currently quoted at two-to-one against.

'Still fifty-to-one', replied Labordette.

Labordette was anxious to leave but Nana wouldn't let him go: she needed advice, and with his contacts in the world of trainers and jockeys he was bound to have inside information on the various stables. His tips had already proved right a score of times; he'd been nicknamed the king of tipsters.

'Which horse shall I back?' the young woman asked. 'What are the odds on the Englishman?'

'Spirit? Three-to-one . . . The same on Valerio II . . . The others are Cosine at twenty-five-to-one, Hazard at forty, Boum at thirty, Pichenette at thirty-five, Frangipani at ten . . .'

'No, I shan't back the Englishman, I'm too patriotic . . . How about Valerio II maybe? The Duc de Corbreuse seemed very pleased with himself a moment ago. Perhaps not, in fact.

What do you think about putting a thousand on Lusignan?'

Labordette was looking at her with a peculiar expression in his eyes. She leaned forward and questioned him in a low voice because she knew that, to give himself a freer hand, Vandeuvres got him to place his bets with the bookmakers. If he'd picked up some information, he could surely pass it on to her. However, without making any attempt to go further into the matter, Labordette told her to rely on his flair: he'd place her thousand francs for her as he thought fit and she wouldn't regret it.

'Any old horse you like', she shouted cheerfully as he at last made his escape. 'Any except Nana, she's a rotten old nag!'

There was a roar of laughter from the carriage; the young men found her witticism highly amusing but Louiset peered at his mother uncomprehendingly through his pale eyes, surprised by all the noise they were making. But Labordette still couldn't manage to get away: Rose Mignon was beckoning to him and gave him some instructions; he took down some figures in a notebook. Then it was Clarisse's and Gaga's turn; they called him over and asked him to change their bets; they'd heard something the crowd was saying and wanted to drop Valerio II and back Lusignan. Labordette blandly continued to make notes and finally succeeded in leaving. He disappeared between two grandstands on the other side of the track.

Carriages were still arriving. They now formed a deep, solid block all along the barrier, set off by the pale splashes of colour of the white horses. All around other carriages were parked higgledy-piggledy, as if they'd been left stranded all over the public enclosure, wheels and teams of horses scattered in every direction, side by side, diagonally, crosswise, head to head. On those parts of the grass still unencumbered, riders were trotting and the black swarm of people on foot constantly on the move. Above this confused and motley fairground mob the grey canvas awnings of the snack-bars stood out, turning white in the bursts of sunshine. But the jostling crowd and its whirlpool of hats was thickest round the bookies, who were standing up in their open carriages waving their arms in the air like dentists, beside the large boards on which they'd written up their odds.

'No, it's really too stupid not to know which horse you're backing!' said Nana. 'I must put something on for myself.'

She stood up to see if she could find a nice-looking bookmaker. However, the sight of a whole crowd of her old cronies put the idea out of her head. Apart from the Mignons and Gaga, Clarisse, and Blanche, in the middle of the mass of carriages now hemming in her landau, she could see, to her left and right behind her, Tatan Néné accompanied by Maria Blond in a victoria, Caroline Héquet in a barouche with her mother and two gentlemen, Louise Violaine all by herself in a little wicker pony-cart with green and orange ribbons, the racing colours of the Méchain stables, Léa de Horn sitting high up on a bench in a mail-coach full of rowdy young men. Beyond them, in a luxuriously aristocratic eight-spring carriage, Lucy Stewart, wearing a very simple black silk dress, was sitting beside a tall young man in a midshipman's uniform, taking good care to look distinguished. But Nana was amazed to see Simonne arriving in a tandem driven by Steiner, with a footman sitting motionless behind them with his arms crossed; she was dressed all in white satin with a yellow stripe and plastered with diamonds from the waist upwards, including her hat; she looked dazzling; flourishing an immensely long whip, the banker was urging on his two horses, a big, showy, chestnut high-stepper behind a dainty gold bay.

'Crikey!' exclaimed Nana. 'That crook must have cleaned out the Stock Exchange again! . . . I say, doesn't Simonne look smart! She'd getting too uppish, we'll have to bring her down a peg!'

Nevertheless, she exchanged a wave from a distance. She was, in fact, waving and smiling all the time, turning round to make sure she didn't miss anyone and that everybody would see her. And she didn't stop chattering.

'But that must be Lucy's son she's got in tow with her! Doesn't he look nice in uniform! . . . That's why she's looking so grand. You know, she's afraid of him and lets him think she's an actress . . . Poor young man, I'm sorry for him . . . He doesn't seem to suspect . . .'

'Nonsense!' murmured Philippe with a laugh. 'She'll find a rich young girl for him in the provinces anytime she wants to!'

Nana stopped talking; in the midst of all the carriages, she'd just caught sight of Tricon. She'd arrived in a cab, and being unable to see anything from there had calmly climbed up to the driver's seat where her tall figure, with its aristocratic-looking face framed in long ringlets, towered over the crowd, looking like the queen of all her women subjects, who were all giving her discreet smiles. She turned up her nose and pretended not to know them. She hadn't come there to work but for pleasure; as a passionate gambler, she went to the races to enjoy herself.

'I say, there's that nit la Faloise!' exclaimed Georges suddenly.

He was a surprising figure. Nana couldn't recognize the la Faloise she'd known before. Ever since he'd come into money he had become extraordinarily smart. He wore his hair in tight coils, had a butterfly collar, and was dressed in a soft-coloured material which clung to his bony shoulders. He had adopted a weary, swaying form of locomotion and spoke in a gentle, drawling tone of voice, using slang expressions and sentences which he couldn't be bothered to complete.

Nana was captivated.

'How splendid!' she exclaimed.

Gaga and Clarisse made a dead set at him; they would have liked to win him back, but after they'd called him over to them he left them straight away with a joke and a scornful wag of his hips. He was dazzled by Nana and went over and stood on the footboard of her carriage. When she made a playful reference to Gaga, he murmured:

'Oh no, my dear, the old guard is definitely out! Nothing of that sort for *me*! And in any case, you know you're the one now, my Juliet!'

He placed his hand on his heart. This sudden declaration of love in the open air sent Nana into peals of laughter. But she went on:

'But there are other things in life than that, you know. You're making me forget that I want to place a bet. Georges, you see that bookie over there, the big red-faced one with curly hair. He's got the sort of flashy look which I like . . . You go over and place a bet with him on . . . Well, what's it to be?'

'Me no patriot, definitely not!' babbled la Faloise. 'Me, put all my lolly on Englishman . . . If Englishman win, good show! Frenchmen go to Jericho!'

Nana was deeply shocked. They discussed the merits of the horses. Pretending to have it straight from the horse's mouth, la Faloise said they were all nothing but hacks. Baron Verdier's Frangipani was by Truth out of Lenora, and the big bay would have had a chance if it hadn't suffered a strain during training. As for Valerio II from the Corbreuse stud, he wasn't ready, he'd had a touch of enteritis in April; of course they were trying to hush it up, but he knew it as a fact, honour bright! His final recommendation was Hazard, a Méchain horse—the most suspect of the lot and a rank outsider. What a rattling good horse Hazard was, by Jove! Didn't he move well! That gee-gee was going to surprise everybody!

'No', said Nana, 'I'm going to put two hundred francs on Lusignan and fifty on Boum.'

La Faloise exploded.

'But you can't possibly, my dear! Even Gasc's not backing his own horse . . . As for your Lusignan, not on your life! He's just a joke. Just imagine, by Lamb out of Princess! What a joke! Lamb and Princess. Not a hope in hell! Far too short in the leg!'

He was almost speechless. Philippe pointed out that in fact Lusignan had won the Prix des Cars and the Producers' Stakes. The other man brushed him aside: what did that prove? Nothing at all! Quite the opposite, it made you suspicious. Anyway, Gresham was riding Lusignan, so don't talk rubbish. Everyone knew Gresham was bad news, he never won!

The argument which had started in Nana's landau seemed to be spreading all round the public enclosure. People were shouting, the gambling fever was gripping everyone, faces were beginning to go red, arms were waving about more wildly, while perched in their carriages the bookies were shouting the odds and furiously scribbling down figures. It was only the small fry that were placing their bets here, the big punters were in the jockeys' enclosure, so these earnest little gamblers with greed written all over their faces were risking five francs with the possibility of winning a few louis.

In the end, the main clash turned out to be between Spirit and Lusignan. Gentlemen recognizably British were walking around among the groups of people, displaying ruddy complexions and already celebrating victory: one of Lord Reading's horses, Bramah, had won last year's Grand Prix, a defeat still rankling in French hearts; it would be a national disaster if France was beaten yet again. So the ladies were all being passionately patriotic and the honour of France was in the hands of the Vandeuvres stables; Lusignan was being boosted, defended, and glorified. Gaga, Blanche, Caroline, and the others were backing Lusignan. Lucy Stewart was holding back because of her son, but there was a rumour that Rose Mignon had told Labordette to put four thousand francs on Vandeuvres' horse. Only Tricon, sitting up beside her driver, was waiting until the last minute; keeping herself completely aloof from these various squabbles, she sat dominating the increasing hullaballoo in which the horses' names were being bandied about in lively Parisian accents or gruff English bellows. She listened majestically, taking notes.

'And what about Nana?' asked Georges. 'Isn't anybody going to back her?'

Nobody was; in fact, no one was even mentioning her name. Lusignan's popularity was completely overshadowing Vandeuvres's outsider. Then la Faloise suddenly flung his arms into the air and exclaimed:

'I've just had a revelation! . . . I'm going to put twenty francs on Nana!'

'Good for you!' said Georges. 'I'm going to double that.'

'And I'll treble it', Philippe added.

The three of them climbed into the landau and playfully started flirting with her, throwing figures about as if they were bidding for Nana at an auction. La Faloise was talking about covering her in gold. Moreover, everybody ought to be betting on her, they'd go out and recruit more support. But as the three young men were making off to do some propaganda for her, Nana shouted after them:

'Remember I don't want to bet on her, won't you? Georges, will you put ten louis on Lusignan, and five on Valerio II?'

They'd already left. Highly amused, she watched them dodging through the crowd, around wheels, ducking under horses' heads, scouting through the whole enclosure. As soon as they saw people they knew, they hurried over and urged them to back Nana. There were great gusts of laughter in the crowd as they kept turning round and tracing numbers in the air with their fingers, while the young woman stood brandishing her sunshade. However, they weren't having much success, though a few men allowed themselves to be persuaded, including Steiner who was thrilled at seeing Nana and decided to risk sixty francs. But the women were very firm: 'Back a certain also-ran? Thanks a lot!' In any case, why trouble to support a little slut who was putting them all in the shade with her four greys, her footmen, and her brazen determination to gobble everybody up? Gaga and Clarisse asked la Faloise if he was trying to pull their legs. When Georges had the cheek to walk up to the Mignons' landau, Rose turned her back in outrage without replying. You had to sink pretty low to let your name be given to a horse! Mignon himself, on the other hand, was following the young men with an amused look, remarking that women always brought you luck.

'Well?' enquired Nana when the young men came back after a lengthy session with the bookmakers.

'You're forty-to-one', said la Faloise.

Nana was flabbergasted.

'Forty-to-one?' she exclaimed. 'I was fifty-to-one a moment ago. What on earth's happening?'

Labordette too had just come back. The track was being closed off and a bell was ringing to announce the first race. During the sudden buzz of interest, she questioned him about the sudden drop in the odds. He was evasive: there must have been further backers. She had to be satisfied with this explanation; moreover, Labordette had a worried look; he said he couldn't stay, Vandeuvres was coming.

In anticipation of the Grand Prix the first race aroused little interest, and just as it was ending there was a cloud-burst over the course. The sun had gone in a few seconds before and the crowd was shrouded in a pall of murky grey; there followed a squall of wind, and the rain bucketed down in enormous drops, falling in solid sheets. In the sudden confusion people were shouting, joking, and swearing and there was a mad rush of spectators scurrying for shelter under the awnings of the drink-stalls. In their carriages women were trying to protect themselves, holding their parasols in both hands while their footmen dashed to put up the hoods. But the shower was already abating and the sun was gleaming through the spray tossed by the gusty wind. Through a rift in the clouds as they whisked away over the Bois a blue streak emerged, a cheerful sun peeped through and the women started laughing in relief; and as the horses snorted and the soaked, bustling, excited crowd shook themselves dry, a golden glow spread over the streaming enclosure, setting it sparkling like crystal.

'Oh, poor little Louis!' said Nana. 'Are you soaked, my precious?'

Without a word the little boy let Nana wipe his hands on her handkerchief. Then she dabbed Bijou, who was trembling more than ever. It wasn't serious, a few spots on her white satin dress but she didn't mind. Freshened up by the rain, her flowers were glittering, snow-white; blissfully, she sniffed one; it was like wetting your lips with dew.

Meanwhile, the sudden downpour had quickly filled the grandstands. Nana was peering through her binoculars. From this distance it was possible to pick out only a confused, compact mass of people piled up on the tiers of seats and forming a dark background speckled by pale, shining faces. Across the corner of the grandstand roofs the sun was casting a slanting beam of light on the seated crowd, turning the dresses of the ladies paler. Nana was particularly amused by the ladies who'd been driven away from their chairs which had been lined up on the sanded area in front of the grandstands. Access to the jockeys' enclosure was strictly forbidden to all tarts, and she was making rude remarks about all these respectable married women who were so plain and dowdily dressed.

The word spread that the Empress was going into the small central grandstand, a Swiss-chalet style of pavilion with a deep balcony set with red armchairs.

'But he's up there!' exclaimed Georges. 'I didn't think he was on duty this week.'

The stiff, solemn figure had loomed up behind the Empress. The young men started joking: what a shame Satin wasn't here to go and dig him in the ribs! But through her binoculars Nana had recognized the Prince of Scotland in the Imperial stand.

'Good Lord, there's Charles!' she exclaimed.

She thought he'd put on weight; he'd expanded in the last eighteen months. She gave a few details: he really was physically well endowed.

All around her, their ladyships were whispering that the count had ditched her. There'd been a fuss, the Tuileries was shocked at the Chamberlain's flagrant carrying-on, and in order to hang on to his job he'd recently broken off the affair. La Faloise wasn't slow to pass on the story and immediately volunteered to take the count's place, again addressing her as his 'Juliet'. She merely gave a loud laugh and said:

'That's completely idiotic . . . You don't know him. I only need to lift my little finger and he'll do anything I tell him.'

For the last few seconds she'd been examining Countess Sabine and Estelle. Daguenet was still in attendance on the two ladies. Fauchery had just arrived and was pushing his way through to join them. Once there, he stood with a smile on his face. Nana continued to talk, waving a scornful hand towards the grandstand.

'You know, that lot up there doesn't impress me anymore . . . I know them all too well. You ought to see them when they take their wrappings off . . . There's no respect anymore! It's all gone. Filth at the top, filth down below, there's nothing but filth and more filth . . . That's why I want to be left alone!'

And she swept her arm around to include the whole scene, from the strappers leading the horses on to the track to the Empress talking with Charles, a prince of royal blood but still a bastard.

'Good for you, Nana! Jolly good show!' exclaimed la Faloise enthusiastically.

The sound of the bell was carried off in the wind. The races were proceeding. They'd just run the Isfahan Stakes, won by Pear Drop from the Méchain stud. Nana called out to Labordette to enquire what he'd done with her hundred louis. He laughed and refused to tell what her horses were, he didn't want to spoil her chances. He'd done the right thing with her money, she'd soon see. And when she confessed that she'd put two hundred francs on Lusignan and a hundred on Valerio II on her own account, he shrugged his shoulders, hinting that you couldn't stop women from doing silly things. She was surprised, she couldn't understand what he meant.

The enclosure was now becoming livelier and livelier. While they waited for the Grand Prix, people were organizing picnic lunches; all around there was a lot being eaten and even more drunk, on the grass, on the raised seats of the four-in-hands and mail-coaches, in the victorias, the coupés, and the landaus. Footmen were unloading the boots to display vast assortments of cold meats and an impressive array of cases of champagne. The sound of popping corks was swept away on the wind; people were exchanging jokes; the cheerful hum of excited voices was punctuated by the jarring tinkle of broken glass. Gaga and Clarisse were tucking in beside Blanche, munching sandwiches on a rug spread out on their laps. Louise Violaine had got out of her dogcart and joined Caroline Héquet, while on the grass at their feet gentlemen friends had rigged up a little bar where Tatan, Maria, Simonne, and the others were going up to be served; nearby, on Léa de Horn's mail-coach, drink was being consumed by a whole group of people sitting in the sun and getting tipsy, blustering and posing perched high up above the crowd. But soon Nana's landau became the centre of attraction. She had got to her feet and was pouring glasses of champagne for the men who were pressing forward to greet her. François, one of her footmen, was passing up the bottles while la Faloise tried to put on a vulgar accent in a stream of sales-patter:

'Walk up, walk up, gents . . . It's all free, gratis, and for nothing . . . Enough for everybody . . .'

'Oh, do be quiet, my dear chap', Nana said eventually. 'You make us sound like a fairground show.'

But she found him very funny and was in high good spirits. For a moment she was tempted to send a glass of champagne over to Rose Mignon, who was ostentatiously refusing to drink; Henri and Charles must be bored to tears, poor little chaps, they'd have loved a glass of bubbly. But not wishing to land himself in trouble, Georges downed the glass himself. Nana now remembered little Louis sitting neglected behind her; perhaps he was thirsty. She made him sip a few drops of wine, which brought on a terrible fit of coughing.

'Walk up, walk up, gents!' continued la Faloise. 'It's not ten cents, it's not five cents . . . we're giving it away for nothing.'

Nana interrupted him.

'Look, there's Bordenave over there. Call him over, oh, please run and fetch him!'

It was indeed Bordenave walking along with his hands behind his back. In the sunlight his hat looked all ruddy; he was wearing a frock-coat with faded seams; a shabby, bankrupt Bordenave but still belligerent in spite of everything, parading his poverty in front of all these smart people and still with the tough look of a man ready to take fate by the throat.

'Well I'm damned! Aren't you looking chic!' he said, gripping Nana's friendly proffered hand.

Then, having emptied a glass of champagne, he said in a voice full of regret:

'Ah, if only I'd been born a woman! . . . But bloody hell, what does it matter! Why not come back to the stage? I've got a bright idea, I'll hire the Gaîté and we'll have Paris on their knees in front of the two of us . . . How about it? You owe me that much at least!'

And he stayed there, grumbling away but still glad to see her again because, as he said, just watching her live was balm to his heart. He felt she was like a daughter, blood of his blood.

More and more people were joining their circle. Now la Faloise had taken over the job of pouring while Philippe and Georges went off rounding up friends. Slowly everybody in the enclosure was pressing round her and for every one of them Nana had a laugh or a joke. The groups of drinkers were coming over, the champagne being consumed all around was gravitating towards her, and soon there was one solid mass of noisy people gathered round her landau while she, with her yellow, wind-swept hair and her snow-white complexion bathed in sunlight acknowledged the homage of all these glasses of champagne toasting her. Then, in order to crush the other women who were infuriated by her success, she stood up, dominating everybody, raised her full glass, and struck the attitude of Venus triumphant which had made her famous.

She felt a touch in the back, and looking round she was surprised to see Mignon sitting there. She slipped down out of sight for a second and took a seat beside him. He'd come to tell her something very serious; he'd always made it plain to everyone that he thought his wife was ridiculous to bear Nana such a grudge; it was stupid and pointless.

'But look', he said in a low voice, 'I wanted to say, take care not to provoke Rose too much . . . I wanted to warn you, you understand, because she's got hold of something that can do you harm and as she's never forgiven you for that business over *The Little Duchess* . . .'

'Harm?' said Nana. 'Why should I worry?'

'But let me tell you, it's a letter written by Fauchery to the Countess Muffat, which she must have found in that swine's pocket, and it leaves no room for doubt, it's all spelt out. So Rose wants to send that letter to the count, to get her own back on you and on him.'

'Why should I worry?' repeated Nana. 'That's funny, that is . . . So that's cooked Fauchery's goose. Well, so much the better, she was getting on my nerves. It'll be fun.'

'No, I don't want that to happen', retorted Mignon quickly. 'What a fine scandal that would be! And anyway, we've got nothing to gain . . .'

He stopped, afraid of saying too much. She exclaimed that she certainly wasn't going to come to the rescue of any respectable married woman. But when he persisted, she looked at him closely. No doubt he was afraid that if Fauchery broke with the countess he would fall back on Rose. That was what Rose wanted too, as well as getting her revenge, because she still had a soft spot for the journalist. Nana became pensive; she was thinking of Monsieur Venot's visit, and while Mignon continued his efforts to convince her a plot began to hatch in her head.

'Let's assume Rose sends the letter, yes? There's a scandal, you're implicated, people will say that you're to blame . . . The first thing that happens is that the count separates from his wife . . .'

'Why should he?' she asked. 'On the contrary . . .'

But this time it was she who broke off; she didn't need to think out loud. Finally, in order to get rid of him, she seemed to come round to his point of view and when he advised her to show Rose a little deference, for instance by paying her a short visit on the racecourse, which everybody would be able to see, she replied that she'd think about it.

A sudden uproar brought her to her feet. Horses were galloping furiously up to the winning-post: it was the City of Paris Cup, which was just being won by Cornemuse. The Grand Prix was next; excitement was rising to fever pitch and the tense, nervous crowd was impatiently swaying and shifting from one foot to another in anticipation. And at this last minute the punters were surprised and dismayed by the continued shortening of the odds on Nana, Vandeuvres' outsider. Fresh information was being brought back all the time: Nana was thirty-to-one, twenty-five-to-one, then twenty, then fifteen. Nobody could explain what was happening. A filly who'd been an also-ran in every race she'd ever run in, a filly who that very morning couldn't even find a backer at fifty-to-one! What could this sudden mad rush mean? Some were laughing and making fun of all those suckers who were being fooled and would be ripped off; but others were looking serious and worried, scenting something suspicious underneath it all. Maybe someone was up to some monkey business? People were remembering things that had happened before and the devious practices people got away with at race-meetings. But the mention of Vandeuvres, one of the great French families, put a stop to such adverse speculation, and in the end the dissenters carried the day, predicting that Nana would finish a good last.

'Who's riding Nana?' asked la Faloise.

At that very moment Nana herself popped up into view again, and seeing her the men broke into loud laughter, giving the question an obscene meaning. Nana gave them a wave.

'It's Price', she said.

This sparked off fresh discussion. Price was a famous English jockey unknown in France. Why had Vandeuvres engaged him when Nana's normal jockey was Gresham? Moreover, people were surprised that he'd put Gresham on

Lusignan, a jockey who, as la Faloise had pointed out, never rode a winner. But all these remarks were being swallowed up in jokes, contradictions, a hubbub of extraordinarily mixed opinions. To kill time, people began emptying their bottles of champagne. Then a murmur ran through the crowd as it opened up to let Vandeuvres through. Nana pretended to be annoyed.

'Well, you're a fine one, arriving now! . . . I'm dying to see the private enclosure.'

'Come on then', he said. 'There's still time. I'll show you round. It so happens that I've got a lady's pass on me.'

He went away with her on his arm. Nana was delighted to see the jealous looks from Lucy, Caroline, and the rest as they followed the couple with their eyes. The Hugon brothers and la Faloise stayed behind in her landau, continuing to do the honours with her champagne. She called out that she'd be back in a sec.

At this moment however Vandeuvres caught sight of Labordette and called him over. They exchanged a few brief words.

'You've put it all on?'

'Yes.'

'How much?'

'Thirty thousand. I've spread it around.'

Seeing Nana pricking up her ears, they stopped talking. Vandeuvres was looking very nervy; his pale eyes had the same bloodshot glare that had so scared her that night when he'd talked of going up in flames with all his horses. As they were crossing the track, she whispered confidentially:

'Xavier my pet, can you explain why the odds on your filly keep shortening all the time? It's causing a tremendous fuss!'

He gave a start and momentarily dropped his guard.

'Oh, so they're nattering, are they? . . . What a bunch those punters are! When I've got a favourite they latch on to it like leeches, and when an outsider begins to be favoured they start squealing like skinned rabbits.'

'I'm asking because you ought to tell me, you know. I've been placing some bets myself. Has Nana got a chance?'

For some strange reason he suddenly flared up.

'What did you say? Don't start bothering me, for goodness

sake! Every horse has a chance. Her odds are shortening because people are backing her, heavens above! Who are they? I've no idea . . . If you have to keep on asking damn silly questions, I'm off!'

Such a tone was unusual and quite out of character. She was more surprised than hurt. He himself was looking ashamed, and when she sharply asked him to mind his manners he apologized. He'd been suffering from this sort of moodiness for some time now. In the smart, raffish circles in which he moved everybody was aware that this was his last fling. If his horses didn't win, if they once again failed to bring home, with interest, the vast sums which he'd been putting on them, it would be a catastrophe, a complete collapse; the whole basis of his credit and grand style of life, undermined and at its last gasp as a result of his debt-ridden and rackety existence, would be demolished in a spectacular crash. And everyone knew equally well that one particular gold-digger, the last in line of all those who'd been gnawing away at his fortune, would suck him dry and throw away the pieces. There were tales of crazy whims, of immense sums tossed airily away, a party at Baden where she hadn't left him with enough to pay the hotel, of one drunken night when she'd thrown a handful of diamonds on to a brazier to discover if they burned like coal. Little by little, the sturdy limbs and vulgar gutter laugh had brought this over-civilized, impoverished scion of an ancient family to his knees, and now he'd been so corrupted by his taste for stupidity and squalor that he'd even lost his capacity for scepticism and was risking everything. A week ago she'd got him to promise her a château on the Normandy coast between Trouville and Le Havre and he had made it a final point of honour to keep his word, even though she got on his nerves and he found her so stupid that he could have thrashed her.

The gatekeeper let them through into the paddock, not daring to stop a woman who was arm-in-arm with the count. As she strolled along in front of the ladies seated at the foot of the grandstands, Nana was carefully calculating her effect and gloating at having finally broken into this forbidden sanctum. These ladies were packed in a solid mass on ten rows of chairs, their brilliant dresses matching their cheerful enjoyment of being in the open air. Chairs were being shifted round, friends were meeting unexpectedly and gathering round in circles as they do under the clumps of trees in public gardens, while their children were going off by themselves, running from one group to the other. Higher up in the packed grandstands, the bright dresses melted into the shadows cast by the pillars supporting the tiers of seats. Nana was staring at these ladies and made a particular point of scrutinizing Countess Sabine. As she passed in front of the Imperial grandstand, she was greatly amused to see Muffat, looking rigidly official, standing close to the Empress.

'Oh, doesn't he look stupid!' she remarked to Vandeuvres in a very loud voice.

She was determined not to miss anything, even though she didn't find this little corner of parkland with its lawns and clumps of trees much fun. An ice-cream vendor had set up a large stall beside the railings. Under a rustic, mushroom-shaped thatched roof there was a whole crowd of men shouting and throwing their arms about: this was the bookmakers' ring. Nearby were empty horse-boxes; Nana was disappointed to find only a police-horse there. Next came the paddock, a circular track a hundred yards in circumference where a strapper was leading round Valerio II with a hood over its head. So there it was: lots of men walking along the gravel paths under rows of trees with their entrance ticket making an orange patch in their buttonhole, a constant flow of people in the open galleries of the grandstand which attracted her interest for a moment or two; but really, it wasn't worth getting het up if you weren't allowed into this place.

Daguenet and Fauchery went by, raising their hats. She beckoned to them to come over and have a word with her. She made rude remarks about the private enclosure. Then she broke off and said:

'Well, if that isn't the Marquis de Chouard! Isn't he looking old! And so decrepit! Is he still crazy about women?'

Daguenet told them of the old man's latest exploit, something which had occurred only a couple of days ago and which wasn't yet generally known: he'd just bought Amélie from her mother Gaga for a sum rumoured to be thirty thousand francs.

'What a revolting old man!' exclaimed Nana disgustedly. 'Who'd want to have daughters! . . . But now I come to think of it, that must be Lili over there on the grass with a lady in a coupé. Yes, I recognized the face . . . The old man must be showing her off.'

Vandeuvres wasn't listening; he could hardly wait to get rid of her. But as he was leaving, Fauchery remarked that if she hadn't seen the bookmakers she hadn't seen anything, so the count was forced to take her over to see them. When they arrived there she was satisfied at last: now that really was something special!

There was a round, open space set between lawns bordered by young chestnut trees with fresh green leaves, under which she saw a row of bookmakers packed tightly together, waiting as if on a fairground for people to come and lay their bets. In order to overlook the crowd, they were standing on benches; their odds were marked up on boards placed against the trees. They were keeping a sharp look-out, picking up a wink here or a signal there and writing down the bets so fast that the curious spectators watching open-mouthed couldn't understand what was happening. There was confusion everywhere, figures were being shouted out, and any sudden change in the odds produced an uproar; adding to the din were men running up to the edge of the ring and yelling bits of information, an announcement of a start or a finish which raised a long buzz of excitement from the punters feverishly crowding together in the sun.

'Aren't they funny!' said Nana, highly amused. 'They look all hot and bothered. Look at that tall man over there, I wouldn't like to meet him alone in a dark country lane!'

Vandeuvres pointed out a bookmaker who was a draper's assistant who'd made three million francs in the last two years. He was slender, fair-haired, a sensitive-looking man who was being treated with the utmost respect; people were smiling as they talked to him and passers-by kept stopping to look at him.

As they were finally leaving the ring Vandeuvres gave a little nod to another bookmaker, who then ventured to call him over. He was one of the count's former coachmen, a huge man, red-faced with shoulders like an ox, who was trying his luck at bookmaking with assets of highly dubious origin. Vandeuvres was giving him a helping hand by placing his clandestine bets with him, making no attempt to hide their connection and always treating him as a former employee. In spite of the count's patronage he'd been losing considerable sums of money in a very short space of time, and he too was staking everything on today's race; his eyes were bloodshot and he looked a candidate for an apoplectic fit at any moment.

'Well, Maréchal', Vandeuvres asked in an undertone, 'how much have you managed to place?'

'A hundred thousand, your lordship', replied the bookmaker in an equally low voice. 'It's good, isn't it? I must confess I lengthened the odds, I'm offering three-to-one.'

Vandeuvres looked put out.

'No, you mustn't do that, put it back up to two-to-one straight away . . . That's my last word, Maréchal . . .'

'Oh, what does it matter to your lordship now', the other man replied with an obsequious, conspiratorial smile. 'I had to do something to attract people to place your ten thousand francs.'

Vandeuvres told him not to talk so much, but as he was going off Maréchal suddenly remembered something and was annoyed not to have questioned him on the shortening of odds on his filly. If that filly really was in with a chance he'd be in the shit, because he'd just taken a bet of four thousand francs at fifty-to-one.

Nana hadn't understood a word of the count's whispered conversation but still didn't dare ask for an explanation. He seemed more jumpy than ever, and suddenly handed her over to Labordette when they met him outside the weigh-in room.

'You take her back', he said. 'I've got things to do here . . . Goodbye.'

And he went off into the room, which was narrow and low-ceilinged with a massive weighing-machine in the middle. It looked like the left-luggage room in a suburban station. Once again Nana was sadly disappointed; she'd pictured something enormous, a colossal machine to weigh the horses. So they only weighed the jockeys! In that case there wasn't much point in making such a fuss about their silly old weigh-in enclosure! On the scales an idiotic-looking man with a saddle and harness on his lap was waiting for a burly fellow in a frockcoat to check his weight, while in the doorway a stable-lad was holding the horse Cosine and a silent throng of people was gathered, watching intently.

They were about to close the track off. Labordette was hurrying Nana along but came back to point out to her a little man talking with Vandeuvres at one side.

'Look, that's Price', he said.

'Ah, the man who's going to ride me', she murmured with a little laugh.

She thought he was jolly ugly. To her all the jockeys looked cretinous, perhaps because they were deliberately stunted in growth. This one, a man of 40, was like a dried-up old child, with a long, thin, deeply creased, dour face, like a death-mask. His body was so gnarled and shrunken that his tunic, blue with white sleeves, seemed as if it had been slung over a bit of wood.

'Not my type, I'm afraid', she said as they went off. 'I can't see myself enjoying him.'

The track was still thronged with people and the trampled wet grass had gone black. In front of the number board high up on its tall cast-iron post, a dense crowd was buzzing with excitement as they watched each horse's number being flashed through from the weighing-room by electric cable. Men were checking them on their race-cards: the withdrawal by its owner of Pichenette raised a flutter of attention. Meanwhile Nana simply walked across the track, while the bell suspended from the flagpole continued to ring to warn people to get off it.

'Well', she said, getting back into her landau, 'that famous enclosure of theirs is just a joke!'

All around people were calling out and applauding her. 'Good for you, Nana! You've come back to join us!' . . . Stupid lot! How could they ever have thought she was the sort of woman to let her public down! And she was back in the nick of time: the big race was just about to start.

However, Nana was surprised to find Gaga in her carriage, with Bijou and Louiset on her lap. Gaga said that she'd wanted to come over and say hallo to the little lad; she adored children! The truth was, she wanted to try and make it up with la Faloise.

'Talking of children, how's Lili?' said Nana. 'It is her in the old man's barouche, isn't it? . . . Someone was just telling me something that didn't sound very nice . . .'

Gaga put on a tearful look.

'Oh, the very thought of it makes me feel ill, my dear', she exclaimed with a pained expression. 'Yesterday I'd been crying so much that I had to stay in bed and I didn't think I'd be able to come today . . . Well, you know my views, don't you? I didn't want it, I'd given her a convent education so that she'd be able to make a good marriage. And I was very strict and gave her good advice and kept my eye on her all the time . . . Well, my dear, it was entirely her idea . . . Oh, you can't imagine what a dreadful row we had, tears and nasty remarks, in fact I had to give her a clip round the ear. She was so bored, she said she wanted to have a go. So when she started saying: "After all, it's not for you to stand in my way!" I said to her: "You're a horrible girl and a disgrace to us, so clear out!" And that's how it all happened. I agreed to fix her up. But that's the end of all my hopes, and I had such dreams of a nice life for her!'

The sound of quarrelling brought them to their feet. It was Georges defending Vandeuvres against the vague rumours that were circulating among certain groups in the crowd.

'Why say he's dropping his horse', he was shouting. 'Why, yesterday in the betting-room,* he put twenty thousand francs on Lusignan.'

'Yes, I was there', Philippe confirmed. 'And he didn't put a single franc on Nana either . . . If Nana's down to ten-to-one, it's nothing to do with him. It's ridiculous to accuse people of plotting like that. What good would it do him?'

Labordette was quietly listening. He shrugged his shoulders:

'Oh, don't stop them, people always like to talk . . . The count has just put another ten thousand francs at least on Lusignan, and if he's put two thousand on Nana it's only because an owner must always appear to have confidence in his horses.'

'And what's all the fuss about anyway?' shouted la Faloise, flinging his arms about. 'Spirit's going to win . . . France'll go down the drain! England for ever!'

The bell announcing the arrival of the horses on the track

started to ring and a thrill ran through the crowd. To get a better view, Nana climbed up on to the seat of her landau, trampling all over the bunches of flowers, the forget-me-nots and the roses, and she could now see round the whole of the wide horizon. First of all there was the empty track with its grey barriers and police lined up at every second post, the turf around her all muddy but stretching out and becoming greener and greener, until in the distance it turned into a velvety green carpet. Then, looking down, in these last, feverish minutes before the start she could see the public enclosure swarming with people on tiptoe, hanging on to their carriages, frantic with excitement; horses were neighing, the canvas tents were flapping, riders were spurring their horses amongst the spectators on foot who were rushing to lean on the barriers. She turned towards the grandstands; on that side the figures were smaller; the solid mass of faces was a gaudy medley of colours filling the avenues, the tiers of seats, and the packed terraces where they were silhouetted against the sky. And beyond, round the racecourse, she looked out over the plain where, behind the ivy-clad mill on her right, there were meadows sloping away, slashed by giant shadows; opposite, right up to the Seine which flowed along the bottom of the dip, there was the network of avenues of the Bois, with rows of carriages waiting at a standstill. Then on her left, towards Boulogne, the countryside opened up again to give a vista of Meudon in a distant blue haze, blocked off by an avenue of leafless paulownias whose tops formed a bright crimson screen. People were still arriving, winding their way through fields on a narrow path like a long trail of ants, while in the far distance, in the direction of Paris, the non-paying public, a herd of people camping in the wood, formed a line of black dots moving along under the trees, down at the level of the Bois.

Suddenly the sun, which had been hidden for the last quarter of an hour, re-emerged, bathing everything in warmth and light, and the hundred thousand souls packed into this bit of meadow like a heaving mass of panicking insects immediately cheered up. Once again the whole scene glowed; above the crowd the women's sunshades gleamed like innumerable golden shields. As the sun came out, people laughed and applauded, waving their arms in the air to brush away the clouds. Meanwhile a solitary policeman was walking down the middle of the track. Higher up on the left a man appeared with a red flag.

'It's the starter, Baron de Mauriac', said Labordette in reply to Nana's question.

The men surrounding Nana, pressing right up to her landau, were making a tremendous din, chattering wildly as they exchanged excited reactions with each other. Philippe and Georges, Bordenave and la Faloise, were all finding it impossible to keep quiet:

'Don't shove! . . . Let me have a look! . . . Ah, the judge is going into his box . . . It's Monsieur de Souvigny, did you say? . . . My goodness, you need sharp eyes to pick out a winner by a short head in that kind of contraption! . . . Don't talk now, the flag's going up . . . Here they come! . . . That's Cosine leading the way . . .'

A red-and-yellow banner was fluttering in the wind at the top of the flagpole. Stable-lads were leading the horses in one by one; the jockeys, sitting on their horses with their arms hanging loose, made bright splashes of colour in the sunlight. Cosine was followed by Hazard and Boum. Then Spirit appeared, bringing a buzz of approval in the crowd; it was a superb chestnut bay and its harsh colours, lemon and black, had a sort of sad look, very English. Valerio II, small and very lively, with its colours of delicate green bordered with pink, made a very favourable impression. The two Vandeuvres horses were keeping the crowd in suspense; then finally, following Frangipani, the familiar blue-and-white emerged. But Lusignan, a very dark bay, an immaculately built horse, was almost overlooked in the surprise caused by Nana. Nobody had seen the sorrel filly looking like this before; she gleamed in the sun like a red-headed blonde, as golden as a freshly minted guinea, deep-chested but with a light head, neck and withers flowing into her long, lean, slender but sinewy back.

'Good Lord! She's got my hair!' exclaimed Nana delightedly. 'I say, you know, I'm proud of her!'

The men were clambering into the landau; Bordenave trod on Louiset whom his mother had forgotten. He hoisted him up on to his shoulder, grumbling in fatherly fashion and muttering:

'Poor little kid, he ought to be able to join in. Hang on, I'll show you your Mummy . . . There, you see over there, look at gee-gee.'

And feeling Bijou scratching at his leg, he picked him up, too. Nana meanwhile, pleased by the sight of this animal which had been named after her, threw a sidelong glance at the other women to see how they were reacting. They were all livid with anger. At that very moment, Tricon, who till now had been standing motionless on her cab, started waving her hand over the heads of the crowd to a bookmaker to lay her bets. She had a hunch: she was betting on Nana.

Meanwhile la Faloise was creating a dreadful row; he'd suddenly fallen for Frangipani.

'I've had an inspiration!' he proclaimed. 'Just take a look at Frangipani. What an action, eh? . . . I'm going for Frangipani at eight-to-one. Any takers?'

'Oh, do be quiet', said Labordette in the end, 'you're making us think we've done the wrong thing.'

'Frangipani's a non-starter', said Philippe firmly. 'He's already covered in lather . . . Wait till he starts to canter!'

The horses had moved on to their right and now came cantering back helter-skelter, in front of the grandstands. This sparked off further heated discussion; everybody was talking at once.

'Lusignan's too long in the back but he's in peak form . . . Not a sou on Valerio II, you know, he's nervy and galloping with his head up, that's a bad sign . . . I say, Burne's riding Spirit . . . I reckon he's weak in the shoulders, that's what you need, well-built shoulders . . . No, Spirit's definitely too lethargic . . . Listen, I saw Nana after the Producers' Stakes, all in a lather, dull coat, chest heaving, a job to breathe! . . . I bet four hundred francs she's not placed! . . . Oh, do keep quiet, for God's sake . . . Christ, he's a bore with his Frangipani! There's no time now anyway, they're off!'

The last remark was addressed to la Faloise who was almost in tears, struggling to find a bookie. They had to try and make him behave sensibly. Everyone was craning their necks.

However, it was a false start; the starter, visible as a thin black line in the distance, hadn't dropped his red flag. The horses galloped on for a second or two and then came back. There were two more false starts before the starter got the horses in line and sent them off so successfully that the crowd shouted their appreciation.

'Magnificent! . . . No, it was a fluke! . . . Never mind, they're away!'

The roar subsided as throats grew tense. Betting had stopped, action was now all on the track. At first the crowd was hushed as though everyone had stopped breathing. People were on tiptoe, white-faced and quivering. Hazard and Cosine had set the pace at the start and were in the lead, followed closely by Valerio II; the rest of the field were straggling behind in a disorderly bunch. When they passed in front of the grandstands in a flurry of wind, making the ground tremble, the field was already spread out over some forty lengths. Frangipani was last, Nana just behind Lusignan and Spirit.

'Well I'm damned!' muttered Labordette. 'Just look how the Englishman's keeping out of the ruck!'

Having recovered their breath, everybody in the landau was on tiptoe, talking excitedly with all eyes fastened on the dazzling specks of colour of the jockeys racing along in the sunlight. Up the slope, Valerio II went into the lead and Cosine and Hazard slipped back, while Lusignan and Spirit were neck-and-neck with Nana still close behind.

'Good Lord, the Englishman's coming up, that's obvious', said Bordenave. 'Lusignan's tiring and Valerio II can't hang on.'

'Well, if the Englishman wins, it's a swizz!' exclaimed Philippe in a sudden pang of patriotic conscience.

The packed crowd was seized by a dreadful foreboding. Thrashed again! A tremendous ground-swell of support of almost religious intensity was rising in favour of Lusignan; Spirit was being showered with abuse, as well as that miserable jockey of his who looked as if he was at a funeral. Among the spectators dispersed round the course enthusiasm was rising to fever-pitch, with partisan gangs rushing at top speed over to the barrier to get a better view; men on horseback were furiously galloping across the enclosure. Twisting round to watch, Nana could see this surging mass of men and animals at her feet, a sea of heads tossed and almost swept away in the whirlwind of the race as the line of jockeys flashed across the horizon. She'd watched the hindquarters of the horses as they tore away; they lengthened their stride, and as their legs disappeared into the distance they looked no thicker than a hair. Along the back-straight they could now be seen from the side, very small and delicate against the distant green of the Bois. Then suddenly they disappeared behind a big clump of trees planted in the middle of the racecourse.

'You mustn't say that!' shouted Georges, still hopeful. 'It's not over yet . . . The Englishman's weakening.'

Meanwhile la Faloise had reverted to his contempt for his compatriots and was shocking everybody by applauding Spirit. Well done! It was a jolly good thing, France needed something like that! Spirit first, Frangipani second! That'd teach the country a lesson! Labordette was thoroughly exasperated and threatened to chuck him out of the landau.

'Let's check on their times', said Bordenave placidly, pulling his watch out while still holding on to Louiset.

One by one the horses were emerging from behind the clump of trees. A long buzz of amazement burst from the spectators, scarcely able to believe their eyes. Valerio II was still in the lead but Spirit was catching him up, and behind them Lusignan was dropping back and another horse was moving into his place. At first the crowd didn't realize what was happening; there was uncertainty over the jockeys' caps. People started yelling.

'It's Nana! . . . Come on, Nana! . . . I don't think Lusignan's slipped back! . . . Yes, it's definitely Nana! . . . It's her colour, she's golden! . . . Just look! . . . What a bombshell! . . . Well done Nana! . . . She's got guts, that girl! . . . No, it doesn't mean a thing, she's playing into Lusignan's hands! . . .'

For a few seconds everybody thought the same, but galloping hard, the filly was slowly gaining ground. The excitement was intense. Nobody was interested in the tail-enders anymore. The final tussle between Spirit, Nana, Lusignan, and Valerio II began. People were stammering incoherently, calling out their names and watching how they progressed or fell back. Nana had climbed up on to her coachman's box, as though lifted up by her excitement, and was standing there pale-faced and suddenly trembling, too nervous to speak. Beside her Labordette was now looking cheerful again.

'How about that!' exclaimed Philippe delightedly. 'The Englishman's in trouble, he's not going so well.'

'Anyway, Lusignan's had it!' la Faloise cried. 'Valerio II is coming up . . . It's between those two now, look!'

Everyone was shouting together.

'What a race! My God, what a race!'

The leaders were now heading furiously up the straight; the rumble of thundering hooves in the distance was growing louder and louder every second; you could almost feel the horses' breath. The whole mass of spectators had flung themselves wildly towards the barrier, and their deep-throated roar was like the boom of an Atlantic breaker crashing ahead of the horses. It was the savage end of a colossal contest, with a hundred thousand fans all fired by gambling fever as they followed these galloping animals, each carrying stakes of millions of francs. People were pushing and being crushed, clenching their fists, open-mouthed, each urging his horse on with words and waving hands. And the roar of the mob, the roar of a wild beast emerging from its lair, hidden under these frock-coats, was becoming plainer and plainer:

'Here they come, here they come, here they come!'

Nana was still gaining ground, she'd overtaken Valerio II and was now up among the leaders, a couple of lengths behind Spirit. The thunder of hooves grew louder and louder. They were coming up to the finish, greeted by a hail of imprecations from the landau.

'Buck up, Lusignan, you bloody slacker! What a hack! Good for you, Englishman! Come on, old man! . . . Valerio's disgusting . . . what a hopeless nag! That's my hundred francs down the drain! . . . There's only Nana! . . . Well done, Nana! . . . well done, you beauty!'

Up on the box seat, Nana had started swaying her thighs and back, as if she herself was in the race, thrusting her hips forward under the impression that she was helping the filly along and with each thrust she heaved a tired gasp and said in a low strained voice:

'Come on! Come on! Come on!'

And now the public was to see something stupendous. Rising in his stirrups, Price lifted his switch and started thrashing Nana unmercifully. This dried-up old child with his long, dour, dead-looking face, came on fire. In a sudden, savage burst of energy, a firm determination to win, he was giving heart to the filly, all covered in lather and with bloodshot eyes, he was supporting, carrying her with him. The whole field flashed by in a thunder of hooves, in a violent gust of air that left the crowd breathless while the finishing judge sat impassively, waiting coolly with his eye on his sighting mark. A tremendous roar went up: with a supreme effort, Price flung Nana past the post, beating Spirit by a short head.

All hell broke loose: Nana! Nana! Nana! The cry rang out, echoing and re-echoing in ever-increasing waves, like a hurricane, gradually sweeping out towards the distant horizon, from the depths of the Bois to Mont Valérien, from the meadows of Longchamp to the plain of Boulogne.

In the enclosure, wild enthusiasm reigned. Long live Nana! Long live France! Down with England! Women were brandishing sunshades, men were screaming and twirling as they danced up and down; others were laughing excitedly and flinging their hats in the air. And the private enclosure on the other side of the track was responding similarly, the grandstands were in a turmoil, though the only thing that could be clearly seen was a sort of quivering in the air, like the invisible flame of a brazier above this living pile of tiny, hysterical figures with writhing arms and open mouths and eyes like black pin-points. The roaring went on and on, swelling until it was taken up at the far end of the distant avenues and among the public camping under the trees, expanding and spreading even up to the excited spectators sitting in the Imperial grandstand, where the Empress herself had been seen applauding. Nana! Nana! Nana! The cry rose up as the glorious sunlight flooded the delirious crowd in a golden glow.

Still perched on top of her landau and looking larger than

life, Nana thought it was she herself who was being acclaimed. For a second she stood stock-still, flabbergasted at her splendid victory, watching as the track was invaded by a throng so dense that the grass disappeared under a sea of black hats. Then, as the crowd drew up forming two lines to cheer Nana again as she made her exit with Price slumped forward weakly on her neck, absolutely drained, Nana, completely forgetting where she was, slapped her thighs and gloated over her triumph in the crudest terms:

'Shit, it's me, really me! . . . Oh shit, what luck!'

And not knowing how to express her overwhelming delight, finally noticing Louiset perched on Bordenave's shoulders, she grabbed him and kissed him.

'Three minutes fourteen seconds', the theatre manager said, putting his watch back into his pocket.

Nana was still listening to her name reverberating over the plain. It was her subjects applauding her while she dominated them all, standing bolt upright in the sunlight, in her blue-and-white dress, the colour of the sky, with her hair glowing like a sun-queen. As he slipped away, Labordette had informed her that she'd just won forty thousand francs, as he'd put her five thousand francs on Nana at forty-to-one. But she was less affected by the money than by her glorious, unexpected win that would make her the undisputed queen of Paris. Their ladyships had all lost. In her rage, Rose Mignon had broken the handle of her new parasol, and Caroline Héquet, Clarisse, Simonne, and even, despite the presence of her son, Lucy Stewart herself, were cursing under their breath in exasperation at the luck of that fat tart; Tricon, who'd crossed herself at the start and finish of the race, was standing erect dominating them, delighted at having followed her instinct and, in the ripeness of her experience, full of commendation for Nana.

Meanwhile, more and more men were crowding round the landau. The mob had erupted into a wild uproar. Georges had continued to shout on his own, in a hoarse, croaking voice. As the champagne was running out, Philippe dashed over to a bar with the footmen to fetch some more. And still Nana's crowd of courtiers was growing; her splendid victory had won over those who'd been holding back, and the movement which had made her landau the centre of attraction of the whole enclosure was ending in the apotheosis of Queen Venus surrounded by her subjects, who seemed to have taken leave of their senses. Behind her, Bordenave was gently swearing under his breath, like a fond father. Even Steiner had succumbed and had left Simonne to come over and hoist himself up on to one of her footboards. When the champagne arrived and she lifted her full glass, people clapped and started chanting: Nana! Nana! Nana! so loudly that the other spectators looked round expecting to see the filly, not knowing whether it was the horse or the woman that had won people's hearts.

Disregarding Rose's black looks, Mignon himself came hurrying over. That damned woman had made him lose his head completely and he wanted to show his feelings. He gave her a fatherly kiss on both cheeks and said:

'What worries me is that Rose will certainly be sending that letter now. She's absolutely livid.'

'Never mind! That suits me!' blurted Nana.

Then seeing his bewildered expression, she quickly corrected herself:

'Of course it doesn't suit me, what did I say? Quite honestly, I don't know what I'm saying! I'm drunk!'

And she was indeed drunk, drunk with joy and from the warm sun. Still clasping her glass, she toasted herself:

'Here's to Nana!' she shouted, bringing a renewed outburst of laughter and cheering and shouting, which by now had spread over the whole racecourse. The last race, the Vaublanc Stakes, was being run. Carriages were leaving one by one. A good deal of squabbling seemed to be going on and Vandeuvres's name kept being mentioned. It now became quite plain that the count had been planning his coup for a couple of years: he'd been instructing Gresham to hold Nana back and had been running Lusignan merely to overshadow the filly. The people who'd lost money were annoyed, those who'd won were shrugging their shoulders: so what? Was it in any way illegal? An owner managed his stud as he thought fit! He wasn't the only one, by a long chalk! Most people thought Vandeuvres had been very smart to have got his friends to pick up what he'd put on Nana, which explained the sudden drop in the odds; there was talk of two thousand louis having been put on, at an average of thirty-to-one, thereby netting one million two-hundred thousand francs; an astronomical sum like that didn't need excuses.

But there were other whispered rumours filtering out of the jockeys' enclosure that were very serious. Men kept filling in the details as they emerged; people began talking more freely, speaking quite openly of a dreadful scandal. Poor old Vandeuvres was down the drain; he'd spoilt his superb coup by an act of crass stupidity, an idiotic attempt at robbery. He'd got a shady bookmaker, Maréchal, to put forty thousand francs on his behalf against Lusignan to offset the paltry twenty thousand he'd backed the horse for publicly—a mere flea-bite. Well aware that the favourite wasn't going to win, he'd netted sixty thousand francs or so on Lusignan. However, not having been given the full picture, Labordette had gone to Maréchal to put two thousand louis on Nana which the bookmaker, left equally in the dark, was still offering at fifty-to-one. As a result, Maréchal had been ripped off for a hundred thousand francs on the filly and was forty thousand in the red on the other horse. He was facing ruin; then he'd seen Labordette and the count confabulating after the race in front of the weigh-in room and suddenly put two and two together. Furious at the plot against him, the count's former coachman, he'd just made a terrible scene in front of everybody, giving the full story, savagely exposing the man who had so callously fleeced him, and arousing universal condemnation. It was also reported that a meeting of the stewards had been convened.

When Philippe and Georges whispered to Nana what had transpired, though she didn't stop laughing or drinking, she made a few comments: Yes, it might well be possible, there were certain things she could recall, and that fellow Maréchal certainly had an ugly mug. All the same, she still had doubts. Then Labordette came up, deathly pale.

'Well?' she whispered.

'He's sunk!' he replied simply.

And shrugged his shoulders. What a child the man was! She made a gesture as if to say: 'What a bore!'

That night Nana had a huge success at Mabille. When she

made her entrance around ten o'clock, the din was already terrific. This traditionally wild ball attracted all the young bloods, all the smart set falling over each other to behave as cretinously and brutishly as their footmen, packed like sardines under the festoons of gaslights. White ties, way-out clothes, the women in low-necked dresses, old ones, so that it didn't matter if they got filthy, twisting and shrieking, crazed with drink. Even a dozen yards away from the band, the brass was barely audible. No one was dancing. Idiotic remarks were being bandied about from one stupid group to the other. People were trying hard to be funny and failing. Seven women had got locked in the cloakroom and were tearfully pleading to be let out. Someone had got hold of a shallot and started auctioning it; it fetched forty francs. At that very moment, Nana appeared, still wearing her blue-and-white race-meeting outfit. Amidst thunderous applause she was handed the shallot, and despite her protests she was hoisted up and carried in triumph out into the garden by three men crashing through the shrubbery and trampling all over the grass. When the band appeared to be in the way, they stormed it, smashing its chairs and its stands. Meanwhile the police were keeping a fatherly eye on the chaotic scene.

Nana didn't recover from the excitement of her win till Tuesday. That morning she was chatting with Madame Lerat, who was telling her about Louiset, poorly from being exposed to so much fresh air at the races. Nana was all agog with a story that had set all Paris talking: Vandeuvres had been warned off every racecourse and that same night blackballed at the Imperial Club. Next day, he'd set fire to his stables and been burnt to death with all his horses.

'He told me he would', the young woman kept saying. 'He's a really crazy man. You can imagine how I got the creeps when they told me about it. You realize he might easily have done me in one night. And don't you reckon he ought to have warned me about his horse? I could at least have made a fortune! He told Labordette that if I knew about it, I'd pass it on to my hairdresser straight away and to a whole lot of men! Polite, wasn't he? No, I really can't feel sorry he's gone . . .'

Thinking about it had made her furious. At that very moment Labordette himself came in; he'd settled all the bets and handed over her forty thousand francs. This made her even crosser: she could have won a million. Labordette, who was pretending innocence in the whole matter, frankly washed his hands of Vandeuvres. Those old families were pooped out, they were coming to an ignominious end.

'No, I can't agree', said Nana. 'It's not ignominious to go up in flames like that in his stables. I think it took real guts to die like that . . . Oh, I'm not trying to defend that business with Maréchal. That was idiotic. When I think that Blanche had the nerve to try and put the blame for that on to me! I said: "Did I ask him to be a thief?" That's right, isn't it? One can ask a man for money without wanting him to turn to crime. All he needed to say was "I haven't got any more" and I'd have said, "OK then, it's goodbye", and that would have been the end of it.'

'Of course', her aunt said solemnly. 'If men will persist, they deserve what they get!'

'But as for his little farewell party, I think it was super!' Nana continued. 'Apparently it was dreadful, enough to make your flesh creep. He'd arranged for everybody to keep away and shut himself in there with some kerosene . . . You should have seen the blaze it made! Just imagine, a building made almost entirely of timber and full of straw and hay . . . The flames were shooting up almost as high as a church tower . . . The best part was the horses who didn't want to be roasted to a cinder. You could hear them lashing out and smashing against the doors and crying out like human beings. Yes, a lot of people had a deathly feeling afterwards.'

Labordette pooh-poohed the whole thing: he didn't think Vandeuvres was dead. Someone swore he'd seen him climbing out through a window. He'd had a brainstorm and set light to his stables, but as soon as it started to get too hot for him he must have come to his senses. A man who was so stupid with women, so played out, would never have had the guts to die like that.

Nana listened to him destroying her illusions. Her only reaction in reply was to say:

'Poor man! It was such a wonderful way to go!'

Chapter 12

It was nearly one o'clock in the morning. In the large bed draped in Venetian lace, Nana and the count were not yet asleep. After sulking for three days, he'd come back that evening. In the light of a single lamp the vague outlines of the silver-encrusted lacquer furniture cast a pale gleam; the bedroom was drowsy with the warm, stuffy smell of love. A curtain had slipped down, casting a shadowy veil over the bed. There was a sigh and the silence was broken by the sound of a kiss; then, sliding out from under the blankets, Nana sat for a moment, bare-legged, on the sheets at the edge of the bed. The count's head had fallen back on the sheets and lay in shadow.

'Do you believe in God, darling?' she asked after a moment's thought. She looked earnest; fresh from her lover's arms, she'd been suddenly assailed by religious qualms. She'd been complaining all day of feeling uneasy, obsessed by what she called her 'silly thoughts', thoughts of death and eternal damnation. Sometimes she had nights like this when she'd lie with wide-open eyes, and her childish fears and all kinds of dreadful fancies would give her nightmares. She said:

'Do you think I'll go to Heaven?'

She gave a shudder. Surprised to hear these peculiar questions at such a moment, the count felt stirrings of his Catholic guilty conscience. With her night-gown slipping off her shoulder and her hair hanging loose, she flung herself on to his chest, sobbing and clutching at him.

'I'm afraid of dying . . . I'm afraid of dying . . .'

He had great difficulty in pulling himself free. He himself was scared of giving way to this woman's hysterical outburst as she clung to his body; her sudden fear of the unknown was infectious. He started reasoning with her: she was perfectly healthy, all she had to do was to behave in such a way that one day she'd earn forgiveness. She shook her head: certainly, she wasn't doing harm to anyone and she even always wore a medallion of the Virgin Mary, which she showed him hanging on a red thread between her breasts; but it was laid down that all those women who went with men even when they weren't married were doomed to go to Hell. Scraps of her catechism kept coming back to her. Oh, if only you could really know, but there it was, you didn't know a thing, nobody ever came back from there to tell you anything. True enough, it would be silly if the priests were all talking nonsense . . . But she still kept devoutly kissing the medallion lying warm against her skin as a magic charm against death, the thought of which made her blood run cold.

Muffat had to go with her into her dressing-room; she was terrified at the thought of being alone there, even for a minute with the door left open. He got back into bed but she continued to prowl around the bedroom, peering into corners and starting at the slightest sound. Suddenly she stopped in front of a mirror and was lost in thought, as always, at the sight of her naked body. But looking at her breasts and hips and thighs only made her more frightened. She started running her hands over the bones of her face, lingeringly.

'You're ugly when you're dead', she said slowly.

She was drawing her cheeks tight, pulling her eyes wide open, and dropping her jaw to see what she'd look like. Then turning towards the count with her face distorted in this way:

'Look, my head will be all tiny.'

He was angry.

'You're mad. Come back to bed.'

He had a vision of her in her grave after she'd been asleep for a hundred years; he clasped his hands and mumbled a prayer. For some time now his faith had been regaining ground and his religious qualms would descend on him like an apoplectic stroke, leaving him utterly overcome. Now his fingers were cracking as he kept repeating just two words: 'Oh God! . . . Oh God! . . . Oh God! . . .', a cry of distress at his utter failure to resist his sinful temptation even although he knew he would be eternally damned. When she went over to him, she found him lying under the blanket with a wild look in his eyes, his hands clasped on his chest, and staring upwards as if seeking heavenly aid. She burst into tears again and they embraced, with their teeth chattering, both caught up in the same idiotic obsession which neither of them could explain. A similar thing had happened to them on a previous occasion, but tonight, as Nana remarked when she had recovered from her fears, they were both behaving like complete imbeciles. Nana suspected that Rose might have already sent him the famous letter and made a cautious enquiry. But this wasn't the problem, it was nothing more than a sudden panic; he was still in the dark over his wife's affair with Fauchery.

Two days later, after again staying away, Muffat came round in the morning, a time when he normally never called. His face was ashen, with bloodshot eyes; he was obviously shaken by an immense inner conflict. But Zoé herself was in a state of great bewilderment and failed to notice how disturbed he was. She ran up to him, crying:

'Oh sir, please come! Madam nearly died last night!'

He asked for details.

'It's incredible, sir! She's had a miscarriage!'

Nana was three months pregnant. For a while she'd taken it to be merely a passing indisposition, and Doctor Boutarel himself had his doubts. When he finally told her definitely, she was so annoyed that she made every effort to conceal the fact. Her predicament had been the root cause of her black moods and nervous fears; she felt ashamed and was anxious to keep it quiet, like any unmarried mother forced to hide her condition. It was a ridiculous and humiliating accident which would make her a laughing-stock. What a rotten sort of joke! And what bad luck, too! Just when she thought she'd finished with all that kind of lark, she had to be caught out! And she had a permanent feeling of surprise, as if her sex organs had let her down: so they produced babies even when you didn't want them to and were using them for quite other purposes? Nature really was infuriating! You were enjoying a bit of fun and had to face up to the serious business of becoming a mother. Nature was making people die all around you and then forcing you to give life. Oughtn't you to be allowed to use your body as your fancy took you without having all that fuss? And where on earth had this little brat come from? She didn't even know. The man responsible would have done better to keep it to himself, for God's sake, because no one would claim the child, it was an embarrassment for all concerned and his life would certainly not have been very happy.

Meanwhile Zoé was relating how the catastrophe had taken place.

'Madam got griping pains round about four o'clock, and when I went into her dressing-room because she hadn't come out, there she was lying flat on the floor, unconscious. Yes, sir, on the floor in a pool of blood as if she'd been murdered . . . So naturally, then I realized what had happened. I was furious, madam could have told me about her troubles. Monsieur Georges happened to be here and he helped me pick her up and at the first mention of a miscarriage, blow me if he didn't pass out himself . . . I've really been in the wars since yesterday!'

Indeed, the whole house seemed upside-down. The servants were scurrying upstairs and downstairs and all over the house. Georges had spent the night in an armchair in the drawing-room. It was he who'd given the news to madam's friends when they'd called at the time madam was usually 'at home'. He was as white as a sheet and still in a terribly confused and emotional state when he explained what had happened, and when Steiner, la Faloise, Philippe, and the others heard what he had to say, they all exclaimed in amazement.

It couldn't be true! It must be a joke! Then they looked solemn and cast irritated glances towards her door, shaking their heads and not finding it funny at all. A dozen men-friends of Nana had stayed on till midnight chatting in low voices round the fireplace, all with the same worrying thought in their minds: they might be the father. They seemed uncomfortable and confused, rather apologetic towards each other. Then they cheered up; it wasn't any concern of theirs, after all, it was her baby. What an extraordinary girl Nana was, wasn't she? You'd never have credited her with a lark like that, would you? And then they'd all tiptoed away as if they were in a death-chamber where it's forbidden to laugh.

'But please come up, sir', Zoé said to Muffat. 'Madam's much better, she'll be able to see you . . . We're waiting for the doctor, he promised to call back this morning.'

The maid had persuaded Georges to go home to sleep. Upstairs in the drawing-room, there was only Satin left, stretched out on a divan, smoking a cigarette and looking up at the ceiling; since the incident, in the midst of the general confusion she'd remained icily angry, shrugging her shoulders and making disagreeable comments. Then, as Zoé went by, still telling the count how much her poor mistress had suffered, she snapped:

'Serves her right, it'll teach her a lesson!'

They turned round in surprise. Satin didn't move, still staring up at the ceiling, clenching her cigarette between her lips.

'That's a nice thing to say!' exclaimed Zoé.

Satin jerked upright, looked angrily at the count, and again snapped:

'Serves her right, it'll be a lesson for her!'

Then she flopped back on the divan and blew out a thin puff of smoke as if she'd lost interest and was determined to wash her hands of the whole business. It was all so stupid!

Meanwhile Zoé had shown Muffat into the bedroom. In the cosy, silent room there was a vague smell of ether in the air; the only sound was the occasional carriage rumbling by in the Avenue de Villiers.

Looking extremely pale, Nana was lying back on her pillow, not sleeping, with her eyes wide open, thinking. Seeing the count, she smiled but didn't move.

'Ah, my pet', she murmured slowly, 'I really thought I'd never see you again.'

Then, when he bent down to kiss her, she became affectionate and spoke of their child, in all sincerity, as if he were the father.

'I didn't dare tell you . . . I felt so happy! Oh, I was building castles in the air, I wanted him to be worthy of you. And now that's all over . . . Ah well, maybe it's better that way, I don't want to cause you any trouble.'

Surprised at the idea of being a father, he stammered a few incoherent words. He'd drawn a chair up to the bed and was sitting with one arm resting on the blanket. Nana suddenly noticed his upset look; his eyes were bloodshot and his mouth was quivering feverishly.

'What's the matter?' she enquired. 'Are you ill too?'

'No', he replied, clearly distressed.

She gave him a searching look. Then, seeing that Zoé was taking her time over tidying away a few medicine bottles, she motioned to her to leave, and as soon as they were alone she pulled him towards her and repeated her question.

'What's the matter, darling? . . . You've got tears in your eyes. Come on, out with it, you've got something you want to tell me.'

'No, I haven't, I promise you I haven't', he stammered.

Then, choking with misery and rendered all the more emotional by the sick-room atmosphere into which he'd been so unexpectedly thrown, he buried his head in the sheets to stifle his uncontrollable sobbing. Nana realized what had happened: Rose had obviously decided to send him the letter. For a while, she let him cry; he was trembling so convulsively that she could feel the bed shaking. In the end, speaking in a motherly, compassionate voice:

'You've got troubles at home?'

He nodded. She paused again; then, in the merest whisper:

'So you've learnt the truth?'

Again he nodded. Once again a heavy silence fell in this bedroom so full of suffering. He'd found Sabine's letter to her lover yesterday after coming home late from an evening party at the Empress's. After an agonizing night full of plans of vengeance, he had left home early in order to escape the urge to kill his wife. Outside, the fresh air and the wonderfully mild June morning had so affected his mind that he'd completely lost the thread of his ideas, and he'd gone round to see Nana as he did at all the harrowing moments of his life. Only with her was he able to surrender to his misery and have the cowardly satisfaction of knowing she would comfort him.

'Come along now, calm down', the young woman said in her kindliest voice. 'I've known about this for a long time. But naturally I'd never want to let you know about it. You remember, you had suspicions last year and then, thanks to my common sense, things worked out all right. In fact, you hadn't got any proofs and now that you have I can see that it's hard for you. All the same, you must be sensible. You've got no need to feel disgraced by it.'

He'd stopped crying but he was too ashamed to speak, even though he'd been telling her the most intimate details of his family life for a long while. She was forced to prompt him: look, she was a woman, he could tell her everything.

'You're ill . . . What's the point in tiring yourself! . . . I was stupid to come. I'm going', he said suddenly, in a barely audible voice.

'No, you're not to go', she said quickly. 'You must stay and perhaps I can give you some good advice. Only don't make me talk too much, the doctor told me not to.'

He'd at last managed to stand up and was walking round the room. She started questioning him.

'What are you going to do now?'

'What do you think? I'm going to slap his face.'

She looked disapproving.

'That's not sensible at all . . . And how about your wife?'

'I'll take her to court. I've got evidence.'

'That's even less sensible, my dear man. In fact, it's stupid. I'll never let you do that, you know.'

And calmly and composedly, speaking in a weak voice, she pointed out how futile it was to cause a scandal with a duel and a court-case. He'd make the headlines in the newspapers for a week. It would jeopardize his whole life, his peace of mind, his high office in the Tuileries, the honour of his name. And for what? To end up as a laughing-stock.

'What does that matter?' he cried. 'I'll have had my revenge!'

'No, my pet', she said. 'In that kind of affair if you don't hit back straight away, you never will.'

At a loss for words, he made no reply. Certainly, he was no coward but he could see that she was right; he felt more and more uneasy; his anger had suddenly subsided into a feeling of shame and a realization of helplessness. He was due for a further shock; she was determined not to let him off lightly.

'And shall I tell you what's really troubling you, darling? It's because you're being unfaithful to her yourself. That's right, isn't it? You don't spend all those nights away from home just twiddling your thumbs, do you? And your wife is bound to suspect that. So how can you blame her? She'll reply that you showed her the way, and that'll certainly make you shut up . . . And that's why you're dancing up and down here instead of going off and slaughtering the pair of them.'

Under the savagery of this attack Muffat fell back into his chair. She paused to recover her breath and then went on more quietly:

'Oh, how tired I am . . . Help me move up a bit. I keep slipping down all the time, my head's stuffed with cotton wool.'

He helped her up and she gave a sigh of relief. She again started talking about the tremendous fun the public would get out of a lawsuit for a legal separation. Couldn't he see the countess's lawyer keeping Paris in stitches with his account of Nana's career? He wouldn't miss a point: her flop at the Variétés, her luxurious residence, her whole life-style. No, she didn't want all that much publicity, really not. Maybe there were nasty women who would have egged him on to get cheap publicity at his expense, but what she wanted first and foremost was his happiness. She'd drawn him close and was holding him with his head beside hers on the edge of the pillow, with her arm round his neck. She murmured gently:

'Listen my pet: you must make it up with your wife.'

He was outraged: no, he couldn't ever do that. He was too deeply hurt, he'd be ashamed. She gently persisted:

'You must go back to your wife . . . Look, you don't want everyone to go about saying I enticed you away from your family, do you? That'd give me a dreadful reputation, what would people think of me?. . . There's just one thing: you must give me your word of honour that you'll love me always, because if you ever go with another woman . . .'

Her tears were choking her. He cut her short with kisses but still insisted:

'No, you're mad, it's out of the question.'

'No, it's not', she retorted. 'You absolutely must . . . I'll just have to grin and bear it. After all, she is your wife. It's not as if you were deceiving me with just anybody.'

She continued to offer good advice in this vein, even bringing God into the argument. He could imagine he was listening to Monsieur Venot when the old man kept preaching at him to give up his life of sin. But she wasn't talking of breaking with her, she was merely advocating a policy of give and take, a friendly sharing of himself between his wife and his mistress, a quiet life to suit everybody, a kind of relaxing snooze amid the unavoidable squalor of living. It wouldn't change their lives in the slightest, he'd still remain her best darling man, only he'd come and see her not quite so often and let the countess have the nights he wouldn't be spending with her. She was by now very tired and finished with a little gasp:

'And I shall be able to feel I've done a good deed . . . You'll love me all the more.'

There was a hush. On the pillow her face looked paler than ever; her eyes were shut. He was now listening to what she was saying, with the excuse that he didn't want to tire her. She remained silent for a good minute; then, opening her eyes again, she said faintly:

'And anyway, how about money? Where will you get that if you don't stay on good terms with her? Labordette was here yesterday asking about that bill . . . As for me, I'm dead broke. I haven't got a stitch to put on my back!'

And she shut her eyes again and lay completely inanimate. An agonized look clouded Muffat's face; in a state of shock from yesterday's events, he'd temporarily forgotten his financial troubles from which he could see hardly any way to extricate himself. In spite of the most solemn assurances he'd received, his hundred-thousand-franc promissory note had been put into circulation. Labordette was pretending to be utterly dismayed and blaming everything on Francis; he'd take good care not to have any future business dealings with someone who wasn't a gentleman. But the note had to be met; the count would never allow his signature to be questioned. However, apart from Nana's fresh demands, his domestic expenditure had suffered an extraordinary upheaval. After coming back from Les Fondettes, the countess had suddenly manifested a taste for luxury and an appetite for social pleasures which was running away with their fortune. People were beginning to talk about her compulsive spending, a whole new and ruinous style of living, half-a-million francs squandered on doing up their old house in the Rue Miromesnil, her extravagant wardrobe and vast sums that had disappeared, melting, or perhaps given, away without any effort to provide justification. Twice Muffat had ventured to comment on her behaviour in an endeavour to discover what was happening, but she'd merely smiled and given him such an odd look that he'd been too intimidated to ask any further questions: her answers might have been too forthright. His acceptance of Daguenet as son-in-law had been motivated primarily by the thought of reducing Estelle's dowry to two hundred thousand francs, even if that involved reaching some agreement on the remainder with the young man, who was quite content to be making this marriage which was like a dream come true.

However, during this last week, faced by the necessity of laying hands on the hundred thousand francs for Labordette without delay, Muffat had hit upon one final scheme which he viewed with extreme reluctance, namely the sale of Les Bordes, a magnificent property with an estimated value of half-a-million francs which had recently been bequeathed to the countess by an uncle. But this sale required the countess's written agreement, and under the terms of her marriage contract she herself couldn't dispose of the property without the count's authorization. He had in fact been intending to raise the question of her agreement with his wife yesterday. And now all his plans were being dashed; in the present situation he couldn't possibly accept that sort of compromise. This thought brought home his wife's adultery to him even more forcibly; and he could quite understand the point of Nana's remarks, for in her increasing domination of him which had led him to keep nothing from her, he had been bewailing his situation and admitting the difficulty he was facing to get the countess to sign.

However, Nana didn't seem to be insisting. She still had her eyes shut, and seeing how pale she was he took fright and gave her a little sniff of ether. She sighed and, without mentioning Daguenet's name, asked:

'When's the wedding?'

'The contract's being signed on Tuesday, in five days' time', he replied.

Then, still keeping her eyes closed, as if she was speaking from the obscure depths of her consciousness:

'So there you are, my pet, you can see what you've got to

do . . . I only want everyone to be happy . . .'

To soothe her he took hold of her hand. Yes, they'd see, the main thing was for her to rest. His feeling of outrage had gone, the warm, drowsy atmosphere of the sick-room, with its lingering scent of ether, had finally lulled him into a mood of relaxed happiness. His male pride, which had been so offended and inflamed, had evaporated in the excitement of her own feverish state and the warmth of her bed which, as he sat beside her, caring for her in her suffering, brought back once again memories of their pleasures. He bent forward and hugged her tightly, while on her impassive face her lips curled in a sly smile of triumph. At this moment Doctor Boutarel came in.

'Well, how's our dear little girl?' he said familiarly to Muffat, whom he treated as her husband. 'Well, we finally managed to get her talking!'

The doctor was a handsome man, still young, who had a superb practice in the world of kept women. Cheerful, lively, and very friendly without ever going to bed with any of them, he charged extortionate fees and made sure they were paid. However, he was always prepared to visit, for the most trivial ailment; being so scared of dying, Nana used to send for him two or three times a week to tell him all about her worries over childish complaints which he treated and at the same time entertained her with gossip and lots of silly stories. His lady patients adored him. But this time the trouble was more serious.

Muffat was leaving in a highly emotional state; his only feeling now was tenderness at seeing his poor Nana so frail. As he was going out she beckoned him back and held up her forehead for a kiss. Then, in a weak voice and with a playfully threatening look:

'You know what I'm letting you do . . . You must go back to your wife or else! . . . I'm going to be very cross!'

Countess Sabine had wanted her daughter's marriage-contract to be signed on a Tuesday to coincide with a party given to celebrate the renovation of her house, though the paint was barely dry. Five hundred invitations had been sent out, to include more or less all levels of polite society. That very morning the decorators had been fixing the hangings to the walls, and as the chandeliers were being lit around nine o'clock the architect was still issuing his final instructions in the company of the enthusiastic countess.

The party took place in a setting full of gentle, spring-like charm; mild June weather had made it possible to open up the double doors of the large drawing-room and to extend the dancing out on to the sandy garden terrace. The first guests, greeted at the door by the count and countess, were quite dazzled; they could remember the icy old Countess Muffat and the old-fashioned drawing-room full of stern piety and solid mahogany Empire furniture, with its yellow velvet hangings and its damp, musty, green ceiling. Now on entering the front hall you saw glittering mosaics picked out in gold, with the marble staircase and its delicately carved banisters gleaming under the high candelabra. The hall led into the magnificent drawing-room draped in Genoese velvet with an immense decorative ceiling by Boucher* for which the architect had paid one hundred thousand francs at the sale of the Château de Dampierre. In this room the chandeliers and crystal sconces lit up a luxurious array of mirrors and fine furniture; Sabine's former single *chaise longue*, with its red silk upholstery which had looked so much out of place in the old days, seemed now to have spawned and expanded, filling the whole grand residence with a mood of idle pleasure and eager enjoyment which had broken out with the violence of a fire that had long been smouldering.

Dancing had already begun. The orchestra had been placed in the garden in front of an open window. It was playing a waltz whose lilting rhythms floated up into the night air and were already dying away before they reached the house. The huge garden was full of gentle shadows cast by Venetian lanterns; at the edge of one lawn a buffet had been set up under a crimson awning. The waltz being played by the orchestra was the vulgar little dance-tune from *The Blonde Venus*, and as its cheerful, saucy rhythm flowed into the house it seemed to send a warm thrill through the old walls, like a gust of gutter sex sweeping away a bygone age in the haughty Muffat residence and dispersing their past, a hundred years of honour and Christian belief which had been sleeping in the dark corners of its lofty ceilings.

Meanwhile, the count's mother's old friends had themselves taken refuge in their usual position beside the fireplace, forming a tiny dazzled and bewildered group in the middle of the steadily encroaching crowd. Madame Du Joncquoy had failed to recognize any of the rooms and had come through the dining-room. Madame Chantereau was looking with a bemused expression at the garden, which now seemed huge. Soon their little corner was buzzing with all kinds of whispered comments.

'I say', muttered Madame Chantereau, 'supposing the countess were to come back, eh? Can you imagine her coming into the room amidst all these people . . . And the ostentation of it all! And the frightful din! . . . It's absolutely dreadful!'

'Sabine's out of her mind', replied Madame Du Joncquoy. 'Did you notice her as you came in? Take a look, you can see her from here . . . She's wearing all her diamonds.'

They stood up for a moment to peer at the count and the countess in the distance. Sabine was in a white dress trimmed with superb Brussels lace, looking young, gay, exulting in her loveliness, and with a touch of intoxication in the permanent smile on her face. Beside her, Muffat was looking somewhat pale; he had aged but he too was smiling in his calm, dignified way.

'And to think he used to be the master in this house', Madame Chantereau went on, 'that not even one tiny seat would have been allowed in without his permission! . . . Well, she's changed all that! It's her house now . . . Do you remember that she didn't want to do up the drawing-room? Well, now she's done up the whole house!'

They paused; Madame de Chezelles was just coming in, followed by a whole bunch of young men making enthusiastic little noises of approval:

'How utterly delightful! It's exquisite! What taste!'

She dashed ahead and turned back to exclaim:

'What did I say! . . . There's nothing like these tumbledown old places when you do them up! . . . They turn out so smart! Ever so Louis XIV, don't you think? . . . Now she can start giving parties.'

The two old ladies had sat down again and were talking in low voices about the marriage, which had taken a lot of people by surprise. Estelle had just gone by in her pink silk dress, as thin and flat-chested as ever, wearing her usual tight-lipped, virginal look. She'd raised absolutely no objection to her marriage to Daguenet, showing neither sadness nor gladness, as cold and white as those winter nights when she used to put more logs on the fire. This party in her honour, with all these lights and flowers and music, left her completely unmoved.

'An adventurer!' Madame Du Joncquoy was commenting. 'I've never met him myself.'

'Look out, here he comes', murmured Madame Chantereau.

Daguenet had caught sight of Madame Hugon with her two sons and was hurrying over to offer her his arm, laughing and looking extremely affectionate, as if she'd been instrumental in engineering his stroke of luck.

'Thank you, my dear boy', she said, sitting down beside the fireplace. 'This is my old corner, you see.'

'You know him, do you?' enquired Madame Du Joncquoy, when Daguenet had moved on.

'Indeed I do. A charming young man; Georges is very fond of him . . . Oh, he comes from a most highly regarded family.'

And the good lady defended him against the veiled hostility which she could sense. Louis Philippe had had an excellent opinion of his father, who had been a Prefect until his death. The son had perhaps been a little wild. People were saying he was ruined. Be that as it may, one of his uncles who owned a lot of land was going to leave him his entire estate. But the ladies were still shaking their heads and Madame Hugon, herself embarrassed, kept coming back to the high regard which his family enjoyed. She was feeling very weary and complaining about her legs. For the last month she'd been living in her house in the Rue Richelieu, having, so she said, all sorts of business to deal with. Her motherly smile was tinged with sadness.

'All the same', said Madame Chantereau in conclusion, 'Estelle could have done very much better for herself.'

A fanfare announced a quadrille and everybody moved to the side to leave room for the dancers. Women in light-coloured dresses were going past, mingling with the dark patches of the men's tail-coats, while the large chandelier gleamed down over the surging heads below with their sparkling jewels and the rustle of white feathers, a whole flower garden of lilacs and roses. It was already hot, the orchestra was playing a lively tune, and a pungent scent was wafting from the dainty tulles and rumpled silks and satins out of which pale, bare shoulders were emerging. Through the open doors at the far end of the adjoining rooms, women could be seen sitting in rows, hiding their discreetly flashing smiles, their glowing eyes, and pouting lips behind the flutter of their fans. Guests were still being loudly announced by the footman, while in the crush of people the men were in the slow process of attempting to find a place for the ladies clinging uncomfortably to their arms, standing on tiptoe to see if there was an armchair free in the distance. The house was becoming overcrowded; the ladies were huddling together with a rustle of skirts, showing the polite resignation of people familiar with such dazzling, crowded gatherings, maintaining their gracious poise as expanses of lace and bows and pouffes occasionally blocked their way through. Meanwhile, in the pink glow of the Venetian lanterns, couples were taking refuge in the depths of the garden from the stifling atmosphere in the large drawing-room; shadowy gowned figures were hurrying along the edge of the lawn as though keeping time with the distant music of the quadrille, here gently muffled by the trees.

Steiner had just met Foucarmont drinking a glass of champagne with la Faloise at the buffet beside the lawn.

'It's all so terribly trendy', la Faloise was saying as he looked at the purple awning supported on gilt posts. 'It's a sort of gingerbread style. That's it, isn't it? A gingerbread style!'

He'd adopted the permanently supercilious pose of the young man who, having seen and done the lot, was perpetually flippant.

'Wouldn't poor old Vandeuvres be surprised if he were to come back now', murmured Foucarmont. 'Do you remember how he was bored to tears round that drawing-room fireplace? My God, wouldn't you have caught it if you'd laughed!'

'Oh, why bring up Vandeuvres?' sneered la Faloise. 'A failure, and he certainly slipped up badly if he expected us to be shocked by his barbecue . . . People have completely forgotten him. Finished, dead and buried, poor old Vandeuvres. Someone else's turn now!'

Then, as Steiner was shaking hands with them:

'Nana's just turned up, you know. What an entrance, chaps! Something out of this world! First of all, she kissed the countess. Then, when the happy young couple came up, she gave them her blessing and said to Daguenet: "Now listen to me, young fellow: if you don't behave, you'll have me to deal with . . ." Didn't you see it? Oh, it was so smart, an absolute wow!'

The other two were listening open-mouthed. Then they burst out laughing. He was very gratified; he imagined he was being very clever.

'You really thought it had happened, didn't you? . . . Well, it's not far wrong, since Nana's the one who's arranged the marriage. After all, she's one of the family, isn't she?'

At this moment the Hugon brothers came up; Philippe told him to shut up. They started to talk about the marriage, in the way men do. La Faloise told his version of the story, which made Georges cross. Nana had certainly landed Muffat with one of her old flames as son-in-law, but it wasn't true that she'd gone to bed with Daguenet the day before. Foucarmont shrugged his shoulders: who could ever tell who Nana was going to bed with? Georges now became even crosser and snapped: 'Excuse me, sir, but I can!', which everybody found highly amusing. In any case, as Steiner pointed out, the whole set-up was very odd.

The buffet was gradually being taken over and they moved away, but stayed together. La Faloise was eyeing the women impudently, as if he was at Mabille. At the far end of an avenue, a surprise awaited them: Monsieur Venot was in earnest discussion with Daguenet. They laughed and made the obvious jokes: Venot was hearing Daguenet's confession and giving him a few tips on wedding-nights. The group then went back to one of the doorways of the drawing-room; they could see the couples swirling round in a polka, cutting a swathe through the men still standing. The gusts of air from the garden were making the candles flare up very high. Each time a ball-gown swept by to the rhythmical tapping of the dance, a puff of fresher air cooled the glow from the chandeliers above.

'It's pretty hot in there, by Jove!' muttered la Faloise.

Having just emerged from the darkness outside, they found themselves blinking. They now noticed the tall figure of the Marquis de Chouard, standing by himself and towering over the bare shoulders all around him. He was pale and looked severe, dignified, and haughty with his crown of sparse white hair. He'd been so shocked by his son's behaviour that he'd recently broken off relations with him and was making a point of not setting foot in his house. It was only because his granddaughter had begged him to come that he'd agreed to be there that evening, despite his indignant objection to her marriage which, in his eyes, reflected the decline of the ruling classes brought about by their shameful compromises with the debauchery of modern life.

'Oh, it's the end of everything', Madame Du Joncquoy was whispering to Madame Chantereau. 'That trollop has bewitched the poor wretched man . . . And we can remember how deeply religious he was, how truly noble!'

'By all accounts, he's ruining himself', remarked Madame Chantereau. 'A promissory note of his came into my husband's hands . . . And now he's moved into that house in the Avenue de Villiers. He's the talk of the town . . . Not that I condone Sabine's conduct, mind you, but you must admit he does give her great cause for complaint, and if she's letting people make free with her money . . .'

'That's not the only thing she's letting people make free with!' the other woman interrupted. 'Anyway, with the pair of them both doing it, it'll be over all the quicker.'

A voice broke in gently; it was Monsieur Venot who'd crept up and sat down behind them, as though anxious not to be too visible. He bent forward and murmured:

'Why despair? God can manifest Himself when everything seems lost.'

He himself was witnessing placidly the downfall of the house which he'd controlled in the past. Ever since his stay at Les Fondettes, fully realizing how powerless he was, he'd been letting the collapse follow its increasingly wild course. He'd accepted everything: the count's uncontrollable passion for Nana, Fauchery's relationship with the countess, and even Daguenet's marriage to Estelle. What did such things matter? And he was showing himself more accommodating, more sphinx-like than ever, never losing sight of the thought of taking charge of the newly-weds as well as of the estranged couple, knowing very well that the more grievous the sin, the greater the repentance. God was biding His time.

'Our dear friend still has a strong religious sense', he went on in his soft voice. 'He's given me the most gratifying evidence of such feelings.'

'In that case', said Madame Du Joncquoy, 'he should start by going back to his wife.'

'Certainly . . . And I have high hopes, in fact, that a reconciliation is not far off.'

The two old ladies began questioning him; he beat a humble retreat: Heaven must decide. His only desire in bringing the count and countess together again was to avoid any public scandal. Religion was indulgent towards many types of weakness providing the proprieties were observed.

'All the same', Madame Du Joncquoy observed, 'you should have prevented this marriage with that adventurer.'

The little old man looked deeply surprised.

'You're mistaken. Monsieur Daguenet is a young man of very great qualities. I know how he thinks. He wants to leave all his youthful errors behind him. Estelle will bring him back into the fold, you may be sure of that.'

'Oh, Estelle', Madame Chantereau snorted. 'I don't think that dear little creature capable of anything. She's completely insignificant.'

Monsieur Venot merely smiled and made no attempt to enlarge on his view of the bride. Closing his eyes as if no longer concerned, he once again retreated behind the ladies' skirts. Madame Hugon, who'd been listlessly lending half an ear to the conversation, now summed up her own view, kindly as always, to the Marquis de Chouard who came over at that moment to pay his respects.

'I think these ladies are being too harsh. Life is so difficult for everybody . . . Don't you agree, my dear Marquis, that we must be very forgiving towards others if we want to deserve forgiveness ourselves?'

For a second the marquis was embarrassed, suspecting an indirect allusion to his own conduct. But seeing the sad smile on her kindly face he was quickly reassured, and replied firmly:

'No, there can be no forgiveness for certain acts . . . That sort of leniency leads to the collapse of society.'

There were still many people dancing. Another quadrille had just started and the floor was gently swaying as if the old house itself was collapsing under the vibration. Amid the blur of pale faces, here and there the head of a woman stood out, bright-eyed, with parted lips, carried away by the rhythm of the dance, her white skin gleaming under the bright chandelier. Madame Du Joncquoy was saying how stupid it was, absolute madness, to cram five hundred people into a space that could barely have held two hundred. Why not sign the marriage contract in the Place de la Concorde? It was the influence of modern ideas, Madame Chantereau claimed; in the old days, solemn occasions like these took place within the family circle but nowadays you had to have a crowd, including anybody and everybody, you had to squash people in or else things wouldn't go with a swing . . . You paraded your luxury and invited the ragtag and bobtail of Paris; and naturally such a hotchpotch of society inevitably led to the destruction of the sanctity of the family. The poor ladies were complaining that they didn't know more than fifty of the guests. Where had all these people come from? There were girls in low-cut dresses flaunting their bare shoulders. One woman had stuck a gold dagger into her chignon, while her jet-bead embroidery made her look as if she was wearing a coat of mail. Another woman was in such a shameless skin-tight skirt that people were following her progress with amused smiles. In this smart, permissive society dedicated purely to pleasure, full of people whom a society hostess would pick up in the course of some short-lived intimacy, where a duke rubbed shoulders with a crook, the opulence of this last ball of the season was blatant; people wanted one thing only: to have fun. And as the dancers performed the symmetrical figures of the quadrille in time to the music, the overcrowded rooms were becoming hotter and hotter.

'A very smart woman, the countess', la Faloise was saying,

still standing in the doorway leading to the garden. 'Looks ten years younger than her daughter. And talking of that, Foucarmont, you can tell us something: Vandeuvres used to bet that her thighs weren't up to much.'

The men were growing bored by his cynical flippancy. Foucarmont merely replied:

'Ask your cousin, my dear fellow. And here he comes.'

'What a good idea!' exclaimed la Faloise. 'I bet ten louis that she has got decent thighs.'

Fauchery was just making his way over to them. As an intimate friend of the family, he'd come in via the dining-room to avoid the crush. However, at the beginning of the winter Rose had managed to lure him back, and as a result he found himself sharing his favours between the singer and the countess; he was a very tired man and unable to devise a way of dumping one or other of them. Sabine flattered his vanity but Rose was more fun. Moreover, the latter was passionately in love with him, and so constant in her affections that Mignon was in despair.

'I say, can you enlighten me?' said la Faloise, catching hold of his cousin's arm. 'You see that lady over there in the white silk dress?'

Ever since he'd come into money, he'd become very self-assured and insolent, and enjoyed poking fun at Fauchery; he had old scores to settle for the way his cousin had teased and patronized him on his first arrival in Paris from the provinces.

'Yes, the lady with all the lace.'

The journalist was standing peering on tiptoe, failing to realize what la Faloise was getting at.

'Do you mean the countess?' he asked eventually.

'That's right, old man. I've got a bet on, for ten louis. Has she got decent thighs?'

And he gave a delighted cackle, pleased to have scored off his dashing young cousin, who'd impressed him so much in the old days when he'd asked him if the countess was going to bed with anyone. Without being flustered in the least, Fauchery merely looked him straight in the face, paused for a second, shrugged his shoulders, and said:

'Do try to be less of a nitwit, will you?'

He then shook hands with the others while la Faloise

sheepishly wondered whether he'd been so funny after all. They chatted. Ever since the races, the banker and Foucarmont had joined the inner circle at the Avenue de Villiers, where Nana was making a rapid recovery. The count called every evening to enquire after her progress. However, while he listened, Fauchery was looking worried. In the course of a quarrel he'd had with Rose that morning, she had openly admitted sending his letter to the count: so now, when he called on his grand society mistress, he'd be sure of a warm welcome. After long deliberation he'd still decided to come, out of bravado, to show he wasn't afraid. But though he seemed calm and collected, la Faloise's silly remark had shaken him.

'What's up with you?' enquired Philippe. 'Aren't you feeling well?'

'No, I'm fine . . . I've been working, that's all. That's why I arrived late.'

Then, with that secret heroism which is the stuff of the tragic climaxes of everyday life, he said calmly:

'But I haven't yet said good evening to our host and hostess . . . We mustn't forget our manners, must we?'

And he even had the courage to make a joke by turning to la Faloise and saying:

'That's right, isn't it, nitwit?'

And he threaded his way through the throng. The footman had stopped bawling out the names of the guests but the count and countess were still standing by the door, chatting to some ladies who had arrived late. When he finally reached them, the men still standing on the terrace all craned their necks to watch what would happen. Nana had obviously been indiscreet.

'The count hasn't yet noticed him', said Georges in a low voice. 'Look out! He's turning round now . . . Here we go!'

The orchestra had just struck up the *Blonde Venus* waltz again. First, Fauchery greeted the countess, who still had her smile on her face; she looked composed and delighted. He then stood very calmly waiting for a moment or two behind her husband's back. The count was tonight displaying his solemn, official persona, with the haughty demeanour of the high dignitary of the Empire. When his eyes finally fell on the journalist his lordly attitude became even more pronounced. For a few seconds the two men eyed each other. Fauchery was the first to hold out his hand. Muffat took it and the two stood with hands clasped. With half-closed eyes Sabine watched them, smiling, while the orchestra continued to churn out the saucy, mocking lilt of the waltz.

'Absolutely painless!' exclaimed Steiner.

'Have their hands got stuck together?' asked la Faloise in surprise, as the two men continued to hold hands.

Fauchery's pale cheeks had taken on a pink tinge; he couldn't help thinking of that moment in the props-room at the theatre, with its greenish light and miscellaneous junk, where Muffat had stood with the egg-cup in his hands taking unfair advantage of his dilemma. And now Muffat's own troubles had come home to roost, his last shred of dignity had been torn away. Relieved of his forebodings and noting the countess's cheerful smile, Fauchery felt an urge to laugh; he found it funny.

'Ah, this time it really is her!' shouted la Faloise who could never let a joke rest once he'd made up his mind that it was a good one. 'Look over there! Isn't that Nana coming in?'

'Oh, do be quiet, you idiot!' muttered Philippe.

'But I'm telling you! . . . They're playing her waltz, for goodness sake, and so she appears . . . And she's responsible for the reconciliation, damn it all! Can't you see what's happening? She's clasping them all to her bosom, all three of them, my cousin Fauchery, my cousin Sabine, and her husband, and calling them all her little pets! God, that sort of family scene turns my stomach! . . .'

Estelle had come up. Fauchery complimented her and she stood there stiffly in her pink dress with her childish, surprised look, silently watching him with a sidelong glance at her parents. Daguenet also shook the journalist warmly by the hand. Everybody was smiling; in the background, Monsieur Venot was fondly eyeing the little group with a blissful smile on his face, enfolding them in his sugary piety, happy to witness these final sinful acts which were preparing the way for Providence to intervene.

The waltz swirled voluptuously on and on, battering at the old house in a rising tide of pleasure. The trills of the piccolos were shriller, the sighs of the violins more and more rapturous; amidst the gilt and the paintings and the Genoa velvet, the chandeliers were glowing like hazy suns and the throng of guests, amplified by the mirrors, seemed to be growing larger and larger, the buzz of their voices louder and louder. The couples dancing with hands on waists, beneath the smiling eyes of the seated women, were making the floor of the drawing-room rock even more giddily. In the garden, the Venetian lanterns looked like the glowing embers of a fire which lit up the shadowy figures of the men and women strolling off to take a breath of air in the remoter paths, with a gleam as if from some distant conflagration. And these quaking walls and this red haze were like a final holocaust consuming the honour of the whole of this ancient house. Those timid bursts of laughter which were just vaguely audible on that night in April in the past when Fauchery had mentally compared them to the tinkle of broken crystal, had become bolder and wilder to culminate in this peak of glittering revelry. Now, the crack was widening and soon the whole house would crumble. In working-class slums, families dragged down by drunkenness finish up in utter destitution, with larders emptied and mattresses stripped* to satisfy the mad craving for alcohol; in this house, where a vast accumulation of wealth was suddenly about to go up in flames and collapse in ruins, the knell of this ancient family was being tolled with a waltz, while poised over the dancers, loose-limbed and invisible, with the smell of her body fermenting in the stuffy air, Nana was turning this whole society putrid to the rhythm of her vulgar tune.

On the night of the church wedding of their daughter, for the first time in two years, Count Muffat went to his wife's bedroom. The countess was greatly surprised and drew back, though she still retained the familiar, delighted smile which now never left her lips. Seeing him embarrassed and groping for words, she gave him a little lecture. Neither of them was keen to speak completely frankly. Their religion taught mutual forgiveness, and they came to a tacit agreement that they should both continue to go their separate ways. Before going to bed, as the countess still seemed hesitant, they talked business, but when he brought up the question of selling Les

Bordes she showed no hesitation: they both needed money badly, they'd split the proceeds. Their reconciliation was complete; the guilt-ridden count felt very relieved.

That very same day, at about two in the afternoon, while Nana was still drowsing, Zoé timidly knocked on her door. The curtains were drawn and the room was in semi-darkness, cool and silent, with a breath of warm air coming in through the window. The young woman was still a little weak but now allowed out of bed. She opened her eyes and asked:

'Who is it?'

Before Zoé could answer, Daguenet pushed his way past her and announced himself. Nana propped herself up on her elbow on her pillow and sent her maid away.

'Oh, it's you? And on your wedding day!'

Confused by the dim light, he remained standing in the middle of the room. Then, as his eyes became accustomed to the half-darkness, he groped his way towards her; he was wearing a white tie and gloves. He said again:

'Yes, it's me. Well, don't you remember?'

No, she didn't remember anything and he had to make the proposal himself, in his usual playful way:

'Look, it's your commission . . . I'm letting you have first go . . .'

At this, seeing him standing beside the bed, she reached out and grasped him in her naked arms, laughing out loud and almost in tears: wasn't that really sweet of him!

'Oh Mimi, you're so funny! . . . And you remembered when I'd quite forgotten. So you managed to slip away, you've come straight from the church . . . Oh, give me a kiss . . . no, harder than that, Mimi darling! Ah well, maybe it's the last time.'

There was tenderness in their laugh; then their laughter died away . . . It was now very hot in the bedroom, where a vague smell of ether still lingered; the curtains were billowing; the sound of children's voices drifted in from the street. They joked: there was no time to lose, the groom was due to leave with the bride immediately after the wedding breakfast.

Chapter 13

LATE one afternoon towards the end of September, Count Muffat called on Nana to tell her that his attendance was suddenly required at the Tuileries and he would be prevented from coming to dinner that evening as arranged. Although dusk was falling, the lights in the house were not yet on; there was a lot of laughing in the servants' quarters. He went very quietly up the stairs in the subdued glow cast by the stained-glass windows. The door of the upstairs drawing-room opened noiselessly. The dying daylight had tinged the ceiling pink; the red hangings, the deep divans, the lacquer furniture, the jumble of embroidered materials, bronzes, and faience-ware were already drowsing in the invading darkness which flooded into every corner, blotting out the gleam of gilt and the glint of ivory. But one large white patch stood out sharply: it was a petticoat spread out wide, on which Nana was sprawling on her back in George's arms.

She sprang to her feet and pushed the boy into her bedroom to give him time to get away.

'Come in here', she mumbled, completely at a loss. 'I can explain . . .'

She was furious at being caught out: she never let a man do that to her in her own drawing-room, with all the doors open. All sorts of things had conspired to cause it: Georges had been crazy with jealousy because of Philippe and made a terrible scene, flinging his arms round her neck and sobbing so much that she'd weakened, feeling at heart very sorry for him and at a loss how to console him. And on the one occasion when she'd let herself go like that, with a little brat whose mother kept him so short of money that he now couldn't even offer her a bunch of violets, the count had to turn up unexpectedly and catch them. It really was bad luck! That's the reward you get for being kind-hearted!

The room into which she'd pushed Muffat was in complete darkness. She fumbled for the bell-pull and tugged it furiously for someone to bring a lamp. It was really all Julien's fault! If there'd been a lamp in the drawing-room, nothing like this would have happened. It was that stupid twilight hour that had made her go all soppy . . .

'Oh, please, my pet, do try and understand', she said, when Zoé had brought a lamp.

The count was sitting with his hands resting on his knees, looking down at the floor, utterly bewildered by what he'd just seen. He couldn't even show any anger. He was shivering as if his blood had run cold with horror. His silent distress touched her heart. She tried to comfort him:

'OK, yes, it was wrong of me, very wrong . . . You can see how sorry I am for what I did . . . It makes me feel dreadful because it's made you cross . . . Oh come on, be nice too, tell me you forgive me . . .'

She crouched down lovingly at his feet and looked meekly up into his eyes to see if he was very angry with her; then, as he heaved a long sigh and began to recover, she started coaxing him. Speaking in an earnest, gentle voice, she offered him one final reason:

'You see, darling, you must try to understand . . . I can't turn down my friends if they're poor . . .'

The count allowed himself to be persuaded, insisting on one thing only: Georges must go. But all his illusions had been shattered; he no longer trusted her promises to be faithful. Tomorrow, Nana would be going to bed with some other man. Only his abject need for her, his fear of life, made him hold on to her despite the torment she was causing him. He couldn't live without her.

This was the period in her career when Nana's star blazed with ever-increasing brilliance and her vicious life loomed even larger on the horizon of vice of Paris. Her shameless luxury, her majestic, total disregard for money, so that whole fortunes melted away before everyone's eyes, had the capital at her feet. Her grand residence was like some glowing furnace where desire was constantly at white heat and her slightest breath could turn gold into fine ash, to be swept away by the wind. Nobody had ever seen such raging extravagance. The house was like a bottomless pit in which men were engulfed with all their possessions; their body and even their name sank without leaving even a tiny speck of dust. This tart with the tastes of an insatiable parakeet, nibbling radishes and sugared almonds and merely pecking at her meat, would spend five thousand francs a month on food for her table. The waste in her kitchen was indescribable, a gigantic haemorrhage, with whole barrels of wine being guzzled and her bills swelling to grotesque proportions as they passed through three or four different hands. The kitchen was under the complete control of Victorine and François; here they would entertain their friends, not forgetting a whole tribe of cousins whose families they kept supplied with cold meats and unlimited quantities of beef-stock. Julien insisted on getting his rake-off from the tradesmen, and every pane of glass, replaced at a cost of one franc, carried a 50 per-cent surcharge for himself; Charles devoured oats by the bushel for his horses, buying double the quantity required and selling off at the back-door whatever was delivered at the front. And at the centre of this wholesale looting operation, like the ransacking of a captured town, Zoé was artfully contriving to save appearances, and covering everybody else's thefts in order to include and protect her own. But even worse was the waste: yesterday's left-overs went straight into the rubbish bin, together with piles of food the servants had got tired of; glasses smeared with sugar, gas-jets left burning full on, threatening to blow up the house; spitefulness, neglect, and bungling, everything that could accelerate the ruin of a household plundered by so many greedy mouths. Upstairs, aided and abetted by the mistress, the collapse was going ahead even more merrily: dresses costing ten thousand francs, worn twice before being discarded and sold off by Zoé; jewellery left mouldering in drawers; stupid purchases, the 'latest thing', forgotten the following day and tipped out into the street. She was incapable of seeing anything expensive without wanting to acquire it, swamping herself in floods of flowers and trinkets, all bought on impulse; and the more expensive these things were, the happier she was. She couldn't hang on to anything: in her dainty white fingers everything disintegrated, withered, or got filthy; strewn around in her wake you'd find tatty, muddy rags, every kind of miscellaneous rubbish. And then, after spending money like water, she was hit by the big bills: twenty thousand francs at the milliner's, thirty thousand for the linen-draper, twelve thousand for the shoemaker; her stables mopped up another fifty thousand; and in six months she ran up a bill for one-hundred-and-twenty thousand francs with her dressmaker. Without making any change in a life-style which Labordette had estimated to cost an average of four hundred thousand francs, in her very first year she got through a million francs. She couldn't believe it herself: where on earth had all that money gone? Not even the barrow-loads of cash from the men lining up to get her to bed could stem the flood undermining the foundations of her opulent mansion, which was tottering under the strain.

Meanwhile Nana still had one last whim up her sleeve: she had set her heart on doing up her bedroom and she thought she had hit on a solution: a bedroom with furniture upholstered in tea-rose pink velvet with silver buttons and hangings draped in a canopy rising up to the ceiling, adorned with cable mouldings and gold lace. It seemed to her that this would be both delicate and rich, a superb backcloth for a girl with red hair and a pink skin. But the room furnishings were intended merely to provide the setting for the bedstead, which would be dazzlingly sensational. Nana had dreams of a bed that would be utterly unique, a throne or altar where all Paris would come to worship her in her naked, equally unique, beauty. It would be made entirely of embossed gold and silver, like some gigantic jewel, golden roses hanging on a silver trellis; along the bed-head a band of laughing Cupids would be leaning forward, surrounded by flowers and peering at the voluptuous delights concealed in the shade of the curtains. She had consulted Labordette, who had brought along two goldsmiths. Designs were already being drawn up. The bed would cost fifty thousand francs, and Muffat was to be giving it to her as a New Year's gift.

One thing that surprised the young woman was that, despite this stream of money flowing through her thighs, she was permanently short of cash. Some days she found herself at a loss to lay hands on ridiculously small sums, a couple of louis. She had either to borrow from Zoé or look around to see if she could scrape something together through her own efforts. However, before resorting to extreme measures she'd try out her friends, extracting whatever they happened to have on their persons at the time, even if it was only a franc or two. For the last three months she'd been mainly milking Philippe, who discovered that in her moments of crisis he could no longer call on her without having his wallet emptied. She soon became more ambitious and asked him for loans, two or three hundred francs, never more, to meet pressing debts or IOUs; and Philippe, who'd been promoted captain in July and put in charge of the regimental funds, would bring the money along the following day, apologizing for not being flush because his dear mother was far from open-handed with her sons. After three months these little loans, regularly repeated, amounted to some ten thousand or so francs. The captain was still emitting his loud guffaw, but he looked thinner and occasionally preoccupied, even somewhat careworn. But a glance from Nana would transform him and throw him into a sort of sensual ecstasy. She behaved very kittenishly with him, driving him crazy with her kisses behind doors and suddenly pouncing on him to give herself to him. Any free time he could get away from his military duties he spent sniffing round her skirts.

One night, as Nana had made it known that she was also called Thérèse and that her name-day was October the first, her gentlemen friends all sent her presents. Captain Hugon brought his round in person: an antique, gold-mounted, Meissen sweetmeat dish and cover. She was alone in her dressing-room, fresh from her bath, wearing only a large blue-and-red flannel bathrobe and busily examining her presents spread out on a table. She'd already broken a rock-crystal scent-bottle while attempting to take the stopper out.

'Oh, you're too kind!' she said. 'What is it? Let me have a look . . . What a child you are to spend your money on little gadgets like that!'

She gently told him off: after all, he didn't earn much money; but she was delighted to see him spending all he had on her; this was the only proof of love that went straight to her heart. Meanwhile she was fiddling about with the dish, opening and closing it, trying to see how it was made.

'Look out!' he exclaimed. 'It's rather fragile.'

She shrugged her shoulders: did he think she was so clumsy? Then suddenly the little lid came off, fell on to the ground, and shattered. She gazed at the pieces on the floor in utter amazement and said:

'Oh, it's broken!'

Then she started to laugh: those little bits on the floor looked so funny. It was a slightly hysterical sort of laugh, silly and rather spiteful, like a destructive child. For a moment, Philippe had a feeling of revulsion; the wretched woman had no idea of the torments the purchase of that knick-knack had cost him. When she saw how upset he was, she tried to restrain herself.

'After all, it's hardly my fault, it was cracked anyway . . . Those old things are always a bit decrepit . . . There was something wrong with the lid, did you see how it slipped loose?'

And she again broke into hysterical laughter. Then, seeing that in spite of himself the young man's eyes had filled with tears, she flung her arms tenderly round his neck:

'What a silly you are! I love you all the same. If things didn't get broken, people wouldn't be able to go on selling them. It's all meant to be broken. Look at this, for example, this fan's not even properly stuck together.'

She snatched up a fan and tugged at it so that the silk tore in two. This seemed to stimulate her, so, to prove that, having just spoilt his present, she didn't give a damn about the others, she treated herself to a massacre, hitting the objects to show that none of them was built to last. She smashed up the whole lot. She had a glint in her vacuous eyes and her lips were drawn tightly back over her white teeth. When everything had been reduced to smithereens, she again broke out laughing, slapped the table with the flat of her hand, red in the face, and lisped in a childish voice:

'All gone, done for, no good!'

Caught up in her sudden frenzy, Philippe started laughing too, pushed her down, and began kissing her breasts. Clasping him tightly round the shoulders, she let herself go delightedly; she couldn't remember having had such fun for ages. Then, still clutching him, she said appealingly:

'I say, darling, do you think you could let me have a couple of hundred francs tomorrow? . . . It's a boring old bill from my baker who won't leave me in peace.'

He went pale; then he gave her a final kiss on her forehead and said simply:

'I'll do what I can.'

There was a pause. She began to get dressed. He was standing with his forehead pressed against the window. After a minute, he went over to her and said slowly:

'Nana, you ought to marry me.'

The young woman found this idea so funny that she stopped tying her petticoats.

'You must be mad, my pet! . . . Are you asking me to marry you because I want to borrow two hundred francs from you? . . . The answer's no, never, I'm too fond of you . . . What a stupid thing it would be!'

And as Zoé now came in to help her on with her shoes, the subject was dropped. The maid's eye had immediately been caught by the fragments of the presents lying on the table. She asked if she was to tidy them away, and when her mistress told her to dump the lot she took them away in a corner of her skirt. They could go through her mistress's rubbish in the kitchen and share it out between themselves.

That day, although Nana had banned him from the house, Georges had slipped in. François had seen him arrive, but by now the servants had reached the stage of treating the scrapes her ladyship kept landing herself in as a joke. Georges had just got as far as the small drawing-room when he heard his brother's voice; he stood rooted to the spot behind the door and heard the whole scene, the kisses and the marriage proposal. Shocked and horrified, he went away looking foolish, without waiting to hear more; he had a terrible, empty sensation in his head. It wasn't until he was back in his room over his mother's flat in the Rue Richelieu that his heart burst and he exploded into wild sobs. This time there could be no doubt, and in his mind's eye the same atrocious vision kept looming up, the vision of Nana in his brother's arms. It seemed to him a sort of incest. Each time he thought he'd calmed down, this memory recurred, and in another frenzy of jealousy he would fling himself down on his bed, chewing his sheets and shouting foul abuse, making himself even madder.

He spent the whole day acting like this; to avoid leaving his room, he explained that he had a migraine. When night came, it was even worse; he tossed and turned in a feverish succession of nightmares; if his brother had been living in the house he would have gone and stabbed him to death. When day broke, he tried to reason with himself: it was he who had to die, he was going to throw himself out of the window, under a bus. However, round ten o'clock he went out and roamed all over Paris, lurked round the bridges, and at the last minute felt an irresistible urge to go and see Nana. Maybe a word from her might save him. It was striking three o'clock in the afternoon as he went into the house in the Avenue de Villiers.

At about noon, Madame Hugon had been shattered by some dreadful news: on the previous day, Philippe had been arrested on the charge of having stolen twelve thousand francs of regimental funds. He had been embezzling small sums of money over the last three months in the hope of returning them at a later date, disguising the shortfall by presenting false accounts; and thanks to the incompetence of the authorities, his fraud had only now been detected. Devastated by her son's crime, the old lady's first reaction was anger directed against Nana. She knew of her son's affair, and this unfortunate situation had been a source of great distress to her, keeping her from leaving Paris for fear of some calamity. But not even her worst fears had led her to imagine such a shameful action, and she was now blaming herself for having kept him so short of money. Her legs gave way under her and she slumped into her armchair, so numbed that she felt completely helpless, paralysed, at death's door, unable to do anything. But suddenly she felt comforted: Georges at least was still there at her side, he could act and perhaps save the situation. So without calling for help, because the affair must remain a secret, she laboriously dragged herself upstairs, buoyed up by the thought that there was still someone who loved her. Upstairs she found his room empty. The caretaker told her that Georges had gone out early. In the bedroom was the hint of a second tragedy: the bed with its chewed sheets spelled suffering, the chair on the floor, overturned amongst a pile of books, had a deathly look. Georges must be with that woman. So, dry-eyed, Madame Hugon went determinedly downstairs: she wanted her sons and she was on her way to claim them.

Nana had been having problems all that day. To start with, at nine o'clock the baker turned up with his account, a mere trifle, a bread-bill for a hundred and thirty-three francs which, with her sumptuous style of living, she had never got round to paying. He'd called a score of times before, annoyed at being replaced by another baker the moment he'd cut off her credit. He had the backing of the servants. François was saying that his mistress would never pay up unless he kicked up a real fuss, Charles was talking of going upstairs himself to get a long-overdue bill for straw settled, while Victorine advised waiting until Nana had a gentleman with her and extracting the money by breaking into the 'conversation' without warning. The servants were quite worked up; they used to keep the tradesmen fully informed and spend hours gossiping, revealing their mistress in all her nakedness, giving every possible detail, with the cantankerous pettiness of servants who are living in clover and haven't enough to do. Only the butler Julien made a point of standing up for his mistress: she wasn't a bad sort, really; and when the others accused him of going to bed with her he gave a fatuous grin which enraged the cook, who wished she was a man so as to be able to spit on the backside of such revolting women . . . Without warning his mistress, François had spitefully stationed the baker in the vestibule so that when she came down to lunch she ran into him face to face. She took the bill and told him to come back at about three o'clock. He took himself off, muttering abuse and promising he'd be back on time and get paid, by hook or by crook.

Nana was annoyed by this scene and didn't enjoy her lunch. This time she really must get rid of that fellow; she'd already put the money aside a dozen times before, but on each occasion it had somehow melted away, one day on flowers, on another for a subscription in aid of an old policeman. Anyway, she had faith in Philippe and was even surprised that he hadn't yet appeared with his two hundred francs. It really was bad luck, only the day before she'd bought a whole outfit for Satin, nearly twelve hundred francs for dresses and lingerie, and now there wasn't a twenty-franc piece in the whole house.

About two o'clock, as Nana was beginning to become worried, Labordette appeared with the sketches for the bed, thereby providing a diversion, and her pleasure made her forget her troubles. She clapped her hands and did a delighted little jig. Bursting with curiosity, she bent over the table to examine them while Labordette explained the details.

'Here's the bed, with curved ends, like a boat, decorated with a bunch of roses in bloom and a garland of buds and flowers. The leaves will be a greeny gold and the roses golden red . . . And this is the big bed-head showing dancing Cupids on a silver lattice-work.'

Nana was ecstatic. She interrupted:

'Oh, isn't that cute, the little one in the corner there who's showing his bottom? Don't you agree? And that saucy little laugh . . . They all look terribly saucy! . . . You know, my dear, I'll never dare get up to any little tricks while they're watching! . . .'

She was purring with gratification. The goldsmith had said that there wasn't even a queen who slept in such a splendid bed. There was, however, a minor complication. Labordette showed her two sketches for the bed-end, one reproducing the bed-head motif, the other a completely different theme, a figure of Night swathed in veils which a faun was lifting up to reveal her splendid naked body. He added that if Nana chose that one, the goldsmiths proposed to depict Night in her own likeness. This spicy suggestion made Nana go pale with pleasure. She could see herself as a silver statuette symbolizing steamy nights of love . . .

'Of course, you'll only pose for the head and shoulders', Labordette added.

'Why? . . . When a work of art's involved, I don't give a damn what the sculptor wants me to do!' Nana retorted calmly.

So that was settled, she'd take the second version. He interrupted:

'Wait a second . . . It's six thousand francs more.'

She burst out laughing.

'Good Lord, what do you think that matters? Don't you

know my little muff is rolling in it?'

With her close friends, she'd taken to referring to Count Muffat as the little muff; and her various men would ask her about him in similar terms: 'Did you see your little muff last night? . . . Goodness me, I expected to be seeing your little muff here! . . .' It was a familiarity which she hadn't yet dared use to his face.

Labordette rolled up the sketches and explained the final arrangements: The goldsmiths would undertake to deliver the bed inside two months, about the twenty-fifth of December; a sculptor would come round next week to make a model of Night. As she was showing him out Nana suddenly remembered the baker, and on the spur of the moment asked:

'By the way, you don't happen to have two hundred francs on you, do you?'

One of Labordette's principles—one which had stood him in good stead—was never to lend money to a woman. He had a stock response:

'Afraid not, deary, I'm broke. But would you like me to go and see your little muff?'

She said no, there was no point, she'd squeezed five thousand francs out of the count only two days ago. However, she soon regretted her qualms, for although it was barely half-past two, hard on Labordette's heels the baker made his reappearance, swearing loudly, and unceremoniously sat down on a bench in the front hall. The young woman could hear him from the first floor. She went pale, particularly when she heard the servants voicing their secret delight at her predicament more and more openly. In the kitchen they were splitting their sides with laughter; outside, the coachman was looking in from the yard, while François for no apparent reason went through the hall and hurried back to pass on the latest news, throwing the baker a conspiratorial grin. They were all jeering at their mistress, and the uproar they were making was echoing through the whole house. Their loathing for her, their spying on her, and their filthy jokes at her expense made Nana feel completely isolated. She dropped the idea which had momentarily crossed her mind of trying to borrow the hundred and thirty-three francs from Zoé; she already owed her money and was too proud to want to risk being refused. As she went back into her bedroom she was in such a state of emotion that she was talking to herself:

'OK, my girl, you'll have to rely on yourself. You've got your body and it's better to take advantage of that rather than be insulted.'

So without even asking Zoé to help her she feverishly got dressed; she'd pay a quick visit to Tricon, her final resort in moments of financial crisis. She was in great demand; the old lady was always pressing her and she would refuse or agree according to her need. On those days, increasingly common, when there were holes in her grand establishment needing to be plugged, she could always rely on picking up five hundred francs at Tricon's; it was an easy option and she went there regularly, in the same way as poor people go round to the pawnshop.

As she was leaving her bedroom she ran into Georges, who was standing in the middle of the drawing-room. She didn't notice how deathly pale he was or the dark glow in his dilated eyes. She gave a sigh of relief.

'You've come from your brother?' she said.

'No', the boy replied, turning even paler.

She made a despairing gesture. What did he want? Why was he standing there blocking her way? Look, she was in a hurry. Then she came back:

'Have you got any money?'

'No.'

'Of course, how stupid of me! Never got a penny, not even the price of a bus fare . . . Mummy doesn't like them to have any, does she? And they call themselves men!'

And she continued on her way. He held her back, he wanted to talk to her. In full career, she again said that she hadn't got the time, but his next remark halted her in her tracks.

'Listen to me, I know you're going to marry my brother.'

This was absolutely hilarious; she flopped down on a chair so that she could enjoy a really good laugh.

'Yes', the boy went on. 'And I don't want you to do it . . . You're going to marry me . . . That's why I've come.'

'For crying out loud!' she exclaimed. 'You too? It must be a family vice! I'll never do such a thing! What queer tastes you have. Did I ever remotely ask you to do such a disgusting thing? . . . Neither you nor your brother, never, never, never, do you hear?'

Georges's face lit up. Perhaps he'd got it wrong? He continued:

'Then swear to me you don't go to bed with my brother.'

Nana abruptly sprang to her feet.

'For Christ's sake, now you're really beginning to annoy me! It may be funny for a while but when I keep on telling you again and again that I'm in a hurry! I'll go to bed with your brother if I feel like it. Are you keeping me or paying my bills? Why should I explain my conduct to you? . . . OK, if you want to know, yes, I do go to bed with your brother!'

He gripped her arm hard enough to break it and stammered:

'Don't say that! Don't say that!'

To make him let go she slapped his face.

'So now he's knocking me about, is he? . . . Just look at the little brat! . . . You'd better get going, my little lad . . . pronto! . . . I've only been letting you stay here out of the kindness of my heart . . . Yes, I have, it's no good looking at me with those sheep's eyes! I hope you weren't expecting me to act as your Mummy for the rest of your life, I've got better things to do than bring up little boys!'

Numb with grief he listened to her unprotestingly, but every word was like a deadly stab to his heart. Nana didn't even notice the pain she was causing him; delighted to be able to get off her chest, at his expense, all the frustrations of her morning, she added:

'You're no better than your brother, who's another queer fish. He'd promised me two hundred francs and, can you believe it, I'm still waiting for them . . . It's not that I particularly want his money, which wouldn't be enough to keep me in face-cream . . . But he's let me down when I happen to be short of cash! Well, let me tell you something! Because of your brother I've got to go out and get five hundred francs from some other man! . . .'

He completely lost his head. Barring her way, he clasped his hands and begged her, stammering with tears in his eyes:

'Oh no, don't do that, please don't!'

'Right you are, then', she said. 'OK, where's your money?'

He didn't have any, he'd have given his life to have some. Never had he felt so miserable and so useless, such a little boy. He was sobbing so much and looked so distraught that she finally noticed what a state he was in. Her heart melted. Gently she pushed him to one side:

'Look, my pet, you must let me pass. Be sensible. You're just a baby and it was very nice for a week or so but now I've got business to attend to . . . Just think . . . After all, your brother's a man . . . I don't say, maybe with him . . . Oh, and do me a favour, there's no point in telling him about all this . . . There's no need for him to know where I'm going. When I'm cross, I always say more than I intend to . . .'

She was laughing. Then she caught hold of him and kissed him on the forehead.

'Goodbye, baby . . . This is the end, it's all over and done with, do you get me? I must be off.'

She left him standing in the middle of the drawing-room. Her last words were ringing in his ears like a death-knell: this is the end, it's all over and done with; he could feel the earth opening up under his feet. In his state of shock, he'd forgotten the man waiting for Nana at Tricon's, he could only see Philippe, Philippe perpetually clasped in Nana's naked arms. She didn't deny it, she loved him, for she wanted to protect him from being unhappy because she was going to bed with someone else. No, this was really the end, everything was really over and done with . . . He took a deep breath and looked round the room; there was a crushing weight on his chest. Memories were flooding back to him one by one: the wonderful nights at La Mignotte; the hours spent being caressed and fondled when he could think of himself as her son; the stolen pleasures he'd enjoyed in this very room . . . And now it was all over, he'd never have such wonderful times again. He was too young, he hadn't grown up quickly enough: Philippe had ousted him because he was able to grow a beard. No, this was the end, he couldn't go on living. His lust had become refined into something infinitely tender, a sensual adoration which had taken complete possession of him. And how could he ever forget, when his brother would always be there? His brother, his double, with the same blood in his veins, whose pleasure was driving him mad with jealousy. No, this was the end, he didn't want to go on living . . .

Having seen their mistress leave on foot, the servants had started scurrying noisily around the house, leaving all the doors open. On the hall bench downstairs, the baker was having a laugh with François and Charles. Dashing through the drawing-room, Zoé was surprised to see Georges and asked him if he was waiting for madam. Yes, he'd forgotten to tell her something. Once he was alone he began to look around and, failing to find anything else, he took out of her dressing-room a pair of sharp-pointed scissors which, with her constant compulsion for preening herself, Nana used to trim off little bits of skin or snip off hairs. Then he waited patiently for a whole hour, nervously clutching the scissors in his pocket.

'Here's the mistress', said Zoé, coming back; she must have been keeping watch from the bedroom window.

Everybody scrambled; the laughter stopped; the doors were shut. Georges heard Nana curtly paying off the baker. Then she came upstairs.

'Still here?' she exclaimed on seeing him. 'Ah, there's going to be big trouble between me and you, young fellow-me-lad!'

He followed her as she made her way towards the bedroom.

'Nana, will you marry me?'

She shrugged her shoulders. The whole thing was too stupid for words, she refused to answer any more. She decided to shut the door in his face.

'Nana, will you marry me?'

She slammed the door. He pushed it open again with one hand, took the scissors out of his pocket with the other, and without saying a word, thrust its points deep into his chest.

Sensing that something dreadful was happening, Nana had turned round. When she saw him stab himself, she spluttered indignantly:

'How stupid can you be, plain stupid! . . . Will you behave yourself, you naughty little boy! . . . And with my scissors, too! . . . Oh, good God, good God! . . .'

She became alarmed. The boy had fallen on his knees. He stabbed himself again and collapsed face downward on the carpet, blocking the doorway. Nana completely lost her head and started screaming at the top of her voice; she was too terrified to step over the body barring her way and preventing her from running for help.

'Zoé! Zoé! Come here quickly, make him stop, it's really too stupid, a little boy like that! And now he's killing himself! And in my house, too! Have you ever seen anything like it?'

He was frightening her. His eyes were closed; he'd gone very white. There wasn't much blood, just a trickle forming a small patch half-hidden by the waistcoat. She was just bracing herself to step over the body when she saw something which made her shrink back: through the drawing-room door opposite, which had been left open, there was an old lady coming towards her. She recognized Madame Hugon. What was she doing here? Nana continued to retreat in horror; she was still wearing her hat and gloves. Terror-stricken, she started to defend herself:

'It wasn't me', she stammered. 'I swear it wasn't me! . . . He wanted me to marry him, I refused, and he's killed himself!'

Pale-faced, dressed in black, the white-haired Madame Hugon continued to approach. In the carriage on the way here, brooding on Philippe's action, she'd completely forgotten about Georges. A plan was shaping in her mind to plead with Nana to give evidence on her son's behalf; perhaps that woman could give the judge some sort of explanation for his conduct that might soften his heart. Downstairs the house had been left open, and she was painfully dragging herself upstairs on her bad legs when shouts of horror had led her to this room where a man in a blood-stained shirt was lying on the ground. It was her other son, Georges.

Nana kept repeating, idiotically:

'He wanted me to marry him, I refused, and he's killed himself.'

Madame Hugon didn't cry out. She knelt down: yes, it was her son, her other boy, it was Georges. One son was disgraced, the other one murdered. As her life collapsed around her, she felt no surprise. She was kneeling on the carpet, not realizing where she was, unaware of anyone, staring intently at her son's face with her hand on his heart, listening. She gave a little gasp: she'd felt a heartbeat. Then she raised her head, examined this bedroom and this woman, and seemed to remember. Her glazed eyes began to blaze; her silence was so impressive, so terrible, that Nana trembled as she continued to defend herself, across the body that was lying between them.

'I swear to you, Madame Hugon . . . If his brother was here he'd be able to explain to you . . .'

'His brother's been caught stealing and has been sent to gaol', their mother said harshly.

Words stuck in Nana's throat. Where was the reason for all this? Now the other man had been stealing! Was the whole family crazy? She felt unable to cope any more. Feeling a stranger in her own house, she let Madame Hugon issue her instructions. The servants had appeared; the old lady insisted on Georges's being carried down, unconscious, to her carriage. She wanted to get him out of this house even at the risk of killing him. Nana watched in a stupor as the servants lifted poor little Zizi up by his legs and shoulders and carried him away, followed by his mother, now exhausted, clutching at the furniture for support, crushed by the loss of everything she held dear. On the landing, she turned and sobbed:

'Oh, the harm you've done us! All the harm you've done us!'

That was all. Still stupefied, still wearing her hat and gloves, Nana sat down. The carriage had left, the house was once again massively silent; and she sat there motionless, her mind a blank, her head buzzing from all these events; and it was here that Count Muffat found her when he arrived a quarter of an hour later. She released her feelings in a flood of words, telling him the dreadful story, going into all the details over and over again, picking up the blood-stained scissors and demonstrating each time how Zizi had stabbed himself. Above all, she was anxious to establish her innocence.

'Look, darling, is it any fault of mine? If you had to judge me, would you condemn me? . . . Of course I didn't tell Philippe to put his hand in the till, any more than I encouraged that poor little wretch to slaughter himself . . . It's me who's suffered most in all this. People come to my house and act stupidly, they hurt my feelings and treat me as if I was a tramp . . .'

She burst into tears; her nervous reaction had left her weak and emotional, extremely sorry for herself and utterly miserable.

'And you don't look very pleased either . . . Just ask Zoé if I had anything to do with it . . . Zoé, do tell the count, explain to him.'

The maid had gone off to fetch a towel and a basin of water from the bathroom, and for the last few minutes had been scrubbing at the carpet to remove the blood-stains while they were still fresh.

'Oh yes, sir', she said, 'madam is really upset.'

Muffat was in a daze, stunned by the drama, thinking all the time of this mother who must be mourning her son. He knew how upright she was and could see her in her widow's weeds slowly sinking into her grave at Les Fondettes. Meanwhile Nana was growing more and more frantic; the image of Zizi falling with a red hole in his shirt was driving her distraught.

'And he was such a sweetie, so gentle and caressing . . . Ah, you know, my pet, I loved my little baby, I'm sorry if that makes you cross, there's nothing I can do about it, I just can't help it! Anyway, it can't affect you now, he's not there any more . . . You've got what you wanted, you can be sure of never catching us out again . . .'

And she was so overcome at this last thought that he ended by comforting her. Come along, she must be strong; and she was quite right, it wasn't her fault. However, she stopped crying of her own accord and said to him:

'Listen, you must go off and find out what's happening about him . . . Be quick, off you go straight away, I want to know!'

He picked up his hat and went off to gather news of Georges. When he came back three-quarters of an hour later, he saw Nana anxiously peering out of a window and he called up from the street that the lad wasn't dead and there was even hope of saving his life. She immediately broke into an exuberant dance of joy, singing and saying how wonderful life was. Meanwhile, Zoé was not pleased with her carpet-cleaning; she couldn't take her eyes off the stain, and each time she went by she'd mutter:

'You know, madam, it's not gone away . . .'

And indeed, it kept reappearing, a pale red stain on a white rosette in the carpet, like a rim of blood blocking the doorway to the bedroom itself.

'Nonsense!' Nana said. 'It'll be rubbed out by people's feet.'

By the next day, Count Muffat too had forgotten about the incident. In the cab taking him to the Rue Richelieu, he had for a moment promised himself not to go back to that woman. It was a warning from Heaven, and he could see Philippe's and Georges' misfortunes as heralding his own downfall. But neither the sight of Madame Hugon in tears nor the boy in a raging fever had affected him enough to make him stick to his promise, and all that remained from this sudden, brief tremor was a secret delight at being rid of the rivalry of this charming youngster who had always irked him. He'd now become utterly besotted by his obsessive passion, the sort of passion experienced by men who've never known what it is to be young. He loved Nana and needed to know that she belonged only to him, to hear her voice, touch her, feel her breath. It was a feeling of tenderness transcending the senses, a pure feeling, an anxious affection jealous of her past; he would sometimes dream of being redeemed and pardoned, and see them both on their knees before God the Father. He was becoming more religious every day, a regular church-goer, going to confession and Mass, always at odds with himself, combining the delights of sin and contrition with feelings of deep remorse. And since his confessor had given him leave to let his love burn itself out, he'd grown accustomed to this daily exercise in damnation, redeeming himself by bursts of religious fervour and humble piety. He was so naive that in expiation of his sin he was trying to offer his own atrocious suffering, which was becoming harder and harder to bear. He was set on his path of martyrdom, an earnest and sincere believer who had fallen into the clutches of an insatiably sensual whore. His greatest torment was the woman's constant promiscuity; he couldn't become used to having to share her with others, nor could he ever understand her idiotic whims. He wanted the eternal, steadfast love which she'd promised him and for which he was paying her. But he could feel that she was a liar, incapable of restraint, giving her body to friends or anyone who happened to come along, nothing but a good-hearted, stupid woman with an inborn compulsion to strip off.

When he saw Foucarmont leaving her house at an unusual time one morning, he made a scene. Fed up with his jealousy, she flared up: she'd already shown him how nice she was several times before, for example that evening when he'd caught her with Georges, she'd been the first to go to him and admit she was wrong and hugged and kissed him to get him to let bygones be bygones. But now it was becoming too much of a good thing, his pigheadedness in refusing to understand women was beginning to get on her nerves. She didn't mince her words:

'OK, fair enough, I've just spent the night with Foucarmont! So what? That puts you out, eh, my little muff?'

It was the first time she'd used her 'little muff' to his face. Her frank admission had taken his breath away, and as he stood there with clenched fists she strode up to him and looked him straight in the eyes.

'So that's enough of that, understand? If you don't like it, you can do me the favour of shoving off . . . I don't want you going about yelling in my house . . . I intend to be independent, so just get that into your head. When I fancy a man, I go to bed with him, it's as simple as that . . . And you'd better make up your mind pretty smartly: you can stay or you can go.'

She went over to the door and opened it. He stayed; and this became her way of attaching him to her more and more; at the slightest disagreement she'd renew her offer, in the most offensive terms: she'd not have any trouble replacing him with someone better, never fear, she could have her pick; and they'd be men with real blood in their veins, not old fusspots. He would cringe and hope for better times, when she'd be in need of money and full of affection; and then, for one night of love that made up for a whole week of martyrdom, he could forget everything. His reconciliation with his wife had made life at home a hell. Abandoned by Fauchery, who'd once more fallen into Rose's clutches, the countess was trying to forget by launching into a series of love-affairs; and in her feverish anxiety as a woman nearing 40 she was constantly on edge and turning their home into a bedlam of mad activity. Since her marriage, Estelle had stopped seeing her father; this insignificant beanpole of a woman had suddenly been transformed into an iron-willed termagant, so domineering that Daguenet was terrified of her. He had been converted and now went to Mass with his wife, and was furious with his father-in-law who was ruining them for the sake of a worthless creature. The only person showing the count some sort of kindness was Monsieur Venot, who was biding his time. He had even managed to worm his way into the Avenue de Villiers, and his permanent smile could be seen smirking behind the doors of Nana's house as well as Sabine's. So, driven out of his own home by shame and boredom, the wretched Muffat still preferred life with Nana, where he was being constantly insulted.

Soon their relationship was reduced to one thing: money. One day, having given his word that he'd let her have ten thousand francs, he dared to turn up empty-handed. She'd been working on him with tender care for the last two days, and his failure to come up to scratch, as well as having wasted so much affection, unleashed a torrent of abuse. She was livid with rage.

'So you've not got the dough . . . In that case, my little muff, you can go back where you came from double-quick! What an oaf! He wanted his oats, did he? Well, no cash, no crumpet, d'you get it?'

He tried to explain that he'd have the money the day after tomorrow; she savagely interrupted him:

'And how about my creditors? I'll be sold up while the noble gent gets a free cuddle . . . Just take a look at yourself, will you? Do you imagine I love you because of your manly beauty? When someone's got an ugly mug like yours, he has to pay any woman who's prepared to put up with it . . . What the hell! If you don't bring those ten thousand francs round this very night, you won't get the chance of sucking even the tip of my little finger . . . I'll send you back to your wife, don't worry!'

That evening he brought her the ten thousand francs. Nana offered him her lips, and the long kiss he planted on them consoled him for an interminable day of torment. The thing which really bored the young woman was having him perpetually hanging round her skirts. She complained about it to Monsieur Venot and begged him to take her little muff back to his wife. What was the point of their being reconciled? And she told him how much she regretted having had anything to do with it, because it hadn't stopped him from falling back on her. Some days she was so angry that she'd lose sight of her own interests and swear she'd play such a dirty trick on him that he'd never want to set foot in the house again. But, as she exclaimed, slapping her thighs, he'd have thanked her and hung on even if she'd spat in his face. So rows over money continued; her demands were quite shameless and she would subject him to the most violent abuse for utterly trivial sums; she was permanently and despicably rapacious, brutally emphasizing that she went to bed with him purely because of his money, that she didn't enjoy it, that she was in love with someone else; and she would add, what hard luck it was for her to have to depend on an idiot like him! And they didn't even want his company at the Tuileries any more and were talking about demanding his resignation. The Empress had said: 'What a disgusting man!' That was certainly true; and Nana would round off their squabble with the same comment:

'God, what a disgusting man you are!'

By now, she'd completely broken free and abandoned any sort of restraint. Every day she would drive round the lake in the Bois, picking up men whom she then got to know far more intimately elsewhere later on. It was hustling on a grand scale, soliciting alfresco, accosting by the most notable Paris tarts, who flaunted their charms amid the glitter and luxury and under the tolerant smiles of the cream of smart society. Duchesses would point her out to each other with a nod, upstart middle-class wives copied her hats; sometimes as her landau drove by it would hold up a queue of prestigious carriages, bankers whose money-bags controlled the finances of Europe, ministers whose thick fingers held France in a strangle-hold; and Nana was one of this smart Bois de Boulogne set and held a place of honour in it; she was known in every capital, every visiting foreigner asked to meet her;

her orgies and wild escapades added lustre to this brilliant crowd; she was its crowning glory, the epitome of a nation's keenest pleasures. Then there were her one-night stands, an endless series of short-lived affairs which she herself couldn't remember the following morning, visits to the smartest restaurants, often the Madrid* when the weather was fine. The diplomatic corps queued up for her, she would dine with Lucy Stewart, Caroline Héquet, and Maria Blond in the company of men who murdered the French language and were paying to be amused, booking them for the evening merely for that purpose, since they were so world-weary and empty-headed that they didn't even touch them. And the girls described it as 'going out for a laugh' and went home glad to have cold-shouldered them and finished the night in the arms of one of their fancy men.

As long as Nana refrained from flaunting them, Count Muffat pretended to know nothing of such goings-on. He was in any case unhappy as a result of the petty humiliations of his daily life in the Avenue de Villiers, which was turning into a sort of inferno, a madhouse where everything was falling apart. Things were in a constant state of crisis; Nana even took to brawling with her servants. For a while, the coachman Charles was very much in her good books; when she was in a restaurant she would send a waiter out with glasses of beer for him; if he got caught in a traffic-jam she would find him very amusing, and sit in her landau laughing and commenting on his 'slanging-match with the cabbies'. Then for no reason at all she said he was an idiot. She squabbled with him constantly over the cost of hay, bran, and oats and, for all her love of animals, claimed that her horses were getting too much to eat. One day when they were settling up the accounts, she accused him of swindling her. Charles flared up and told her bluntly that she was a slut, he preferred her horses to her because they didn't go to bed with all and sundry . . . She replied in kind; the count had to separate them and sack the coachman. However, this was the signal for a general stampede amongst her staff. Some diamonds were stolen and Victorine and François left. Julien too disappeared, and there was a rumour that the master himself had appealed to him and offered him a considerable sum of money to go, because he was sleeping with madam. Every week there were fresh faces in the servants' quarters. Everything was in a mess; the house turned into a sort of passage along which employment agencies' unemployables hurtled at startling speed. Only Zoé stayed on, looking prim, anxious to bring some sort of order into this chaos merely until such time as she'd put sufficient on one side to set up on her own, a plan which she'd had in mind for a long while.

These were only relatively mild problems. The count bore with Madame Maloir's stupidity and played bezique with her, although she smelt like a stale sock; he also put up with Madame Lerat and her tittle-tattle and with the miserable little brat Louis, always complaining of feeling ill, who was afflicted with some unsavoury secret disease inherited from his unknown father. But Muffat had worse things to bear than these. One evening, behind a closed door, he'd heard Nana raging to Zoé that she'd just been diddled by a man claiming to be a millionaire, a handsome man, yes, who said he was an American and owned gold-mines over there, a dirty swine who'd bilked her by slipping out while she was still asleep without leaving a cent; he'd even gone off with a block of cigarette paper. Not wanting to hear any more, the count had crept away downstairs on tiptoe, as pale as death. On another occasion, he'd been forced to face the truth: Nana had become infatuated with a baritone, a singer in a café, who'd then ditched her, leaving her in such an hysterical, heart-broken state that she'd melodramatically decided to commit suicide by drinking a glass of water in which she'd dissolved a handful of matches; this made her very ill but failed to kill her. The count had to look after her and suffer in silence as she retailed the whole passionate story, accompanied by sobs and vows never to fall in love again. She declared all men were pigs and she despised them; however, she still couldn't remain heart-free and always had some fancy man or other in tow, in one unaccountable infatuation after another; her jaded body had acquired perverse tastes. Ever since Zoé had been letting things slide the whole household was in a state of chaos, so much so that Muffat didn't dare open a door, draw a curtain, or look into a wardrobe; nothing was working any more, there were men all over the place, constantly bumping into each other. He now coughed before going into a room; one evening when he'd been out of the dressing-room for a couple of minutes, ordering the carriage to be hitched up, he came back and nearly caught Nana with her arms round Francis's neck as he was putting the final touches to madam's hair. She'd suddenly give herself to the first man who happened to be around, taking her pleasure on the spur of the moment behind the count's back, in any free corner, whether she was dressed up to go out or in her chemise. She'd come back to him flushed and radiant from her stolen pleasure. What a chore it was making love with him!

The wretched man had been reduced to such agonies of jealousy that he felt positively relieved when Nana was with Satin. He'd have encouraged Nana in this vice if only to keep men away. But in this department, too, things were going wrong: Nana was being as unfaithful to Satin as she was to the count, hurling herself enthusiastically into wild passing affairs. She'd pick tarts up from the street; driving home, she'd take a fancy to some slut walking along in the road; she'd feel randy, her imagination would take over, she'd invite the little slut up to her room, pay her, and send her away. She would disguise herself as a man and have orgies in brothels; watching people doing it helped relieve her boredom. Annoyed at being continually deserted, Satin was constantly turning the house upside-down with dreadful scenes; she'd at last succeeded in completely dominating Nana, who respected her. Muffat even had hopes of making an ally of her; when he was too intimidated he'd get her to tackle Nana on his behalf, and she'd already forced her darling Nana to take him back a couple of times. In return he did things to help her, giving friendly warnings and retreating into the background at the slightest hint from her. However, their pact didn't really last very long: Satin was equally crazy. Some days she'd go completely berserk in uncontrollable fits of rage or love which left her half-dead, but still looking pretty. Zoé must have been egging her on, because she'd have quiet chats with her in out-of-the-way corners, as if she was looking forward to recruiting her for her grand design which she hadn't yet divulged to anyone.

However, oddly enough, there were still certain things that

stuck in Count Muffat's throat. While he had put up with Satin for months and finally come round to accepting Nana's unknown sexual partners, the constant stream of males leaping in and out of her bed, he was furious at the thought of being deceived by someone belonging to his own set or even by someone he knew. When she had admitted her affair with Foucarmont he'd been so hurt, and thought the young man's duplicity so abominable, that he'd wanted to challenge him to a duel. As he didn't know where to find seconds in this sort of matter he turned to Labordette, who was dumbfounded and couldn't help laughing.

'A duel over Nana? The whole of Paris would laugh at you, my dear count. Nobody fights over Nana, the idea's ridiculous.'

The count went very pale. He made a violent gesture.

'Very well then, I'll slap his face in public.'

It took Labordette a whole hour to make him see reason. A slap in the face would give the whole affair a very ugly turn; that very same evening, everyone would know the real reason for the duel; the press would have a field-day. And his arguments always led to the same conclusion:

'It's out of the question!'

Each time his words were like a stab in the heart for Muffat: so he couldn't even fight for the woman he loved; everybody would have roared with laughter. Never had the pathetic nature of his passion been brought home to him more painfully, its deep seriousness lost in the wasteland of cynical hedonism surrounding him. So he gave up the struggle and accepted the inevitable; from now on he watched a steady stream of friends, all the men who lived there, making themselves at home in his house.

In the space of a few months Nana gobbled them up one by one; her luxurious tastes had sharpened her appetite; she could clean them out in one bite. It was Foucarmont's turn first; he didn't even last a fortnight. He'd been hoping to retire from the navy, and over his last ten years at sea had managed to put by thirty thousand or so francs to use for speculation in the United States; but his instinctive caution, or indeed miserliness, was thrown to the winds and he gave her everything, even signing bills of credit mortgaging his future. When Nana discarded him, he was penniless. But she was very kind to him and advised him to go back to his ship: what was the point of persisting? Now he was broke, they couldn't possibly stay together, he must surely realize that and be sensible. A ruined man dropped through her fingers like a ripe fruit, to rot quietly on the ground, by himself.

Nana next moved on to Steiner, without repugnance but equally without affection. She called him a dirty Jew, seemingly satisfying an age-old hatred which she hardly realized. He was fat and stupid and she hustled him along, keen to get shot of this Prussian as quickly as possible. He'd given up Simonne. His Bosphorus venture was beginning to look shaky, and Nana's crazy demands hastened its demise. Miraculously, he managed to hold out for one more month, covering the whole of Europe with notices, prospectuses, and advertisements in a colossal publicity campaign, squeezing money out of the remotest countries. And all these funds, the speculators' reserves of gold and the tiny nest-eggs of the poor, were engulfed in the Avenue de Villiers. He'd also gone into association with an iron-master in Alsace; in a corner of that province there were miners black with coal-dust and dripping in sweat who were straining their muscles and wrenching their limbs to satisfy Nana's pleasures. She consumed everything like some great fire, the fruits of honest toil and the dishonest profits of currency sharks. This time she finished Steiner off and put him back on the street after sucking him so dry that he didn't even have the strength to think up any further skulduggery. His bank collapsed, he went in fear and trembling of the police, he wandered around mumbling incoherently. He'd just been made bankrupt, and at the mere mention of money this man who'd been used to handling millions flew into a panic like a little child. One evening in Nana's house he burst into tears and asked if she could lend him a hundred francs to pay his maid. Amused to see such an end to this terrible character who'd been ruthlessly exploiting the market for the last twenty years, Nana, out of the kindness of her heart, handed him the money, saying:

'You know, I'm letting you have this because it's very funny . . . But listen, you're too long in the tooth for me to keep you . . . So do find another job, there's a good chap . . .'

Nana immediately turned her attention to la Faloise, who'd been clamouring for the honour of being ruined by her for a long while; this would consecrate him as the smartest man about town; it was a blemish in his career, he needed a woman to launch him. Paris would learn all about him, in a couple of months he'd be reading his name in the papers. However, Nana took only six weeks. La Faloise's inheritance consisted of property, land, pastures, woods, farms. He had to dispose of the lot, one after another. Each acre provided just one mouthful. The leaves quivering in the sunlight, the tall, ripe wheat, the golden September vines, the long meadow-grass in which cows stood munching up to their bellies, everything went, as if swallowed up in an abyss. There was even a river, a cement quarry, and three mills; they all vanished. Nana shot through like a cloud of invading locusts, a devastating fire flattening a whole province. Wherever she set her little foot, there was burnt earth. Farm by farm, meadow after meadow, she gobbled up his inheritance without even noticing, just as she gobbled up a bag of sugared almonds on her lap between meals. It was quite unimportant, just so many lumps of sugar-candy. But one night the only thing left was a tiny area of woodland. She swallowed it scornfully; it was hardly worth opening your mouth for. La Faloise would give an idiotic laugh, sucking the silver knob of his stick. He had crushing debts, his income was less than a hundred francs, he was faced with the prospect of going back to the provinces and living with a crotchety old uncle; but it didn't matter, he was 'smart', his name had twice appeared in the *Figaro*, and with his scrawny neck sticking out between the points of his turn-down collar, his slouching shoulders covered by a jacket that was too short, he shuffled round screeching like a parrot, putting on a wooden, world-weary air, like a puppet incapable of any real emotion. Nana found him so irritating that in the end she thumped him.

Meanwhile Fauchery had come back, brought round by his cousin. Poor Fauchery was now caught up in domesticity: after breaking with the countess, he'd fallen into the hands of Rose, who treated him as her real husband; Mignon was merely her ladyship's factotum. Since he'd become head of the family, every time the journalist went to bed with other women he was obliged to lie to Rose and take careful precautions, like some scrupulous, good-hearted husband intending to settle down in the end. Nana's great achievement was to lay hands on him and gobble up a newspaper of his which he'd set up with money from a friend. She didn't flaunt herself with him in public, in fact she enjoyed treating him as a man who needs to stay in the background. Whenever she mentioned Rose, she referred to her as 'poor old Rose'. Fauchery's paper set her up in flowers for a couple of months; she had subscribers in the country; she took the lot, from feature news-reports to theatre gossip-columns; then, having run the staff off its legs and thrown its whole management into chaos, she satisfied a major whim of hers, a water-garden in part of her house in the Avenue de Villiers; this put paid to the printing-press. In any case, the whole thing was just a joke. When Mignon, delighted at the affair, hurried round to see if he couldn't persuade her to take Fauchery over completely, she asked him if he was pulling her leg: a fellow without a penny to his name, making a living from his articles and plays? Definitely not! That sort of silliness was good enough for a talented woman like 'poor old Rose'. She became suspicious that Mignon might try to play some dirty trick on her, such as splitting on them to his wife. And, as Fauchery's only means of paying her now was by giving her publicity in his articles, she gave him the sack.

However, she still kept pleasant memories of him: they'd both had a good time at the expense of that idiot la Faloise. Perhaps the thought of getting together again might never have occurred to them but for the pleasurable excitement of making fun of such a cretin. What a lark it was! They'd kiss each other to his face and go on outrageous sprees which he paid for; they'd send him off on errands to the other side of Paris, and when he returned they'd crack jokes and make innuendoes which he couldn't understand. One day, egged on by the journalist, she'd made a bet that she'd slap la Faloise's face and she did it, that very evening; then, warming to the task, she went on doing it, delighted to prove what cowards men are. She nicknamed him her 'punchball' and ordered him to come forward and take his medicine; it made her hand smart, she hadn't yet quite got the knack. La Faloise was laughing, with his dead-beat look and tears in his eyes. He was delighted that they were on such intimate terms; it was marvellous.

'Do you know', he said one evening, all excited after she'd been boxing his ears, 'you ought to marry me. What do you think? We'd have lots of fun together!'

It was a genuine proposal. He'd been quietly planning to marry her; he wanted to stagger Paris: Nana's husband, eh? Wouldn't that be smart! A pretty smashing way to crown his career, what? Nana quickly put him in his place:

'Me marry you? . . . Good God, if I'd have had something like that in mind, I would've found a husband ages ago! And someone worth twenty of you, my boy . . . I've had masses of proposals. Listen, just count them up: Philippe, Georges, Foucarmont, Steiner, that's four to begin with and that's without all the others you don't know. They all sing the same song . . . As soon as I start being nice to them, off they go straight away: "Will you marry me, will you marry me?" . . .'

She was becoming heated and finally exploded in indignation:

'No, I don't want to! . . . Do you think I'm made for that sort of caper? Just look at me, if I got saddled with a man for good, I wouldn't be Nana any more. And anyway, it's all so sordid . . .'

She gave a gulp of disgust and spat, as if she'd suddenly seen all the foulness of the world in front of her.

One evening, la Faloise was missing. A week later they learned that he was in the country, at the house of an uncle who was a passionate botanizer; la Faloise was mounting his specimens for him and was in the running to marry a very ugly and very pious cousin. Nana didn't shed many tears on his account; she simply said to the count:

'Well, my little muff, there's one rival less . . . You're gloating now, but let me tell you, he was getting earnest. He wanted to marry me.'

He went pale. She put her arms round his neck and said laughingly, emphasizing each barbed word with a kiss:

'That makes you cross, doesn't it? Because you can't marry

me . . . While they're all boring me stiff as they fall over each other to marry me, you have to sit seething in your corner . . . It's no go, you've got to wait till your wife kicks the bucket . . . Ah, if your wife really did peg out, how you'd come crawling to me on your hands and knees straight away, you'd give me the whole works, sighs, tears, solemn promises . . . It'd be nice, darling, wouldn't it?'

She was speaking in a softer voice, cruelly playing up to him, leading him on. He blushed and returned her kisses, full of emotion. Suddenly she burst out:

'Jesus! I guessed as much, he's waiting for his wife to kick the bucket! Well, that takes the cake, he's an even bigger bastard than the others!'

Muffat had resigned himself to accepting the other men, but in an effort to retain some last remnant of dignity he expected to be treated with respect by the servants and by the regular visitors to the Avenue de Villiers; he wanted to show that, as the chief provider, he was her official lover. His passion for Nana never weakened and he maintained his position by paying; it cost him a lot, even for a smile; he was also fleeced and never got value for money; but it was like some dread disease and he couldn't cure himself. When he went into Nana's bedroom, he merely opened the windows for a moment to get rid of the smell of other people, the stench of all the men, fair-haired or dark, the acrid cigar-smoke that stifled him. The bedroom was being made into a public right-of-way; lots of feet were being wiped on the doorstep and none was deterred by the blood-stain on the threshold. This stain had become a permanent challenge to Zoé, an obsession for a tidy-minded girl irritated that it wouldn't go away; she found it impossible to take her eyes off it, and every time she went into her mistress's bedroom she'd say:

'It's odd, it's still there . . . And it's not as if there aren't enough people walking over it.'

Nana had been getting better news about Georges, who was convalescing at Les Fondettes, and she invariably made the same reply:

'Well, it takes time . . . It *is* getting paler as people walk on it.'

Indeed, each of her men, Foucarmont, Steiner, la Faloise,

and Fauchery, had taken away some of the stain on the soles of their shoes. Muffat took the same anxious interest in it as Zoé, and in spite of himself kept scrutinizing it to detect, in the gradual fading of the pink stain, how many men were going through the door. He himself was secretly afraid of the stain and always stepped over it, filled with the sudden dread that he might crush something living underfoot, a naked limb lying on the floor.

Then, as soon as he was in the bedroom, his head would swim, he'd forget everything, the males scrambling to come in, the tragedy still lurking in the doorway. Sometimes, in the fresh air outside in the street, he would rebel and shed tears of shame, swearing he'd never go back in there. Yet as soon as the door-curtain closed behind him he would fall under her spell, he could feel himself dissolving in the gentle warmth of her room, his body impregnated by her scent, thrilling with lust and a desire for obliteration. This pious man whose experiences of heavenly bliss normally occurred in splendid chapels was gripped here by the same religious ecstasy as when he surrendered to the exaltation of solemn organ music or the scent of incense, kneeling in front of a stained-glass window. This woman possessed him, body and soul, with the despotic power of a jealous God of wrath, terrifying him and offering him brief spasms of joy followed by hours of torment, of fearful visions of hell and eternal damnation and suffering. He would stammer the same prayers, feeling the desperation and above all the humility of a mortal man cursed and crushed by the burden of his earthy origin. The desires of his flesh and the needs of his soul had become intertwined and seemed to be springing from the depths of his being, in the same way as the tree of life opens out into a single blossom. He capitulated to love and religion, those two mainsprings of human existence; but the madness which overcame him in Nana's bedroom always conquered the struggles and scruples of his reason; he would plunge trembling into the all-powerful maw of her sex in the same way as he collapsed overwhelmed by the mystery of the almighty heavens.

When she realized his utter abjection, Nana's triumph turned to tyranny; she had a passionate and instinctive desire to degrade; not satisfied with destroying things, she had to debase them. Her dainty hands carried foul infection and anything they broke went rotten. And, idiot-like, he went along with her, with vague memories of saints devoured by lice and eating their own excrement. When she'd got him behind closed doors in her bedroom, she gave herself the treat of celebrating the depravity of mankind. In the beginning it was just a joke; she would hit him, gently, and order him to do odd things, such as use baby-talk in finishing his sentences:

'Now say like me: . . . and diddles can't be bothered . . .'

Or else she'd get down on all fours on her fur rugs, in her chemise, and pretend to be a bear, going round growling as if she wanted to eat him up; she even playfully nipped his calves. Then she'd stand up and say:

'Now it's your turn . . . I bet you're not half as good a bear as me!'

It was still quite charming. As a bear, she amused him with her shock of red hair and her white skin. He'd laugh and go down on all fours himself growling and snapping at her calves while she ran away from him, pretending to be scared.

'Aren't we stupid, really?' she'd say to him eventually. 'You just can't imagine what a sight you are, my pet! If they could only see you now, at the Tuileries!'

But soon the sport turned nasty. With her, it wasn't cruelty, because she was still a good-natured girl; it was as if a growing wave of violence was sweeping through the closed bedroom and making wild beasts of them both, filling their minds with delirious sexual fantasies. Their earlier pious fears, when they would lie awake at night, had been replaced by bestial impulses, a mad urge to get down on all fours and bite. Then one day as he was pretending to be a bear, she gave him such a violent shove that he fell against a piece of furniture, and when she saw the bump on his forehead she couldn't help laughing. From then on, with pleasant memories of what she'd done to la Faloise, she took to beating and kicking him about like an animal.

'Gee up! Gee up! . . . You're a horse . . . Gee up, you rotten old hack, keep going! . . .'

Sometimes he was a dog. She'd throw her scented handkerchief to the other side of the room and he had to scamper over and retrieve it with his teeth, crawling on his hands and knees.

'Come on, Fido! Look out, if you don't make it snappy, you're going to catch it! Well done, Fido! You're a nice obedient dog . . . Now sit up and beg!'

And he enjoyed being humiliated and liked being an animal; but he wanted to sink even lower. He'd shout:

'Hit me harder! Wouf! Wouf! I'm a mad dog, thrash me!'

She suddenly took it into her head that he must come along one evening wearing his grand chamberlain's uniform. When he appeared in all his finery, with his sword and hat, white knee-breeches and flashy, embroidered, red dress-coat, and the symbolic key of office hanging down from its skirt on the left, she hooted with laughter. She found the key particularly funny and launched into wildly obscene speculations as to its purpose. Still laughing uproariously and carried away by her lack of respect for the great of this world and her pleasure in degrading them in the shape of this pompous official uniform, she shook and pinched him, shouting: 'Off you go, Chamberlain!' and accompanying her words with a series of kicks up his backside which were also directed enthusiastically at the Tuileries Palace and the high and mighty Imperial court lording it over the cowardly grovelling people of France. That's what she thought of high society! She was settling old scores and satisfying an inherited, unconscious, family grudge. Then, when the chamberlain had undressed and his clothes were strewn all over the floor, she yelled at him to jump on them: he jumped on them; she yelled at him to spit on them: he spat on them; and she yelled at him to stamp on the gold and eagles and his insignia: and he stamped on them. Crash! It was a general demolition, nothing was to be left standing, she was smashing a chamberlain in the same way as she would smash a scent-bottle or a sweetmeat dish, turning it into rubbish, just so much garbage for the gutter.

Meanwhile the goldsmiths hadn't kept their word and the bed wasn't delivered till towards the middle of January. Muffat happened to be in Normandy, negotiating the sale of what remained from the wreckage of his estate; Nana was demanding four thousand francs immediately. He expected to be away for two days but, having completed his business early, he hurried back and went straight round to the Avenue de Villiers without bothering to call in at the Rue Miromesnil. It was striking ten o'clock. He had a key to a side-door opening on to the Rue Cardinet and went upstairs without being seen by anybody. In the drawing-room he came across Zoé busy polishing some bronzes; she looked stunned and completely at a loss. In an attempt to delay him she launched into a long rigmarole about Monsieur Venot, who'd been trying to get hold of him for the last two days; he'd looked very upset and had already begged her a couple of times to ask the count to go round to his house if he went straight to the Avenue de Villiers. Muffat listened without understanding what she was talking about; then, noticing her embarrassment, he was suddenly overcome by a fit of jealous rage, something that he thought he had become incapable of. He rushed over to the bedroom door, through which he could hear laughter. The double-door burst open and Zoé withdrew, shrugging her shoulders; she couldn't help it if her mistress had taken leave of her senses; this time she'd have to get out of it on her own.

When he saw what was going on inside Muffat uttered a cry:

'Oh God! Oh God!'

The new bedroom was glittering with an opulence that was truly royal. The velvet drapes, flesh-coloured like the tea-rose pink sky on fine evenings when Venus is gleaming against the soft glow of the setting sun on the horizon, were dotted with the bright stars of silver buttons, while the barley-sugar gilt mouldings descending from each corner and the gold lace round the central panels seemed like darting flames, tresses of red hair floating loose, half-veiling the stark simplicity of the room and emphasizing its voluptuous cool tints. Opposite stood the gold and silver bed with its glittering new carvings, a throne fit to display the royal beauty of her naked limbs, an altar Byzantine in its luxury, a worthy setting for the irresistible power of the curved slit of her sex, which she was flaunting shamelessly with the divine arrogance of some awe-inspiring idol. And lying beside her, against the snow-white breasts of this all-powerful goddess, there was a floundering, sordid, comical, miserable wreck, the Marquis de Chouard in his night-shirt.

The count had clasped his hands together, shuddering in every limb and kept repeating:

'Oh God! Oh God!'

The golden roses of this elegantly curved bed, these bunches of golden roses blooming amongst the golden green foliage, were flourishing in honour of the Marquis de Chouard; it was in his honour that these Cupids, laughing like love-sick little boys, were bending forward from the bed-head and tumbling round on their silver lattice-work, while at his feet a Faun uncovered the figure of Night, a nymph asleep, exhausted by pleasure, copied from the famous nude statue of Nana, even in the detail of her over-fleshy thighs which made her instantly recognizable to all. A limp rag, rotten with decay from sixty years of debauchery, he looked like a death's head at this feast celebrating Nana's all-conquering flesh. On seeing the door open, he'd shot up, a terrified, senile old man; this last night of love-making had made him lose his wits, he was falling into second childhood; speechless and half-paralysed, he lay there babbling and shivering with his night-shirt rucked up round his skinny, cadaverous body, trying to escape, with one leg out of the blankets—a ghastly leg, purplish in colour and covered in grey hairs. Annoyed though she was, Nana couldn't help laughing.

'Oh, do lie down and cover yourself up', she said, pushing him down on his back and burying him under the sheet like something dirty that ought not to be seen.

She jumped out of bed to close the door. She was definitely having bad luck with her little muff! He was always turning up like a bad penny! And why had he gone off to get money in Normandy anyway? The old man had supplied her with her four thousand francs and so she'd let him have what he'd come for . . . Pushing the double-door to, she shouted:

'Hard luck! It's your own fault, you know you shouldn't just turn up out of the blue like that. Well, we've just about had our bellyful of that, so now get going and don't come back! Enjoy your trip!'

Muffat stood in front of the closed door, paralysed by what he'd just seen. His legs started quivering more and more violently and the trembling spread upwards to his chest and head; like a tree shaken in a gale, he swayed and fell on his knees as his limbs gave way. He held out his hands, mumbling incoherently:

'It's too much, O Lord, it's too much!'

He'd put up with everything but this was too much, he hadn't the strength to go on any longer, he had been cast into that bottomless pit where man loses control of his reason. Lifting up his hands, in a wild burst of fervour, he searched the heavens for God:

'No, I refuse! . . . O God, come down to me, come to my aid, let me die rather than go on living in the way I now do! This is the end, O God, give me a haven, take me away to a place where I shan't hear or see anything any more. I belong only to Thee, O Lord . . . Our Father which art in heaven . . .'

And he continued to pray, full of passionate belief and fervour. Someone touched him on the shoulder; he looked up. It was Monsieur Venot, surprised to see him praying in front of a closed door. Then, as if God had indeed answered his prayer, the count flung himself into the arms of the little old man and at last found release in tears, sobbing and exclaiming over and over again:

'O brother . . . My brother . . .'

All his human suffering found comfort in this cry. As he kissed him, his tears poured down Monsieur Venot's cheeks. He stammered:

'O brother, take pity on me, I can't bear any more! O my brother, take me away for ever, you're the only help I have left in the world! For pity's sake, take me away with you!'

Monsieur Venot took him into his arms and called him his brother, too; but he had yet another blow for him: since yesterday he'd been trying to find him to tell him that, in a final act of lunacy, his wife had just run away with the head of a department of a large drapery-and-fancy-goods store, an appalling scandal which was already the talk of the town. Seeing him in this mood of extreme religious exaltation, he sensed that this was the right moment to tell him straight away about the affair, this final, tragically banal event in the fall of the house of Muffat. The count was unmoved; so his wife had left, that meant nothing to him, they'd look into it later. He again became very distressed, casting frightened glances towards the door, at the walls and ceiling, mumbling all the time:

'Take me away! . . . I can't bear it any longer, please, please, take me away!'

Monsieur Venot led him away like a little child, and from then on Muffat was completely in his power. He lived entirely in accordance with strict religious doctrine and discipline. His life was blasted: the Tuileries Palace was outraged and Muffat had to resign as Chamberlain. His daughter Estelle filed a lawsuit against him, claiming sixty thousand francs, a legacy from an aunt which should have come to her on her marriage. Muffat was ruined and lived frugally on the few remaining scraps of his great fortune, which the countess gradually dilapidated as she squandered what little Nana hadn't bothered to help herself to. Corrupted by the example of the promiscuous little tart, Sabine had cut loose herself; she became the agent of his final collapse, the running-sore of the family. After various escapades, she returned to the marital home and Muffat, with Christian resignation, forgave her; she was the constant living reminder of his shame; but he was growing increasingly indifferent to such matters and had reached the stage of no longer being affected by them. Heaven was taking him out of the hands of women and putting him into the hands of God Himself. The sensual delights of Nana were being carried over into the prayers, the stammered ejaculations, as well as into the despair and humility of a sinful man crushed by his weight of original sin; as he knelt on the icy flagstones in hidden corners of churches, he was satisfying the same obscure needs of his body and his soul and enjoying his former raptures, the violent muscular contractions, the same delectable commotion in his brain.

In the evening of the same day that Nana and Muffat parted for ever, Mignon called at the Avenue de Villiers. He'd been getting used to Fauchery and had come to the conclusion that there were very many advantages in having found a husband for his wife; he could leave little domestic matters for him to attend to, rely on him to keep a wary eye open and use the money he earned from his theatrical ventures, when successful, to meet day-to-day expenses; and as, on the other hand, Fauchery was proving sensible, not ridiculously jealous and as accommodating as Mignon himself towards the occasional windfalls which came Rose's way, the two men were getting on better and better, enjoying an association which was proving a rich source of pleasure of all sorts, each in a cosy niche, side by side as part of a family where they were no longer getting in each other's way. The whole thing was running as smooth as clockwork, with not a single hitch, and they were both making every possible effort to ensure that everyone was being looked after. In fact Mignon was calling, on Fauchery's advice, to see if he couldn't snaffle Nana's maid, who had greatly impressed the journalist by her outstanding intelligence. Rose was at her wit's end; for the last month she'd been having to cope with inexperienced girls who were continually landing her in embarrassing situations. As Zoé herself let him in, he immediately cornered her in the dining-room. At his first words, Zoé gave a smile: out of the question, she was leaving her mistress to set up on her own; and looking quietly smug, she added that offers were coming in every day, the ladies were falling over each other to get her; Madame Blanche had promised her a large sum to get her back. However, Zoé herself intended to take over Tricon's business, a plan which she'd been hatching for a very long time, in an ambitious bid to make her fortune that would take every penny of her savings; she was full of grandiose ideas, she had dreams of expanding the business by renting a splendid mansion which would provide every sort of amenity. It was with this in view that she'd recently tried to recruit Satin, but the silly little girl was now lying fatally ill in hospital as a result of the messy life she'd been living.

When Mignon tried to dissuade her by pointing out all the risks involved in such a venture, Zoé, without being too explicit as to the exact nature of her plans, merely smiled, pursing her lips as if she was sucking a sweet, and said:

'Oh, luxury businesses always do well . . . You see, I've been in other people's houses long enough, I want other people to come to mine.'

She bared her teeth savagely: she'd finally be 'madam' herself, and for a few hundred francs those women whose basins she'd been rinsing out for the last fifteen years would be crawling to her.

Mignon asked to be shown up to Nana, and Zoé left him for a moment after informing him that her mistress had had a very bad day. Having called on Nana only once before he didn't know the house, and was amazed by the dining-room with its Gobelins tapestries, its sideboard, and all the silver. He made himself at home, opening doors, inspecting the drawing-room and winter garden before returning to the front hall. Such massive opulence, all this gilt furniture and silk and velvet, was filling him with admiration; his heart was beating fast. When Zoé came to fetch him, she volunteered to show him the other rooms, the dressing-room and the bedroom. The bedroom made Mignon's heart overflow; he was sent into a paroxysm of emotion. He was an expert in such matters but that bloody Nana was still capable of amazing him. With all its waste and the blood-letting of the decamping servants, the house might be foundering but there were still immense treasures brimming over in the damaged vessel and plugging any leaks. Viewing this colossal monument, Mignon was reminded of other splendid man-made structures: near Marseilles he'd once been shown an aqueduct spanning a deep gorge, a cyclopean work which had cost millions and taken ten years of arduous labour; and in the new port of Cherbourg he'd seen an immense building, with hundreds of men sweating in the sun, machines filling in the sea with huge rocks and erecting a wall which had sometimes reduced workers to bloody pulp; but that all seemed petty, Nana's performance was more glorious. Her achievement filled him with the same respect which he'd once felt at an evening party given in a château built by a refiner, a veritable palace whose truly royal magnificence had been paid for by one simple commodity: sugar. Nana had used something else, a tiny object, a little thing that people made jokes about, a dainty, naked titbit, a tiny slit, unmentionable and yet possessing the power to shift worlds, so that by its unaided efforts, without any help from workmen or machines invented by engineers, she had sent Paris tottering and built up a fortune on buried corpses.

'Jesus, what a tool!' exclaimed Mignon, unable to restrain his ecstatic delight as he recalled his own personal debt to it.

Nana had gradually sunk into a state of deep depression. The encounter between the marquis and the count had given her a nasty nervous shock, even if causing her some amusement. Then the thought of this poor old man going off half-dead in his cab and of her little muff, whom she was seeing for the last time after causing him so much exasperation for so long, had put her in a gloomy, maudlin mood. In addition, she'd been annoyed to hear of Satin's illness; she'd gone off a fortnight ago and seemed likely to die in Lariboisière* as a result of Madame Robert's horrible treatment of her. As the carriage was being hitched up to go to visit her, Zoé had calmly given notice. She felt desperate; it was like losing a member of the family. Heavens above, what would become of her on her own? She pleaded with Zoé, who was highly flattered to see her mistress's despair and ended by giving her a kiss to show that she wasn't leaving because she was cross with her; she just had to go, business came before sentiment. So today was definitely not Nana's lucky day. In disgust she'd decided not to go out after all, and she was lounging around in her little drawing-room when Labordette came up with news of a golden opportunity to buy some magnificent lace; he then casually let fall the information that Georges had died. Her blood ran cold.

'Zizi's dead?' she cried.

Without thinking she looked towards the pink stain on the carpet, but it had finally vanished, rubbed off by the tread of feet. Meanwhile Labordette was giving her some details: nobody quite knew what had happened, some people were saying his wound had reopened, others were talking of suicide, that he'd jumped into a pond at Les Fondettes. Nana kept saying:

'He's dead! He's dead!'

Then the pent-up emotions of the morning found release in a burst of tears. She felt immeasurably sad, overwhelmed by a shattering sense of loss. When Labordette tried to comfort her, she motioned to him to be quiet and said brokenly:

'It's not just him, it's everything, absolutely everything . . . Oh, I'm so utterly miserable . . . And I realize that people will be saying once again that I'm a bitch. There's that mother who'll be grieving for her son down there at Les Fondettes, and that poor man who was on his knees moaning outside my door this morning, and all those other people now ruined because they squandered their money on me . . . That's right, blame Nana, blame that beastly girl . . . Oh, I always get the blame, I can just hear them talking: that dirty little tart who goes to bed with everybody, who cleans some of them out and causes the death of others, who brings unhappiness to so many people . . .'

She was choking with tears, unable to go on talking, so distressed that she'd fallen on to a divan and was burying her head in a cushion. All the unhappiness surrounding her, the harm she'd caused, were drowning her in emotional self-pity; she was uttering faint moans, like a little girl.

'Oh, I feel dreadful, so dreadful! . . . Oh, it's unbearable, I can't breathe! It's so hard to be misunderstood, to see everybody against you because they're stronger than you . . . And yet you've done nothing wrong, you've got a clear conscience . . . No! No! It's not right!'

Her anger was boiling over into bitter resentment. She sprang to her feet, wiped her eyes, and started walking agitatedly up and down.

'No, they can say what they damn well like! It's not my fault! Am I unkind? I give away everything I've got, I wouldn't hurt a fly. It's them, it's always them! . . . I didn't ever want to be unkind to them. And they were forever sniffing round my skirts and now they've kicked the bucket or they're begging or pretending to be desperate . . .'

She stopped in front of Labordette and tapped him on the shoulder:

'Look, you were there, tell me truthfully: did I ever encourage them? Weren't there always a dozen of them falling over each other to think up the dirtiest possible thing to do? They were revolting! I did all I could not to go along with them, I was afraid . . . Look, take one example: they all wanted to marry me. There's a nice idea, isn't it? Yes, my dear man, if I'd wanted I could have been a baroness or a countess twenty times over . . . Well, I refused because I was sensible . . . Oh, how many times I've stopped them doing disgusting things, from committing crimes! They'd have stolen and murdered, killed their father and mother, I only had to say the word and I refused to say it . . . And today you can see the reward I get . . . Take Daguenet, I fixed up his marriage for him, a pauper whom I set up after keeping him for nothing for weeks and weeks. I saw him yesterday and he cut me dead! How's that for a pig? I'm a bloody sight better than him!'

She'd started pacing up and down again. She banged her fist down on a little table.

'Bloody hell! It's unfair! Society's all wrong! They set on women when it's the men who demand that sort of thing . . . Look, I can tell you one thing now: Whenever I went with them, you know, well, I never enjoyed it, I got absolutely no pleasure out of it at all, it was just a chore, I tell you honestly . . . Well, I ask you, am I in any way to blame for all that? . . . Yes, they bored me stiff! But for them, my dear man, but for what they made me do, I'd be a nun praying to God, because I've always been religious . . . And if they lose their money or their lives, it's their own fault, they can go to hell . . . It's nothing to do with me!'

'Of course not', said Labordette solemnly.

Mignon was shown in by Zoé; Nana greeted him with a smile; she'd had a good cry, it was all over now. He was still overwhelmed with enthusiasm for her set-up and congratulated her on it; but she gave the impression of being tired of her splendid life-style, she was beginning to dream of other things, maybe one of these days she'd sell up the lot. Then, when he gave as pretext for his call a benefit performance in aid of old Bosc, who was paralysed and confined to an armchair, she was very sympathetic and agreed to book two boxes. At this point, Zoé came back to say that her carriage was waiting; she asked for her hat and, while she was tying her ribbons, told them about poor Satin's escapade and added:

'I'm off to the hospital to see her. Nobody loved me like she did. Oh, people are right to accuse men of being hard-hearted! . . . I may never see her again, who knows . . . Never mind, I'll try and see her, I want to give her a last kiss and a hug.'

Labordette and Mignon smiled. She wasn't sad any more; she smiled too, because those two didn't matter, they'd understand. And the two men stood watching her, in solemn, speechless admiration, while she buttoned up her gloves: there she stood, by herself, amidst all her treasures, with a whole horde of men grovelling at her feet. Like those dreaded monsters of old whose lairs were littered with bones, she was walking on skulls and surrounded by cataclysms: Vandeuvres' mad holocaust, the melancholy Foucarmont languishing in oblivion in the China seas, the downfall of Steiner, condemned to having to make an honest living, la Faloise's idiotic conceit, and Georges's bloodless corpse now being watched over by his brother Philippe, just released from jail. She'd completed her work of death and destruction; the fly which had taken off from the cesspit of the slums with its germs capable of putrefying society had poisoned those men merely by settling on them. It was fair, justice had been done, she'd avenged her world, the world of beggars and the underprivileged; and while the fiery red of her pubic hair glowed triumphantly over its victims stretched out at her feet, like a rising sun shining in triumph over a bloody battlefield, she herself remained, a superb, mindless animal, oblivious of what she'd done, never anything but a 'good sort of girl', a big, fat wench bursting with health and the joy of life. All this now meant nothing to her, her mansion seemed too small, full of furniture that was standing in her way, something quite trivial, just a starting-point for further ventures. She had dreams of bigger and better things. And so she went off, dressed as if for a ball, to give Satin a last kiss, looking neat, durable, in mint condition, untouched by human hand.

Chapter 14

ALL of a sudden, Nana disappeared; she'd taken off on a new venture, a flight into lands weird and wonderful. Before leaving she offered herself the thrill of selling up all her possessions: her grand residence in the Avenue de Villiers, her furniture, her jewels, even her dresses and lingerie. Vast sums were mentioned: over the five days the sale made more than six hundred thousand francs. Paris saw her for the last time in *Mélusine*, a pantomime at the Gaietés, put on by Bordenave, broke but always game to have a go. She was cast with Prullière and Fontan; it was only a walk-on part, but she made a great hit in her three 'artistic' poses as a formidable but silent fairy princess. Then, one fine morning, in the middle of this fantastic success, just as the publicity-mad Bordenave was flooding Paris with his colossal posters, it was learned that she must have gone off to Cairo the previous day; a difference of opinion with her manager, a remark which she took amiss, a sudden whim by a woman too rich to stand being thwarted. Anyway, it was just one of her mad ideas: she'd been longing to get to know the Turks for ages . . .

Months passed. People began to forget her. Whenever her name was mentioned amongst her former set, wild rumours circulated, with everybody producing conflicting and fantastic reports. She'd captivated the viceroy, who'd ensconced her in a palace with two hundred slaves at her command, and she was cutting their heads off for a bit of fun. No, not a bit of it: she'd come to grief with a big black man, a passionate and sordid affair which had left her destitute in the dissolute squalor of Cairo. Then, a fortnight later, to everyone's amazement, somebody swore he'd met her in Russia. She was becoming a legend; she was the mistress of a prince; her diamonds were out of this world. Soon all the women knew about them, though none of them could quote the exact source of her information; but there were rings, bracelets, ear-rings, a necklace two inches wide, and a queen's diadem with a brilliant in the middle as big as your thumb. The very remoteness of these exotic lands invested her with a mysterious lustre, like an idol laden with precious stones. People now spoke of her in hushed tones with awed respect, as befitted such a fortune acquired amongst barbarians.

One evening in July, at about eight o'clock, Lucy was driving along in her carriage and caught sight of Caroline Héquet walking down the Faubourg Saint Honoré on an errand to a local retailer. She called to her and asked point-blank:

'Have you had dinner? Are you free? Oh, in that case, my dear, you must come with me, Nana's back.'

The other woman got in and Lucy went on:

'And do you know, my dear, while we're sitting here talking, she may be dead.'

'Dead? What a strange idea!' exclaimed Caroline, unable to believe her ears. 'Where is she? And what's wrong with her?'

'At the Grand Hotel . . . She's got smallpox. Oh, it's a long story.'

Lucy instructed her coachman to drive fast, and while they trotted quickly along the Rue Royale and the boulevards she told Nana's dramatic story in breathless, disjointed phrases.

'It's absolutely incredible . . . Nana arrives here from Russia, don't ask me why, some squabble with her prince . . . She deposits her luggage at the station and goes off to stay with her aunt, you remember, that old woman . . . Well, so she finds her baby has got smallpox and he dies next day and she has a terrible row with the aunt over the money she was supposed to be sending and which the other woman never saw a penny of . . . Apparently that caused the child's death, you know, a child left on its own and neglected . . . OK, so Nana clears out and goes off to a hotel and then just as she was thinking of seeing about her luggage, she runs into Mignon . . . She comes over all queer and shivery and wanting to vomit, so Mignon goes back with her to her room promising to look after her stuff. Isn't it funny how things turn out? But here's the most extraordinary thing of all. Rose hears about Nana's illness, gets mad when she discovers that she's all alone in a cheap hotel, and dashes round to look after her, with tears running down her cheeks . . . Do you remember how the two loathed each other's guts? Well, my dear, Rose arranges for Nana to be taken to the Grand Hotel so that she can at least die in smart surroundings, and she's spent the last three nights there at the risk of catching her death of smallpox . . . It's Labordette who told me all this. So I wanted to go and see . . .'

'Oh yes', exclaimed Caroline excitedly, 'let's go up and see.'

They had reached the hotel. On the way, the driver had to slow down as the boulevard was jammed with carriages and pedestrians. The Legislative Body had that day voted to declare war; people were crowding the streets, streaming along the pavements, and overflowing across the roadway. Over by the Madeleine, the sun had gone down behind a blood-red cloud and the tall windows were glowing crimson in its reflection. Dusk was falling, the avenues were turning into gloomy and melancholy dark holes still unlit by the sparkling pin-points of their gas-jets. And in this popular commotion, a hubbub of voices could be heard in the distance; a gale of dismal foreboding was sweeping through people's minds, their faces were pale, their eyes gleaming.

'Look, there's Mignon', said Lucy. 'He'll be able to tell us what's happening.'

Mignon was standing under the large porch of the Grand Hotel. When Lucy asked him, he flared up:

'How can I know anything? I've been trying to get Rose to come down for the last two days . . . It's really idiotic to be risking your skin like that! She'll look nice if she catches it and ends up with her face all pitted! That's all we need!'

He was enraged at the thought that Rose might lose her good looks and wanted Nana to be left on her own, double-quick. He couldn't understand the stupid way women stuck together. At this moment Fauchery came over from the other side of the boulevard, looking equally anxious. He enquired what the situation was and the two men started urging each other to go up and see. They had by now become bosom friends.

'No news, old chap', said Mignon. 'You ought to go up and force her to come down.'

'It's all very well for you to say that', the journalist replied. 'Why don't you go up and do it yourself?'

Lucy asked her room-number and they both appealed to

her to persuade Rose to come down or else they'd get really cross. Lucy and Caroline didn't go up immediately, for they'd just caught sight of Fontan loafing around with his hands in his pockets, amusedly watching the stupid faces of the crowd. When he heard that Nana was upstairs ill, he put on a solicitous air.

'Poor girl . . . I'll go up and say hallo. What's wrong with her?'

'Smallpox,' Mignon replied.

The actor was already setting off towards the entrance. He came back and with a shudder muttered simply:

'Shit!'

Smallpox was no joke. Fontan had almost caught it once when he was 5. Mignon mentioned a niece of his who'd died of it. As for Fauchery, he knew all about it, he still had the marks of it, three spots at the base of his nose; he showed them and Mignon again started pressing him, pointing out that you could never catch it twice; Fauchery vehemently rejected that theory, quoting examples and saying that doctors were callous quacks. They were interrupted by Lucy and Caroline, surprised at the increasingly large throng of people.

'Just look! What a lot of people!'

The light was fading fast, and in the distance the gas-jets were coming on one by one. People could now be seen watching the scene from their windows while the crowd under the trees was swelling every minute. From the Madeleine to the Bastille there was one vast stream of people; carriages were having to crawl along. From this solid mass tramping round like a herd of animals, a dull rumble was rising; they were still silent but they were working themselves up to the same pitch of excitement. There was a sudden commotion, and as they drew back a band of men wearing caps and workers' smocks roughly forced their way through the crowd, chanting monotonously as they advanced, like a hammer on an anvil.

'On to Berlin! On to Berlin! On to Berlin!'

People watched them glumly and suspiciously, yet already caught up and stirred by heroic thoughts, as when a military band goes by.

'Yes, go and get your blocks knocked off!' muttered

Mignon, suddenly bursting into philosophy.

But Fontan thought it was splendid and talked of joining up. When the enemy was at the gates, every true citizen ought to spring to the defence of the fatherland: he struck the attitude of Bonaparte at Austerlitz.*

'Well, are you going to come up with us?' Lucy asked him.

'You must be joking!' he replied. 'Why run the risk of catching something?'

On a bench in front of the Grand Hotel a man was sitting, hiding his face in a handkerchief. As Fauchery had come up, he'd drawn Mignon's attention to him with a wink. So he was still there; yes, he was still there. Fauchery held the two women back for a second to point him out to them. At that moment the man raised his head and they exclaimed in surprise, recognizing Muffat as he looked up towards one of the windows.

'You know, he's been squatting there ever since this morning', said Mignon. 'I saw him at six and he's not gone away . . . As soon as he heard the news from Labordette, he came here with a handkerchief over his face . . . Every half-hour, he drags himself along over here to ask if the person upstairs is any better and then goes back and sits down . . . After all, it's not very healthy in that bedroom . . . However much you love someone, you're still not keen to kick the bucket.'

The count was sitting looking upwards, seemingly unaware of what was happening round him. No doubt he didn't know that war had been declared; he was in a complete daze, he couldn't hear the crowd.

'Look!' said Fauchery. 'Here he comes, you'll see.'

The count had stood up and was making his way into the hotel; but the door-keeper had come to recognize him, and anticipated his question.

'She passed away a moment ago, sir', he said abruptly.

Nana was dead. Everybody was stunned. Muffat went back to his bench, his face covered in his handkerchief. The others were making a great commotion but their exclamations were cut short by another band of people going by shouting:

'On to Berlin! On to Berlin! On to Berlin!'

Nana was dead! Such a lovely girl! Mignon gave a sigh of relief: now Rose would be coming down at last. A sudden chill fell. Fontan, longing to play a tragic part, had put on an expression of grief, with drawn lips and eyes turned heavenwards in their sockets, whereas, for all his cheap journalist's flippancy, Fauchery was genuinely moved and was chewing nervously away on his cigar. The two women were continuing to exclaim. The last time Lucy had seen her was at the Gaietés; yes, it was the same for Blanche, in *Mélusine*: oh, it was absolutely wonderful, my dear, in that crystal grotto! The men also remembered the scene very well. Fontan had been taking the part of Prince Cockalorum. They all started recalling the details. Wasn't she out of this world in that crystal grotto, eh? She'd certainly got what it takes! She didn't say a word, the authors had even cut out her only speech because it spoilt the effect; no, she didn't do a thing, it was grander like that, all she had to do to get the audience on the edge of their seats was to show herself. A figure you'll never see the like of again, those shoulders and legs and that lovely slim waist! Wasn't it queer to think she was dead? You know, over her tights she wore only a gold belt that barely covered her, front or rear . . . The grotto round her, made up entirely of mirrors, was glittering with cascades of diamonds, streams of white pearl necklaces amongst the stalactites of the vaulted roof, and in this sparkling mountain spring, gleaming in a broad beam of electric light, with her skin and fiery hair she seemed like the sun. Paris would always see her like that, blazing with light in the middle of all that crystal, floating in the air like an image of the good Lord. No, for someone in her position it was just too stupid to have to die! A pretty sight she'd look now, up there!

'And to think of all that pleasure down the drain!' said Mignon sadly; he was the sort of man who can't bear to see good things going to waste.

He asked Lucy and Caroline if they were still intending to go up. Of course they were, they were even more curious now. At that very moment Blanche arrived, out of breath and exasperated because the crowd was blocking the pavement. Her arrival led to a further spate of explanations and exclamations and then the good ladies made their way towards the stairs, with a great swishing of skirts. Mignon went after them to call out:

'Tell Rose I'm waiting for her . . . Straight away, OK?'

'They don't know exactly whether it's more catching at the beginning or at the end', Fontan was explaining to Fauchery. 'One of my doctor friends who works in a hospital was even telling me that the most dangerous time is after the patient's died . . . There are all sorts of noxious fumes . . . Oh, I'm sorry the climax came so suddenly, I'd been so looking forward to going up to shake hands with her for the last time to say goodbye.'

'What's the point now?' replied the journalist.

'Yes indeed, what's the point?' the other man echoed.

There were more and more people crowding the streets. In the bright lights from the shop-windows and the flickering patches of the gas-jets you could see the stream of hats flowing along on both pavements. The fever was beginning to spread and people were constantly dashing into the road to join the gangs of men in smocks forcing their way along with the same insistent shout:

'On to Berlin! On to Berlin! On to Berlin!'

A room on the fourth floor of the Grand Hotel costs twelve francs a night; Rose had wanted something decent but not too luxurious: suffering doesn't need luxurious surroundings. The room was hung in a large, Louis XIII floral cretonne with the traditional mahogany hotel furniture and a red carpet with a pattern of black leaves. A heavy silence reigned, broken by whispers: suddenly loud voices were heard in the corridor.

'I'm sure we've gone wrong . . . The boots said turn right . . . What a barracks!'

'Hang on, let's see . . . Room 401 . . . 401.'

'Ah, here we are . . . 405, 403 . . . This must be it . . . Yes, 401, come along. Sh! Sh!'

The voices died down. There was some coughing as they composed themselves for a second; then, slowly, Lucy opened the door and went in, followed by Caroline and Blanche, only to come to a halt as they saw five women already there. In the light of a shaded lamp standing on the corner of the chest-of-drawers, Gaga sat sprawling in the only armchair, a low one upholstered in red velvet with a high back. Simonne and Clarisse were standing in front of the fireplace talking with Léa de Horn who was sitting on a chair, while to the left of the door Rose Mignon was perched in front of the bed on the edge of a wooden coffer, staring at the body lost in the shadow of the curtains. They looked like ladies paying a social call, for all except Rose were wearing hats and gloves; she, pale and tired from her three sleepless nights, was sitting dazed and utterly forlorn from this sudden confrontation with death.

'What a dreadful tragedy', murmured Lucy as she shook hands with Rose. 'We were hoping to be in time to say a last goodbye.'

She turned her head, trying to see Nana, but the lamp was too far away and she was afraid to bring it any nearer. On the bed a grey mass lay stretched out; only the bunch of red hair was visible and a pale patch which must have been her face. Lucy added:

'I hadn't seen her since that grotto scene at the Gaietés!'

'Ah, she's changed now, she's changed now.'

And without another word or sign she went back to her contemplation. They might be able to take a look at her in a minute, perhaps. The three women joined the others in front of the fireplace. Simonne and Clarisse were talking in a whisper about the dead woman's diamonds. Did they in fact really exist? No one had ever seen them, it must be a joke. But Léa de Horn knew somebody who had actually seen them; oh, they were absolutely gigantic . . . And that wasn't the lot, she'd brought all sorts of precious things back from Russia, embroidered cloth, valuable trinkets, a golden dinner-service, even furniture; yes, my dear, fifty-two enormous crates, enough to fill three railway wagons. It was all being held at the station. Bad luck, wasn't it? Dying without even having time to unpack; and don't forget, she had masses of money as well, something like a million. Lucy asked who would be inheriting it all. Distant relatives, no doubt the aunt. An ill wind that'd be blowing a lot of good to that old woman. She didn't know anything about it yet, the sick woman had insisted on not letting her know because the death of her son Louis still rankled. The women all said how sorry they were for the little lad, recalling that they'd seen him at the races: a sickly little fellow who looked terribly old and sad, in fact one of those poor little kids who'd never asked to be born.

'He's better off underground', said Blanche.

'You've put your finger on it', remarked Caroline. 'And the same thing applies to her . . . Life's not much fun . . .'

In this austerely furnished bedroom, a feeling of gloom was descending on the ladies. They began to be frightened, it was stupid to stay here chatting for so long, but they felt riveted to the spot by the urge to look. The room was in shadow, stiflingly hot and muggy; the lamp was casting a moon-shaped patch of light on the ceiling. There was a sickly smell coming from a soup plate of carbolic acid under the bed. Little gusts of air kept making the curtains billow out at the window opening out on to the boulevard, where a dull roar could be heard.

'Was she in much pain?' enquired Lucy, who'd been absorbed in contemplating the decoration of the clock representing the three Graces, naked and smiling like ballet-dancers.

Gaga seemed to rouse herself.

'Yes, she certainly was . . . I was here when she passed away. I can tell you it's not pretty at all . . . You see, she gave a terrible jerk . . .'

But she was unable to go on with her account as loud shouting from outside drowned her words:

'On to Berlin! On to Berlin! On to Berlin!'

Lucy couldn't breathe; she opened the window wide and leant over the sill. It was pleasant outside; under the starlit sky the air was cool. Opposite, windows were blazing with light, the flickering gas-jets were reflected in the gold lettering of the shop-signs. Down below it was fascinating to watch the crowd thronging the pavements and flooding on to the roadway in the middle of the confused crush of carriages, great shadowy waves with glittering pin-points of light from their lamps and the gas-jets. But the mob now coming along shouting was carrying torches; from the Madeleine onwards there was a red gleam, like a burning fuse glowing its way through the crowd and spreading out over them in a broad sheet of flame. Forgetting where she was, Lucy called out to Blanche and Caroline:

'Do come over here . . . You've got a wonderful view from this window.'

All three of them leaned out, greatly intrigued. The trees partly blocked their view and at times the torches were hidden behind the foliage. They tried to get a glimpse of Nana's men waiting below, but the porch was obscured by a projecting balcony and they could only pick out Count Muffat, a black bundle sitting slumped on the bench and holding his handkerchief in front of his face. A carriage had driven up and Lucy recognized Maria Blond; one more woman come to see what was happening. She wasn't by herself; behind her, a fat man could be seen getting out of the carriage.

'Good Lord, it's that crook Steiner', exclaimed Caroline. 'Haven't they packed him off back to Cologne yet? . . . I'd like to see his face when he comes in!'

They turned back into the room, but when Maria Blond appeared later, having twice taken the wrong stairs, she was by herself and when questioned by a surprised Lucy:

'Him? Oh my dear, if you think he'd ever come up . . . It's astonishing that he's even brought me as far as the door . . . There are about a dozen of them down there, smoking cigars.'

Indeed, it was turning into a general meeting of all Nana's men-friends. Having set out for a stroll along the boulevard in order to take a look at what was happening, they were calling out to each other, exclaiming when they heard of the poor girl's death. Then they began talking politics and strategy. Bordenave, Daguenet, Labordette, Prullière, and numbers of others joined the group. They listened to Fontan explaining his plan of campaign to take Berlin in five days flat.

Meanwhile, distressed by the presence of the dead woman, Maria Blond was whispering like the others.

'Poor pet! Last time I saw her was in the grotto at the Gaietés.'

'Ah, she's changed now, she's changed now', Rose Mignon said again, giving her sad, grief-stricken smile.

Two more women arrived: Tatan Néné and Louise Violaine. They'd been combing the Grand Hotel for the last twenty minutes, following the directions of various members of its staff; they'd been up and down thirty storeys or more, caught up in the mad rush of travellers scurrying to get out of Paris, in panic at the thought of war and the commotion on the boulevards. As a result, when the ladies came in, too exhausted to worry about the dead woman, all they could do was to flop down on their chairs. And in fact at that very moment a tremendous din arose in the room next door; trunks were being shoved around, people were colliding with furniture, and loud voices could be heard speaking in uncouth accents. It was a young Austrian couple. Gaga informed them that while Nana was in her death-throes they'd been playing at chasing each other round the room, and as the two bedrooms were separated only by a locked door, you could hear them laughing and kissing when they'd caught each other.

'Look, we must get out', said Clarisse. 'We're not going to bring her back to life . . . Are you coming, Simonne?'

They all looked sideways at the bed but made no move to go, though giving their skirts little taps in preparation for their departure. Lucy was again leaning with her elbows on the window-sill, away from the others. A lump was slowly forming in her throat, as if the yelling crowd outside was itself making her miserable. Torches were still being carried past, throwing out sparks; in the distance, the groups of people were rippling in the gloom like long flocks of sheep being led by night to the slaughter, and this confused, whirling mass of people streaming by created a feeling of terror and immense pity for the massacres to come. They were bewildered, their voices cracking in the frenzy of their intoxication as they hurtled towards their unknown fate beyond the dark wall of the horizon.

'On to Berlin! On to Berlin! On to Berlin!'

Lucy turned and leaned back against the window, deathly pale.

'Oh, my God! What's going to become of us?'

The ladies shook their heads, looking very serious and worried by the situation.

'Well, as for me', said Caroline Héquet with her usual calm, 'tomorrow I'm off to London . . . Mummy's already there, setting up house for me . . . I'm not going to wait and be slaughtered in Paris, you can bet your life on that!'

In her prudence, her mother had prevailed on her to move her money out of the country: you can never tell how a war's going to end . . . Maria Blond was angry: she was patriotic and talked of following the army:

'What a coward you are! . . . If I thought they'd have me, I'd dress up as a man and take pot-shots at those Prussian pigs! . . . And even if we all died, our lives aren't worth all that much, are they?'

Blanche de Sivry was livid:

'Don't you dare say nasty things about the Prussians! . . . They're men like all the rest, and not forever on the look-out for women, like Frenchmen . . . They've just expelled the little Prussian who was with me, a very rich, very gentle little boy who wouldn't hurt a fly. It's disgraceful, I shall be ruined . . . And I want to warn you, I don't want anybody getting on my back or I'll be off to Germany after him like a shot!'

As they were all squabbling with each other, Gaga muttered sadly:

'Well, for me it's the end. I've got no luck at all . . . I've just finished buying my little cottage in Juvisy, you can't imagine all the sacrifices I've had to make to get it, Lili had to help me out . . . And now war's been declared and the Prussians are going to come and set fire to everything . . . How can I start again at my age?'

'That's nonsense', said Caroline, 'I don't give a damn! I'll always find some way or other.'

'Of course', agreed Simonne. 'It's going to be fun . . . Maybe it'll work out all right, in spite of everything . . .'

She completed her sentence with a smile. Tatan Néné and Louise Violaine were of the same view. The former spoke of the fantastic binges she'd had with soldiers, really good sorts who'd do the craziest things for women. But the ladies were now raising their voices so loudly that Rose, who was still sitting on the coffer, told them to shush. There was a shocked hush and they cast a sidelong glance towards the dead woman, as if the request had issued from behind the shadow of the curtains. In the profound silence which ensued, a deathly silence in which they could sense the corpse stretched out stiff and cold beside them, the yells of the crowd burst out once more:

'On to Berlin! On to Berlin! On to Berlin!'

But they quickly forgot where they were again. Léa de Horn, who ran a political salon where former ministers of Louis-Philippe delivered themselves of witty epigrams, shrugged her shoulders and continued in an undertone:

'What a mistake this war is! Sheer homicidal stupidity!'

Lucy at once sprang to the Emperor's defence. She'd been to bed with a prince of the Imperial house; for her it was a family matter.

'Oh, come on, my dear, we just couldn't allow ourselves to go on being insulted! It's France's honour which is at stake in this war. Oh, I'm not saying that just because of my prince, who was a stingy beast if ever there was one! Just imagine, when he got into bed with me at night he'd hide his money in his boots, and whenever we played bezique together, he'd use beans for stakes because one day, purely as a joke, I pretended to grab the kitty . . . But all the same I must be fair, I reckon the Emperor's done the right thing.'

Léa was wagging her head and looking very superior, like a woman who's repeating the views of very important persons. Raising her voice, she said:

'It's the end of the road. The people in the Tuileries are mad. In fact, the best thing the French could have done yesterday was to kick them out . . .'

They all violently interrupted her. What on earth had got into that crazy woman's head to attack the Emperor like that! Wasn't everyone happy? Wasn't business flourishing? Paris would never experience such fun again.

Now Gaga was becoming roused.

'Don't say that sort of thing, it's idiotic!' she snorted indignantly. 'You don't know what you're talking about . . . I've seen Louis-Philippe, it was an age of skinflints and people who hadn't got a bean. And then came the '48 Revolution. And a wonderful thing that was, their famous Republic! Absolutely revolting! After February, I was reduced to starvation, as true as I'm sitting here! . . . If you'd gone through all that, you'd go down on your knees to the Emperor, he's been a father for us, a real father! . . .'

They tried to calm her down, but in a sudden burst of religious fervour she cried out:

'Dear God, try to make the Emperor victorious! Save the Empire for us!'

They all echoed her prayer. Blanche confessed that she'd been burning candles for the Emperor. Caroline had even fallen for him, and for two whole months had placed herself so as to be close to him when he passed but without succeeding in attracting his attention. The others all furiously attacked the Republicans and talked of killing them all off at the frontier, so that when Napoleon III returned victorious from the battle he'd be able to reign undisturbed amidst universal rejoicing.

'That horrible man Bismarck, there's another real swine for you!' remarked Maria Blond.

'And to think I knew him!' exclaimed Simonne. 'If I'd been able to see what was going to happen, I'd have slipped poison into his glass.'

But Blanche, still smarting under the expulsion of her little Prussian boy-friend, found the courage to stick up for him. Maybe Bismarck wasn't such a bad sort after all. Everyone had his job to do; and she added:

'You know, he's mad about women.'

'What good is that to us?' cried Clarisse. 'It's not as if we're queuing up to get into bed with him, is it?'

'There are too many men like that at any time', declared Louise Violaine solemnly. 'Better do without than have any truck with monsters like that!'

The discussion continued: they gave Bismarck his marching orders and with Napoleonic fervour despatched him with a kick up the backside. Tatan Néné kept saying:

'Oh, that man Bismarck! . . . People get on my nerves with him. How I dislike the man! . . . Not that I ever knew him, one can't know everybody.'

'All the same', remarked Léa de Horn finally, 'the fact remains that Bismarck is going to thrash us.'

She couldn't go on; their ladyships all flung themselves on her: What was that? Did she say thrash *us*? . . . No, it was Bismarck who was going to be thrashed and sent home with his tail between his legs. So she'd better shut up, she didn't deserve to be called a Frenchwoman!

'Sh!' Rose Mignon whispered, offended by all the noise.

Embarrassed by the presence of the dead woman, and remembering their secret fear of the disease, the thought of the corpse immediately froze them into silence. On the boulevard the mob was still going by with its raucous shouts of 'On to Berlin! On to Berlin! On to Berlin!'

Just as they were finally making up their minds to leave, a voice called out from the corridor:

'Rose! Rose!'

Surprised, Gaga went over to the door and disappeared. In a moment she returned and said:

'My dear, it's Fauchery at the end of the corridor, he doesn't want to come any further, he's beside himself because you're staying so near to the body.'

Mignon had finally succeeded in prevailing on the journalist. Lucy, who was still at the window, leaned out and saw the men on the pavement below, looking up and signalling wildly. Mignon was brandishing his fists in exasperation, while Steiner, Fontan, Bordenave, and the others were holding their arms out with a worried and reproachful look on their faces. Not wanting to be compromised, Daguenet was merely smoking his cigar and holding his hand behind his back.

'It's true, my dear', Lucy said, leaving the window, 'I promised to fetch you down . . . They're all calling up to us.'

Painfully Rose got up from the wooden coffer and muttered:

'All right, I'm coming. She doesn't need me any more, of course. We'll get a nun in . . .'

She looked around, trying unsuccessfully to find her hat and shawl. Without thinking, she filled a basin on the wash-stand and stood washing her hands and face. She went on:

'I can't understand, it's given me a terrible shock . . . We weren't exactly the best of friends yet, you know, her death's given me all sorts of silly ideas . . . Oh, all kinds of things, the feeling of wanting to go the same way, that the world's coming to an end . . . Yes, I certainly need some fresh air.'

The corpse was beginning to stink. Their previous unconcern suddenly changed to panic.

'Come on, let's get out, my dears', Gaga was saying. 'It's not safe in here.'

They left hurriedly, casting a final glance towards the bed. But seeing Lucy, Blanche, and Caroline still there, Rose took a last look round the room to make sure everything was tidy. She drew the curtain at the window; then the thought occurred to her that a lamp wasn't the proper sort of light and she took a candle out of one of the brass candlesticks standing on the mantelshelf, lit it, and placed it on the bedside table beside the body, suddenly bringing the dead woman's face into full view. It was a horrifying sight. They shuddered and fled. Rose was the last to leave, whispering:

'Ah, she's changed, how she's changed!'

She went out, closing the door. Now Nana was left alone, lying face upwards in the light of the candle, a pile of blood and pus dumped on a pillow, a shovelful of rotten flesh ready for the bone-yard, her whole face covered in festering sores, one touching the other, all puckered and subsiding into a shapeless, slushy grey pulp, already looking like a compost heap. Her features were no longer distinguishable, her left eye entirely submerged in discharging ulcers, the other one a sunken, fly-blown black hole. A thick yellowish fluid was still oozing from her nose. Starting from the left cheek, a reddish crust had overrun the mouth, pulling it into a ghastly grin. And on this horrible and grotesque death-mask, her hair, her lovely hair, still flamed like a glorious golden stream of sunlight.

Venus was decomposing; the germs which she had picked up from the carrion people allowed to moulder in the gutter, the ferment which had infected a whole society, seemed to have come to the surface of her face and rotted it.

The room was empty. From the boulevard below there came a great desperate gasp, making the curtains billow.

'On to Berlin! On to Berlin! On to Berlin!'

EXPLANATORY NOTES

1 *Variétés*: founded in 1807, this well-known theatre was one of the many small theatres on or near the *grands boulevards*. A number of Jacques Offenbach's operettas were put on there, including *La Belle Hélène* and *La Grande Duchesse de Gérolstein*, in which the notorious Hortense Schneider played. Similar theatres mentioned in the novel are the Folies Dramatiques, L'Ambigu, and the Bouffes; the latter, taken over by Offenbach in 1855 for his operetta *Orphée aux Enfers* (Orpheus in the Underworld), was originally in the Champs-Elysées and later transferred to the Boulevard des Italiens.

2 *World Fair*: *L'Exposition Universelle* was held in Paris in 1867.

3 *Figaro*: this most important Paris newspaper became a daily in 1867; it was particularly well known for its dramatic and literary criticism and its witty society gossip-columns.

9 *early thirties*: the first years of the 'bourgeois' King Louis-Philippe's reign; he came to the throne in 1830 and was removed by the February 1848 Revolution.

10 *Conseil d'État*: the State Council had, under the 1852 constitution of the Second Empire, the most important function of initiating all laws to be presented to the Senate (the Upper House) and the Legislative Body (the Lower House; see pp. 56, 412). Its members were all appointed by the Emperor.

16 *Casino de Paris*: a place of popular entertainment and a haunt of prostitutes.

18 *King Dagobert*: king of all France from AD 628 to 638. Last Frankish king of the Merovingian dynasty; there is a very popular comic song about him.

Postilion of Longjumeau: the handsome, irresistible hero of the comic opera of that name by A. Adam (1803–56), better known for the ballet music *Giselle*.

19 *head-pad*: a sort of wicker crash helmet put on children's heads to protect them if they fell.

21 *Rue de Provence*: street-walkers' territory, just north of the Boulevard Haussmann. Fauchery lives nearby.

31 *Wallachia*: a Danubian principality which, until 1918, formed, with Moldavia, the kingdom of Romania.

32 *Rambouillet*: some 35 miles south-west of Paris, well known for its forest and palace.

Batignolles: a district in the north-west of Paris.

35 *Rue de la Goutte d'Or*: Nana grew up in a dingy tenement house in this slummy area of the Chapelle district (see p. 226), east of the Boulevard Barbès and north of the Boulevard Rochechouart, described at length in *L'Assommoir*: Rue Polonceau (p. 294) and the Rue des Poissonniers (p. 227) are just round the corner.

37 *Bercy*: district in the twelfth arrondissement, on the right bank of the Seine, notable as an area of wine warehouses.

54 *Rue Montmesnil*: in the smart eighth arrondissement, just north of the Champs-Elysées.

55 *Nazar Eddin*: Naser ed-Din, born 1831, Shah of Persia from 1848 until his assassination in 1896.

57 *recent successes*: in 1866 Prussia had defeated Austria in a short war.

58 *Mexico*: French troops had fought in Mexico in support of the Austrian Archduke Maximilian as Emperor of that country. In 1867 Maximilian was shot and a republic set up in Mexico.

59 *coup of December the second*: two coups brought Napoleon III to power: the first on 2 December 1851, when as President of the Second Republic he had seized power, the second on the same date next year, when he abolished the Republic and had himself proclaimed Emperor.

60 *Queen Augusta*: wife of King William of Prussia.

Madeleine: the grandest and smartest of modern Paris churches, built in the style of a Greek temple between 1762 and 1842, at the west end of the *grands boulevards*. The Muffats' house is nearby.

65 *Legitimists*: die-hard royalist supporters of the 'legitimate' line of French kings, the elder Bourbon line, deposed in the 1830 Revolution, as opposed to the Orleanist King Louis-Philippe (see note to p. 9 above).

Montauban: in the south-west of France, a comfortably safe distance—nearly 400 miles—from the prying eyes and gossipy tongues of the capital.

69 *Wagner*: the Paris public had not taken kindly to Wagner's music: in 1865 *Tannhäuser* and in 1867 *Rienzi* were badly received.

Patti: the brilliant Adelina Patti (1843–1919) often sang at the Paris Opéra.

71 *Prince of Scotland*: for the Prince of Scotland we can read the son of Queen Victoria, the notoriously lecherous Prince of Wales, the future Edward VII, an ardent admirer of women of high or low degree, but the Prince of Scotland is depicted as taller and rather more handsome than his real-life model.

73 *Viroflay*: a village south-west of Paris, not far from Versailles.

77 *Brébant*: a very well-known smart caterer; Zola is scattering authentic detail.

83 *Meursault . . . Chambertin and Léoville*: the caterer has sized Nana up: these are the most obvious top-class white and red Burgundies and claret.

89 *Saint-Aubin-sur-Mer*: Zola himself spent time at this Norman seaside resort.

Faubourg Saint-Antoine: a working-class suburb of Paris, east of the Bastille.

Pouilleuse: literally 'lousy', the dry western part of the province of Champagne, considered at one time fit only for grazing.

92 *Juvisy*: a few miles south of Paris.

93 *Landes*: a swampy district extending inland from the Atlantic and south from the vineyards of the Bordeaux region to just north of Biarritz; reclaimed in the nineteenth century as a vast pine forest.

96 *Coromandel coast*: on the east coast of India in the Bay of Bengal.

103 *Peters*: a well-known restaurant on the *grands boulevards*

116 *Loiret*: a *département* south of Paris: chief town, Orléans.

132 *PS and OP*: PS is the prompt side, the side of the stage where the prompter is, usually to the actors' left in the UK, to the right in the USA; OP is the side opposite the prompter.

134 *practicable*: a piece of stage equipment, for example, doors and the like, capable of actual use in a play or that can be operated on stage. Zola is showing off his theatrical expertise.

150 *Bougival*: an outer western suburb of Paris, on the Seine.

162 *fortifications*: built along the northern limits of Paris beyond the outer boulevards. Nana used to roam around there in search of fun as a precocious little girl; a rather boring and insalubrious countryside.

165 *Parmentier*: a French agronomist (1737–1813), best known for furthering potato-growing in France.

169 *Victoria*: a low, light, four-wheeled carriage with a folding hood.

181 *Mâcon*: a town in southern Burgundy on the Saône, about 250 miles south-south-east of Paris.

185 *Vendôme columns and obelisks*: the column is a tall one of bronze, forged from captured enemy guns and depicting the victories of Napoleon's Grande Armée; it stands in the Place Vendôme, north of the Tuileries Gardens. The obelisk, brought from Luxor in Egypt in 1836, stands at the end of these Gardens in the Place de la Concorde.

186 *Café Anglais*: in the Boulevard des Italiens, a haunt of expensive prostitutes; the Cafe Riche (p. 237) was opposite.

198 *Opéra building-site*: Garnier's grandiose Opera House was under construction from 1862 until 1874.

214 *Twelfth-cake*: an ornamental cake eaten on the evening of the twelfth day of Christmas; it contained a bean, and if the person receiving the slice containing the bean was a woman, she could choose the Twelfth Night king.

222 *Europe district*: the streets immediately to the east, west, and north of the Gare Saint-Lazare are named after European capital and other large cities.

226 *La Chapelle*: the district adjoining Montmartre to the east; see note to p. 35 above.

232 *Talma*: Napoleon's favourite actor, who lived from 1763 to 1826.

236 *Asnières*: now a north-western suburb of Paris.

Bullier: a very well-known dance-hall in the Latin Quarter, at the end of the Boulevard Saint Michel, where it runs into the Avenue de l'Observatoire. It was frequented by students, whereas the Bal Mabille (pp. 288, 339) on the Champs-Elysées was more up-market.

237 *Rue du Faubourg-Montmartre*: the girls are moving into the sleazier streets north of the main boulevards.

239 *register as a prostitute*: this would entail, amongst other restrictions, having to attend regular medical examinations.

Saint-Lazare: a medieval leper hospital, later a monastery, this was now a women's prison and reformatory in the Faubourg Saint Denis; a specially large section was reserved for prostitutes, with a hospital annexe for the treatment of VD. In 1868, 4,831 prostitutes were held there in squalid conditions in overcrowded dormitories; lesbianism was rife.

242 *Mademoiselle Mars*: 1779–1847, the most renowned comic actress of her age who distinguished herself at the Comédie

Française until 1841.

261 *Parc Monceau*: in the seventeenth arrondissement, still one of the smartest parts of Paris.

267 *Rue de Lappe*: a seedy street running eastwards from close by the Place de la Bastille.

279 *Philippe Auguste*: King of France from 1180 to 1223.

304 *Queen Pomaré*: this decrepit old courtesan's nickname comes from the contemporary queen of Tahiti, which had become a French protectorate in 1847.

329 *betting-room*: before race-meetings, a room for laying bets was opened in the Grand Hotel in the Boulevard des Capucines. Ironically, Nana lies ill in a room there in Chapter 14.

353 *Boucher*: François Boucher (1703–70), Rococo painter, associated with frivolous and erotic themes.

364 *mattresses stripped*: in desperate times, people stripped their mattresses to get money for the stuffing; Nana's mother had done this in *L'Assommoir*.

388 *Madrid*: the smartest of smart restaurants in the Bois-de-Boulogne.

406 *Lariboisière*: a recently built hospital in the district where Nana grew up; in fact, her father had been one of its roof-tilers.

414 *Bonaparte at Austerlitz*: his victory in 1805 over a combined Austro-Russian army had often been a subject for painters; the best-known is by Baron Gérard (1770–1837).